Praise for *Murder at Morrington Hall*

"You will love this delightful debut novel to what promises
to be a winning series. An unlikely duo, Stella and Lyndy
make a great team, both as sleuths and in life, and I can't
wait to see them again. I couldn't put it down!"
—Victoria Thompson, bestselling author of
Murder on Trinity Place

"A successful series needs a great premise plus a landscape
that is fraught with possibilities for future stories, and by
choosing an 'American dollar princess' as her heroine,
McKenna sets the stage well . . . Readers will enjoy getting
to know the affianced pair, watching them solve the mystery,
and will undoubtedly look forward to their next adventure."
—*Criminal Element*

"It will take more than an arranged marriage and a murder
to thwart Stella Kendrick in this compelling mystery filled
with twists and turns, intriguing characters, and rich historical
detail. I fell in love with the clever and spirited Stella and her
charming fiancé Lyndy as they navigate the perils posed by
both romance and intrigue; I cannot wait to see what the
future holds for them!"
—Ashley Weaver, author of *An Act of Villain*

Books by Clara McKenna

MURDER AT MORRINGTON HALL

MURDER AT BLACKWATER BEND

Published by Kensington Publishing Corporation

MURDER AT MORRINGTON HALL

CLARA McKENNA

KENSINGTON BOOKS
www.kensingtonbooks.com

KENSINGTON BOOKS are published by

Kensington Publishing Corp.
119 West 40th Street
New York, NY 10018

All Kensington titles, imprints, and distributed lines are available at special quantity discounts for bulk purchases for sales promotion, premiums, fundraising, educational, or institutional use.

Special book excerpts or customized printings can also be created to fit specific needs. For details, write or phone the office of the Kensington Sales Manager: Attn.: Sales Department. Kensington Publishing Corp., 119 West 40th Street, New York, NY 10018. Phone: 1-800-221-2647.

Kensington and the K logo Reg. U.S. Pat. & TM Off.

First Kensington Hardcover Edition: June 2019

ISBN-13: 978-1-4967-1780-1 (ebook)
ISBN-10: 1-4967-1780-5 (ebook)

ISBN-13: 978-1-4967-2555-4
ISBN-10: 1-4967-2555-7
First Kensington Trade Paperback Edition: June 2020

10 9 8 7 6 5 4 3 2 1

Printed in the United States of America

To my intrepid travel companion, pink hair and all.
Who loves ya, Mom!

ACKNOWLEDGMENTS

I would like to thank Liz Galton, Dr. Katherine Walker and the staff at the Christopher Tower Reference Library at the New Forest Heritage Centre in Lyndhurst, Hampshire, UK. They guided me through the treasure trove of their collection. They answered my questions (literally for hours) while I was in their library and through thoughtful emails after I was back home. I relied heavily on the material I discovered with their assistance for authenticity, accuracy and detail. Any errors are mine alone.

I would like to thank Kathryn Whalley of the Cornucopia Bed and Breakfast in Brockenhurst, Hampshire, UK for providing the support and sustenance for my long research days, as well as introducing me to her church, St. Nicholas'. She made my (and my mother's) visit to the New Forest a joy.

Anette Engel at the Thoroughbred Racing Center in Lexington, Kentucky was extremely knowledgeable and patient as she guided me and my family through her facility. Meeting Thoroughbred racehorses up close and personal was an experience I'll never forget.

I'm grateful to my agent, John Talbot and my editor at Kensington, John Scognamiglio, for their faith in my writing. A huge thank you to the members of Sleuths in Time, both past and present for their critiques, their encouragement and their unfailing support. And finally, to my family, especially Maya, Mom and Brian. I hope they know how much their love and support means.

CHAPTER 1

May 1905
Hampshire, England

"Americans are different, Mother."

Lyndy pulled on the lapels of his morning coat and paced the room, studying the portraits lining the walls, as he had since childhood. The pale faces stared down at him with disapproval, or so he always thought. Some wore lace ruffs; others, long curly wigs; two were in full dress uniform; and one countess clutched a silver, pearl-encrusted cross. All his ancestors, God forbid, dour and boring to the last. Not unlike the many prospects his parents had paraded past him during the Season in London over the years. Was different too much to hope for?

"Not this one. I have your father's assurances."

Papa looked up from the map he'd spread out on the small satinwood inlaid table between the French windows, the vase of pink peonies he'd displaced near his feet on the floor. Lyndy glanced over his father's shoulder at the map, a partial sketch of a region in the American West called Wyoming.

"Yes, Frances. She's quite the young lady, or so I've been told." Lord of the manor he may be, but Papa was far too willing to give Mother her assurances.

"Perhaps Miss Kendrick will be one of these radical Americans we've all heard of," Lyndy said, peering out the window. A pair of ponies emerged from the woodland and drank from the grassy edge of the pond. "Maybe she'll drink Irish whiskey instead of coffee after dinner." That would be a bit much even for Lyndy, but Mother needn't know that.

Papa, bent over, studying his map again, laughed.

"I don't know how you can find any of this humorous, William. If it were not for your . . . hobbies"—Mother waved an accusing finger at Papa's map—"we might not be in this predicament."

"The boy was only joking."

"Was I?"

Mother raised her eyes, appealing to a higher power for forbearance.

What would be so wrong with a woman taking a sip of whiskey now and then? Like so many of society's rules, it seemed archaic. Like the one not allowing them to sell any land. It was their land, wasn't it? Or the one enabling his parents to determine his fate. It was his life, wasn't it?

"Lyndy, why must you always—" Mother began.

"My lord, the guests have arrived." Another quarrel averted. Fulton always did have impeccable timing.

"Move over," Daddy grumbled. "You're too far to the left."

Stella ignored him. She was having too much fun. Digging her heel in, she lifted as far out of her seat as she could. The chimneys of Morrington Hall, reflecting in the first rays of sun in days, jutted up in the distance, above the ancient trees, and she wanted to see more.

But Stella wasn't used to driving from the right side of the car. Feeling the wheels pull toward the middle of the road again, she steered sharply to the right, instead of the left. The vehicle swerved to the right, crossed the lane, and headed straight for the open heathland, a rolling patchwork of ferns, heather, bright green grazing lawns, and yellow flowering gorse bushes, before she corrected the wheel.

"For God's sake, sit down!"

Stella plopped back down into the black leather seat of the brand-new 22 hp Daimler automobile and stole a glance at Daddy. He stared straight ahead, nose in the air, gray hairs protruding out of his ears. With his bottom waistcoat button undone to accommodate his considerable girth, he clutched his leather bag tighter to his chest. Too bad she wasn't leaving him at Morrington Hall instead of Tully. She sighed.

Oh, Tully.

Pushing aside the pale pink motoring veil billowing around her face, she pictured the parade of wagons following her. Daddy had spared no expense in assuring the comfort and safety of his prize thoroughbreds: fresh air and fresh hay on the ship; a refitted first-class carriage on the train; the customized ambulance wagons for the trip from Southampton; and a groom, Roy, to tend to them personally. She'd enjoyed every minute of the ten-day trip from Bronson Ridge Farm, their home in Kentucky. It was her first trip to England. It was her first trip anywhere besides New York and Newport. But the adventure was bittersweet. Even now, with Morrington Hall within sight, she couldn't reconcile losing her best friend. When she returned home, she'd be leaving her horse behind.

"Watch out for that buggy up ahead," Daddy warned.

Orson, the stallion inside the lead wagon, snorted and stomped as the skittish bay mare pulled the buggy past. Stella waved, but the buggy's driver scowled at the strange conveyance.

"Tell me again why you're giving Orson, Tupper, and Tully to this viscount, Lord Lyndhurst?" Stella asked.

"If Cicero wins the Derby at Epsom this week, Orson, being his sire, will be the most valuable stud in England."

"Then why give him away? And why give up Tupper? You expected her to win the Belmont Stakes this year." Daddy might breed some of the best racehorses in the world, but even so, prospects like Tupper were rare.

"Because it suits me."

"But why Tully, Daddy?" He knew she was Stella's favorite.

Silence.

Stella gripped the steering wheel as tightly as she could. The automobile glided down the wooded lane, its blue metallic fenders gleaming in the sunlight that filtered through the leaves. Gnarled oak, redwood, ancient beech, yew, and holly towered above them. Silence. Having lost all feeling in her fingers, Stella loosened her grip and inhaled. The air smelled fresh, earthy, and sweet after the morning's rain. How could she be upset on a day like this?

"Don't you want to ride Tully while you're here?" Daddy said.

"You know I do." Could Daddy have brought the horse to please her? "You're not giving Tully to the viscount?"

"Why would I do that?"

Truly? The kind gesture was so unlike him. But then, so was inviting her to accompany him on this trip. What brought about this change? Whatever it was, she couldn't be more grateful for it.

"I haven't thanked you for bringing me along on this trip, Daddy."

"No need. Just drive," Daddy said as Stella smiled at him. Daddy had never been one for any demonstration of affection.

"Like this?" Stella, biting her lip, pushed down on the accelerator. How fast could this car go?

Stella laughed as she caught a glimpse in her side-view mirror of Great-Aunt Rachel in the backseat. The old lady, wrinkles deep around her puckered mouth, clutched her hat, the plume of black ostrich feathers flapping in the breeze. Her squinting eyes—dark blue, like Stella's own—popped open.

"Whoa, girlie!" Aunt Rachel shouted.

Stella snapped her attention forward. A cluster of ponies, a mix of chestnut and bay, with powerful hindquarters, stood rooted to the middle of the road a few yards away. As one, they bolted, scattering in every direction. Stella yanked hard on the steering wheel and veered around the slowest of the bunch. The wheels bumped up over a small boulder, sending everyone bouncing out of their seats. The car plunked down, brush and twigs crunching beneath the tires.

Whack! Daddy yelled something inaudible as the side of the Daimler connected with a long, sharp branch of a tree. As Stella struggled to control the steering wheel and keep them from careening off the road, the ponies trotted out of harm's way. With a final swerve and swish of the back wheels, the car straightened in the lane again.

Stella laughed with relief.

"What the hell was that?" Daddy said.

"New Forest ponies," Roy said from the backseat. Leave it to the groom to know about every breed of horse and pony in the world.

Like a creature from a mythical land: unicorn, centaur, New Forest pony. Stella looked at the groom in the side-view mirror. He'd pushed his goggles onto his high forehead, exposing two clean rings around his eyes, where the dust hadn't settled. Although gripping the edge of his seat, he studied the ponies as they passed.

"The New Forest region is famous for them," he said.

Stella smiled at the term the *New Forest*. On the ship, Roy had told her all about it and its mythical ponies. An odd name for a place created as a royal hunting ground by King William the Conqueror over eight hundred years ago.

"The Ancient Forest is more appropriate, don't you think?" Stella said.

"Wild ponies?" Daddy said. "Shouldn't they be rounded up? They look hardy enough to be good workhorses. Left to wander, they're a nuisance."

Stella waited for Roy to say more—to tell Daddy that New Forest ponies weren't wild at all and were rounded up on occasion, or to explain why the region was called "new" when it was ancient or "forest" when it was mostly heathland. Stella had even overheard the locals say 'on the forest' like they would say 'on the range' back home. But the groom had fallen silent again.

"Actually, Daddy," Stella began, "the ponies—"

"Finally," Daddy grumbled. Stella gazed up at the arch as she passed through the wrought-iron gates. "I thought we'd never get here."

"Me neither." Stella eagerly glanced around her.

As she drove the mile-long gravel drive, passing more ponies grazing out on the lawns, Morrington Hall came into full view. Stella was used to luxurious homes. The Kendricks had a town-home on Fifth Avenue in New York, a summer cottage in Newport, and a three-story white-pillared "farmhouse" in Kentucky. But nothing rivaled Morrington Hall, which was more reminiscent of Grand Central Station in New York City than any home Stella had ever seen, in opulence and grandeur. The large bricks of gray and yellow stone that made up the house, if one could call it that, spoke of its unquestionable permanency. With a half a dozen gables and four turrets, the building rose four stories, like a castle. Chimneys, haphazardly placed and too numerous to count, climbed at least a dozen feet more. Stella guessed it would take her several minutes, walking swiftly, to cross from one end of the house to the other. Surrounding the colossal home were sculptured gardens, a large pond, wooded park-lands, rolling pastures, extensive grazing lawns, fenced pad-docks, and heathland as far as she could see. The stables, tucked away on the edge of the woodland and made of the same stone as the house, were almost as large as her house in Kentucky. She couldn't wait to explore.

"Slow down," Daddy said.

Stella let the car coast as they approached the house. Waiting for them on the front steps and in the gravel drive were the Searlwyns, owners of this grand estate, and their household staff.

The Earl of Atherly, in contrast to Daddy, fit his morning coat impeccably, with his lean, athletic build. Only the silver threading through his dark brown hair attested to his being Daddy's peer. Beside him stood his wife. Lady Atherly's high-necked collar, the lace brushing the bottom of her chin, her curled hair mounded on the crown of her head, and her Roman nose tilted up created the impression that the countess nearly matched her husband in strength and height. Standing beside them, clutching the lapels of his morning coat, was a man in his midtwenties. With the addition of a dimpled chin and high cheekbones, he was a younger and more dashing version of Lord Atherly. Viscount Lyndhurst, no doubt. Unlike his father, who stood as erect as a rooted tree, Lord Lyndhurst exuded barely contained energy, like a cat ready to pounce. Beside Lord Lyndhurst stood a wisp of a girl a few years younger than Stella. With a sweet face and rounded shoulders, she withered in the shadow of the others around her. She had to be the vis-count's fiancée. Stella didn't envy her.

Lined up in single file off to the side on the gravel drive were members of the household staff, or at least some of them—the butler, his nose rivaling his mistress's in heightened angle; the housekeeper, her eyes darting about, noticing everything; a lady's maid perhaps, with a tidy, stylish coiffure; a handsome footman in full livery; and two housemaids in black dresses and crisp white aprons. With a house this big, there had to be an army of servants out of sight.

Without exception, every face wore a stern or, at best, blank expression. Stella couldn't understand it. Wasn't there to be a wedding in a few days? Weren't they receiving two champion racehorses from Daddy as gifts? Not to mention the excitement of the upcoming Derby at Epsom Downs. She'd heard about the race all her life. Why weren't they all giddy with excitement?

As Stella untied the motoring veil from her chin, a slight breeze caught it, and it floated in front of her face. It turned the world—the clouds, the sky, the gravel drive, the close-cut lawn, the towering stone mansion, Lord Atherly and family, even Daddy—into a pale pink haze. How lovely it all was.

And then Daddy smiled. Nothing good ever came when Daddy smiled.

Reverend John Bullmore came to a decision. He set his empty teacup on the square oak inlaid side table and stuffed the last lemon biscuit in his mouth.

It will be awkward once the Americans have arrived, but needs must.

He pulled out his pocket watch; he still had a few minutes. He snapped it closed and approached the glass-paneled mahogany display case set against the one wall of the library not lined with floor-to-ceiling bookshelves. He'd been staring at the birds in the display case while he sipped his tea, while he considered what to do next. Each bird specimen had a label. Each had been collected on or near the grounds of Morrington Hall by the current Earl of Atherly and his father: honey buzzard, sparrow hawk, curlew, lapwing, hawfinch, stonechat, even a tiny, rare Dartford warbler. Unable to decide which was more reminiscent of himself, the scrawny purple heron or the gray-feathered shrike, Reverend Bullmore bent over to look at the magpie in the case. Its glass eyes stared back. He'd always been fascinated by the black-and-white bird. A crick in his back forced him upright.

If only life were black and white.

The vicar hobbled to the fire. Warming the spasms out of his back, he licked the glistening butter off his fingers, the scent of lamb and roast chicken mingling with the tea on his breath. It would be sinful to let even a taste of such a lovely meal go to waste. He appreciatively patted his slightly bulging stomach. A rare treat indeed.

When was the last time he'd committed the sin of gluttony? He couldn't remember. He couldn't remember the last opportunity. Three years at Everton Abbey had seen to that. Had it been worth it? After yesterday, he had his doubts. Either way, he hadn't been this satiated or this comfortable in years, thanks be to God.

And thanks be to Lord Atherly for allowing him to officiate at his son's approaching nuptials. Reverend Bullmore eagerly anticipated the invitations to many more sumptuous meals. He'd been unpacking down at the vicarage when he received his first summons here. Was he worthy of such a sacred task? Lady Atherly had asked as he bit into an exquisite slice of Victoria sponge. He'd faltered a moment. Did she know about the trouble? No, if she did, the bishop would've been sipping Lord Atherly's port last night, and not he. Yes, Lord and Lady Atherly would be remembered in his prayers this night.

Sufficiently warmed by the fire, he settled into a well-worn leather club chair to wait. Shunning the thousands of books surrounding him, he picked up the crumpled copy of the *Sporting Life*, left behind on the table. The Derby was two days away, and he was woefully uninformed. He flipped through the pages but saw nothing. Had he made the right decision? He still had time to change his mind.

Reverend Bullmore raised his head when the door creaked

open. Who could that be? Surely, it wasn't time to meet with the marrying couple. The Americans hadn't even arrived yet. Sucking the last of his lunch from his thumb, he set down his racing paper to greet the new arrival. With a smile and butter on his lips, he never saw the blow coming.

CHAPTER 2

"Is that a woman driving?" Lyndy said, a hint of amusement in his voice.

His Majesty the King rode in a Daimler like that at the Newmarket races a few weeks ago. Lyndy was envious. Several of his friends were driving about London in the new conveyances. Due to the financial straits his family found themselves in, he hadn't been allowed to get a motorcar, yet.

"Don't be ridiculous, Lyndy," Mother said. Without looking at him, she added, "Calm yourself and stand still. Don't act so nervous."

Lyndy stopped shifting his weight from one foot to the other. His mother was wrong, though. He wasn't nervous. He was thrilled, the wedding notwithstanding. The champion thoroughbreds in those wagons were soon to be his, all his. A childhood dream come true.

Mother expected him to act like a gentleman. Now he could ride like one. He was already composing his excuse for missing afternoon tea. Better still, he'd no longer be just a punter, wagering on other people's horses; he'd have a chance at the winner's circle himself. Grandfather would be proud.

Was he going to get to keep the Daimler as well?

"Look again, Mother."

She squinted at the procession slowly making its way up the drive, strange ambulance wagons led by the blue Daimler motorcar. The driver sported a wide-brimmed motoring hat and veil.

"It *is* a woman," Mother said in disbelief. "William, you don't think . . ."

"That it is Miss Kendrick?" Papa said, finishing her sentence. He pulled out the lorgnette he used at the opera from his breast pocket, held the eyepieces up to his face, and peered through. "I'm afraid I do, my dear."

"No, it cannot be. That woman is driving. Americans are strange beasts. They must have hired a woman chauffeur."

Mother abhorred any deviation from her rigid expectations. Hence, her displeasure at retreating down to the country with the Season in full swing. Quite the boon in Lyndy's opinion, who preferred riding or fishing to listening to prattle in a ballroom. Hence, his mother's perpetual disappointment in Lyndy.

"There are no women chauffeurs, Frances," Papa said, folding his lorgnette and slipping it back into his pocket. Papa didn't like strangers to know he had a weakness; he couldn't see beyond a few yards.

"What about the other woman, the one in the backseat? That must be Miss Kendrick."

"Now who's ridiculous, Mother?" Lyndy said, tugging on his lapels to keep his feet from moving. Despite the distance, even Papa should be able to tell the woman in the back was not in the bloom of youth.

"But . . . ?" Mother was stunned into silence.

Lyndy took a step forward in anticipation. *This might be more fun than I thought.*

As the car pulled up and stopped, he couldn't decide which was more compelling—the Daimler or its driver.

"I suppose we must do this, mustn't we?" Mother sighed,

smoothing the lace-embellished brown silk of her tea gown. She always wore such dreary colors. Must his mother always dress to match her mood?

"Yes, dear," Papa said. "It was inevitable."

"No, William. If you'd—"

"Mother, they're here," Lyndy whispered, cutting off any further bickering.

Mother pinched her lips as the young woman alighted from the car. Her figure obscured by the tan duster coat, the American swept the veil away from her face.

"She's lovely," Lyndy's sister, standing transfixed beside him, whispered. "Like a Gibson girl."

"A gibbon?" Mother said. "How ungenerous of you, Alice. The young woman looks nothing like a monkey."

"No, a Gibson girl, Mummy, not a gibbon. You know, like in the American magazines?"

With a long neck, flawless alabaster skin, red bow-shaped lips, and a flash of mischief in her blue eyes, the young woman was indeed striking. But was she the American heiress? His mother's scowl confirmed it.

Miss Kendrick's eyes sought out Lyndy and she smiled. For a moment Lyndy forgot who and where he was. He forgot his manners; he forgot to breathe.

"Someone get the door!" barked the rotund man in the Daimler.

The young woman, not waiting for the footman, stepped around the front of the motorcar, her large coat swishing about her slender figure, and opened the door for the grumbling graying man in the passenger's seat. He waved away her offer to help him and, clutching a dark leather bag with both arms, clambered awkwardly out of the car. With a considerable paunch and bowed legs, he stood a few inches shorter than the young woman. He stomped toward Lyndy and his waiting family.

"Welcome, Mr. Kendrick. It is good of you to come all this way," Papa said.

"Good to be here, Atherly. Quite the journey over, but you know, I had to make sure everything was in proper order." Mr. Kendrick tapped the leather bag. "By the way, Professor Gridley sends his regards."

Mother scowled at the name.

"Yes, jolly good," Papa said. "I received word from him yesterday. Everything is going according to plan."

"Speaking of plans . . ." Mr. Kendrick glanced at the greeting party. "Where's the vicar?"

"Yes, ummm . . . well," Papa said, "I don't believe you met my wife, Lady Atherly. My dear, this is . . ."

"Elijah Kendrick. At your service, ma'am." He shoved out his hand.

Mother grimaced but offered up her fingers. Mr. Kendrick grabbed Mother's hand and pumped it heartily. Mother wrenched it back, as if she'd been bitten by a viper. Mr. Kendrick then approached Lyndy, stopping within inches of his face. The man smelled of peppermint and tobacco. It was not a pleasant combination. Lyndy would've shoved the American away, but for what was at stake. Tugging harder on his lapels, Lyndy held his ground.

"So, this must be the viscount." Mr. Kendrick examined him with such scrutiny, Lyndy half expected the man to pull back his lips and examine his teeth.

"I am not one of your horses, sir," Lyndy said, brushing his hand through his hair.

Mr. Kendrick laughed. "No, you aren't. But you'll do just the same."

"Well, I never . . . ," Mother muttered.

Miss Kendrick thrust herself in front of her father. Her scent, a heady mix of floral and woody tones, like a walk in the forest in spring, wafted in the air. With a flourish, she curtsied, as if being presented at court.

"I'm pleased to meet you, sir," the young woman said to Papa, not waiting to be introduced. "I'm Stella Kendrick, the daughter."

Papa smiled at Miss Kendrick's attempt and utter failure at acceptable manners. Mother rolled her eyes and sighed. Lyndy chuckled. To think he'd worried about Mother making a fuss when he chose to go riding instead of taking tea.

The second man in the motorcar, a servant, judging by his dress and demeanor, clambered out and joined Gates, the head coachman, who had arrived to take charge of the horse wagons. Lyndy could barely contain his excitement. The sun, like a lantern in the dark, highlighted a horse inside the lead wagon as it turned toward the stables. The horse's silky coat was the color of night, and its intelligent eyes stared back at him.

Just you wait, you beauty. Then we'll see what you can do.

"Pleased to meet you, Miss Kendrick," Papa said. "May I introduce my wife, Lady Atherly?"

"Pleased to meet you, ma'am," Miss Kendrick said. She curtsied deeply again.

Alice stifled a giggle.

Lyndy didn't mind the American's awkwardness. *There's nothing wrong with a woman who is eager to please.*

"My husband is not sir, but Lord Atherly. You shall address me as Lady Atherly or my lady," Mother said. "And you will not curtsy to me like that again."

"No, ma'am. I mean, of course not, Lady Atherly." Instead of the expected flush on the cheeks, the tips of Miss Kendrick's ears blossomed bright red.

"You can curtsy like that to me," Lyndy said, smirking.

Miss Kendrick feigned a partial smile and decided, correctly, to ignore his jest.

"As your father so astutely assumed, I am Edwin Searlwyn, Viscount Lyndhurst, but everyone calls me Lyndy."

"Yes, well . . . pleased to meet you, Lord Lyndhurst, sir."

Mother flashed another scowl in Miss Kendrick's direction. The look of dismay on the young woman's face was disarming. She genuinely seemed to be trying her best.

"Ignore Mother. I think you're charming."

Miss Kendrick frowned, not the reaction Lyndy was expecting. Didn't all women love flattery? He flashed her his smile. Though he was never one to overuse this gesture, women, be they ladies or maids, adored it when he bestowed it on them. Only Mother seemed immune, and Miss Stella Kendrick. Her frown deepened.

"Should you be . . . ? Isn't this your . . . ?" She stole a glance at his sister, and he realized his omission at once.

"May I introduce my sister, Lady Alice Searlwyn?" Lyndy said, hoping to see Miss Kendrick's smile again, big, unabashed, and sincere. He didn't know women ever smiled like that.

Miss Kendrick tilted her head. "But I thought . . . ? Please excuse me. I'm sorry," Miss Kendrick stammered. "I'm pleased to make your acquaintance, Miss Searlwyn."

What had Miss Kendrick thought? Something had surprised her about Alice. But what? Lyndy looked at Alice, who shrugged her shoulders, naturally wondering the same thing.

"And I you, Miss Kendrick. You can call me Lady Alice," his sister said, without the displeasure in Mother's tone.

"Shall we go in?" Mother said.

Mother didn't wait for an answer. With Mr. Kendrick on her heels, Mother turned her back on everyone and started for the house. Papa and Alice followed. Lyndy hung back, hoping to slip off to the stables.

"Wait," Miss Kendrick called, drawing everyone's attention back to her. "Daddy forgot to introduce Great-Aunt Rachel." Miss Kendrick held the hand of the old crone who Mother had impossibly hoped was Miss Kendrick. The lady had yet to utter a word.

"Welcome to Morrington Hall, Mrs. . . . ?" Papa said with his utmost sincerity.

"It's just miss, Your Lordship, sir. Miss Rachel Luckett," the woman said as she hobbled up toward the front steps. "Pleased to meet y'all."

"My mother's sister," Mr. Kendrick said. "I don't understand why you insisted I bring a chaperone."

"Pity I did not also insist you bring manners," Mother muttered.

"Where did you say the vicar was?" Kendrick said, ignoring Mother's retort.

"He'll join us for tea at half past four," Papa said.

Kendrick grunted his acknowledgment.

"We have already had our luncheon, but Mrs. Cole can arrange to have something brought up if you haven't eaten and can't wait for tea," Mother said.

"Good," Mr. Kendrick said. "We missed our lunch."

By the look of him, the vulgar American could miss a month of meals and not be worse for wear. By her grimace, Mother believed so too.

"Yes, sir, I could definitely put a nose bag on," Miss Rachel Luckett, the chaperone, said.

"Yes, well . . . ," Papa said. How did one respond to that? "We've arranged for you all to stay at Pilley Manor, the dower house on the other side of the estate. Fulton will send your servants on ahead, and you and the ladies can settle in there after tea."

"There's no need for that, Atherly. We'll stay here," Kendrick said. "Unless, of course, you don't have the room?" He laughed at his joke.

"But it would be highly . . . irregular for Miss Kendrick to stay here," Mother said.

"But there's nothing regular about our visit, now is there?"

Kendrick said, winking. Mother couldn't contradict him. He was right about that. "Don't worry. Aunt Rachel knows her job. Besides, we didn't bring any servants."

"But we don't . . . ," Mother began. "We couldn't possibly . . ."

How could Mother tell Mr. Kendrick we didn't have enough staff to care for us, let alone them? She couldn't.

"You are most welcome to stay with us, Mr. Kendrick," Papa said.

Mother jutted her nose in the air, turned on her heel, and led the way into the house.

Before Lyndy crossed the threshold, he had planned his escape. Orson, was it? Sounded like a horse to be reckoned with.

Lyndy had taken the new thoroughbred stallion across Beaulieu Heath in his mind before he realized Miss Kendrick wasn't behind him. He glanced over his shoulder and stood transfixed at the scene beyond. Miss Kendrick chatted with the servants in the driveway, introducing herself to them one by one. Lyndy could see Fulton's jowls droop as the butler hid his disapproval. The maids giggled and shifted their feet nervously at Miss Kendrick's ignorance of protocol. Millie, one of the housemaids, unsure how to respond, bowed her head. Her cap, which was not fastened securely enough, slipped to the ground. It landed upside down in the gravel. With a flick of her hand, Mrs. Nelson, Morrington's housekeeper, motioned for Millie to retrieve it. But Millie, the housekeeper, and the entire line of servants froze as Miss Kendrick bent over and picked it up. She brushed the white cap against her hip and handed it back to Millie.

Good thing Mother didn't see that. She would not have approved.

Oh, but this American is a pretty thing to look at, especially bent over. Miss Kendrick had shed the duster coat, revealing a slender frame with a small waist but a less ample bust and narrower hips than he'd hoped for. Lyndy shrugged. *One can't have everything.*

As Fulton dismissed the servants, and Mrs. Nelson scolded the housemaids for their tittering, Lyndy stepped into the shadow of the deep doorway. Miss Kendrick, unaware of his prying eyes, unpinned her hat and tossed it into the backseat of the Daimler. Windblown and crushed by her hat for hours, tendrils fell from the silky light brown hair piled on top of her head. Tucking them behind her ear, Miss Kendrick strode away from the house.

"The *Sporting Times* arrived for you, my lord," a footman said, standing respectfully several feet behind Lyndy in the entrance hall. Lyndy took the pink-papered racing newspaper, still warm from the iron, and absentmindedly tucked it under his arm.

Now where is she off to?

CHAPTER 3

Stella strolled to the stables, struck again by the landscape. Rolling green pastures dotted with towering, stately trees were not unlike those at home, yet at the same time, it was the wildest place she'd ever been. Not a single fence—barbed, picket, or stone—anywhere to be seen. A trio of New Forest ponies grazed on the next hill. *Familiarity and freedom tied up in one landscape. What a novel place this is.*

Stella reached the gardens. From a distance, they had looked like pictures of impeccable tidiness and tranquility. But as Stella passed through them, she noticed dandelion weeds sprouting between stones in the path; clusters of last years' roses, which needed to be deadheaded or pulled out altogether; and branches of yew that jutted haphazardly from the hedge, which needed to be clipped. The fountain, an algae-covered marble statue of a cherub holding a basket of round fruit, spurted out a peaceful trickle of water, but brown leaves clung to the bottom of the pool. A bit of disorderliness she hadn't expected. She didn't like it.

When she arrived at the stables, Stella caught Tully's eye as a stableboy led the horse off the wagon. The horse's ears flicked back and forth. Orson and Tupper were already in their box stalls, munching hay. The stables were as impressive up close as they had been from the lane. Nothing slipshod here. A formidable, sprawling two-story stone building with well-swept cobblestone floors, she would soon learn that the stables contained spacious mahogany box stalls for more than two dozen horses, a hayloft, an ample coach house, a washing yard, and rooms for the stable hands to live in. The scent of fresh hay filled the air. It smelled like home.

She approached Tully and patted her horse on the shoulder. "You're going to enjoy your stay here, Tully, girl," Stella cooed. The luxurious stables were all the testimony she needed that the otherwise disapproving Searlwyns would take good care of her beloved horse. "I wish I could say the same."

Tully's muscles rippled beneath her hand. Stella rested her forehead against the dapple gray's sleek shoulder. Daddy had said they'd be welcomed guests. He'd insisted that the Searlwyns didn't care how he'd made his money, that this time it was going to be different. She'd been excited to come. She should've known better.

The disdain showed her by the Searlwyn family was nothing new. English nobles had nothing on the American elite, though here the servants snickered at her too. Thank goodness, she wasn't staying long. In a few days' time, when the wedding was over, she and Tully would go home to Kentucky. In the meantime, Stella would do as she'd always done when Daddy attempted to force his way into society: spend as much time in the stables and on horseback as possible. But she had dared to hope for more. Maybe next time.

"Oi!" the stableboy yelled. "Mind your step."

She looked down. Clutched in her hand, the hem of her lavender walking-suit skirt was in no danger of dragging on the ground. But her heel was inches from a pile of fresh manure.

She chuckled. That would be from Orson. He always liked to leave his mark whenever he descended from a horse box.

She stepped around the pile and reached out to Tully again, tracing the blaze from the filly's forehead all the way down to her muzzle. Tully nuzzled against Stella's hand, hoping for a treat.

"Do you have any apples?" she asked the stableboy who was holding Tully's lead.

"Oi! You, boy, get that horse inside," a man called. He wore tan trousers, a white shirt, and suspenders. A groom without his coat, no doubt.

The stableboy yanked on the lead. Tully pinned back her ears and tossed her head. The boy tugged again and tried to pull the resistant Tully with him.

"Go easy," Stella said. "You're upsetting her." Tully was a gentle creature, but after everything she'd been through, Stella wouldn't blame her if she was a little stubborn.

"Ah, miss," the groom said, pointing at Stella with the dandy brush in his hand. "Does Lord Lyndhurst know you're here? The stables are no place for a lady."

"I'm Stella Kendrick. These are my horses, until Lord Lyndhurst is married, that is."

"You say you're the master's fiancée?" The groom scoffed, pointing to her kid-leather button boots. His mop of curly black hair bobbed as he unsuccessfully stifled a laugh. Despite her best efforts, Stella had stepped in something, anyway. "All the more reason to let us bring the horses to you, miss," the groom said, composing himself, "and for you to stay out of the stables."

With his gaze, the man took in the stableboys, who had gathered like pedestrians at a carriage wreck. "Aren't I right, boys?"

No one dared say a word.

The familiar burn stung the tips of Stella's ears. Nothing had gone right since the moment she stepped onto the estate. She'd been embarrassed, belittled, and now mocked. She had sought solace here, as she had often done at home, among the horses and the hay. Was she to be denied even that? She kept her calm. Her father had taught her well to take ridicule with aplomb.

"You are mistaken. I am not . . . ," Stella began. She patted Tully once more for reassurance. The horse lowered her head and nibbled on Stella's fingers, hoping for a treat. "If you'll excuse me."

"Herbert!" A stocky, fair-haired man, his skin taut as a drum but for the wrinkles spreading from the corners of his eyes, rounded the corner. With his top hat under his arm, the coachman who had taken charge when she and Daddy arrived led a beautiful Cleveland bay toward them. "Pray what are you doing? Don't you know who this is?"

"Yes, Mr. Gates. I do. I was reminding her how the stables aren't suited for a lady."

"I won't tolerate such insolence." Mr. Gates, a head shorter than the groom, smacked him in the back of the head while retaining his grip on the bay's lead. "Apologize, or you'll be packing your bags."

"What?"

"Now, Herbert!"

The groom flashed a scowl at Stella and then at Mr. Gates before hurling the dandy brush to the ground. "Pardon me, miss," Herbert said sarcastically before storming off.

"Please accept my most humble apologies, Miss Kendrick," Mr. Gates said. "Herbert's behavior is inexcusable. He will be off the estate by daybreak."

"No, no. Mr. Gates is it? You don't have to do that on my account. I've lived around stable hands my whole life. Some don't take kindly to a woman invading their realm."

"You are too kind, Miss Kendrick. I won't soon forget it. As Lord Atherly's stable manager and head coachman, I can assure you, neither will Herbert."

"It's nothing. I do have horse manure on my heel, after all."

Mr. Gates scrunched his eyebrows. Had her self-deprecating jest offended him? Had she made another faux pas? Then the coachman chuckled. The stableboys let out a collective giggle.

"Let this be a lesson for you, lads!" Mr. Gates said, nodding in approval. "Not all ladies shun the honest smell of the stables. Close your mouth, Charlie. She isn't a horse with two tails." The boy who was gawking at her snapped his mouth shut. "But don't for a moment think that means she doesn't deserve your respect. Quite the opposite, if you ask me." Mr. Gates smiled.

She gladly returned the favor.

The boys as one bobbed their heads and said, "Aye, Mr. Gates."

"Now get back to work."

Stella patted Tully on the back as the boy led the filly away. She'd change and go riding as soon as she could slip away.

"I appreciate your allowing me access to your stables, Mr. Gates. I do, as you put it, like the 'honest smell.' I grew up around horses. I dare say I've spent almost as much time in a stable as you have."

Mr. Gates scratched a bushy eyebrow. He didn't believe her.

"I raised Tully from a foal myself," Stella said. "I fed her and groomed her. I trained her myself too."

"That is impressive." Highly irregular or highly unladylike was more like it. But he didn't say that, and she didn't care. She loved this horse. Even Daddy, who was oblivious to Stella's desires and wishes, knew how much.

"Tully is like a member of my family. That's not to say I'm not attached to the other two horses. It will be strange not to have them around."

Mr. Gates crinkled his brow again. "They'll be around, miss, unless Mr. Kendrick has plans for Orson he hasn't mentioned. You can visit any of these fine horses every day if you like. You'll always be most welcome."

"Thank you. But I was talking about after the wedding, when I leave . . ."

"Honeymoons don't last forever. Don't I know it. And you can rest easy while you're gone, knowing we'll treat these lovelies like the King's own." He patted the Cleveland Bay he'd been leading soundly on the neck. "Isn't that right, Lister?"

Honeymoon? She wasn't the one going on a honeymoon. Herbert, the groom, had confused her with Lord Lyndhurst's fiancée. Why would Mr. Gates do the same? A sick feeling rose from the pit of her stomach. Lady Alice was Lyndy's sister, not his bride to be, as Stella had assumed. *Where is she, this fiancée? Where is her family? Is she in London, only days before the wedding? Why don't I know her name?*

Because Daddy had never mentioned it.

"Miss Kendrick, are you well?"

Stella struggled to retain her composure as she tasted bile in her mouth. "Would you mind telling me the name of the viscount's fiancée?"

Alarm flashed across the coachman's face, and Stella knew the truth. It all made sense: Daddy's generous invitation to her to accompany him to England, his insistence that Tully be brought along, the need for Aunt Rachel to chaperone, the reaction of the Searlwyns, everything.

Daddy's wealth couldn't gain him respect in American high society, so he had arranged to secure the one thing that would accomplish that: a British title. Quite the coup for the son of a coachman. But she was to pay the price.

"Her name is Miss Stella Kendrick, of Kentucky, of course," Lord Lyndhurst said, stepping out from the shadows. "It might've been Miss Gladys Vanderbilt—Papa was introduced to her uncle William some time ago—but she's not out yet. For that I'm glad. You're by far the prettier of the two."

His jest fueled her anger. It was a jest, wasn't it? His attempt at flattery was insulting. She looked to Mr. Gates to confirm what the viscount claimed. The pity in his eyes emboldened her. Daddy wasn't going to make her do this.

"Be glad you have an alternative in Miss Vanderbilt, Lord Lyndhurst. I'm not an option!" As she swiveled around, she caught the heel of her boot in a crack in the cobblestones and fell to her knees. Though she was angry and had never felt more wretched in her life, she had no choice but take Lord Lyndhurst's offered hand. She brushed at the clumps of mud and bits of straw clinging to her skirt, hoping to salvage what little dignity she had left.

"He's not going to make me do this," she muttered as she took off running toward the house, tendrils of hair loosening and flying about her head. Clutching her skirt in her fists, she lifted it to run faster. Gravel kicked up behind her as she raced around a bend in the lane and ran right into her father. Bouncing backward off his protruding belly as he stood his ground like a mule, Stella flapped her arms about, trying to maintain her balance. She looked ridiculous. If she wasn't so upset, Stella would've laughed.

"What on earth? Look at you. You're a mess."

"You've gone too far this time, Daddy," she said, finding her balance and planting her boot heels on the gravel path.

"Where have you been? The stables, no doubt."

"I won't do it, Daddy. I won't marry Lord Lyndhurst."

"What woman wouldn't want to? He's an excellent match."

He stepped closer and smiled. It sent a chill up her back, but she was too angry to be afraid. Stella's chest tightened; it was difficult to exhale. Her father gave her his sharp tongue more than his affection, but she'd always hoped it was because he wanted the best for her. Now she knew the truth.

"But you tricked me. You made me believe you wanted me on this trip."

"You were the reason for the trip."

"But Tully, Daddy! You gave Lord Lyndhurst my horse."

"I brought that horse all the way from Kentucky for you." To ride while she was in England, he had said. Because he never intended for her to leave. "Would you rather I had left her in Kentucky?" They both knew the answer to that.

"I'd rather—"

"Why aren't you thanking me? I gave you Tully. Now I'm giving you to Lord Lyndhurst." Like a horse. "You know, I did this for your own good. Someone had to see to your future. You certainly weren't making much of an effort. Time is running out, girl. You are twenty-two years old. What do you think happens to old maids? Do you want to end up like Rachel? Is that what you want?"

Great-Aunt Rachel had lived at the whim of others her entire life, always being expected to care for others, first, her elderly parents, then an ailing cousin, and then Stella, after her mother died. She'd never had a permanent home. She'd never had children of her own.

"But here you'll be a viscountess. You'll have everything you could ever dream of."

"I won't," Stella whispered. Despair had replaced her anger. If he was going to treat her like a horse, she was going to be as stubborn as one.

"And don't worry. After you've done your duty and given the man an heir, he'll find someone else's bed to sleep in," he said, as if promising Lord Lyndhurst would take a mistress was supposed to make her feel better.

"I won't marry the viscount, Daddy."

"You ungrateful little brat!"

Stella winced, preparing for the blow as Daddy's hand swiftly rose toward her face.

"Oi! Everything okay, Miss Kendrick?" Mr. Gates called. He and two stableboys had rounded the corner, walking two gray Hanoverian horses. The one with white half-cannon markings on its hind legs was chewing on something. One of the boys held up the last piece of an apple to the horse with the star on his forehead. Lord Lyndhurst strolled a few yards behind them.

"Everything is fine. Carry on." Daddy dropped his hand and his voice. "Do you know how much this is costing me? Do you think those horses are all I'm giving that family for the marriage settlement? No. I'm saving this magnificent estate for these high-and-mighty Searlwyns in order to benefit you. If they can treat me with respect, is it too much to ask from my own daughter?"

The stableboys held their heads together, whispering, as Mr. Gates released the horses into the paddock. Rumors of her and Daddy's argument would be general knowledge within minutes.

"I'm not a prize horse you can sell to the highest bidder."

Daddy grabbed her hand so quickly, Stella didn't see it coming. Gripping her hand by the knuckles, he squeezed until her joints rolled under the pressure. He looked to see if the stable hands were still watching. They were. He dragged her toward him.

"You should be thanking me for my generosity," he whispered between his teeth, "thanking me for securing your future, not causing a scene."

"I won't marry Lord Lyndhurst, Daddy."

Daddy squeezed harder. Stella met his gaze and steeled herself. He sighed, shaking his head, as he took a step back. He hadn't let go. "Why do you make me do these things?"

"Aaahhh!" she screamed as Daddy crushed her hand. The pain sent her to her knees.

Shouts arose around her.

"Oi, Mr. Gates!"

"Oi!"

Dust flew as Lord Lyndhurst dashed toward them. The horses in the paddock snorted and sprinted around after the boys startled them with shouts for the head coachman. A squirrel bounding across the grass scampered away as Mr. Gates rushed from the paddock to help. But it was too late.

"I'll see you in the drawing room for tea," Daddy said, releasing Stella's hand. "I know how you love your sweets."

Bloody hell. Lyndy had never seen a woman in such disarray. Her hair had all but fallen haphazardly about her shoulders. Bits of straw clung to her knees, and her skirt was smeared with muck from the stable floors. Puffy red eyes and streaks of tears on her cheeks marred her lovely face. It was startling to see.

He'd been pleased while spying on the young woman, unseen, in the stables. He'd caught her unguarded, alone with her horse. He'd been impressed with her ease among the stable hands, her handling of the confrontation with the groom. A flicker of rare admiration and pride had swelled in his chest, and not solely for the magnificent beast. They were both to be his. He wouldn't have made that bet, but there it was. He loathed having to admit it, and never would if pressed, but perhaps Papa was right. Perhaps this would work out.

Lyndy had stayed in the shadows of the empty horse stall until he'd heard Miss Kendrick's question about his fiancée's name. He'd joked about Miss Vanderbilt to flatter the woman, not upset her. How was he to know she was in earnest and didn't know? What kind of man didn't inform his daughter of her fate?

When she'd dashed from the stables like one of the horses, he'd had no intention of following her. He had new thoroughbreds to inspect. But his curiosity and compunction had led him down the path after her, nonetheless. He'd waited a few moments before following, allowing distance to shield him from her eyes. He'd damned his childish spy game the moment Mr. Kendrick raised his hand to her. He was Lord Lyndhurst, after all. Why was he hiding in the bushes like a poacher? Lyndy had leapt into action, but he'd been too late. Even Gates hadn't been close enough to stop the brute. Mr. Kendrick, seemingly unconcerned with the spectacle he created, had strolled away before Gates or Lyndy got there.

As Lyndy approached now, the stable hands surrounding

Miss Kendrick parted. He looked down at her, anger threatening to seep through his calm veneer. He knelt beside her, the pebbles on the path jutting into his knee. She slumped over farther, curling forward in on herself, bravely choking back tears.

"What has that wretch done?" Lyndy asked his head coachman.

"It's her hand, my lord."

"Miss Kendrick? Are you all right? Did that cur harm you?" Hell, this miserable creature was to be his wife. Surely, he could take some liberties. She flinched when he lightly touched her shoulder. "Stella?"

Without looking at him, she whispered, "I'm not a horse to be prized or commanded."

Had she caught him spying on her, after all? The pang of guilt that accompanied the thought surprised him. Lyndy was not one to feel guilty about anything.

"My father may think so, but I assure you, Lord Lyndhurst, I am not," she added.

What could he say? Hadn't he just congratulated himself on winning her as his prize? Yet hadn't he objected to the same treatment when he and Mr. Kendrick were introduced? Bloody hell, what was wrong with him? He'd known the woman for less than an hour, and already he was suffering from a crisis of conscience.

"You've provided me with three fine horses. What need I of another?" Lyndy quipped.

Her countenance remained neutral as she weighed his comment. Did she think he was mocking her? What did he care if she did?

"As I said before, do call me Lyndy." He smiled. A sincere one this time. Despite the pain it must've cost her, the corners of Miss Kendrick's mouth rose.

Now, that's better.

A maid came rushing toward them, the new one. There always seemed to be a new one. Someone from the house, presumably Mother, had noticed their absence and had tired of waiting.

"Miss, are you all right?" the maid asked.

"Yes."

A tension left his shoulders at her affirmation. Was he concerned that his grand trophy had been damaged, or was he genuinely concerned for this woman's welfare? A little of both, perhaps?

"Thank you, Lillian," Miss Kendrick added.

Lillian? He didn't know all the servants' names. Yet this "uncultured" American knew this one's after a single introduction? The maid bent down to help her. Lyndy, acting on his proprietary rights, waved the maid aside and held out his hand. Cradling the injured hand against her chest, Miss Kendrick held out her other. Lyndy swiftly took it and pulled her gently to her feet.

"It will be time for tea by now. Several of the wedding guests staying at the house will be there. The vicar, too, is quite eager to meet you." Lyndy reached out and touched her hair, the only clean thing about her. It was soft and silky in his hand. A thrill shot through his body. He couldn't wait to comb his fingers through her tresses. "Why don't you go and change?" he whispered. "Underneath it all, you really are quite striking."

She stared straight into his eyes. "I pity you, Lord Lyndhurst," she whispered back. It was not what he'd expected her to say. He prepared his retort, but the brightness in her eyes stayed his tongue. "I will go and change and wash off the manure, but you, sir, will always be full of it."

Lyndy burst out laughing.

She turned her back on him, took the maid's offered arm, and proceeded toward the house. Lyndy, captivated by the strength in her retreating back and the slight sway to her curving hips, stood rooted to the ground.

"Well, I'll be damned," he said, still chuckling at her wit. He spied the pink racing sheet tucked into his pocket as he turned back toward the stables. He pulled it out, snapped it to its full length and glanced down at yesterday's numbers. Tiresome had come in fourth. "I owe Westwoode a guinea."

And I owe Papa an apology. That little American might be a good match for me, after all.

CHAPTER 4

Tom Heppenstall dried the pint glass with his fist and towel pressed inside until it squeaked. With a quick glance at the clock on the shelf behind him, he set the glass upside down in the wooden cabinet with the others. He grabbed for the next, but there were none. With no more glasses to dry, he set to vigorously rubbing down the same two feet of the wooden bar in front of him. The publican's eyes weren't on his task but on the door. It was half past, and that good-for-nothing boy who was supposed to be working for him hadn't arrived yet. That made four times late in so many days. Of course, the boy always had an excuse: ponies were blocking the road; his dad had him weeding the vegetable patch, and he'd lost track of time; his mum burnt his pasty, and he had to wait for her to bake another. Tom didn't care what the boy was really up to, though he suspected the butcher's daughter might have something to do with it, but he couldn't have someone unreliable working for him. No matter the excuse the boy had prepared for him today, he might have to let him go.

Tom took his eyes off the door and looked about the pub.

Luckily, it was quiet yet. Only Old Joe at the end of the bar and that grockle in the corner, nursing a half. Tom glanced again at the door—*where is that boy?*—and then back at the grockle. With his cap pulled low on his forehead, the stranger stared into his bitter. How long had the grockle been coming in here? Two, three days? Outsiders wandered in now and then, but this grockle seemed different. He sat in the taproom when, by the cut of his tweeds, the bloke should prefer the lounge. He came, too, when it was quiet, and left as soon as the men arrived in from the fields. Rarely spoke and hardly drank anything either.

In Tom's twenty-two years behind the bar of the Knightwood Oak, he'd seen his share of troubled souls. He was as sure that the timbers above his head would be holding up the ceiling long after he was gone as he was that this fellow was one of those troubled souls. Today the bloke's hands had been trembling when he'd placed his tuppence on the bar. What caused a grown man to shake like an oak leaf in the winter wind? "Grockles bring trouble, bring change," his dad used to say, and Tom found it too often to be true. The publican didn't know what this fellow had done, and didn't want to know, for that matter, but something told him the sooner this fellow moved on, the better. Tom glanced at the clock again as the door flew open and crashed against the wall, making a bloody racket, like a gale off the Solent wanting in. And in with it came the boy, ducking his head as he stepped through.

"I'm sorry, Mr. Heppenstall. Pigs escaped their pen, and I had to round them up."

The publican threw his towel on the bar and planted his fists on his hips. Grockles nothing. This local lad was enough trouble for him to deal with.

With her gloves in her lap, Stella dug her nails into the palms of her hands. Otherwise, she'd cry, and she hated it when she cried. After the fiasco at the stables, she'd changed into her favorite linen and lace tea dress; the embroidered lavender flower swirls usually made her feel like a walking garden. But trapped in the drawing room, a chilly room with vaulted ceilings and dark, heavy furniture, surrounded by portraits of men and women in lace collars or redcoat uniforms with the same stony gaze as that of the woman sitting across from her, Stella decided that the swirls on her dress reflected the nausea in the pit of her stomach.

"Ah, Mrs. Westwoode, Miss Westwoode." Lady Atherly set aside the book in her lap, *Wellington, Soldier and Statesman*, and addressed two women Stella hadn't met yet.

The matron, Mrs. Westwoode, her pale green and gray dress cleverly paired with the gray streaks in her golden blond hair, sashayed into the room. The congenial smile faded quickly from her face. Her daughter's gaze never left the bold red and gold patterned carpet. Miss Westwoode, several years Stella's junior and endowed with an enviable hourglass figure, would never be the beauty her mother was. Her hair was mousy colored, her nose was bulbous, and her cheeks were plump.

"May I present Miss Stella Kendrick . . ." Lady Atherly hesitated, as if the words were difficult to form in her mouth. "My son's intended." Stella flinched at those words. None of the women seemed to notice. "Miss Kendrick, may I present my good friend Mrs. Caroline Westwoode and her daughter, Miss Elizabeth Westwoode?"

"It's nice to meet-," Stella began as the Westwoode women arranged themselves on adjacent green velvet, carved mahogany chairs.

"Likewise, I am sure, my dear," Mrs. Westwoode said, glancing in Stella's direction before patting her daughter's knee. "My daughter is fiancée to Lord Hugh, second son of the Duke of Tonnbridge."

What did Stella care about the betrothal of a stranger, considering her own unbearable situation?

Mrs. Westwoode added, "Who will marry first? I wonder."

Stella bit back the retort on her tongue. *Not me. I'm never going to marry Lord Lyndhurst.* She welcomed the anger that washed over her. If nothing else, it kept the self-pity and the tears at bay. But Mrs. Westwoode apparently never intended to wait for Stella's reply.

"Where are the men?" The matron glanced about the drawing room, as if Lord Atherly, Lyndy, and the others were hiding behind the couch and she had missed seeing them upon her arrival.

"I requested the gentlemen join us at quarter past so that we ladies may get acquainted," Lady Atherly said.

"Isn't your vicar joining us?" Mrs. Westwoode said, looking around the room again.

"Yes, as I said," Lady Atherly said. "At quarter past."

"He was quite charming at luncheon, but I admit I was quite surprised to learn you're allowing him to officiate at Lord Lyndhurst's wedding. The Duke of Tonnbridge insists we have no one less than the Bishop of Winchester."

"Is that so?" Lady Atherly said. "I had no idea His Grace took such an interest in his youngest son's wedding arrangements."

"But why shouldn't the bishop officiate when my darling daughter, the granddaughter of a baron, marries the son of a duke?"

"Why indeed?"

As the two older women continued to discuss the merits for and against the bishop performing the Westwoode wedding, Lady Alice set aside the magazine she'd been reading and sorted through the stack on her lap. Titles like *Life*, the *Ladies' Home Journal*, *Cosmopolitan*, *Vogue*, *and Harper's Bazaar* flickered by. Miss Westwoode stared out the French windows. Stella followed the young woman's gaze. From her vantage point, all Stella could see was the sky, peppered with darkening clouds. She shivered. Why hadn't she brought a shawl?

Hoping to commiserate with a fellow sufferer, Stella leaned over and whispered, "Are you fond of the outdoors, Miss Westwoode, or planning your escape?"

Miss Westwoode gasped and glanced in her mother's direction. "Whatever do you mean, Miss Kendrick?"

Are you marrying for love, Miss Westwoode, or are you being forced to marry by your family, as I am?

"For me, it's a bit of both. I've always preferred the outdoors or the stable to drawing rooms," Stella said. "Much to my father's chagrin, I'm afraid, I like to ride, cycle, swim, play tennis, what have you. I'm not good at sitting about discussing last month's ball or who wore what to the World's Fair." *Or a wedding that is never going to take place.* Stella rubbed her hands up and down her arms. "Is it always this cold in here?"

Miss Westwoode stared at the carpet again. Mrs. Westwoode stopped her conversation with Lady Atherly to stare at Stella. Lady Atherly sighed, as if her forbearance was near its end.

"Did I say something wrong?" Stella asked.

No one responded.

"As I was saying, Mrs. Westwoode . . . ," Lady Atherly continued.

Stella looked to the other women for an explanation. Elizabeth Westwoode examined the vase on the octagonal table next to her, as if she'd never seen a bouquet of roses before. Aunt Rachel dozed in the overstuffed armchair by the unlit fireplace. Lady Alice had a smirk on her face while appearing buried in her magazines. Stella took their cue and sat wallowing in frustrated silence, digging her nails into her palms again, as the two matrons discussed wedding cakes. Then Lord Lyndhurst strode purposefully into the room. He was arrogance personified, and she despised him—he was complicit with her father in this wretched engagement, after all—but his presence brought much-welcomed energy to the room.

"Mrs. Westwoode," he said. "I trust you and Mr. Westwoode had a pleasant journey?"

"Yes. Thank you, Lord Lyndhurst," Mrs. Westwoode said. "We missed you at luncheon."

"My son considered it more important to go fishing than to entertain our guests," Lady Atherly said.

"But I came back in time to welcome the Kendricks, did I not?" Lady Atherly rolled her eyes as her son addressed another lady in the room. "Miss Westwoode, you look as lovely as ever."

Miss Westwoode batted her eyelids and smiled the way women seemed to do here, thinly and without showing their teeth. Could all English women have particularly poor teeth? Why else would they smile so?

"Lord Hugh is a lucky man," Lord Lyndhurst said.

Miss Westwoode's cheeks reddened, and her tight-lipped grin widened before she shyly lowered her gaze. Her mother beamed at him, nodding enthusiastically.

"I see you have met Miss Kendrick," Lyndy noted.

"Yes. Charming, I'm sure," Mrs. Westwoode said, her words belying her fading smile.

Unlike Mrs. Westwoode, who had already focused her attention back on her daughter, Lord Lyndhurst's focus remained on Stella. If he expected her to demurely look away, as Miss Westwoode had, he was surely disappointed. Stella held his gaze and continued to as he strode toward her and presumptuously took her hand. His dark brown eyes never left hers.

"Yes, she is," he whispered as he lifted her hand to his lips.

Her relief in seeing him dissipated instantly. How did he know if she was charming? How did he know anything about her at all? She cringed in shame just thinking about the confrontation he'd witnessed between her and Daddy. He'd looked down upon her, kneeling in the dirt, with horse manure on her boots and skirt. She'd insulted him. How could he call her charming? He was mocking her, and she didn't like it.

"As if you would know," Stella said.

His eyebrows rose, and then he laughed. Stella yanked her hand away. Daddy expected her to spend the rest of her life with this man?

"Well, that's all settled," Daddy announced as he followed Lord Atherly into the room. Daddy pinned Stella with his eyes and smiled like the cat that ate the canary. A sour taste filled Stella's mouth.

Daddy spied Mrs. Westwoode and her daughter and waddled over to them. "And who might these two such fine, beautiful ladies be?"

Mrs. Westwoode, unmistakably alarmed by Daddy's approach, leaned back in her chair, trying to create distance between them. He stared down at her, his hands on his hips, his belly protruding, waiting.

Fulton, the butler, inadvertently coming to Mrs. Westwoode's rescue, announced, "Tea is served, my lady."

"Thank you, Fulton," Lady Atherly said as a footman arrived with a silver tray laden with tea sandwiches and scones. "As to your question, Mr. Kendrick, may I present Mrs. Westwoode and her daughter, Miss Westwoode? They are our guests for the wedding."

"Charming. Elijah Kendrick, the soon-to-be father-in-law to the viscount here, at your service, ma'am, miss." Not having a hat, he pretended to tip his hat, nonetheless.

"Yes, well," Mrs. Westwoode said, trying to calculate the appropriate response. "Pleased to meet you, Mr. Kendrick. Does anyone know where my husband is?"

"No, I'm afraid I haven't seen him since luncheon," Lord Atherly said.

"And Lord Hugh?" Mrs. Westwoode said. "Where is my daughter's fiancé?"

Lady Atherly looked at her son, who shrugged.

"Where is the vicar?" Daddy asked. "Isn't he supposed to be here too? I want to see if the man's up to the task."

"I can't imagine what's keeping him," Lord Atherly said. "Reverend Bullmore does love his food."

"I am certain everyone shall join us soon," Lady Atherly said, a forced smile on her face. "And I can assure you, Mr. Kendrick, that Reverend Bullmore is 'up to the task.'"

"Don't be offended if I don't take your word on that, Lady Atherly. I always need to meet eye to eye with every man I do business with."

"Pity. You must have to carry a step stool around with you, then."

Lady Atherly's retort evoked snickers from several members of the group.

As Mrs. Westwoode stifled a giggle with her hand, Daddy snapped, "Stella, you're just sitting there. Why don't you go find him?"

Since the moment her father arrived, Stella had been staring at him, at the small bald circle on the back of his head, to be precise, as if challenging him to acknowledge her, apologize to her. He hadn't. *What a surprise. But now what?* She'd love a chance to explore this fantastic house, if you could call such an enormous building a house, but her father had demanded she search for the vicar. Stella gently rubbed her sore hand. She was done doing his bidding.

"Why don't I give Miss Kendrick a bit of a tour of her new home?" Lord Lyndhurst offered unexpectedly. "Perhaps we'll find the vicar while we're at it."

"As long as you bring back the vicar," Daddy said. "We have a lot to discuss, and time's ticking."

"As long as you bring Miss Luckett with you," Lady Atherly said.

Aunt Rachel, having stirred at the pronouncement of tea, rose from her chair and grabbed her cane. "I'm game if you are, girlie," she said.

"Shall we?" Lord Lyndhurst said, leaning down and offering his arm to Stella.

Stella studied him. Why had he interceded? Without a hint in his eyes, his countenance, or his manner, she was quick to disregard any thoughts of his sincerity. But she'd made her decision. Stella took the viscount's arm and rose from the chair. He smiled, a thin smirk of a thing. Was he mocking her again? Had she made the wrong choice to go with him? No, for a moment the smile reached his eyes. Stella pushed down the fear, the bitterness, the self-pity, the anger, the doubt, and the determination and forced herself to smile back as Lord Lyndhurst led her and her hobbling chaperone in search of the wayward vicar.

"This is the music room, or what I like to call the Blue Room."

Stella could see why he called it that. Apart from the marble fireplace, the piano, and the crystal chandelier, everything in the room was a shade of blue. It reminded Stella of the ocean voyage she'd taken to get here. Yesterday she would've liked it.

"I don't have much occasion to spend time in here, though Mother insists I attend when she hosts a musical night or a ball. Hasn't been one of those in quite some time."

"You don't have to play tour guide for me, Lord Lyndhurst," Stella said. "Our parents aren't watching." Neither was Aunt Rachel, who'd readily agreed to be left to rest in the conservatory, with a bit of sun on her face.

"Thank goodness for that." He chuckled.

"Why did you offer to come with me to find the vicar?"

"We can't have you getting lost, now can we?"

"That's not why. I'm guessing either you want to ingratiate yourself with my father by compelling me to do his bidding—"

"Never." The viscount's vehemence surprised her.

"Or you dislike drawing-room chitchat as much as I do."

He said nothing. Instead, he leafed through the sheet music on the Blüthner piano. It was Mozart's "Dans un bois solitaire." Since the viscount had admitted he wasn't much of a musician, who played? Stella couldn't play at all and certainly didn't aspire to sing Mozart, but she enjoyed singing the likes of "Daisy Bell," "After the Ball," and "My Old Kentucky Home" for Daddy back home. Her singing performances were one of the rare times Daddy praised her.

Lord Lyndhurst leaned over and began tapping on the keys with his index finger, one key at a time. It was a slow, choppy melody Stella didn't recognize. The notes, filling the room, were discordant in her ears. She wanted him to stop.

"When did you know?" she asked.

"Know what?"

"About this arrangement?"

"Which arrangement? The Mozart piece?" he said, continuing to play.

"This arrangement." She wagged her finger back and forth between them.

"That we tour the house or that we seek out our tardy vicar?"

Stella, frustrated, reached over to block him from playing another note.

Clang!

She banged down on the piano keys. The viscount's head snapped up in surprise. He stepped back from the piano.

"You know what I'm talking about."

"Pity you won't speak of it, then."

"I didn't think I needed to."

"And here I thought Americans were forthright."

"And here I thought English sensibilities were too delicate to handle American frankness."

"I can assure you, Miss Kendrick, I am not so delicate."

"Very well. You want me to be frank? I'll be frank. Our engagement. I'm talking about our engagement. I'm talking about the fact that I have not agreed to it. I'm talking about how everyone expects me to marry you, and I don't even know you. I'm not sure I even like you. I'm talking about how I don't want to marry you, and given a choice, I won't marry you. Is that straightforward enough for you?" Stella, her hands on her hips, glared at him, daring him to respond.

"I don't suppose you shall be wanting this, then?"

He pulled something from his waistcoat pocket. A flash of a sparkle glistened above his fingers as he held it out toward her. It was a ring, an engagement ring. The delicate filigree platinum setting held a large round-cut diamond encircled by smaller diamonds. It was stunning. She didn't know what to say. The viscount laughed.

"You find this funny?"

He shook his head. "Funny, no. Amusing, yes."

"Aren't they the same thing?"

"No, indeed. This marriage arrangement is not 'funny' at all. I, too, had no choice in the matter. It was marry an heiress or give up everything. I, for one, have no intention of forfeiting my ancestral home, my title, or those lovely horses your father brought. So, unless you know a better way, we must abide by our families' wishes."

Stella didn't know a better way. What would Daddy do if she disobeyed him? Would he disown her, deny her an inheritance? But there had to be a way out of this, didn't there?

"As to your frankness, as you call it, it is most refreshing and, dare I say, amusing," Lord Lyndhurst said. "I've been bored to distraction by English heiresses. Do you have anything else you wish to say?"

"No. I think I've said quite enough already."

"Then follow me."

After leaving the music room, he led her through the grand central hall, or grand saloon, as he called it, an expansive room with carpeted parquet floors, marble pillars, and a forty-foot-high fresco-painted vaulted ceiling that was more reminiscent of one in a cathedral than in a home. Stella resisted the urge to look up. The viscount stopped in front of one of several closed doors leading off the main hall.

"This is the library." He opened the door.

Stella, drawn in by the floor-to-ceiling bookshelves, entered the room first. Her home in Kentucky had a library. The room had once been the log cabin Grandpa Kendrick built before Daddy had it incorporated into the bigger house. But as Daddy collected books, as he collected everything, exclusively buying the rare and most expensive ones, Stella hadn't been encouraged as a child to peruse them. But she'd persisted in getting her hands on less expensive volumes, nagging first her mother, then her governesses, and then Aunt Rachel to satisfy her insatiable appetite, especially for adventure stories and romance novels. Daddy would respect the cost of such an extensive, and presumably priceless collection. Stella couldn't wait to see what treasures it held.

"He's not here," Stella said, glancing around.

She could see why the vicar had asked to wait in this room. It was a masculine room, decorated with leather chesterfield chairs and couch, dark red walls, and a dark red and gold carpet, and was by far the warmest in the house. The glowing embers in the fireplace glinted off the gilded frame of a bird painting above the mantel.

"That's probably his," she said, noticing the empty cup and saucer on the square side table. "He must've already left."

A few steps farther in, she caught a glimpse of a glass-paneled mahogany display case, against the side wall, filled with dozens of exotic birds of all shapes and sizes, many mounted on perching limbs. She eagerly strolled toward it. A glass dome filled with colorful butterflies sat in the front parlor at home. Each specimen had been collected and mounted by her mother before she died. Stella had peered into it every day when she was little, more often than not leaving behind fingerprint smudges, much to the maids' chagrin. Yet no one had ever scolded her. The collection was one of the few reminders of Katherine Kendrick left in the house.

Stella stopped short. A wave of regret threatened to overwhelm her. She'd left so much behind. Tully and the trunks Daddy had allowed her, packed with the usual clothes, hats, shoes, jewelry, gloves, books, and the souvenir spoons she'd bought in Southampton and Hythe for a collection she no longer owned, were all that was left of her belongings, of her life back home.

I have to figure a way out of this.

"Where do you think the vicar is?" she asked, with a glimmer of hope. Perhaps the vicar could help her. Maybe he could dissuade Daddy and Lord Atherly from insisting on this ill-conceived marriage. If only she could talk to the vicar before Daddy did.

"Perhaps he's fallen asleep on the sofa. I do hope he thought to remove his shoes." Lord Lyndhurst frowned. "Reverend Bullmore," he called, "you are late for tea, dear fellow."

Stella and the viscount approached the high-backed couch from opposite sides. It was empty. But there on the carpet, a dark blotch seeping into the fibers that cushioned his graying head, was a gaunt man lying on his side. His unblinking eyes

were open, and cookie crumbs clung to one corner of his up-
turned mouth.

"Oh!" Stella gasped, her hand covering her mouth. "Oh my
God. Is that . . . ?"

"The vicar?" Lord Lyndhurst said. "Yes, I'm afraid it is."

CHAPTER 5

"At what time did you discover the body, Lord Lyndhurst?"

Stella stared at the worn bottom of Inspector Brown's left shoe as the kneeling policeman examined the body of Reverend Bullmore, crumpled on the library carpet. From where she sat, leaning against the bird display case, the couch hid the unfortunate vicar from view. But close her eyes and Stella could see every minute detail of the scene: the cookie crumbs on the vicar's lips, the strands of gray hair sticking to the damp blood on his forehead, his left pant leg pushed up enough to expose his sock garter, his right eye partially open and staring at her, the starkness of the white collar around his neck. When had she first noticed the smear of blood on the side table? When had she moved from the couch to this distant chair? While Lord Atherly had been there, she'd stayed with the vicar, planting herself on the couch and nearly sitting on an open copy of the *Sporting Life*. She prided herself on having a strong constitution. She wasn't one to faint at the slightest sight of blood or injury. Hadn't she been the one who assisted when Tully was born? Hadn't she nursed Daddy when he was thrown from

Onondaga the day the stallion lost its shoe? How was this any different?

"Bloody hell. I don't know," Lord Lyndhurst said, combing his fingers through his hair. The other policeman, Constable Waterman, stood off to the side, near the fireplace, pad and pencil in hand, scribbling down whatever was said. He looked at the viscount expectantly. "I don't remember."

"Fulton had called us to tea," Stella said. "It must've been around four o'clock."

Lord Lyndhurst walked away from his position near the vicar's body to stand next to Stella.

The inspector sat back on his heels and looked over the couch at them. He had a round, weathered face with a high forehead. Gray peppered his tidy mustache. He regarded Stella for a moment, a flash of anger in his wary eyes. Yet his tone was respectful and restrained when he spoke.

"Why is this young lady here? Shouldn't she be with the others, my lord?"

"Yes," Lord Lyndhurst said. "But she insisted, and she can be quite persuasive. Even Papa couldn't get her to leave."

When Lord Atherly had insisted she leave when he did, Stella had refused. Now she looked up at the viscount, standing with his hand resting on the back of her chair, almost protectively. He'd supported her decision to stay. *Why?*

"Miss Kendrick is my fiancée. We discovered the body together," he said, as if answering her unspoken question.

"I wanted to . . . I needed to . . ." She stumbled over the words. "I thought . . ." She didn't know what to think. A dead man lay on the other side of the chesterfield couch. "I couldn't leave him alone. Not until you arrived. Not until someone could stay with him."

"Right! Well, we're here now. We'll see to the vicar," Inspector Brown said, not unkindly. "Any questions I have for you can keep. Thank you and if you would please, my lord . . ." He indicated Stella with a nod. "She's had quite a shock."

Lord Lyndhurst held out his hand. Stella took it without thinking and allowed him to help her rise from the chair. As he led her toward the door, she questioned her passive acquiescence. She had the use of her own two feet, as Daddy liked to say, didn't she? She had a mind of her own and had been determined to use it, hadn't she? She remembered how it had been between them when they entered the library. Why did it feel like something had changed?

Stella had a sudden urge to see the vicar again. She took a step toward the couch that hid the body from her. Lord Lyndhurst wrapped his arm around her shoulder and pulled her back.

"Let's remove ourselves from the ugliness, shall we?"

Wretched tears, which she'd fought off since she'd learned of her father's betrayal, welled in her eyes as Stella let Lord Lyndhurst guide her from the room. His hold was firm but warm. When was the last time someone had touched her without malintent? Her hand still ached from her father's cruel squeeze.

As she crossed the threshold, Inspector Brown said, "What do you think, Waterman? Did he crack his skull open on the side table?"

"Fulton said the vicar had an accident," Mother said. "Has someone called the doctor?" Lyndy nodded.

How extraordinary. Everything was as it had been when he and Miss Kendrick left the drawing room, except now Mother and the other ladies held cups of partially sipped tea in their hands. *As if nothing had happened.* Lyndy led Miss Kendrick toward the needlepoint chair next to his sister.

"The vicar is dead," Lyndy said, rubbing his hands together.

Someone gasped.

"Why is it so bloody cold in here?" he asked. Miss Kendrick was shaking. "Shall we have a fire lit?"

Mother nodded to the footman, who disappeared to inform Fulton.

"Oh dear! What happened?" Mrs. Westwoode asked.

"The vicar was in the library. He'd hit his head. Dr. Johnstone has already left for Epsom, so Papa called in the police."

Another gasp.

"Where is your father?" Mother asked. "He rushed off and hasn't come back."

"How should I know?"

The moment he'd noticed the blood—on the carpet, on the vicar's head and clothes, next to the teacup on the side table— Lyndy had rung for Fulton. He and Miss Kendrick had waited in silent vigil over the vicar, Miss Kendrick seated on the sofa next to the body, Lyndy pacing the room. Minutes, which had seemed like hours, had elapsed before Papa finally arrived. When Fulton announced the doctor was unavailable, Papa had insisted Fulton contact the police. But unable to persuade Miss Kendrick to withdraw, Papa had remained in the libary only long enough to speak with the detective in charge. Lyndy had assumed Papa had returned to the drawing room.

"Are you all right, Miss Kendrick?" Alice asked, offering her a cup of tea.

Miss Kendrick declined the tea with a slight shake of her head and rubbed her sore hand as she stared at a point on the wall. Alice put the teacup on the table in front of Miss Kendrick, just in case. Mother offered Lyndy a cup. He took it, noticing his hands were shaking, and gulped the tea down. It was sweet. He held out his cup for more.

"I say Miss Kendrick should be commended for her composure," Lyndy said.

"She's a Kendrick," her father said. "We're all tough when we need to be."

Miss Kendrick's eyes remained focused on the wall. She didn't look so tough right now. Could Lyndy draw her out? Could he rally her? Her silence was unnerving.

"You should've seen her. She insisted on staying until the police arrived. And through it all, not one tear or shriek of despair."

He didn't mention the tears that had streaked down her cheeks as they'd left the library. Were they for the vicar or herself? Lyndy didn't care; the tears had been his excuse to caress her fine features with his handkerchief. Lyndy studied her expressionless countenance now. Did she even remember him doing it?

"You must drink your tea, Miss Kendrick," Mother said, not unkindly, "and eat something, if you can manage it." Mother indicated a plate laden with smoked salmon sandwiches, scones, and an iced Dundee fruitcake.

"I dare say she was more composed with a dead body than with a group of women talking about weddings," Mrs. Westwoode whispered behind her hand to her daughter but loud enough for all to hear.

Splotches of red bloomed on the tips of Miss Kendrick's ears. She stirred and focused her gaze on her disparager. Then, without a word, she bolted from her seat, dashing past Papa as he returned to the drawing room.

"What did I say?" Mrs. Westwoode asked, looking around the room.

"Wedding," Lyndy said, masking the relief that washed over him. He much preferred Miss Kendrick angry than sullen or in shock.

"Speaking of weddings," Kendrick said, "who do we get to do it now that your vicar's dead? The bishop?"

Another gasp. Had that one come from Mother?

"I've seen to it that the bishop knows of Reverend Bullmore's passing," Papa said. "It will be up to him who will officiate the wedding." Mother, her lips white from holding her tongue, handed Papa a cup of tea.

"What about the police? Are they still here?" Mr. Kendrick asked, lacking the tact to stay silent.

"Police? What's this about the police?" A man had appeared in the doorway.

"Lord Hugh!" Mrs. Westwoode and Miss Westwoode chorused. Several other voices rose in delight and relief.

Lyndy strode over to greet the newcomer. Dimples on the rascal's cheeks deepened as Hugh smoothed his thick blond mustache and grinned.

"Mr. Kendrick," Papa said, "may I introduce Lord Hugh Drakeford, who is engaged to be married to Miss Westwoode? Lord Hugh, Mr. Kendrick is our American guest."

"Pleased to meet you, Lord Hugh," Mr. Kendrick said.

"And I you," Hugh said, raking his fingers through his windswept hair. "I hear you come bearing gifts, Mr. Kendrick. Some of the finest thoroughbreds ever to cross the pond, if the rumors are true."

Mr. Kendrick laughed. "If I do say so myself."

"Where have you been, old chap?" Lyndy slapped his best friend on the shoulder. He was relieved that his hands had stopped shaking.

"Didn't Elizabeth tell you? I went into Rosehurst this morning. Why?"

"Brace yourself, Lord Hugh," Mrs. Westwoode said, fluttering across the room and taking Hugh's arm. "The local vicar is dead. Died right in Lord Atherly's library."

"The reverend from this morning? He seemed fit enough when I met him."

"Lord Hugh, dear," Mrs. Westwoode said, pouting, "he met with a terrible accident, and Lord Lyndhurst and Miss Kendrick found him."

Mrs. Westwoode stared at Lyndy, as if a glare could command him to explain. But Lyndy had never liked Mrs. Westwoode. She fussed and fluttered and spoke to her husband like he was a child. For Hugh's sake, he hoped her daughter was made of more sympathetic stuff.

"Bloody hell. Pardon me, ladies. But that's ghastly. Where is Miss Kendrick? I haven't even met her yet."

"She is in her room, recovering from the ordeal," Mother said, offering Hugh a cup of tea.

Ordeal? Which one? Finding the vicar who was to officiate over her wedding dead or being forced to wed in the first place?

"What happened?" Hugh asked.

"He hit his head," Lyndy said.

"As I said, a senseless accident," Mrs. Westwoode said.

"I'm afraid it's more nefarious than that," Inspector Brown said, strolling into the room, hat in hand, as if he'd been invited. "The good vicar was murdered."

Mrs. Westwoode swooned, lost her grip on Hugh's arm, and fell back onto a chair.

CHAPTER 6

Papa's study was a small, dark room at the back of the house. The inspector had requested that the men gather somewhere private, and this was the perfect place. From the half-empty teacups and the full waste bin, it was evident Papa hadn't allowed a maid entry in weeks. The engraved oak partners desk was covered with a small microscope and an array of fossilized horse teeth and was bestrewn with papers pertaining to his expensive "hobby," paleontological expeditions in search of extinct horse fossils. A leather cylinder containing the map of Wyoming sat propped up in the spindle-backed desk chair. The desk dominated one half of the room, forcing the men to cluster near the mantel. With only a single north-facing window to allow the sun in, a chill permeated the room, and not only because the fire grate stood empty. Papa preferred the cluttered, closed-in space to anywhere else in the house. To Lyndy, it was as cozy as a cave.

"Reverend Bullmore was murdered, then?" Papa said.

"There will have to be an official inquest, of course, but yes," Inspector Brown said. "He was hit on the head with a hard, sharp object."

"That wouldn't be enough to kill him," Mr. Kendrick said. "I smacked a hapless gamekeeper in the head with the butt of my shotgun once. All it gave him was a lump as a reminder to be more diligent."

The inspector stared at Mr. Kendrick, his expression unreadable.

"I assumed he hit his head on the corner of the table," Lyndy said, trying to ignore the American. He picked up a fossilized horse leg bone from the mantel. A shape in the dust marked its place. Papa snatched it from Lyndy's hand and gently put it back in its place.

"We did, too, at first," Inspector Brown said. "But no, the wound is far too deep for that. I'm sure the coroner will confirm it. We believe someone hit him with the fire iron. It's heavy enough, hard enough, and has gone missing. We're assuming the killer took it with him."

"But who would want to murder Reverend Bullmore?" Hugh said, picking up and examining a sheet of paper bearing Professor Gridley's signature that had fallen to the floor. Hugh spoke for everyone. It was inconceivable why anyone would want to kill a man of God.

"That is what I hoped you'd be able to tell me," Inspector Brown said.

"I won't be much help, I'm afraid, Inspector," Papa said, plucking the paper from Hugh's fingers. "Reverend Bullmore was a friend of a friend, I admit, but we knew him more by reputation until he moved into the vicarage a fortnight ago."

Papa yanked open a drawer that was a bit stuck and dropped the papers from his desk in it. Lyndy had had no idea Papa had any connection, however distant, to the dead vicar. Who was this friend of a friend? Papa shut the drawer with a bang.

"You know of no enemies, no altercations, no recent arguments with anyone?" the inspector said.

"No, not that I know of," Papa said.

Lyndy's breath caught in his throat. He glanced at Hugh.

Like everyone else, Hugh shook his head. But Lyndy had over-heard Hugh and the vicar involved in a heated discussion. Why was Hugh lying?

"Right," Inspector Brown said. "I'm sorry to inconvenience you, my lord, but I'd be obliged if I could have a small space to set up as an interview room." The inspector looked about him with a sour expression. "Not anywhere that will inconvenience you, of course." He undoubtably didn't want to have to be cooped up in this hovel any more than Lyndy did. "I will have to speak to the servants, your guests. I will have to ask for your assistance, as well, Lord Lyndhurst."

Lyndy nodded. He'd expected as much. Papa had not.

"No one in this house would do such a thing," Papa said.

"Be it as it may, my lord, I would be most grateful," the inspector said.

"If it will help, speak to Fulton, our butler, about it. I'm sure he can accommodate you." Papa was not about to offer up his study, to the inspector's obvious relief.

The inspector tipped his hat. "Thank you, my lord, for your cooperation. We'll speak again soon."

"It's all such a damn inconvenience," Mr. Kendrick muttered as he bent to peer into Papa's microscope. "Never would be too soon."

"What now?" Silas Gates, the stable manager and head coach-man, looked up from his accounts.

He'd been interrupted twice already today, and he had a long night ahead of him. The provender bill was due by morning. Gates had expected the first interruption; the Americans had arrived with the new horses. He'd welcomed the break. Not every day did a man add champion thoroughbred racehorses to his fold. The second time had been shocking; a stable lad had run about yelling something about the vicar dying up at the house. Gates had met the vicar only this past Sunday. After a single sermon, he hadn't had time to form an opinion. This time someone lingered outside the harness-room door.

Who could it be at this hour? The others were having their dinner. No one should be about. If any of his lads were where they shouldn't be, he'd find out right quick.

"Hello?" Gates called.

No answer. He didn't give much credence to the rumor that someone had murdered the vicar, but just the same, he didn't relish someone lingering silently outside his door.

Gates slid back from the workbench. Firelight gleamed off the harnesses hanging in neat rows along the walls. Although Lord Atherly had provided him with a small office of his own, Gates preferred to do his accounting in here. *An organized room for an organized brain*, he'd reasoned. But, in fact, it was the nicest room in the stables: wood-paneled walls, parquet-tiled floor, and the immense two-sided stone fireplace that guaranteed the horses' comfort year-round, which was more than he could say for his office or the bedrooms upstairs. Lying in his bed at night, he often suspected the hayloft would be warmer.

Gates stepped out of the harness room. "Hello?" No one was about.

But someone had been.

He walked past the empty standing stalls, making a note to have the brass ball finials on the stable posts polished. The scent of nothing but fresh hay assured him the lads had done their work before heading to their dinner. He passed the loose boxes, which were occupied for the first time since Lord Atherly's late father died years ago, their mahogany walls newly scrubbed. The horses followed him with their gaze but showed no other sign of interest. Only the new thoroughbred stallion, Orson, stomped and snorted as Gates passed. *He's going to be a handful, that one.*

Gates continued past the wash stall, the sick box, and the

coal room. All appeared in hand. All was quiet. He entered the coach house. The vast room was filled with Lord Atherly's family carriages, cleaned, polished, and ready to go at a moment's notice. The Americans' motorcar was parked in the far corner. Gates had looked the contraption over while the lads were cleaning it. If the American expected him to service the machine, he'd have to request help. What did he know of motorcars?

A shadow darted between the victoria and the dog cart.

"Hello? Who's there?"

A man's figure skirted around the carriages and dashed toward the door. Lamplight briefly illuminated the side of his round face. Blond stubble dotted his chin. Gates didn't recognize him. It wasn't one of his lads. It wasn't Roy, the Kendricks' groom, either. Then who could it be? Who would be poking around the coach house, uninvited and unannounced? The appearance of Lord Lyndhurst's fiancée earlier had taken him by surprise; the family never visited the stables. Perhaps this was someone from her party he didn't know of. Everyone knew the Americans did things differently. After his groom's mistake, Gates had to tread lightly.

"Sir?" Gates's call went unheeded. The stranger shoved the door open and disappeared.

No gentleman would act so, not even an American one. Must be a local lad, then, who'd heard about the motorcar and wanted a peek. Two years ago, the miller from Rosehurst's youngest boy had been discovered sleeping in the hayloft after a fight with his brother. A local lad. That had to be it.

"Oi!" *I'll teach him to creep about my coach house.*

Gates weaved his way through the carriages, in pursuit. By the time he reached the washing yard, the lad was gone. As Gates debated which direction to take, Herbert rounded the corner.

"Herbert! Did you see a village lad come by here?"

"No, I haven't seen anyone. Everyone's at dinner. Why? Do you think it was the vicar's killer? Everyone's saying he was murdered, you know."

Dragons in Burley Beacon, kingly ghosts in Hurst Castle, and now vicar-slaying murderers. What will these lads think up next? Gates was not going to dignify Herbert's speculation with an answer.

"Why aren't you at dinner?" Gates asked.

"Leonard's still sick, so I came to check on the thoroughbreds. The stallion wasn't eating earlier."

"Then off you go."

Gates stood a moment or two after Herbert left, his palm against his forehead and his eyes closed. His head was pounding. It was no small feat preparing for the new horses with one of his grooms sick in bed, and what with news of the vicar's death . . . The strain of the past few days had caught up with him. Now this. Either way, the lad was long gone by now.

Gates retraced his steps, reassuring himself that the intruder, whoever he was, had caused no mischief. Tomorrow he'd inform Lord Atherly about the incident, just the same. But back in the harness room, odd Americans, mischievous village lads, and rumors about murderers slipped from his mind as he sat back down to finish his infernal accounts.

CHAPTER 7

"Saddle up the new filly," Lyndy said to the first stable hand he encountered. Frustrated and restless, he'd headed for the stables instead of waiting for a horse to be brought to him.

Lyndy had intended to ride the new stallion this morning. He'd been in a foul mood. What better time to pit his skills against the feisty horse? But when he'd approached the stallion's loose box, the horse was stomping inside, sending bits of straw flying. The ornery animal had already chewed a chunk of wood off a corner of his box's door post. Until the angry horse had adjusted, why risk getting bitten or worse?

"Which filly, sir?" the groom asked. "Tupper or Tully, the one Miss Kendrick is with?"

Miss Kendrick? His mood brightened. So, this was where she was. He'd waited for Miss Kendrick to appear at breakfast until the servants came to clear everything away. She'd never come. Who would've guessed she'd be here? He couldn't help but smile.

"Tupper."

Lyndy strode behind the groom, passing empty loose box

after empty loose box. It had been too long since the stables were at even half capacity. There were the carriage mares, Sugar and Spice; and Lister, Papa's horse, a gift from the board of Rosehurst Cottage Hospital when Papa inherited his title; and Lyndy's horse, Beau, a striking chestnut Irish Hunter. But now his family would have thoroughbreds again, racehorses to ride, to race, to breed.

As it should be.

Grandfather, the seventh Earl of Atherly, had owned Augustine, a champion thoroughbred filly, among others. He'd cultivated a love for the Turf in Lyndy, as his own son cared more about discovering fossils of ancient horses than about the racehorses in his own stables. As a small boy, Lyndy had wanted nothing more than to follow in Grandfather's footsteps. But soon after Grandfather died, Papa had discovered the estate no longer paid for itself. Unwilling to give up his fossil-hunting expeditions, Papa had sold Augustine and the other racehorses, as well as let go of several of the staff, to fund his hobby. Lyndy hadn't forgiven him. Until now.

Lyndy stopped short of Tully's loose box. Miss Kendrick was inside it, with her back to him, checking the balance strap on the horse's sidesaddle. She was stunning, the tailored lines of her black riding jacket clinging to her curves, the top hat accentuating her long, pale neck.

"Do you think I'm doing the right thing?" she said.

Who was she talking to? The groom was over in Tupper's loose box. She couldn't have seen or heard Lyndy approach. He leaned against the wooden wall, waiting for her to say more. He brushed aside the shame of spying on her, not once but twice in so many days.

"I can't think of anything else to do," she said. With one hand on the horse's back and the other one over her eyes, she began to weep, and not, Lyndy suspected, for the vicar.

A surge of unexpected emotions flowed through Lyndy:

confusion, misery, compassion, empathy, guilt. Their engagement had come as a bit of a shock to her, yes, but marriages between the better families were always arranged like a business transaction, each getting something from the alliance. In their case, Mr. Kendrick got a title in the family, Papa got Mr. Kendrick's money, Lyndy got champion thoroughbred racehorses, and Miss Kendrick gained an eminently charming husband. Why was she so upset?

"At least I have you, Tully," she whispered.

She was talking to the horse! With a sudden urge for her to talk to him instead, Lyndy pushed away from the wall and stepped into Tully's loose box.

"Lord Lyndhurst," she said, swiveling around at the sound of crunching straw beneath his boots.

"Miss Kendrick. I'm surprised to see you here."

She brushed away tears from her cheeks with the back of her gloved hand. "Why would that be? Because you don't expect a woman in the stables or because you already pay good money to a stable hand to do this?"

"Well, yes to both, but mostly because we expected you were in your room, recovering from yesterday's shock. You didn't come down to breakfast."

She turned away from him and began tugging at the balance strap again. "I don't always do what's expected." She needn't tell him that.

"No, in fact, you haven't done a single thing since you've been here that was as we expected." She stopped her adjustments of the saddle. Lyndy expected her to deny it or to protest, but as he should have predicted, she did neither.

"I can imagine. You and your family aren't what I expected either."

What had she expected? Warmth, humor, kindness, acceptance, perhaps? Instead, she had gotten barely veiled disapproval, feigned interest, and obligatory civility. If the former was what she'd imagined of her reception, then, yes, he could understand her disappointment.

"More's the pity, since we might be stuck with each other," she added.

Might? This wasn't going the way he'd planned. And she still wouldn't call him Lyndy. After yesterday, they should be on less formal terms.

"I'm so sorry about the vicar." She faced him and laid a hand on his arm. The gesture was so like another, it made him flinch. But nothing but sincere sympathy shone from her eyes. "Your family must feel horrible about his accident."

She didn't know. Lyndy dreaded being the one to tell her.

"It's worse than you know. Reverend Bullmore was the victim of more than fatal clumsiness. He was murdered, bludgeoned to death."

Lyndy held her gaze, brushing his hand methodically down the filly's neck. How would this unpredictable woman respond to such a pronouncement? She didn't faint. She didn't swoon. She didn't burst into a fit of tears.

She did that only when she contemplated spending eternity with him.

"Besides me, perhaps, who would benefit from the vicar's demise?" she asked.

Lyndy sputtered as he stifled an undignified guffaw. Her words were, yet again, completely unexpected.

"Do you find the poor man's death funny, Lord Lyndhurst?"

"Certainly not. But I am taken aback by your confession that you had motive to kill him."

"I do have a motive, and everyone knows it. You do, too, if you're entering into this marriage against your will."

How did he answer that? This marriage was to save Morrington Hall from Papa's folly, to acquire the thoroughbreds, and bring pride back to his family. It was his duty. But how did he tell her that now that he'd met her, he had no objections to wedding, and bedding, her at all?

"I don't fancy myself a murderer, Miss Kendrick," was all he could say in his defense.

"I'm glad to hear it," she said. "Neither do I."

"I'm glad to hear it."

She studied his face. Wondering whether he was teasing her, no doubt. He willed his expression not to give him away.

"But someone did kill him," she said in earnest, "and they must've had a reason, presumably one far more compelling than trying to stop a wedding."

"Presumably."

"She's ready for you, my lord," the groom called, walking Tupper toward them. Lyndy strolled back into the aisle and took the horse's reins from the groom.

Miss Kendrick led her horse out of its loose box and mounted it in the aisle with the aid of the groom as Lyndy flung his leg across Tupper's back. He'd decided to join her, whether she wanted his company or not. A quizzical expression crossed her face as he and Tupper fell in beside her. Maybe he was as unpredictable to her as she was to him. What an intriguing notion.

"By the way, where are we going?" he asked as they walked the horses through the stable doors.

"To the vicarage," she called over her shoulder as she and her horse trotted across the yard.

"I wouldn't know. That was the last time I saw him."

Inspector Archibald Brown nodded curtly to his constable in disgust. He rested his elbow on the edge of the small oval oak center table serving as a makeshift desk and pinched the bridge of his nose.

Hours of interviewing maid after footman after housekeeper and . . . nothing. No one had noticed anything, heard anything, would admit to anything. No one knew the vicar well, but all had heard his sermon about the faith of the centurion on Sunday and had agreed it was uplifting. No one knew of any enemies he might have had, any disagreements he might have had, or any reason why anyone would have wanted to do him harm. Yet someone had gone into the library and bashed the poor bugger's head in.

"Thank you," Constable Waterman said. "We'll let you know if we need to speak to you again."

The footman—a tall, fair-haired fellow, indistinguishable from all the other tall, fair-haired footmen on these country estates—in his morning livery of a black double-breasted coat, striped waistcoat, black trousers, and small black tie, got up without a word and left.

From his interviews of the staff, all Brown could confirm was that the vicar was alive and well in the library at about quarter past two, when a maid brought him tea and lemon biscuits. From his examination of the crime scene, all Brown could conclude was that the murder weapon was most likely the fire iron. They hadn't found it, yet. They had found the vicar's pocket watch; the glass had been smashed beneath him. It had stopped at 2:47 pm. Was that when the vicar fell on it and died? Or had it stopped before he fell? Brown didn't know. What he did know was that by teatime, the vicar was dead and not a single bloody servant had seen or heard a thing.

"Who is next on our list, Waterman?" Brown grumbled.

It didn't do taking his frustrations out on his constable, but someone had to take it. If their luck didn't change soon, they were finished. Lord Atherly was most cooperative, giving up his rarely used—according to the butler—smoking room for them, but even the most reasonable aristocrat had his limits. Brown had already put most of the household staff through the paces. He wouldn't be able to do it again, not without just cause. Interviews with the family, beyond the two who had found the body, were hardly guaranteed. Brown peered around at the large antlers of roe, fallow, and red deer mounted above him on the dark wood-paneled walls. His head might be mounted up there if he didn't come up with something soon.

"Miss Ethel Eakins, chambermaid," the constable said, skimming down the list. They were almost out of names.

A small, big-eyed, freckled woman in her midtwenties, wearing a plain gray dress and starched white apron, entered the smoking room. A white cap covered her tidy ginger hair. She kept her eyes cast down as she covered the distance between them.

"Thank you for helping us with our investigations, miss," Brown said, indicating for her to sit in the seat across from his constable.

Was she like the others, who had refused to sit in their master's chair, or could this one be different? The girl looked at the dark leather-covered captain's chair.

"I'd rather stand."

Constable Waterman shrugged. "As you may know, Miss Eakins, Reverend Bullmore was found dead yesterday in the library," the constable said.

The maid cast a brief glance at the inspector before shifting her gaze back to the swirling green, brown, and black leaf pattern of the carpet. Her hands were clasped tightly at her waist, with her pinkie fingers oddly intertwined on top.

"Yes . . . I heard."

Brown, slouched against the back of his chair, sat up. His seventeen years in the Hampshire Constabulary might not end in disgrace, after all. This maid knew something.

"Could you tell us where you were between half past two and four yesterday afternoon?" the constable asked. The maid twisted her pinkie fingers again.

"I saw a stranger running away from the library," the maid blurted.

Brown was on his feet. Within half a second, he loomed over the girl. Despite his exhilaration, Brown hadn't failed to notice that she didn't answer the constable's question.

"When was this?" the inspector asked.

The maid, her large green eyes wide open, cowered under Brown's scrutiny. "I . . . I don't remember." She sunk down onto the edge of the chair behind her, despite her previous inhibitions, and stared at her lap.

Brown strode back to his seat in silence, not wanting to intimidate the maid further. He nodded to his constable to continue.

"Can you tell us what the stranger looked like?" Constable Waterman said.

"I caught but a glimpse of him as he turned the corner of the grand saloon," she said, looking up.

"What type of build did he have? How tall was he?"

"Average build, I think, and taller than me, maybe." That wasn't saying much. Brown was starting to lose his enthusiasm.

"What color was his hair?"

"I don't remember."

"Can you think of any identifying characteristics of the fellow?"

The maid bit her lip as she considered the question. She cast a furtive glance at Brown. "His boots and his trousers were black."

A man of average height and build, wearing black boots and trousers. That could be any number of men: Lord Atherly, his guests, visiting tradesmen, the butler, the footmen, even the vicar. It all seemed a bit too vague, a bit too convenient, this barely seen "stranger." Was the maid making it all up to avoid telling the truth? Or had she honestly not gotten a good look at the fellow? Brown studied every twitch of the maid's face and had the sneaking suspicion she wasn't telling them everything.

"If you caught only a glimpse, how do you know this wasn't someone you've seen before?" his constable asked.

"I don't, I suppose. But at the time that's what I thought. None of the family would be running in the house."

"But it could be a footman, perhaps?" Brown asked. Didn't footmen wear black shoes and trousers? Could she be wrong about the height?

The maid blanched, and her lip trembled before she stared into her lap again.

Now we're getting somewhere. "Or a guest visiting for Lord Lyndhurst's wedding?"

"Yes, one of the Americans, maybe," she said, latching on to Brown's suggested alternative.

"Did you speak to this stranger or hear him say anything?" Constable Waterman said.

"No. But I did wonder about the vicar."

"You did?" The surprise in Constable Waterman's voice reflected Brown's own.

"We were specifically told not to disturb him," the maid explained. "But the library door was ajar."

"You feared this stranger might have disturbed the vicar?" the constable said.

The maid nodded. "That's why I peeked into the library."

"You went into the library after the stranger left?" Brown demanded, unable to contain himself.

The maid's shoulders bowed, and she shrank into herself, clutching part of her apron in her lap.

"You did nothing wrong, Miss Eakins," Brown said, commanding the softest tone his rough voice would allow. "But we want to learn the truth."

The maid looked at the constable and then at the inspector again, both of whom nodded encouragingly.

"I didn't go into the room. But I did push the door open a bit more and peek in."

"What did you see?" Brown said, cooing to the frightened maid.

"Nothing. The room was empty."

Brown remembered the position of the body, hidden from view, at the foot of the chesterfield sofa. She wouldn't have seen the dead man. So that much of her story was true.

She went on. "So, I didn't worry about it again, until I heard what happened. You won't tell Mrs. Nelson I peeked into the library, will you?"

Could this be her cause for alarm? Why she appeared so nervous?

"But you never did, did you?" Brown said.

The woman looked blankly at him for a moment before her eyes lit up with understanding. "No, I didn't."

"What time was this?" Brown asked again.

"About the time the Americans arrived."

Brown nodded and smiled. "Thank you, Miss Eakins. You have been most helpful. You may go."

The maid scurried away like a scared rabbit. She knew exactly when she'd entered the library. The clock ruled life in these country houses. So why not say so? Because she was still holding something back. Had she seen a man running through the saloon? It was worth checking into. The inspector sat back in his chair, steepling his fingers together. Finally, they were getting somewhere.

CHAPTER 8

Tully snorted, impatient to run. Stella filled her lungs with the fresh, cool breeze. Its scent of damp earth and a slight fragrance of coconut wafted up from the flowering gorse. She wanted to run as much as the horse did, to sweep over the grassy heath, to leap over puddles, to startle the free-ranging ponies and the deer as she and Tully galloped toward the sea. After yesterday, the chilling oppression of the stonemanor house, the murder of the vicar, and Daddy's pronouncement that threatened to turn her life upside down, she was prepared to fly on Tully toward the clouds and never look back.

But she did look back. As they passed the last of the exercise paddocks, Lord Lyndhurst overtook her, encouraging his racehorse to run. Tupper bolted. Her speed, taking him by surprise, violently thrust him backward. His derby hat flew off and landed yards away, on a cluster of prickly gorse bushes. Clamping his legs as tight as he could, he leaned forward, trying to stay in his seat. He shouted and pulled on her reins, but Tupper wouldn't have it. She'd been idle for too long. Lord Lyndhurst gave up trying to slow the horse and simply held on. His whooping and hollering and laughter rang across the heath.

So, the stuffed shirt can have fun, after all.

Stella made chase, following him across the heath, toward a small cluster of trees on the far hill, the spire of a church rising above them. With a brisk wind in her face, Stella concentrated on keeping her sights on the pair far ahead as they navigated the unfamiliar landscape. Tully was no match for Tupper. When Tupper slowed down to a canter, Stella and Tully caught up. They reached a gravel lane and trotted side by side past a cottage with a thatched roof. Stella marveled at how what looked like tightly bound dark brown hay could keep the rain out.

"Was the filly more difficult to handle than you expected?" she asked as they halted in front of a redbrick building.

He combed his fingers through his windswept hair and brushed the front of his jacket. "It wouldn't be the first time," the viscount said, looking meaningfully at Stella.

She laughed. After that ride, she couldn't help feeling better. She slipped down unaided from Tully's saddle. She flipped the reins around the hitching post as Lord Lyndhurst did the same. "Don't worry. Tupper will trust you eventually. She just has to get to know you first."

"I hope that goes for the other filly as well."

"Don't worry, girl," Stella said, patting Tully's neck. "I won't let the Englishman ride you." Stella slipped Tully a piece of peppermint, which she always kept in her pocket.

"I wasn't talking about the horse."

Stella's eyes widened, and she laughed again. "We'll see about that."

Lord Lyndhurst's smirk widened into a smile as he checked the girth and billets of Tupper's saddle and adjusted them after his wild ride. He whispered something to the filly while patting her neck. Stella smiled at the gentle gesture. Seemingly unaware of her scrutiny, he gestured toward the vicarage.

"Shall we?" he said.

Stella studied the cozy two-story redbrick building with thick white crosses decorating the windowpanes. A gravel path lined with vibrant blooms of delphinium, iris, and peonies led to the whitewashed door. Shiny green ivy thickly covered the walls, and smoke curled from one of two chimneys. Only in England would a fire need to be lit in June.

I wish they'd light more back at Morrington Hall.

A chill ran up Stella's spine, and her lighthearted mood evaporated as quickly as the smoke. Why had she come here? After finding the vicar yesterday, she had to do something. But what? Give her comfort and condolences to those he had left behind? Of course. To learn about Reverend Bullmore, whose life and death were so intimately and suddenly thrust upon her? Yes. But now, on the threshold of the vicarage, her determination wavered. She realized what she'd really come for. Answers. But what answers did she expect to find? Why anyone would want to harm a vicar? Or how his death might affect her fate?

Stella joined Lord Lyndhurst at the door and, before her courage failed, lifted the brass knocker, then rapped it twice. She stared straight ahead, willing the door to open. Lord Lyndhurst's gaze was fixed on her, and she wasn't sure what to make of it.

The door creaked open. A woman well past middle age, with a long face and a lace cap on her thick, curly gray hair, peered out at them with squinting green eyes, red and swollen from crying. Her dress was black crepe.

"Yes?" she said before noticing Stella's companion. She swung the door open. "My lord!"

"Good morning, my dear, Miss Judd," he said.

Miss Judd bowed, her head quivering slightly. She held her left arm tight against her side, her hand twitching uncontrollably.

"Now, now, I'll have none of that."

Lord Lyndhurst took the old woman's trembling hand, bent down, and gently kissed the woman's cheek. Miss Judd's face lit up, her toothless grin stretching across her face. Stella regarded the pair with fascination. Who was this woman that evoked such tenderness?

Miss Judd patted him on his cheek. "Do you remember the last time you were here?"

Lord Lyndhurst nodded.

"Did Lady Atherly ever find out about it?"

He grinned sheepishly. "No, she didn't. Thanks to you."

Stella would have to ask him to tell her that story.

"Do come in. Come in," Miss Judd said, backing up and moving aside to allow them passage into the narrow hall.

When the old lady closed the door behind her, stifling hot air akin to that in Kentucky in July enveloped Stella. After the drafty manor house, Stella should've appreciated the warmth, but she could barely breathe. Thankfully, Lord Lyndhurst cracked the door open again as Miss Judd shuffled down the hall.

"Please do make yourselves comfortable," she said.

They followed her into a small drawing room, the one without the roaring fire, filled with lush ferns and multiple wooden crosses mounted on the wall. Stella sat on the chintz-covered couch, leaving the overstuffed armchair for the old woman. But she refused to sit.

"Can I get you anything, my lord? A cup of tea, perhaps? I baked a loganberry tart yesterday for the vicar's supper, but . . ." She stopped and stifled a sob.

"No, nothing. Please put yourself at ease, Miss Judd," the viscount said, indicating the armchair.

The old woman nodded and, with the aid of his arm, hobbled over to it.

"Miss Judd, our lovely hostess here," Lord Lyndhurst said, "served at Morrington Hall during my grandfather's day, before she became the vicar of Rosehurst's housekeeper. No one was kinder to this awkward young lord than her. She's been terribly missed."

The old woman waved off the comment with a hand, but she

was grinning again. Lord Lyndhurst snatched a green hand-knitted blanket from the back of the chair and tucked it around the woman's lap, like a baby. Then he moved one of two wooden ladder-back chairs positioned on either side of the fireplace and set it beside her.

"How are you holding up?" he asked.

"I've been better, my dear boy."

Stella watched the viscount. So haughty, pretentious, and smug back at the house, so gentle and considerate here. Who was this man?

"And who is this, my lord?" Miss Judd said, blatantly scrutinizing Stella.

"How foolish of me. Miss Judd, this is Miss Stella Kendrick."

The old woman's eyes widened. "The American."

Stella struggled to keep the smile on her face. She was American and proud of it, but why did she feel every time anyone said it that the speaker was surprised she didn't have two heads?

"Yes. I'm from Kentucky," Stella said. "I'm pleased to meet you, ma'am. Though I wish it could've been under happier circumstances."

The old woman openly stared at Stella. "You're . . . Reverend Bullmore was to marry you and my lord on Saturday." It wasn't a question, but her words were spoken with such obvious disbelief, Stella cringed. She wasn't the only one not reconciled to the idea. "It must be postponed now, though, won't it? Until a new vicar arrives." Tears welled in the housekeeper's eyes again. "That poor, poor man."

She lifted a plain white threadbare handkerchief and dabbed her eyes. The viscount pulled a crisp new one from his waistcoat pocket. It had an *L* embroidered on it in navy blue. He handed it to the old housekeeper.

"I told him not to wear that belt."

Lord Lyndhurst and Stella shared a look.

"What belt would that be, ma'am?" Stella said.

"The vicar's money belt," the housekeeper said, shaking her head. "He called it his 'price of penance,' whatever that meant. He insisted on wearing it everywhere. Wearing it under his trouser leg, no less. I knew it would cause nothing but trouble."

"You think someone killed him for his money?" Stella asked.

"Why else? He was a man of the cloth. He had no enemies. What else could it be?" The housekeeper pulled the hand-knitted blanket tighter across her lap. "His prayer book had gone missing, but no one is going to kill for that."

"But surely no one would kill the vicar for a pittance?"

"Ah, but, my lord, I didn't say a pittance," Miss Judd said. "I said a penance."

"How much money was in the belt, Miss Judd?" Stella said.

Lord Lyndhurst pursed his lips, as if he'd bitten into a lemon. She'd seen his mother do that whenever Stella made a faux pas. Was it her persistent questions or the mention of money that was so off-putting? With her luck, it was both.

"We mustn't speak of such things," he said, confirming that any discussion of money offended him.

"That's all right. The dead have no secrets," the housekeeper said. "If the reverend died because of that money, it's right that someone should know."

"It must've been a great deal of money, then," Stella said, ignoring the viscount's frown. "But was it enough to die for?"

"Enough to die for, no," Miss Judd said, staring at Stella again. Stella shivered despite the oppressive heat. "Enough to kill for? Oh, aye, indeed."

Millie fluffed the pillows and smoothed the ivory lace bedcover. With Miss Kendrick's bed finished, the housemaid straightened the stack of books on the nightstand. She couldn't read the titles, but the top book had snow and dogs on the cover.

What a curious one Miss Kendrick is.

In the servants' hall, the talk was of two things: the vicar's death and Miss Kendrick, her lovely new clothes, her kind face, her horrible father, her appetite, her need to learn the house's rules, her gruesome discovery. Millie wasn't put off by Miss Kendrick's familiarity, like some downstairs. Millie liked her.

Millie retrieved the carpet sweeper and pulled and pushed it in rhythm across the floor as she sang.

> " *'Twas on a Tuesday morning,*
> *When I beheld my darling.*
> *She looked so neat and charming,*
> *In ev'ry high degree.*
> *She looked so neat and nimble, O,*
> *A-hanging out her linen, O,*
> *Dashing away with the smoothing iron,*
> *Dashing away with the smoothing iron,*
> *Dashing away with the smoothing iron,*
> *She stole my heart away."*

On her knees, sweeping under the bed, Millie heard voices in the hallway. She hushed. It wouldn't do to be caught singing. She needed this job, especially now that her mum was bedridden with a cough. Someday she and Mum would visit the seaside, maybe take the ferry to the Isle of Wight. Millie pushed up off the floor and listened for the voices to fade before taking up her song again.

> " *'Twas on a Wednesday morning, when I beheld my*
> *darling . . . "*

Millie lifted the thick ivory window curtain to sweep along the baseboard. A motion outside cut off her song again. She'd caught a glimpse of a man lurking in the back garden. Could it be the killer? She leaned the handle of the carpet sweeper against the wall and peered down. No, it couldn't be; the man was wearing posh tweeds. But she'd never seen him before.

He wore his tweed cap pulled down low over his brow. He skittered across the lawn and hid behind the tall hedgerow. He peered around the hedgerow and, seeing no one about, skittered across the open lawn again. Millie followed his progress until he disappeared beneath the window's eave. He seemed to be heading for the trade entrance door.

Now, why would a gentleman do that?

She shrugged. Must be one of the Americans. One never knew with them. After retrieving the carpet sweeper, Millie resumed her cleaning and her song.

CHAPTER 9

"It's Harry Finn, isn't it?" Constable Waterman said, indicating the chair in front of him to the newest arrival.

According to the butler, Harry Finn was the first footman and also served as Lord Lyndhurst's valet. He'd also been assigned to Mr. Kendrick during his stay. The fellow must be busy. But too busy to murder the vicar? Brown would have to see about that.

Staring at a point on the opposite wall, the footman said, "I prefer to stand."

Brown studied the footman—tall; slim; hooded blue eyes; dark hair carefully combed with pomade; dressed in dark gray trousers, a high-buttoned black waistcoat, a short black coat without tails, and a black tie. Not a hair or a thread out of place. Brown subconsciously brushed his hand across his forehead and receding hairline and then brushed the front of his dark blue uniform tunic. He'd never get used to the myriad tall, handsome men in service that were crawling about a place like Morrington Hall. He wasn't a short man, but his bulbous nose and the twenty years he had on all the lads set him apart. Brown looked at Constable Waterman, a man, like him, who had spent his youth hiking the heath and wrangling with pigs and ponies. But Brown came off the better in comparison. Since getting married last year, Constable Waterman had put on more than two stones. Mrs. Brown was a good enough cook, but Mrs. Waterman was rumored to have won more than thirty ribbons for her steak and pork pies.

"Where were you between half past two and four yesterday afternoon, Mr. Finn?" the constable asked.

"I was in my lord's dressing room."

"Doing what exactly?"

"Lord Lyndhurst had instructed me that he wanted to go riding. In addition to putting away his morning attire, setting out his evening attire, and attending to his fishing equipment, I needed to brush and press his riding clothes."

"Were you alone?"

"Who would be with me? Lord Lyndhurst didn't dress for dinner until Mr. Fulton sounded the gong."

The footman's tone had an edge to it. Was he offended by some perceived slight, as these lads who moved up in the world too fast often were, or was he hiding something? Brown wasn't a betting man, as many around here were, but if pressed, he'd bet the latter. Brown hadn't moved up in his world without a sense of when someone was lying.

"Can anyone verify that you were in Lord Lyndhurst's dressing room at that time?" Constable Waterman asked.

"No. No one else saw me."

"Isn't it usual to have maids coming in and out, doing this and that?" Brown added.

The footman's eyes flickered toward the inspector before focusing in front again. "Yes, but yesterday the Americans arrived. Most of the staff was consumed with settling them in."

"Constable, read back what the housemaid Millie said when we asked where she was from half past two until four yesterday." Brown studied the footman as Constable Waterman flipped through his notebook. Staring straight ahead, the footman blinked a bit too much.

"I was out on the drive when the Americans arrived," Constable Waterman read. "Then, since it was Monday, I cleaned the glass lamp and chandelier globes in all the rooms upstairs." Constable Waterman flipped the notebook closed with a flick of his wrist.

"We've checked all the rooms upstairs, Mr. Finn," Brown said. "If I remember correctly, there is a glass globe in Lord Lyndhurst's dressing room. So how is it that the maid didn't see you there?"

Brown waited. He counted to the ticking of the mantel clock for the footman's reply. *One, two, three, four—*

"Perhaps that's when I stepped out to retrieve Mr. Kendrick's trunk."

Got him! Brown silently congratulated himself. He was right. The footman was lying. But the footman was also clever. Four seconds was all he had needed to come up with the reasonable lie. But why? Was Harry Finn the "stranger" Ethel, the housemaid, saw? If she was to be believed. Or was Harry guarding another secret? Brown would have to bide his time and be patient if he wanted to learn the truth. Pushing the footman further would only stimulate more lies. Brown nodded to his constable to continue.

"Had you ever met Reverend Bullmore before yesterday?" the constable continued.

"Yes, once. After his sermon on Sunday."

"Can you think of any reason why anyone would want to kill the vicar?"

Harry Finn looked over at the constable and frowned. "No, I can't."

Did Brown believe him? The footman had stopped his blinking, and his reaction seemed genuine enough, but then again, he was on to them now. Brown would be extra cautious not to give himself away again.

"And before you ask, I wasn't anywhere near the library. I didn't have an idle chat with the vicar or pick up a book to read in my spare time. I didn't see anything. I didn't hear anything," the footman said, looking Brown in the eyes. The words, poured out of him in a quiet but clipped voice. He clenched his jaw and stared again at the wall, but Brown knew the footman was losing his patience or his nerve. Brown just didn't know which.

Brown scrutinized the calluses on the palm of his hand. Constable Waterman tapped his pencil in counterpoint to the clock ticking on the mantel. If Brown hoped the silence or the constable's insistent tapping would unnerve the footman, he was disappointed. Harry Finn matched his silence, staring ahead as before. It was time to try another tactic.

"Did you kill Reverend Bullmore?"

Harry Finn's steely exterior cracked, and he flinched.

"Absolutely not!" he declared. Harry Finn's brow glistened with perspiration. "If that's all?"

It wasn't. Not by a long shot.

"Where have you been all afternoon, Augustus?" Mrs. Westwoode said. "We could've been killed, and you were nowhere to be found."

"Now, now, Caroline," Augustus Westwoode said, blandly chiding his wife. He took a sip of his sherry. He didn't answer his wife's question.

Stella regarded Mr. Westwoode. She had been introduced to him and Lord Hugh when she arrived downstairs for dinner. Two men couldn't look less alike. Lord Hugh, with a tall, muscular build and thick blond hair, had a boyish face, even with his mustache. Gray peppered Mr. Westwoode's bushy brown mustache, and he lacked most of the hair on the top of his head.

He stood several inches shorter than his wife, the tops of his ears protruded outward, his grayish-green eyes were dull, and he had a habit of chewing on his upper lip. He was doing it now.

"The police still don't know the identity of the killer, then, Lord Atherly?" he asked.

Stella's and Lord Lyndhurst's eyes met. They'd been interviewed by Inspector Brown earlier in the afternoon, recollecting everything again and again: why they were in the library the day of the murder, what time it was when they entered the library, exactly what they saw in the library and when and where, what they heard while in the library. It was the least they could do. But they hadn't been able to recall anything new. Stella had been disappointed when the inspector stifled a yawn; she'd wanted to help. So, she'd mentioned their visit to Miss Judd, the vicar's housekeeper. The inspector had sat up straight at the mention of the money belt and had immediately dispatched his constable to interview Miss Judd. But despite Stella's cooperation and her persistence, Inspector Brown had evaded answering a single question. She didn't know any more than anyone else about the police's progress. Perhaps he'd been more forthcoming to Lord Atherly.

"I'm afraid I have no news," Lord Atherly said. "But they seemed confident they would apprehend the fellow in due course."

"Glad to hear it," Daddy said. "I trust the wedding won't be postponed?"

Stella, with a surge of anger at her father rising, pictured the pathetic face of Miss Judd grieving the vicar's death. She pictured Reverend Bullmore lying in a pool of blood. She couldn't hold her tongue. But the viscount beat her to it.

"Mr. Kendrick, a man has died," he said, as if reading her mind. "Don't you think that's more important than marrying your daughter off as fast as possible?"

Mrs. Westwoode gasped. Lord Hugh sputtered, attempting to hold in a laugh. Lady Alice looked up from her magazine.

"Lyndy, that is quite enough," Lady Atherly said. No one appreciated Stella's forthrightness, but coming from the heir of the house, it was clearly unexpected and intolerable.

Lord Lyndhurst watched Stella, his expression unreadable. This morning he'd surprised her, treating Miss Judd with such obvious affection. And that look of exhilaration on his face while riding was encouraging. And now this. She offered him a faint smile.

Perhaps he isn't like Daddy. That oaf leaned back in his green crushed-velvet armchair and swirled the sherry in his glass. He put the glass to his nose to appreciate the wine's aroma before gulping down its entire contents. He snapped his fingers and held up the glass for more.

No, no one was like Daddy.

"Yes, the vicar has died. That's why I asked about the wedding," Daddy said, unfazed by Lord Lyndhurst's admonishment. "It's what's best for everyone."

"A postponement is inevitable, I'm afraid," Lord Atherly said.

"That is too bad. Isn't Professor Gridley expecting funding for his next expedition, Lord Atherly? Is it true what my valet says, Lady Atherly? That you are short on staff and can't afford to hire more?" Daddy brushed lint from his pant leg. "Your garden would certainly benefit from some regular weeding."

Shock and shame froze on Lady Atherly's face, flaring blotches of red on her pale cheeks; her eyes widened in horror. Everyone else averted their eyes.

"I say that was—" Lord Lyndhurst, his teeth clenched, stepped forward, knocking against an end table. His mother's book, a biography of the Duke of Wellington, slipped from the top of a stack and fell with a thud to the floor.

"Dinner is served, my lady," Fulton's voice rang from the front of the room.

"Oh, good," Aunt Rachel said, as if she hadn't noticed the

tension in the room. "I'm as hungry as a bear coming out of hibernation."

"As everyone knows, my bet's on Cicero."

"I can't say as I blame you, Mr. Kendrick," Mr. Westwoode said, "but I'm going to put my money on Golden Measure."

"I don't know, Mr. Westwoode," Hugh said, helping himself to the platter of asparagus in hollandaise sauce held out to him by the footman. "I've had a hot tip about Jardy, the French colt."

"Yes, but Jardy has a cough, which might affect his form," Lyndy countered. Despite the earlier tension, Lyndy couldn't resist when the discussion turned to the Derby.

The meal had begun in silence, but Mother, whatever her faults, and there were many, was nothing if not an exemplary hostess. She'd led the way by asking Mr. Kendrick if President Lincoln hadn't been born in Kentucky. To her dismay, the conversation about Mr. Lincoln had led to bourbon and horses.

"What is the difference between the horses?" Miss Westwoode asked. "I've never been one to follow the races."

Lyndy pitied Hugh. Woe to the gent whose wife knew nothing about horses. He resisted the urge to glance at his bride-to-be across the dining table.

"Lady Yardley attended the opening-night performance of *Pagliacci* at the new Waldorf Theatre in Aldwych last week," Mother said, attempting to redirect the conversation.

Despite its popularity with polite society, not to mention that it was a favorite pastime of His Majesty King Edward, Mother preferred all talk of racing to be confined to the stables. Mother didn't like anything about horses. She never rode, preferred taking the train or walking to riding in a carriage, and might embrace the idea of a motorcar. Lyndy could only hope. Papa's obsession with finding a complete horse fossil, and the excessive funds that that task required, were much to blame for it.

Mother went on. "I read that it is managed by your fellow countrymen, Mr. Kendrick, the Messrs. Shubert of New York. Yet Lady Yardley had a lovely time. She couldn't say enough in praise of it."

Lyndy knew Lady Yardley. She could never say enough about anything, good or bad. The woman talked incessantly.

Mr. Kendrick ignored Mother. "The difference, Miss West-woode," he said, reaching over and pushing the silver candelabra against the floral centerpiece greenery to see her better, "is that Cicero has an outstanding pedigree, not least of all his sire, my stallion, Orson. Pretty good for a son of a coachman, eh?"

"Hear, hear," Miss Luckett, the aunt, agreed.

"Don't you mean *my* stallion?" Lyndy said.

"Orson's mine until my daughter holds the title of Lady Lyndhurst," Mr. Kendrick said, never taking his eyes off Elizabeth Westwoode. "Like I said, I'm thinking of everyone when I push for this wedding."

Mother's eyes widened at the American's audacity in bringing up the subject again. Poor Mother, having to entertain this barbarian at her dining table. But it was her own fault. She'd agreed with Papa to tie their fate to this "son of a coachman." The man was boorish and had been nothing but dastardly toward Miss Kendrick since they'd arrived, something that angered Lyndy in a way he couldn't describe. But had it been the poorest choice? Mr. Kendrick was an exceptional horse breeder and was worth millions, after all. Besides, Lyndy wasn't marrying the father, was he?

Lyndy stole a quick glance over the centerpiece, a dense cluster of pink hydrangeas. Miss Kendrick was seated next to Papa. Papa was retelling his famous story of killing the roseate spoonbill when he was a boy. The bird, not a native of the area and presumed to have escaped from a passing ship, had frequented the neighboring Solent for over a week, with many a gunman stalking it. Papa, out in the punt, had come across the bird at the entrance of the Beaulieu River and had bagged it for himself. It was the last bird he'd collected. Two weeks later he'd found his first fossil.

And that was that.

The candlelight flickered across Miss Kendrick's porcelain skin, the diamond combs tucked into her silky light brown hair, and in her attentive, attractive blue eyes as she listened to Papa's story.

If only Lyndy could get her to look at him like that.

"If Cicero wins the Derby, that will make Orson the sire of all three winners of the English Triple Crown races," Mr. Kendrick boasted. "He'll be the most sought-after stud in England. The King will be demanding Orson cover his mares."

"Getting ahead of yourself, aren't you, Mr. Kendrick?" Hugh said. "Cicero has to win tomorrow at Epsom Downs first."

Mr. Kendrick laughed before emptying his glass of claret.

"What a shame to have to miss the race this year," Miss. Westwoode said.

Mrs. Westwoode nodded solemnly in agreement. Lyndy didn't believe for a moment that the matron was sincere.

"Don't be foolish, Elizabeth!" Mr. Westwoode said, holding his fork in midair, spears of asparagus dangling from its tines. "Why would we do that? I always attend the Derby."

"There is the delicate matter of the vicar, my dear," his wife reminded him. "Have you finished already, Miss Kendrick?" Mrs. Westwoode said, noticing that the American woman's plate was empty, again. "I think you misunderstood the lesson of 'eat like a bird.' They meant like a sparrow, not a vulture."

Miss Kendrick set down her fork, dabbed the corner of her mouth with her napkin, and allowed the footman to clear away her plate. Without a word, she turned her attention back to Papa.

Did all American women have such hearty appetites? He'd admired her slim, subtle curves on more than one occasion. Where did she put it all? But leave it to Mrs. Westwoode to remark upon it—despite Miss Kendrick's dining etiquette otherwise being beyond reproach—hoping to change the subject at the young woman's expense. The tips of her ears burned red while everyone else ignored Mrs. Westwoode. Miss Kendrick would be wise to follow their lead.

"Lord Atherly? Is this true?" Mr. Westwoode said. "Are we expected to abstain from this year's Derby because of the vicar's murder?"

Papa, who had been smiling, having found an earnest listener in Miss Kendrick, frowned. "What's this? I say. We aren't talking about the vicar's . . . at the table, are we?"

"The discussion about our new thoroughbred stallion has led to whether we were abandoning our plans to attend the Derby or not," Lyndy said, as eager as Mr. Westwoode to know his father's decision on this matter. He had never dreamt the vicar's death would impact tomorrow's trip to Epsom.

"Why not go?" Lord Hugh said flippantly. "Reverend Bullmore would've postponed my funeral to go to Epsom Downs and not have thought a thing of it." Lyndy shot a glance at his friend. It wasn't like Hugh to be callous. But then again, it wasn't like Hugh to argue with anyone.

The night before the murder, Lyndy, approaching the pond to go fishing, had heard two raised voices, carried across the water from the folly on the other side. He'd recognized one immediately. But Hugh never lost his temper. Even after Hugh returned from South Africa and everyone expected him to show signs of battle fatigue, he'd smiled and laughed, as if he'd never left. Yet there he'd been, red in the face, fists clenched, mere inches from the vicar, shouting, "Either give it to me or leave me alone!"

Lyndy tried not to think of it now. But how could he not, with Hugh's tone of voice, his heartless attitude? What did Hugh have against Reverend Bullmore? How well did he know the man?

Others noticed it too. Mrs. Westwoode held her ring-covered

fingers over her mouth like a bejeweled fan. Miss Westwoode stared at the gloves in her lap. Mother puckered her lips. Hugh was such a congenial chap. It was why Lyndy liked him so much. Even when Hugh was in his darkest mood, Lyndy found his friend to be excellent company. So why the sudden rancor?

"I don't relish speaking thus about the dead," Papa said after dabbing his lips with his napkin, "but you are correct, Lord Hugh. If the situation were reversed, I suspect Reverend Bullmore would attend Derby Day."

Was there a more nefarious side to this man of the cloth? Until this moment, Lyndy had assumed the vicar had been killed for his money. How would his father know about any of it?

Mr. Kendrick chuckled. The man was obscene.

"William, you are not suggesting . . . ?" Mother said, despite her own rules about what was and was not appropriate to discuss at the table. "It would be unseemly."

"If our guests wish to attend the races, Frances, I don't see why the death of our vicar should prevent them."

If Lyndy didn't know better, his mother's nostrils flared like a horse's. She raised her chin and looked across the table at Papa through narrowed eyes.

"If our guests wish to attend, I shall see to the arrangements." Mother lifted her wineglass to her lips and took a deliberately slow sip. She wasn't happy, and she wasn't going to speak on the subject again.

Another pall of silence hung over the gathering. The quiet clinking of silverware on china plates accompanied the rustling of fabric as one and then another shifted in their seats. Only Westwoode grinned as he nudged a bite of his mutton cutlet onto his fork with his knife.

"Well, if you insist on going, Mr. Westwoode," his wife said, "I must too. Forgive me, Lady Atherly, but someone has to keep an eye on him." Hugh laughed, but Mrs. Westwoode's half smile told the truth. She hadn't been joking.

"I'll keep an eye on him for you, Mrs. Westwoode," Lyndy said.

Westwoode chuckled; his wife did not.

"No, Lyndy," Mother said. "I cannot allow you to go."

Lyndy balked at his mother's declaration. "I'm going," Lyndy said, raising his wineglass without taking his eyes from his mother's.

"I promised the girl she could go," Mr. Kendrick said, cutting into his mutton cutlet with his fork in one hand and then laying down his knife and switching his fork to the other hand. "She's been looking forward to it for some time. So, I say, 'What's good for the goose is good for the gander.'"

Mother's lip curled. Was she incensed by the inelegant American custom of switching silverware from hand to hand or by Mr. Kendrick's contradicting argument? Knowing Mother, both.

"Then it's settled," Papa said before Mother could object again. "Lyndy will accompany all our guests who wish to attend, and will represent us in the box."

CHAPTER 10

With the balconies of the towering multitiered white grandstand behind her and the bright green mile-and-a-half turf racetrack before her, Stella gazed out across the white rails on a sea of tents, their white roofs flapping in the gentle breeze; a scattering of painted covered refreshment wagons, their windows propped open to showcase their food and drink; and thousands of people dressed in their finest top hats and feathery, wide-brimmed creations as far as she could see. Stella had never seen so many people. Ever.

Stella had heard about the Derby all her life. It was the most prestigious horse race in the world. She'd visited Churchill Downs in Louisville twice, when Daddy had a horse in the Kentucky Derby, but that hadn't prepared her for the crowds, the noise, the excitement of Epsom. It was as if the entire nation had descended on Epsom Downs to take part in the festivities. She said as much.

"Yes, quite the challenge, these crowds," Mr. Westwoode said, sitting next to her, biting his upper lip. His top hat tipped precariously as he studied his racing form. His casual attitude belied his words; he was oblivious to the mass of people everywhere. The crush wasn't as pronounced here in the "members' enclosure," as Lord Lyndhurst had called it, a protected space reserved for members of the Jockey Club, the governing body of British horse racing. Lord Atherly, as well as Lord Hugh's father, the Duke of Tonnbridge, were members.

"Thank goodness we don't have to subject ourselves to the ruffians and pickpockets among them," Mrs. Westwoode said, sitting across the table from Stella. "If they charged an entrance fee, one wouldn't have every shopkeeper and his son to deal with."

Lady Atherly had arranged a lavish picnic for them. Enormous hampers filled with cold veal and ham pie, a joint of cold boiled beef, a variety of sandwiches, cucumbers, stewed fruit, fresh fruit, biscuits, strawberry tartlets, sponge cake, petit fours, champagne, silver, china, linens, and glasses had been loaded up and, along with the servants necessary to serve the picnic, transported with them from Morrington Hall and reassembled under the open sky.

Stella dabbed the corner of her mouth with a napkin. If only they could have every meal outside.

"My father's box is over there, near the Royal Box," Lord Hugh said, waving in a vague direction to the right. "His might be farther from the shopkeepers, but I much prefer the company in this one." He lifted his champagne glass, as if in a toast.

"Hear, hear," Lord Lyndhurst and Mr. Westwoode said, raising their glasses in response.

Bubbles tickled Stella's nose as she took a sip of champagne. Stella had never seen the viscount in a jovial mood. He'd ridden beside her on the train. With the tension of the night before forgotten, he'd eagerly questioned Daddy about American horse races—the Kentucky Derby, the Kentucky Oaks, the Belmont Stakes, the Preakness Stakes, the Travers Stakes. He'd suggested Stella describe Kentucky and their farm. He'd listened attentively as she described the endless rolling hills of bluegrass, the stone fences she and Tully liked to jump, the mighty rivers, like the Ohio and the Mississippi, and the warm, humid days, which she missed most on this pleasant but cool last day of May. When he'd asked whether every man in Kentucky carried a holstered revolver out on "the range," Aunt Rachel and Daddy had laughed at him. He'd joined in. His cheerfulness was unflappable.

"We adore your company, as well, Lord Hugh, dear. Such a shame Elizabeth decided to stay behind and keep Lady Alice company." Mrs. Westwoode took a dainty bite of her petit four. "Finished already, Miss Kendrick?"

The tips of Stella's ears burned. Why must the matron always comment on what was or wasn't on Stella's plate? What was so remarkable about a woman who enjoyed her meal? Other women picked at their food, taking a minuscule bite or two before their plate was whisked away. Stella wasn't like that. She never overate, like Daddy was inclined to do, but if she liked a dish, she relished every bite. Was that so bad? Stella smoothed her dress's buttery-yellow linen and Battenberg lace across her lap. A dressmaker had once advised her never to wear yellow; Stella's complexion was too pale. She hadn't listened to the dressmaker, and she wasn't going to listen to Mrs. Westwoode either.

"The tartlets were delicious, weren't they?" Lord Hugh said. "Would anyone care for another?"

"I think I might," the viscount said, winking at Stella before popping an entire tartlet into his mouth.

Lord Hugh laughed. Stella did too.

Lord Lyndhurst smiled at her as he motioned for the footman to pour more champagne. In three days, she had been betrayed by her father, had been thrown in with this strange family, and had stumbled upon a murder. All morning Stella had been overwhelmed with emotions: guilt, confusion, anticipation, excitement, resentment, curiosity, consternation, hopefulness. A man was dead, and her life was in limbo. How could she be enjoying herself?

But she was. She loved the boisterous crowds, the smell of the turf mingling with the scent of champagne, the glaring sun in a sky unblemished by a single cloud, the gleam in the viscount's eye. And the race hadn't started yet.

"Where are you, O eminent one?" Daddy said, holding a spyglass to his eyes with one hand and raising the last slice of sponge cake to his mouth with the other. He had his eyes pinned on the paddock area.

"He, Mr. Kendrick," Lord Lyndhurst said, "is referred to as His Royal Majesty King Edward, and you won't find His Royal Majesty out there."

Daddy lowered the spyglass. "The King? I meant Cicero, the stallion. But for God's sake, point the King out to me, will you?"

"His Majesty's up there, Mr. Kendrick," Lord Hugh said, pointing and laughing. "If you see him, save me the trouble and wave to my father for me, will you? The Duke is never far from His Majesty's side when a wager is involved."

Daddy focused his gaze in the direction Lord Hugh pointed, at a private balcony above and behind them. Stella, as intrigued by the famous royal as Daddy was, knew better than to ask to borrow his spyglass.

"The horses are out in front, Mr. Kendrick," Mrs. Westwoode sneered, even as she stole a glance back toward the Royal Box.

"Already?" Daddy swiveled his spyglass toward the racetrack, then searched for the thoroughbreds. "They aren't in the paddock yet." He turned back around and continued spying on the King.

A parade of people, as interesting as any king, passed by as the servants cleared away the picnic things. They were all shapes and sizes: tall men in top hats; buxom ladies in summery white cotton dresses, carrying parasols; gaunt farmers in their best suits; a wizened old fortune-teller in flowing black lace, bent over the palm of a pudgy gentleman with a pair of spectacles perched halfway down his nose. Stella looked down at her hand, the etched lines of her palm hidden beneath her glove.

What would the fortune-teller see in my palm?

As the footmen folded up the table, a man with a jet-black mustache and a swagger approached the group. Lord Lyndhurst and Lord Hugh stood, then greeted the newcomer with handshakes. Mr. Westwoode frowned and reluctantly addressed him with a nod.

"Harris," he said, distaste evident in his tone.

Mrs. Westwoode carefully kept her gaze elsewhere, as if her not seeing the newcomer would make him disappear. Mr. Westwoode returned his attention to his racing form.

"Who is that?" Stella asked Mrs. Westwoode.

Mrs. Westwoode waved her hand dismissively. "No one of any consequence," she scoffed.

The newcomer smiled and tipped his hat at them. Mrs. Westwoode rebuffed his attention, purposefully returning her attention to the track. Stella, uncertain how to react, smiled at the newcomer briefly before following Mrs. Westwoode's gaze across the rails. The field was gathering for the first race of the day.

"It's starting!" Stella said, leaping up from her chair. She never tired of the thrill of anticipation when the starter shouted the preliminary warning. But all the men in their party, including Harris, the newcomer, had left their box. Stella scooted past Mrs. Westwoode and headed down the way the men had gone.

"Miss Kendrick, you mustn't go alone," Mrs. Westwoode called.

Aunt Rachel struggled to get past Mrs. Westwoode and then to navigate the crowd as she shuffled her way toward Stella. Why had Lady Atherly insisted the old lady join them? Wasn't Mrs. Westwoode sufficient as a chaperone? The poor lady shouldn't have to traipse around Epsom Downs. But her sympathy wasn't enough to compel Stella to wait. She wanted to be next to the rails when the starting bell sounded.

* * *

"Brewster's Lad, ten to one. Isoldash, thirty to one."

The rush and roar of a dozen horses' feet pounding on the turf as they raced by Stella and across the finish line had barely faded when the hoarse cry of a bookmaker, already taking bets for the next race, lifted above the cheers and applause of the crowd.

"Dutch Love, seven to one," another shouted.

The bookmakers, some perched on wooden stools, some standing next to tall poles with the next races' odds tacked to them, all of them shouting, were clustered in the betting ring, a crowded area adjacent to the members' enclosure. Gathered about a certain bookmaker, a man with a tan top hat, a thin blond mustache, and a large white carnation in the buttonhole of his tan jacket, were the men from Stella's party. With Aunt Rachel finally at her side, Stella left the rails and headed toward them. Bits of conversation caught Stella's attention as they made their way through the crowd.

"If he starts fast and runs at a good clip . . ."

"With last night's rain, there's bound to be cut in the ground."

"Pity their first-string has turned out to be a non-runner."

"Is that her?"

Stella spied a woman, her pink parasol opened above her, whispering behind her hand. The woman's companion, a stout matron with a flourish of tall gray feathers on her hat, nodded. The two women were staring straight at her. Caught gawking, the pair promptly focused their attention elsewhere.

"What was that about?" Stella said.

Aunt Rachel shrugged. "Who knows, girlie. Some people don't have the sense God gave a bedbug."

Stella and her chaperone reached the bookmaker with the white carnation in time to see Lord Hugh hand the bookie three one-hundred-pound notes.

"Not feeling lucky today, Lord Hugh?" Mr. Westwoode said, stepping up beside his future son-in-law.

"I'm always feeling lucky, Mr. Westwoode," Lord Hugh said, taking his ticket from the bookmaker's clerk. "That was a bet to place on Commerce, the long shot. The horse is going at ninety-nine to one."

"Then five hundred on Commerce, each way," Mr. Westwoode said, handing the bookmaker a white one thousand-pound note. The bookie's clerk scribbled something down in his black book and tore off the ticket.

Lord Hugh laughed. Lord Lyndhurst shook his head in bemusement. Daddy mumbled something about "good money after bad" as he walked past Stella and Aunt Rachel without a word of acknowledgment. Stella was stunned. She'd never seen such a cavalier attitude toward betting before. Daddy didn't rise from his humble beginnings by taking foolish risks. He raised and sold racehorses; he seldom bet on one.

"Bless your heart," Aunt Rachel said. "You have no idea how betting works, do you, Mr. Westwoode?"

"If Lord Hugh is feeling lucky," Mr. Westwoode said in his defense, "then so am I."

The men placed their bets for the stakes race.

Stella, wanting nothing to do with their recklessness, faced the crowd. So many people! Nearby a weathered man in a checkered waistcoat missing two buttons solemnly parted with half a crown, handing it to another bookmaker. A woman in a dark, tattered shawl, a decades-old straw hat, and stained gloves tucked a ticket into her boot. Several boys in suspenders and caps raced back and forth, imitating the last race. A white-haired gentleman in a gray frock coat and top hat, with a paunch bigger than Daddy's, slapped another on the shoulder, laughing. A short, round-faced man wearing a straw boater with a wide brown ribbon nodded appreciatively at his companion's remark. His companion had a jet-black mustache. It was Mr. Harris.

Stella spotted Mrs. Westwoode in the crowd as the matron slipped behind a bearded gentleman leaning on a distinctly topped rabbit-headed cane.

"Dutch Love, nine to two!"

The bearded gentleman turned his head at the shout. The wide brim of Mrs. Westwoode's hat caught the man square in the face. He threw up his hand to brush it away, entangled his fingers in the festoon of pink silk cabbage roses adorning the brim, and pulled the hat partly from her head. Mrs. Westwoode, drawn forward, tripped on his cane and dropped her handbag. The gentleman bent to retrieve it. Mrs. Westwoode, her face flush with embarrassment, yanked the bag from his hand. With a silk cabbage rose loose and flopping about on her hat, she stomped away and headed directly for Mr. Harris.

Hadn't Mrs. Westwoode shunned Mr. Harris? A man of no consequence, indeed!

Mr. Harris's companion stepped aside as Mrs. Westwoode approached, and engaged his attention with a lady with a white ostrich-feather boa draped around her neck. Mrs. Westwoode spared little time in conversation, slipping an envelope out of her bag and into Mr. Harris's outstretched hand. He tucked the envelope into his waistcoat pocket before retrieving a small black book from the opposite pocket. Mrs. Westwoode didn't wait. She navigated her way to another bookie on the far end of the ring. After a moment's discussion, Mrs. Westwoode continued to the next bookie and spoke to him. To this bookmaker, she handed several banknotes. Stella couldn't tell how many.

"Make a bet, miss?" said the bookmaker with the white carnation, drawing her attention back to Lord Lyndhurst and the other men.

Until that moment Stella had had no intention of betting. But if Mrs. Westwoode could do it, why couldn't she?

"Yes. I'd like Dutch Love, across the board, for five pounds, and Cicero, in the Derby Stakes, on the nose for five pounds." Stella pulled a ten-pound note from her handbag.

"That's the spirit," Lord Lyndhurst said, smiling.

"From your lips to God's ears, Miss Kendrick," Lord Hugh said as the bookmaker's clerk took her banknote and wrote up the ticket. Seeing how much Lord Hugh had bet on a long shot, she could imagine how much he had wagered on the favorite.

Mr. Westwoode and Lord Hugh strolled away, laughing, toward the members' enclosure.

"Kendrick?" the bookie said as he handed Stella her ticket. "As in Elijah Kendrick, the American horse breeder?"

"The same," Stella said.

"Good luck, Miss Kendrick!" the bookie called as the viscount offered his arm and led them back toward their seats. "I've got the odds on you."

Stella glanced over her shoulder at the bookmaker and caught sight of the fortune-teller again, bent over the palm of a woman who openly wept as her fortune was read.

What did he mean by that?

CHAPTER 1 1

The crowd in the betting ring swelled as the post time of the next race approached. Stella held tightly to Lord Lyndhurst's arm as he deftly dodged the punters focused on getting their wager in before the bell. He regaled her with details of the pedigree of Dutch Love, the horse she'd bet on. It was a direct descendant of Augustine, the champion filly that belonged to the viscount's grandfather, the seventh Earl of Atherly. As he spoke of this cherished horse, his face lit up as she'd never seen it. Smiling, animated, and waving his free hand about as he talked, he recounted his first attempt to ride the filly as a boy, and his subsequent broken ribs. He fondly recalled how he'd sneak into the stables at night to spoil the filly with treats he'd taken, unbeknownst to Mrs. Cole from the kitchen. He was delighted, he said, that Stella had the acumen to bet on Augustine's progeny. Stella didn't have the heart to tell him she'd made the bet on a whim.

"Tell me about the last time you visited Miss Judd," she asked.

Lyndy laughed.

What incident, what boyhood foible had he and the old house-keeper kept from Lady Atherly?

"It was all the fault of a donkey," he said. "Headley, Alice nicknamed him, on account of his disproportionally large—"

"Lord Lyndhurst!"

Harris, the man with the jet-black mustache, stepped out in front of them. They barely avoided bumping into him. Aunt Rachel, a few steps behind, wasn't as fortunate. Taken by surprise by the abrupt halt, she wobbled precariously as she used her cane to regain her balance on the soft grass. But it wasn't enough. She had teetered forward too far. Lord Lyndhurst, seeing her distress, reached out as she began to fall. Harris, taking the viscount's cue, dashed to take Aunt Rachel's other arm, and between them, they set the old lady on her feet again.

"Thank you kindly, sirs," Aunt Rachel said. "I thought I was a goner."

Harris tipped his fedora hat at Aunt Rachel and then at Stella and smiled. "Lord Lyndhurst, I don't believe I've had the pleasure."

The viscount, although taken aback by the man's sudden appearance, was willing to oblige.

"Mr. Harris, this is Miss Kendrick, my fiancée." Stella was still not used to hearing it said out loud, and her fingers momentarily clenched his arm. "And her great-aunt, Miss Luckett." The old lady smiled with gratitude and then stepped respectfully back several feet. "Miss Kendrick, this is Mr. Clyde Harris, a . . . well-known figure on the Turf."

"Mr. Harris," Stella said.

Who was this man? A bookie, yes, but obviously much more.

"Congratulations are in order, Miss Kendrick," Mr. Harris said.

Stella feigned a smile. She wasn't sure about that.

"Doubly so if Cicero wins," Mr. Harris added.

"Ah, so you know Orson is now at Morrington Hall," Lord Lyndhurst said.

"I have heard it mentioned a time or two, among other things." Clyde Harris chuckled.

"What other things?" Stella said.

Mr. Harris hesitated, as if deciding what he should say next. He leaned in a bit too close and said softly, "That your vicar was most unkindly prevented from attending today."

"We feared as much," Lord Lyndhurst said. "We were hoping to avoid the topic altogether."

"To be honest, the recent events at Morrington Hall have been on everyone's lips all day," Mr. Harris said, shrugging, "and not all of it pertaining to the vicar's demise."

"Such as?" Stella asked.

Again, he hesitated. "Some of the more disreputable bookies have been taking wagers on whether the wedding will take place, many taking ten to one, against. Without an announcement in the *Times*, it's been quite the topic of speculation."

Stella didn't know what to say. Was he joking?

"I say. That is most shabby of them," Lord Lyndhurst said. He wasn't joking.

The cryptic comment from the bookie about the odds being on her now made sense. Stella was appalled. Those gossiping women, the ones she had passed in the crowd, had been whispering about her? Her heart sank as she glanced around and caught more than one person gawking at her.

"Shabby?" Stella said, pulling away from the viscount. Her fingers began to tingle as the hurt, shame, and anger made her head ache. "That's not the word I'd use for it. A man has been murdered, and people are betting on whether Lord Lyndhurst and I will get married or not?"

Lord Lyndhurst stole a quick glance at her. She couldn't look him in the eye. Men were betting on her wedding. How could anyone treat her fate with such callousness? All the fun and excitement of the day was gone. She had allowed it to distract her from her wretched predicament but couldn't anymore. Lord Lyndhurst hooked his arm around Stella's again. She didn't pull back but found no comfort in his steady hold.

"Shall we go back?" he asked.

She nodded, wishing she had never left the privacy of the box. With Miss Luckett shuffling behind, Lord Lyndhurst guided her away from the betting ring. Clyde Harris, oblivious to her distress, stepped in beside her. Why wouldn't the man go away?

"If I may speak plainly, as you Americans do," he said, "I think the word you might be looking for is *befitting*. Bully no doubt would've appreciated the irony."

Bully? Stella had never heard Reverend Bullmore called by that nickname before. As gaunt as he'd been upon his death, the nickname couldn't have been further from the truth.

"He would probably even bet a quid in your favor, being the gambler that he was."

Curiosity and surprise lifted Stella out of her despondency long enough for her to ask, "He was?"

Mr. Harris nodded. "Got him into a heap of trouble with the church too. I hear that he did penance for it somewhere, to atone for his . . . sins."

"For being a punter?" Lyndy said. "That seems a bit harsh, doesn't it?"

Harris shrugged before exchanging pleasantries with a man who had a thick neck and wore a white top hat. Clyde Harris seemed to know everyone.

Could this have anything to do with his murder? Perhaps the vicar's sins went beyond gambling?

When the stocky man moved on, Mr. Harris continued, as if

they'd never been interrupted. "But interestingly enough, from what I hear, Bully hadn't placed a wager in over three years. He hadn't once graced my offices in Cork Street. Maybe he'd learned his lesson."

"But?" Stella said expectantly. "You know more than you're telling us, Mr. Harris."

Clyde Harris looked at Lord Lyndhurst, surprise in his eyes. The viscount shrugged. Stella was beginning to get used to Englishmen reacting this way to her. What had she done now?

"As you rightly assumed, Miss Kendrick, there is more to the story."

"But?" Stella said.

Still, Clyde Harris hesitated. He looked at Lord Lyndhurst, cast a glance at Stella, and then regarded the viscount again. "It is of the most delicate nature," he whispered behind his hand.

"If you're concerned about my delicate nature, don't be." Lord Lyndhurst nodded his concurrence. "After all," Stella said, "Reverend Bullmore wasn't just to marry us. We found him."

"You . . . both . . . found . . . ?" Clyde Harris stammered. He wagged his finger back and forth between them. This was news to him. But if Stella read the man right, it wouldn't be a secret for long.

"What is it you aren't telling us, Mr. Harris?" Stella said, her troubles forgotten.

"I can't confirm or deny it, but I've heard his name connected with a certain house party and a certain game of baccarat."

"Are you telling me Reverend Bullmore was at Carcroft House?" Lord Lyndhurst said. He sounded skeptical. Was that also a hint of worry in his voice?

"Bully was quite the favorite on the Turf back then," Mr. Harris said. "He went to all the best houses."

"What happened at Carcroft House?" Stella asked.

Harris looked at her sideways. "You've never heard of the Carcroft House scandal? It was in all the London papers for weeks. The parties involved were subject to the most virulent accusations of ungentlemanly conduct. I assumed news of it reached our cousins across the pond."

If it had, Stella wouldn't have heard of it. It would have been the topic of gossip at balls, tennis parties, and teas. Stella rarely attended any of these. If Daddy had known, he wouldn't have talked about it to her.

"Well, if the rumors are true," Mr. Harris said, "someone cheated at baccarat, a card game that already met with widespread disapproval, during a house party held at Carcroft House for the St. Leger Stakes a few years back. A game instigated by His Majesty himself, I might add. The parties involved attempted to cover it all up. The rumor says several were paid for their silence, including the bloke that cheated."

"If the rumors are true," Lord Lyndhurst said.

"Reverend Bullmore?" Stella asked.

Clyde Harris shrugged. "It's what I've heard."

As they approached their private box, a group of men below them called Harris's name.

"That's me, then." Mr. Harris tipped his hat. "Good day, Miss Kendrick, Miss Luckett, my lord."

Lord Lyndhurst scowled as Clyde Harris skipped down the stairs to join his friends. Stella wasn't the only one glad to see Harris go. But he'd left behind so many unanswered questions. Could the hush money from the baccarat game be one and the same as the money stolen from the vicar's hidden money belt? Who else suspected Reverend Bullmore's involvement in the scandal? Did the police know? Did his killer know?

"Was there a great deal of money involved?" Stella asked. "Who else knows about this?"

Suddenly, the muscles of Lord Lyndhurst's jaw tightened.

He tugged forcefully on his frock coat. Stella braced for the reprimand about mentioning money, but his attention was focused elsewhere. She followed his gaze. Was he looking at Daddy, cigar dangling between his lips as he rested the end of the racing program on his protruding belly, or at Mr. and Mrs. Westwoode, who were in a private discussion, their heads bent toward each other, her hand shielding their mouths from lipreaders? No, his eyes moved to follow the man who stood, a welcoming smile on his face as he motioned for them to join him. Why was Lord Lyndhurst scowling at Lord Hugh?

Herbert Kitcher wiped his forehead with a handkerchief. He tucked it back into the pocket of his apron, stained and smelling of saddle soap and silver polish, and adjusted the saddle in his lap again. The sun was high, and the glare off the stirrup iron blinded him if he didn't move it periodically. But he didn't mind. These late spring days were unpredictable; misty rain could dampen him at any moment. He'd brought the saddles into the washing yard, the open-air space next to the coach house, which always smelled of wet cobblestones, to clean and polish them. Mr. Gates insisted Herbert clean the saddles in the harness room, but Mr. Gates wasn't here. Herbert lifted his face to the sky and savored the sunshine.

Herbert liked it when the family was away. Mr. Gates, if he didn't accompany them, would drive them to the train station before visiting a niece and her family in Christchurch. That left Herbert in charge, to harry the stable lads, to linger over his chores wherever and whenever he wanted, and to take a short kip if time allowed. Today, of all days, he counted on being left to his own devices. After the scrape he got into with the American lady, Herbert had worried he'd ruined everything. How could he have been such an idiot? Would he ever be free of Mr. Gates's watchful eye? But then the family had packed up for

Epsom—surprising, considering they had discovered a dead man in their library two days ago—and Mr. Gates had left for Christchurch. Herbert could relax. He was alone, and he wasn't going to let this opportunity slip by.

"Oi, Leonard!" Herbert called for the second groom for the second time. Leonard was sluggish and was feeling poorly, but that didn't excuse him from not answering when Herbert called. A shaggy-haired boy appeared around the corner, but it wasn't Leonard.

"Where's Leonard?"

"Leonard is exercising the new fillies, sir," the lad said.

Herbert nodded. The thoroughbreds had been carted across an ocean. The fillies needed to gallop about and stretch their legs as much as possible. Herbert would see to the new stallion later.

"Have all the horses been fed, and the loose boxes mucked out?"

"Yes, sir. Did you hear who won the Derby yet, sir?"

"Not yet, but my money is on Cicero." Herbert wasn't kidding. He'd put two pounds, more than a month's wages, on the horse to win.

"That would be good, wouldn't it, sir?"

"Yes, Charlie, that would be good. Now go fetch me a cup of tea and be quick about it."

"Yes, sir."

The lad rushed off as Herbert polished the solid gold nameplate on the back of the saddle's cantle. The etching read ORSON. Yes, it would be very good if Cicero won. Herbert would win a few pounds without lifting a finger, and Morrington Hall's new thoroughbred stallion would be the most sought-after stud in England. Vigorously rubbing silver polish onto the stirrup iron, he studied the reflection of his ruddy, round face. Being the famous horse's groom should carry with it some privileges, shouldn't it? Before Mr. Gates got back from Christchurch tonight, Herbert meant to take advantage of some of those privileges.

Herbert smiled, despite the clouds that drifted across the sky, threatening to block out the sun. He had more than sunshine to look forward to.

CHAPTER 12

"Come on, Cicero. Come on!" Stella shouted at the toll of the starting bell.

On the far side of the track, the horses bolted from the gate. Quickly, the field became a blur of jerking, bobbing slick brown bodies ridden by streaks of men in bright white and colored silks. As they raced along toward the top of the hill and rounded the first turn of the track, Stella trained her eye to find Lord Rosebery's primrose yellow and pink. The murmur of the crowd rose to a dull roar as the horses approached Tattenham Corner. The jockey of the horse trailing the pack was bareheaded. Somewhere on the top of the hill lay his helmet, a dot of white-and-yellow checks. Cicero was ahead on the downhill into the stretch; Jardy and Signorino fought neck and neck for a second.

"Pump him! Pump him!" Daddy shouted, holding his spyglass and clutching his ticket in his fist. The horses thundered down the home straight toward the winning post.

"Come on! Come on!" Stella yelled. "Come on!"

A deafening din of applause, cheers, and shouts burst out of tens of thousands of people as Cicero crossed the line, three-quarters of a length ahead of the others. Less than a head separated Jardy and Signorio as they finished second and third. The rest of the field thundered by.

"Attaboy!" Aunt Rachel called, stomping her cane on the ground.

"We did it! We did it!" Daddy shouted, as if he were Lord Rosebery, Cicero's owner.

Stella, cheering and clapping until her hands hurt, had to stop herself from hugging Lord Lyndhurst, who was standing beside her. A wide grin crossed his face. He and Daddy shook hands with anyone offering their congratulations. Lord Hugh slapped Lord Lyndhurst on the back with a rolled-up program. But the others were more subdued than she'd expected. Mr. Westwoode tore up his ticket. Mrs. Westwoode, fussing with the broken embellishments on her hat, was outwardly annoyed. Could they have bet against Cicero? Stella couldn't fathom why.

"Isn't it thrilling?" Stella said.

"Yes," Lord Lyndhurst said as he accepted another hearty handshake from a well-wisher. "Well done, I'd say."

"My ears are ringing from all the hullabaloo," Mrs. Westwoode shouted, holding her hands over her ears. She glared at Stella and then looked around at the people around them.

Stella followed her gaze. Despite the many well-wishers, more than one gentleman and lady of the Jockey Club had fixed their eyes on Stella, their heads shaking in disapproval, their mouths pinched in displeasure, or their heads bent together as they whispered behind fans. Was this more of the same, gossiping biddies speculating about whether she and Lyndy would marry? Or had she done it again, broken yet another unspoken rule of aristocratic etiquette?

"I can't imagine why anyone yells and screams," Mrs. Westwoode said. "The horses can't hear you."

Stella had been so caught up in the excitement of the race, she hadn't realized until now that she, Daddy, and Aunt Rachel had been the only ones in the members' enclosure, shouting at the top of their lungs. She had again done the unacceptable. But this time, she didn't care. She wasn't going to deprive herself of one of her few joys simply to appease someone else's sensitivities.

Who decided these rules, anyway?

"I can't imagine standing there as if you're watching the grass grow," Stella said, spying Cicero, surrounded by a mass of well-wishers, being led to the winner's circle.

"Well, I never," Mrs. Westwoode gasped.

Stella could feel the matron's cold stare on her back, but she kept her spine straight and her back turned. She fixated on the happy, cheering crowds of shopkeepers, farmers, and tradesmen celebrating on the other side of the rails. They understood. *What fun is a horse race if you can't imagine yourself the jockey and will your horse to win with shouts of encouragement?*

"Congratulations, Lyndy, dear boy," Lord Hugh said, playfully shaking his friend by the shoulders. "This makes your new stallion quite the stud."

"How many times do I have to say it?" Daddy said, watching the events in the winner's circle through his spyglass. "The horse isn't his until my daughter and Lord Lyndhurst marry."

Daddy's pronouncement thwarted Lord Hugh's attempt to ease the tension. Why did Daddy have to harp on the subject, reminding her again and again? He was as bad as Mrs. Westwoode. With all the distress of the past few days, why couldn't everyone just enjoy this triumphant moment?

"Pardon me, Lord Lyndhurst?" Standing next to the box was a tall man who had a waxed mustache and wore a beige top hat and matching frock coat. He pushed his spectacles in place with the tip of his index finger. "Am I correct in saying that you are the owner of Orson, sire of Cicero?"

"I'm the owner of Orson," Daddy said. "Elijah Kendrick, at your service." He thrust out his hand. "And you are?"

Gaping at Daddy's outstretched hand, as if he were holding a wriggling fish, the man continued to address the viscount. "I apologize, my lord. I was told you were the horse's owner."

"Not quite yet," Daddy said, pulling back his hand and tucking his fingers into his waistcoat pocket.

"Sir, you have me at a disadvantage," Lord Lyndhurst said. "Have we met?"

"I beg your pardon, my lord. I am Sir Devlin, an emissary of His Royal Majesty King Edward."

"I'll be damned," Daddy said, glancing up at the Royal Box. As he raised his spyglass to look, Lord Lyndhurst pushed it down. "What the devil—?"

The viscount, ignoring Daddy's bluster, faced Stella. "Sir Devlin, may I introduce my fiancée, Miss Stella Kendrick?"

That was twice now in less than half an hour. Would she ever get used to hearing it?

"Cicero's sire is to be a wedding gift from her father."

Sir Devlin lifted his hat and tipped his head forward. "Pleased to meet you, Miss Kendrick."

"And I, you, Sir Devlin."

Sir Devlin smiled.

Daddy, his arms crossed over his chest, glared at Stella and then at Lord Lyndhurst before turning his disapproving gaze to Sir Devlin. Did he expect a proper introduction?

"This is my father, Mr. Elijah Kendrick," Stella said, obliging him.

"I already said that," Daddy grumbled. "I don't need you to introduce me, girl."

Sir Devlin's eyes widened at Daddy's sharp words.

"What can we do for you, Sir Devlin?" Lord Lyndhurst said. Stella wished she could so easily ignore her father.

"His Majesty would like a word with Orson's owner."

"Then lead the way," Daddy said, pushing his way in front.

Sir Devlin, his wide eyes appealing to Lord Lyndhurst, had no choice but to scuttle after Daddy as he stomped his way toward the Royal Box. Lord Lyndhurst deftly looped his arm around Stella's, much to her surprise, and, guiding her, followed.

"Her father will be her chaperone this time, Miss Luckett," Lord Lyndhurst said when Aunt Rachel stood, clearly intending to follow.

Aunt Rachel winked.

"What are we doing?" Stella whispered.

"Where are you going?" Daddy asked over his shoulder when he realized they were behind him.

"We're going to be presented to His Majesty," Lord Lyndhurst said.

Nervous fluttering filled Stella's stomach. She tightened her grip on the viscount's arm. She'd never met a king before. He patted her hand.

"No, that's kind of you, Lord Lyndhurst, but it will make the girl cocky," Daddy said. "Go back to the other women."

Stella looked at the viscount. What would he do? Would he send her back, as Daddy demanded? Or would he escort her back, giving up his chance to greet his king?

"Miss Kendrick may and will accompany me to the Royal Box," he said. Stella smiled at him. He'd defied Daddy with such ease, and on her behalf. She wouldn't soon forget it. "Isn't that right, Sir Devlin?"

"Yes, my lord, you and Miss Kendrick are most welcome." He pushed his spectacles up with his finger as he cast an appreciative glance at Stella, making her blush. "His Majesty will be charmed, I'm sure."

Lord Lyndhurst frowned. He understood the courtier's meaning, maybe more than Stella did. If King Edward's reputation with the ladies was notorious back home in Kentucky, it must be scandalous here.

The balcony of the Royal Box, draped in garlands of pink, red, and white blossoms, had a spectacular view of the finish line. At the balcony railing, surrounded by several gentlemen holding glasses of champagne, was a heavyset man in his sixties, his back ramrod straight. He was impeccably dressed in a black frock coat and matching top hat and wore a tidy pointed white beard. In his fingers, he held a cigar. From the aroma that wafted toward them, it was a good Havana cigar, like the ones Daddy enjoyed. It was Edward VII, the King of England.

"Your Majesty," Sir Devlin said when the King nodded, allowing them to approach. "May I present Lord Lyndhurst, his fiancée, Miss Stella Kendrick, and her father, Mr. Elijah Kendrick? The owners of the sire of Cicero."

Lord Lyndhurst gave His Majesty the proper nod of his head. Daddy bobbed his head as if he had a twitch in his neck, but Stella, having mistakenly curtsied to Lord and Lady Atherly, didn't waste the opportunity to use what she'd practiced so hard to perfect before they left Kentucky. She dipped gracefully and low. To Stella's surprise, the King leaned down and took her hand. He smelled of expensive eau de cologne.

"My dear." His voice was unusually accented.

"Your Majesty," Stella said as she allowed the King to raise her up with his hand.

"I've heard about your American betrothed, Lord Lyndhurst," the King said. Although he addressed Lord Lyndhurst, the King's eyes never left Stella. Under his inquisitive gaze, she kept her eyes lowered, or else he'd see how the blood had rushed to her cheeks.

Why had they been summoned? To satisfy the royal's curiosity about her? What was he thinking? Did he appreciate her feminine beauty? Was he wondering how the Earl of Atherly could align his family's fate with these upstart Americans? Was he pondering the gossip that had preceded her? Did he know about Reverend Bullmore's murder?

"How delightful she is. I'd wed her soon, Lord Lyndhurst, or you might find she's found a more attentive suitor."

The King laughed as he released Stella's hand, and turned to the gentleman beside him. The audience was over.

"What'll it be?"

"Burton, pale," Inspector Brown said, leaning against the wooden bar, taking in the taproom of the Knightwood Oak pub.

It wasn't as old as his own local in Lyndhurst but was cozy enough: thatched roof outside and low ceilings, hand-hewn wooden beams, and sturdy wooden tables within. None of those pretentious paintings of French landscapes or New Forest ponies grazing the heathland he'd seen in pubs of late. A few posters advertising Guinness stouts, Bass Ales, and Wrexham Lagers hung behind the bar, and over the mantel was a recent portrait of the pub's famous namesake, the Knightsbridge Oak, an English oak said to be over five hundred years old and more than twenty-four feet around. The pub was quiet before the local lads rewarded themselves after a hard day's work. Just the way Brown wanted it. The publican put the Burton ale on the bar and went back to cleaning pint glasses with a cloth.

"How much do I owe you?"

"Tuppence."

Cheaper than my local too. Brown fished out his coin. He took a sip of the brown ale, a bit of froth clinging to his mustache. It was good but a bit too hoppy for his tastes. He wiped his mouth with the back of his hand.

"Any news on the Derby?" he asked.

He already knew the answer. Constable Waterman had a cousin who worked at Epsom Downs and who'd telephoned the police station right after the race. Apparently, the constable had bet against Lord Rosebery's horse and now owed his cousin more than a few shillings.

"I sent one of my lads to find out."

Brown took another sip of his ale. He'd hoped the question would loosen the publican's tongue; the fellow had hardly uttered a word. The subtle approach having failed, Brown tried being more direct.

"Have you heard the news about the vicar?"

Brown had come not only to drink a pint but also to glean from the locals anything that might help his case. After interviewing everyone at Morrington Hall he'd been allowed to, the housekeeper at the vicarage, and the occupants of its neighboring houses, he'd learned two important facts: two members of Lord Atherly's staff were lying (about what he hadn't figured out yet) and Reverend Bullmore had worn a money belt, supposedly containing thousands of pounds, which was still missing. Brown assumed the vicar's money was the motive. But so far, besides the housekeeper, no one had admitted knowing about it.

"Who hasn't?"

"What have you heard?"

The publican looked Brown in the eye for the first since he'd sat down. "Who wants to know?"

Brown frowned. He'd hoped to avoid identifying himself. Men like the publican talked more if the conversation was friendly and unofficial. But there was no avoiding it now. He pulled out his warrant card.

"Inspector Archibald Brown, Hampshire Constabulary. I'm investigating Reverend Bullmore's death."

The publican put up the glass he was drying and started wiping down the bar. "Should've known."

"Why is that?" Brown had specifically changed from his uniform into his brown suit.

"I know all the regulars that come at this time of day." They both glanced over at a shaggy, white-haired man wearing spectacles and a wool sack coat, with three empty glasses and one three-quarters full by his elbow on the bar. His attention was focused on the broadsheet he'd spread open in front of him. "Like Old Joe."

"What have you heard?" Brown prompted.

"That the reverend was murdered up at the manor house."

"Anything else?"

"Sure. There's plenty of talk."

Brown stared at the publican in anticipation. But the publican said nothing more. Was he going to have to prompt the fellow for every sentence?

"Such as?"

"It's just talk, you know."

"About the vicar?"

"He'd been in Rosehurst only a fortnight."

"Any speculation as to why someone would want to kill him?"

"No. That's got folks stumped. Who would want to kill a vicar?"

Since he hadn't asked directly about the money belt, Brown had to assume no one knew about it, or at least had blabbed about it, at the pub.

"If not about the vicar, then what?"

"I wouldn't want to spread gossip about the family."

"Lord Atherly's family?" Brown asked.

The publican nodded. His loyalty was commendable but didn't help Brown one bit. "Or those American guests they have visiting," the publican volunteered.

Brown looked over the rim of his near-empty glass. This was promising. "What have you heard about the Americans?"

"That Lord Lyndhurst is to marry the daughter. An heiress, they say."

Brown nodded. Maybe if he gave a little, the publican would reward him in return. "That's true."

"Oh?"

Brown sighed and took another sip of his beer. Suddenly, the door flew open, and a lad of no more than eighteen came tumbling in, as if he'd tripped over his feet when they crossed the threshold.

"Cicero won the Derby, Mr. Heppenstall," the boy shouted.

The old man looked up from his newspaper. "Ah, the local horse beat the Frenchie, did he?" Old Joe said.

The boy nodded.

"What took you so long?" Mr. Heppenstall, the publican, said. "It should've taken you no more than half an hour. What'd you do? Ride up to Epsom to get the news?"

"I, ah . . ."

"I know all about the butcher's daughter, lad. Just get back in there." He pointed behind him with his thumb. "Those bottles aren't going to stock themselves."

The boy's face flushed a deep red. He stared at Mr. Heppenstall and then glanced at Brown and then at Old Joe before rushing past and disappearing through a door behind the bar.

"Cicero, huh?" Mr. Heppenstall said. "That reminds me, Inspector."

Brown looked at the publican with anticipation. The arrival of the boy hadn't ended his chances of getting more out of Mr. Heppenstall, after all.

"One of those rumors is about the horses the Americans brought with them. Three thoroughbreds is what I heard told."

"Yes, that's right."

"One of them is related to the Derby winner."

"That's right. The stallion the Americans brought was the sire."

The publican nodded. "It will be good to see racehorses at Morrington Hall again."

The publican fell into silence again. The old man went back to his newspaper, and Brown downed the last of his beer. This hadn't gone as he'd hoped. The entire investigation hadn't gone as he'd hoped. But he wasn't about to give up. He wasn't called Bloodhound Brown for nothing.

"Ever get anyone from Morrington Hall in here?"

"What? The family come into my pub?" Mr. Heppenstall chuckled. "I don't think so."

"No, I meant more like the household staff."

"Bavage, the gamekeeper, comes in, and I see some stable lads now and again."

"Seen any strangers lately?"

"Besides yourself?"

Brown smiled and nodded.

The publican glanced over at a corner of the room. "Now that you ask, I have."

"And?" A surge of energy filled Brown, and it had nothing to do with the strong ale. He'd shake the fellow to get it out of him if he had to.

"A grockle came in for several days in a row. Fancy tweeds, always ordered a half, never said anything."

Fancy tweeds? That didn't match up with Brown's assumptions about the maid's stranger in black trousers and boots. If he believed her at all.

"What did he look like?"

"Couldn't tell you. He wore his cap low and kept himself to himself, you know."

"Was he tall, fat, blond?"

The publican shrugged his shoulders. "He was a grockle. I try not to mix myself up with grockles. Outsiders bring nothing but trouble."

"Did he say anything? Like where he's from, why he's in the area?"

The publican shook his head.

"Can you tell me anything unusual about the stranger?"

Mr. Heppenstall looked up at the ceiling, as if he were studying the old spiderweb that dangled from the side of the nearest beam. "His hands shook," the publican said, "like he was sick or nervous or something."

"Did he come in on Monday at all?"

"Aye, Monday afternoon," the publican said without a moment's hesitation. "Left around the time we heard about the vicar. Haven't seen the grockle since."

CHAPTER 13

"Is that it?" Mr. Kendrick said as Sir Devlin escorted them away.

Lyndy didn't look at the horse breeder. Mr. Kendrick was a boor. His ingratitude was astonishing. A lack of acknowledgment by His Majesty was more than Mr. Kendrick deserved. Lyndy only had eyes for Miss Kendrick. She was on his arm, her head held high, and in that creamy yellow linen and lace dress that accentuated her long neck, she positively glowed. A slight breeze ruffled the feathers on her hat. When she caught his eye, she smiled, that wide, unabashed smile Lyndy preferred to any other. He became acutely aware of the beating of his heart.

"But what about the horses? What about Orson?" Mr. Kendrick said, plodding behind them. "The King is a racing man, and he didn't talk to me about the race."

Didn't Mr. Kendrick know anything? The audience wasn't about the horses or the race. As Sir Devlin led them back to their box, everyone watched them, or to be more precise, watched the woman on Lyndy's arm. Behind parasols, gloved hands, fans, and hats, whispers followed them. Lady Arabella Brice-Campbell, whose husband owned last year's third-place finisher, was among several elderly ladies who held spyglasses up to their wrinkled faces to catch a better glimpse. After the audience with the King, nothing would be the same.

"That's her. Isn't she lovely?"

"But I'd heard she was an American."

"She must have English blood."

"I always knew Lady Atherly would find a suitable match for her son."

Lyndy sought out the speaker of the last comment, but the members' enclosure was too crowded, and there were too many onlookers, to tell. He'd never had any doubt of his worth. He was the most eligible bachelor in Hampshire and had rightly questioned the match his parents had made. Until he'd met his match. He looked at Miss Kendrick again. A few strands of silky curls brushed against her cheek. The charming smile hadn't left her face. The murmurs and whispers continued.

"Did he actually take her hand?"

"She is delightful, isn't she?"

"I wonder why we haven't seen her in London?"

As they approached their box, Mrs. Westwoode rushed out to greet them. She was beaming. Lyndy didn't know the lady was capable of such a wide smile.

Mrs. Westwoode grabbed Miss Kendrick's hand. "Miss Kendrick, dear. We heard what the King said. We're so happy for you."

And for yourselves, of course. The association with one praised by the King couldn't do the Westwoodes any harm.

"Already?" Miss Kendrick said, gently slipping free of the woman's hold.

"Good news travels fast," Mrs. Westwoode said, a giddy lilt to her voice, which Lyndy had heard her use solely with her daughter or Hugh.

"Bad news travels faster," Mr. Westwoode muttered.

Mrs. Westwoode scowled at her husband before flashing a bright smile at Miss Kendrick again.

"Well, ain't that something," Miss Luckett, the chaperone, said, patting her niece's cheek.

"I never have met a king before," Miss Kendrick admitted.

"He called you 'delightful,'" Mrs. Westwoode said. "That's high praise, indeed. Of course, we all already knew that."

What a hypocrite.

"Just don't let it go to your head, girl," Mr. Kendrick said. "*Delightful* is not the word I'd use to describe you."

Miss Kendrick's smile disappeared.

How dare he? His daughter had been triumphant, converting her staunchest naysayers, including Mrs. Westwoode, and all Mr. Kendrick could do was criticize? She'd risen to the challenge, risen above her humble roots. Didn't Mr. Kendrick want society to accept her? For Mr. Kendrick's part, wasn't that what this was all about? Lyndy would never understand the heel.

"Well, I agree with His Majesty. Miss Kendrick is delightful," Lyndy said.

Hugh regarded him with a smirk, his eyes full of questions. His friend knew Lyndy was not one to pay compliments, at least not with any sincerity. Miss Kendrick scrutinized him. Did she think he was teasing her, as he had when they first met? Or did she hear the honesty in his words? How frustrating not to be able to read her thoughts. Most women were so transparent. But then again, he didn't even know his own mind right now.

"Glad to hear it, Viscount," Mr. Kendrick said, waving to someone in the box above, "since she's to be your wife. Like the King said, sooner than later, vicar or no vicar."

"The vicar was murdered, Daddy," Miss Kendrick chided.

"Tragic, yes, but why should it affect our plans, eh, Viscount? You do want full ownership of Orson, don't you? Your own valet again?"

Lyndy cringed as Mr. Kendrick included him in the collusion to bargain away his daughter in exchange for her fortune and a horse. As Mr. Kendrick waved to someone else in the crowd and tottered over to greet them, Miss Kendrick frowned. Miss Luckett frowned. Mrs. Westwoode frowned. They all glared at Lyndy. He hadn't done anything, and the women were against him. Moments ago, everyone had been cheerful and lively. He wanted to see Miss Kendrick smile again.

"Any more on who the police suspect?" Westwoode said, redirecting the conversation. Though Lyndy was grateful, it was a poor choice of topic.

"If you'd been around more, you'd know they don't know anything," his wife scolded.

"I say, he's become quite the popular chap," Hugh said, deflecting the talk away from the vicar's murder. All eyes followed his gaze. Several people Lyndy recognized and should know by name were gathered around the American like flies on steaming horse dung. Mr. Kendrick shook hands with every one of them.

"Wonders never cease," Miss Kendrick whispered.

When her father returned, she said, "That was nice of them to congratulate you on Cicero's win, Daddy."

"No," Mr. Kendrick said, a smug, satisfied grin on his face, "they were congratulating me on making such a fine match for my daughter. So, let's keep your mouth shut. We wouldn't want them changing their minds."

"Like the proverbial gift horse, Daddy?" she said through clenched teeth.

"Gift? Ha! This horse cost me millions."

Lyndy, like Hugh and the Westwoodes beside him, blanched at the vulgarity. No one spoke of money or the delicate details of a marriage arrangement, especially not in public.

Mr. Kendrick waved his betting ticket about before sauntering down toward the betting ring.

"Well, I'm glad to hear I am worth something to you, Daddy," Miss Kendrick grumbled bitterly. She glanced at Lyndy but hastily shied away. The pain in her eyes was piercing. Lyndy had to do something.

"If you'll excuse us." He grasped her hand and pulled her away from the Westwoodes, Lord Hugh, Miss Luckett, and any other prying eyes. He counted on the old chaperone's fragility to get Miss Kendrick away before the aunt caught up with them.

"What are you doing?" Miss Kendrick said.

Lyndy led her up the stairs until they were under cover, away from the crowds, and snuggly behind one of the wide pillars that held up the grandstand. A swallow's nest perched under the eaves above their heads. It was empty. Lyndy stopped abruptly, and the brim of her hat collided with his chest. Before she could retreat, he flung his arms around her and filled his lungs with the scent of her, that mix of floral and woody tones that reminded him of the New Forest in spring. She didn't struggle, she didn't complain, nor did she pull away. She tilted her hat back to look up at him.

"What are you doing?" she asked again.

"I'm taking the advice of my monarch." He'd seen the way the men looked at her. She was natural, she was honest, and she was strikingly beautiful. But Lyndy didn't get jealous, except over a horse, perhaps. Did he? "I wouldn't want you to find a more ardent suitor."

"As if I have a choice."

Her comment stung, the cruelty of it, the truth of it, and he considered letting her go. But something—lust, definitely, and maybe hope and curiosity too—kept his arms around her.

"Neither of us does. Daddy has made sure of that."

Lyndy leaned into her ever so slightly, relieved that she was aiming her bitterness at Mr. Kendrick, where it rightfully should be, and not at him.

"I wasn't joking about feeling like a gift horse. Is that all I am to you?" Her blue eyes stared at him in earnest; not a hint of animosity tainted her voice. "Be honest."

"If you weren't, could I do more than look you in the mouth?"

Her eyes widened, and her back stiffened. He couldn't decide if she was mortified by what he'd said, the way he'd said it, or its implication. He didn't care. He'd been staring at her lips for too long.

"Lord Lyndhurst, are you asking—"

He didn't let her finish. She wanted him to be honest. So, he would be. He pulled her to him in a tight embrace.

"Do call me Lyndy," he said. Then he kissed her.

"Herbert?"

Having ridden all the way from Christchurch, Gates's legs were weak and his balance was off. Despite the improvements they'd made to the road, enough ruts remained to make the journey a bumpy one. Give him hours on horseback to a carriage any day. But the journey, despite its discomforts, was always well worth it. Annie, his niece, and her husband, John, were pleasant people who fed him well, plied him with jars of John's homemade cider, and were always eager for news of Morrington Hall. With his feet up and the baby on his lap, he'd regaled them with the story of the Americans' arrival and their peculiar behavior. Annie had had him retell the story of Miss Kendrick appearing unannounced in the stable yard three times. But this visit had naturally been dominated by talk of the Derby races, the new thoroughbred horses, and the vicar's murder. He'd told that tale but once, and due to Annie's sensitive nature, he'd told it with as few gruesome details as possible. He hoped he'd never have to speak of it again.

"Herbert?" Gates called again, purposefully stretching and shaking his legs out, one at a time, as he strode into the yard. It was late, but he'd left the groom in charge. Someone should be about. He looked up at the second-story windows. They were dark. Had all the lads gone to bed?

Gates longed for his bed, but without reassurances from Herbert that all was well in hand, he'd have to check. But where was Herbert? Despite the incident with Miss Kendrick, Herbert was normally a reliable lad. It wasn't like the groom not to be here to greet him.

Gates glanced about the yard. It was swept, and the lamps had been dampened. He tugged on the coach-house door. It was latched. He unlatched a side door and strolled past the feed box, the coal room, and the standing stalls. He nodded with approval. Everything was as it should be. He passed the loose boxes. They'd all been mucked out, clean water had replaced the day's dirty water, and clean, fresh straw covered the floors. All the doors were secure. Beau and Lister were sleeping. Sugar and Spice, the Hanoverian carriage mares, were drowsy but content to take the pat Gates offered.

When Gates reached the loose boxes that housed the new thoroughbreds, Tully, the gentle filly Miss Kendrick favored, approached him and whinnied in greeting. He reached through the iron grating of the sliding door and patted her neck. Tupper, the three-year-old, stuck her head out of her loose box.

"Don't worry, girl. I won't forget you."

Gates stepped over to the other filly and rubbed behind her ear. She pushed against his hand to get a deeper rub. Gates listened for the stomping and snorting from Orson, which he knew would come. The stallion wasn't one to let the fillies get all the attention. But the ruckus never came. Gates glanced across the aisle as the filly nibbled his coat sleeve, hoping for a bite of apple or one of the peppermints Miss Kendrick gave her. Orson wasn't at the door. Could he be sleeping? Gates dismissed the thought as swiftly as he crossed over to the stallion's loose box. He wasn't a man to panic, but the hairs stood up on the back of his neck.

If anything happened to this horse . . .

At the Jockey Club, they were celebrating Cicero's win. Tomorrow Annie would be boasting to her neighbors about how her uncle cared for the most valuable stud in England. Lord Lyndhurst and the Americans would return from Epsom, triumphant. The irony of the timing wasn't lost on him.

In less time than it took to cross the aisle, Gates considered every conceivable reason why Orson wouldn't be responsive—shock, fever, blood loss, dehydration . . . death—and what immediate steps he must take in each case. In his haste to open the door, he laid his hand on the jagged edge of the doorjamb, where the stallion had gnawed the wood.

"Ow!" He jerked back his hand and teased a splinter from his finger with his teeth.

He heard a muffled response from inside. The horse was alive. *Thank God!* Gates blew out a pent-up breath. He hadn't realized how much he'd feared the worst.

With extra caution, Gates slid the box door open. He stepped into the dark, bracing for what he would find. Fresh hay crunched beneath his boots. He stared down at the figure on the floor. It wasn't the stallion lying in the fresh straw, spread thickly less than an hour ago, whimpering in pain or struck by fever. It was Herbert, lying on his side, his hands and feet tied, his mouth gagged with a polishing cloth. Orson, the stallion, was gone.

CHAPTER 14

"If only my darling Elizabeth had been there," Mrs. Westwoode said, for the tenth time, as they alighted from the carriage that had met them at the train station. Neither the evening spent in Epsom the night before, dining late into the night at the Jockey Club's Derby Day dinner, nor the journey back to Morrington Hall this morning had diminished the lady's regret that Stella, and not her daughter, had been granted an audience with the King. The warmth and affection she had shown Stella at the time had lasted only as long as it took her to realize the opportunity missed. "Why give an audience to an American, after all?"

Stella wasn't listening. Instead, she savored everything around her: the dark line patterns crisscrossing between the stone bricks of the sprawling house; the burst of lavender, pink, yellow, green, and white popping from the peony, hydrangea, and rhododendron bushes and the rosebushes; the ripples across the pond as a fish surfaced to catch a low-flying dragonfly; the individual pebbles, like a sea of stone, beneath her feet; the ripples in Spice's sleek gray coat as Stella rubbed the carriage horse's neck. Stella's lips remembered the pressure of Lyndy's. She swore she could still taste the champagne on his breath. His kiss had startled her, shocked her even. But was it his audacity or her own ardent response that surprised her more? She couldn't say.

"Welcome back," Lady Atherly said, stepping forward to greet the returning travelers. Was that a smile on her face? "Quite the coup, I must say."

"I knew you'd be pleased," Lyndy said to his mother, then placed a light kiss on her cheek.

He and Stella had spoken little since their kiss. At dinner, they'd been seated far from each other, and Stella, exhausted by the excitement of the day, had retired early. On the train ride home, he'd diverted himself by discussing the relative merits of flat racing versus steeplechase with Lord Hugh. Stella had stared out the window at the miles and miles of rolling fields of green, stone walls, and flocks of sheep, trying to puzzle out what had happened, while half listening to Mrs. Westwoode complain. Was she pleased he had kissed her? Would she regret it? Could she trust him? She didn't know. But neither the distance across the dining table nor the divergent discussions had kept them from stealing glances. What was he thinking?

"A coup is winning at ninety-nine to one. Cicero was favored to win," Daddy said.

Lady Atherly pinched her lips. Stella knew the smile wouldn't last.

"I'm sure my wife meant Miss Kendrick's audience with His Majesty," Lord Atherly said. "We've had a dozen cards left this morning. All our neighbors want to meet you, Miss Kendrick."

"The girl did nothing but stand there. What's so special about that?" Daddy said as he stomped past Lord Atherly and into the house.

Daddy had relished his role last night as society's newest welcomed member, accepting toasts, handshakes, and congenial pats on the back. That was, until all the questions, all the compliments were directed at or were about Stella, and not him. He'd tried all evening to recapture some of his early glory, telling his rags-to-riches story to anyone who would listen. As the evening had worn on, few would.

"Have the police told you any more, Lord Atherly?" Stella asked. Despite the distractions, Lyndy's kiss the greatest of them all, she hadn't forgotten for a moment about the vicar.

Lord Atherly shook his head.

"I do wish Elizabeth had been there," Mrs. Westwoode muttered.

Mr. Westwoode rolled his eyes and chewed on his upper lip.

"Where is my darling daughter, anyway?" Mrs. Westwoode asked.

"Taking a stroll in the garden," Lady Atherly said.

"Welcome back, my lord, Miss Kendrick," Fulton said. He and Mrs. Nelson, along with two maids and the footman that hadn't accompanied the party to Epsom, prepared to orchestrate their party's smooth return.

Lyndy nodded in acknowledgment, Aunt Rachel winked as she hobbled by, but Stella stopped in front of the butler, then placed her hand on his arm.

"Thank you, Mr. Fulton. It is so nice to feel welcome."

The butler raised an eyebrow.

Lady Alice stepped over and looped her arm in Stella's. Unlike the butler and the housekeeper, who would have bitten their tongues off before losing their composure, the maids' and the footman's faces betrayed their bewilderment. As Lady Alice led Stella through the front door, Stella glanced over her shoulder. The two maids, despite having been dismissed, stood rooted to the gravel drive, their eyes following Stella. Stella smiled at them, and the girls, wide-eyed, hastily retreated toward the servants' entrance around the side.

"Did I do it again?" Stella said.

"Do what?" Lady Alice asked.

"Break some unspoken rule of etiquette? I smiled at the maids, and they stared at me as if I'd grown antlers."

"We aren't familiar with the servants. They were surprised, is all."

"It seems I'll never learn to act like everyone else."

Lyndy handed Fulton his hat and leaned in toward Stella. "And I hope you never do."

He didn't smile. He didn't wink. His face betrayed no emotion. Like the pompous man she'd met that first day. If Stella hadn't felt the pressure of his hand on the small of her back as he kissed her yesterday, she'd think he was mocking her again now.

"Don't mock, dear brother," Lady Alice said, believing the same thing. "Miss Kendrick is genuinely trying to fit in."

"And I urge her to resist the temptation."

"She is to be Countess of Atherly one day," Mrs. Westwoode said, piling Fulton's arms with her cape, hat, and parasol. "Miss Kendrick must be the picture of English gentility, despite her . . . upbringing."

"With all due respect, Mrs. Westwoode, she's going to be my wife, not yours."

Mrs. Westwoode glared at Lyndy but held her tongue. Her husband, however, did all he could to stifle a chuckle.

Lord Hugh glanced at his future in-laws. "To have His Majesty's blessing is most fortuitous."

Mrs. Westwoode nodded vigorously.

Lord Hugh went on. "I say, lucky you that she is to be your bride."

"That she's to be my wife is not up for argument," Lyndy said.

Stella flinched. Must he remind her? They'd shared one kiss. It guaranteed him nothing.

"And, as your wife, she will have to learn how to conduct herself properly," Lady Atherly said. "And she can start this evening. I've invited a few friends over who are most eager to meet you, Miss Kendrick."

One comment from the King and everyone wants to meet me? Gawk at me, more likely.

"I don't think that's a good idea," Stella said. For her, social events tended to end badly. She said so.

"Pity. It has all been arranged," Lady Atherly said, dismissing Stella's concerns. "Now, I'm sure the ladies would like to rest before we must change for luncheon."

Now, that sounded good. Stella longed to soak in the bath, to let the neck-deep hot water steam away all thoughts of Lyndy, their kiss, their future, and this evening's party, and to feel warm again, finally. She still wasn't used to the damp, cool air inside or out. Would she ever be?

But as she followed Mrs. Westwoode and Aunt Rachel up the stairs, she heard Lord Atherly say, "I didn't want to say this with the ladies present, but the police are waiting for us in my study."

When she reached her room, she splashed cool water on her face from the basin, grabbed the woolen shawl Lady Alice had lent her, and hurried back down the stairs. A bath could wait. If the police had caught the vicar's killer, she had to know.

"We think the two crimes, the horse theft and the vicar's murder, might be related," Inspector Brown said.

Lyndy was beside himself. How could this have happened? Grandfather must be turning in his grave. As the inspector had related the details of the thoroughbred's theft and the discovery of the groom tied up in its loose box, Lyndy had wanted to pace, but the room was too small. Instead, he'd picked up one of the many fossilized horse bones and fiddled with it in his hands. Papa had cringed but had said nothing. Lyndy had returned it to its place.

"How?" Stella asked. "The horse didn't belong to the vicar, and he was dead before the horse was taken."

The men turned at the sound of her voice. They'd convened in the privacy of Papa's study to hear what the police had learned. She must've slipped in unseen.

"Miss Kendrick," Papa said, startled to find a woman in his study. Neither Mother nor Alice ever entered Papa's private sanctum. "I don't think you should be here."

"But I'd like to be, Lord Atherly, if it's all the same to you," she said, holding a wool shawl tight around her shoulders. She looked about the room, her eyes darting from fossil to fossil.

Papa looked at Mr. Kendrick, who shrugged, then at the inspector, and then at Lyndy. None offered their objections.

"I do hope you'll tell me more about your expeditions to Wyoming sometime, Lord Atherly." She was studying the map Papa had tacked up on the wall.

Papa's expression softened. He turned his face away and feigned a cough, as if needing to clear his throat. But Lyndy knew his father. Stella had won Papa's heart.

"Yes, well, Miss Kendrick did find the vicar's body," Papa said, then again tried to clear his throat. "And the horse is part of her inheritance. If she desires to stay, I have no objections."

Stella smiled. It didn't matter that it was a simple upturn of her lips; only she could distract him from such a tragic turn of events. Lyndy stared at it. He'd adored her wide, bold smile before, but now that he'd tasted her lips, sampled their softness . . . he'd be more diverted by any of her smiles than what was good for him. He turned his attention back to the inspector and the dreadful matter at hand.

"I agree with Miss Kendrick," Lyndy said. "It doesn't follow that the two crimes are related."

"From our preliminary investigation, I'd say the theft was planned," the inspector said. "Perhaps the vicar participated in that plan but was betrayed and murdered by his accomplices."

"Or the horse thief wants you to think that," Stella said.

The inspector nodded. "Perhaps. Or perhaps it is, as you say, Lord Lyndhurst, a coincidence."

"It doesn't matter," Mr. Kendrick said, swiveling back and forth in the desk chair, staring hard at the inspector. "Just get me back my horse."

Lyndy was ashamed to admit he partially agreed with the brute. The vicar's killer must be brought to justice, and Orson must be returned. *But let the police figure out the why and where and when and how.*

"We will do our best to find your horse, sir," the inspector said. "As we will do our utmost to find who killed Reverend Bullmore."

"Vicars are commonplace, like sheep in your fields. I wanted the bishop to marry off Stella, anyway. But Orson . . . he's the most valuable horse in this damn country."

Papa raised an eyebrow at Mr. Kendrick's blatant disregard for the vicar's violent end. Yet, to his distaste, Lyndy understood what the vulgar man meant. Any parish priest had the power to marry a couple, but the horse was unique. If Mother and Papa considered its theft a breach of promise, Mr. Kendrick wouldn't be able to supply another suitable replacement. The wedding would be canceled. Would Mother and Papa do such a thing?

"All our ponies and horses are valuable, sir," the inspector said. "This is the New Forest. But I, myself, put more value on human life."

Mr. Kendrick ground the butt of his cigar in the silver tray on the desk, pushed himself up from the chair, and shoved his face within inches of the inspector's. He poked the inspector in the chest with his thick, stubby finger.

"I don't give a damn about what you think. Find my horse."
Without a backward glance or a word of courtesy to Papa, the
American left the room.

The inspector sputtered incoherent curses.

"You were saying?" Papa said, as if Mr. Kendrick's outburst
were a mere distraction from the matter at hand. The inspector
stiffened his back, pulled out a small notebook, and flipped it
open. He didn't consult it once.

In a clear and concise manner, Inspector Brown summarized
everything the police had done to investigate the vicar's death:
examined the library, sent the body to the coroner's office, con-
ducted interviews with the Morrington Hall household staff,
the vicar's housekeeper, the vicar's neighbors, and key members
of the village community. He detailed the few facts they'd discovered: that the blows to his head were the confirmed cause of
death, that the wrought-iron fire iron was missing, and that the
time of death was between half past two and four that afternoon. He explained that they were investigating two possible
leads: the fellow, described by the maid, seen running away
from the library and a stranger spotted in the local pub. They'd
also expanded their inquiries to include the stable staff and any
relevant connections to the theft of the horse.

Inspector Brown flipped his notebook closed. He didn't
look happy.

"A stranger at the pub?" Stella asked. "Is that so unusual?"

"In these parts, yes," the inspector said.

Mr. Westwoode blanched.

"Nothing to worry yourself about, sir," the inspector said,
seeing Westwoode's reaction. "I promise you, if he was involved in the vicar's murder, we'll have him."

Mr. Westwoode nodded.

"Our biggest lead so far has come from the vicar's housekeeper."

The inspector glanced at Lyndy and then at Stella as he explained about the vicar's missing money belt but said nothing about their involvement in the matter. Stella, the shawl pulled as tightly around her shoulders as possible, rubbed her hands up and down her arms. Lyndy glanced at the fire grate. It was cold, as he'd expected. Perhaps with Stella's inheritance, they'd be able to heat this old house properly.

"It contained ten thousand pounds. Were any of you aware of this?"

"No, most certainly not," Papa said. "I'd never heard any such a thing."

Judging by the negative responses, this was a secret the vicar had kept well. If Hugh's argument with the vicar had been about the money, he gave no hint of it.

"Ten thousand pounds. That certainly could be a motive, if someone knew," Lyndy said.

"Most definitely," the inspector said, "and I regret the money is still missing, my lord."

"What about the housekeeper?" Mr. Westwoode asked. "Is she reliable?"

"Miss Judd served in this house before taking the position at the vicarage," Lyndy said, offended he should ask.

"She's quite a sweet elderly lady," Stella said. "I can't imagine her doing anyone any harm."

Mr. Westwoode still seemed skeptical. To further exonerate her, the inspector explained that Miss Judd had an alibi for the entire day of the murder and that they found no indication that she'd spent any sum greater than a few shillings in the past few days.

"There it is, then," Papa said. "Someone came into the house, killed the vicar for his money, and then stole the horse."

"No disrespect, my lord," Inspector Brown said, "but we don't think a stranger wandered into Morrington Hall, or its stables, for that matter."

"What are you saying?" Papa said.

"We believe it was someone connected to the estate."

"I don't believe it." Papa never could conceive of anyone he knew being guilty of a crime, be he a gamekeeper or a duke. Lyndy admired that about him.

Lyndy didn't want to believe it any more than his father, but an outsider would be noticed. "But who?"

"We're focusing on the staff, both inside the house and out," Inspector Brown said. "My constable is searching the stables as we speak. We will then be interviewing the coachman, the grooms, and the stable lads."

"But haven't you already questioned all the house staff?" Lyndy had been annoyed to learn they'd questioned his valet. It reflected badly on him. His man was beyond reproach, and Lyndy didn't appreciate having his judgment of character called into question.

"Yes, and we will need to do so again, considering the new developments."

"Very well," Papa said. "But I will not have my guests or my family disturbed by your investigations."

"I will endeavor to be discreet, my lord."

"Then if that's all, Fulton will see you out." Papa rang the bell.

At being dismissed, the inspector tipped the rim of his hat and followed the butler. But as he passed, Stella said, "We know you're doing your best, Inspector. Please know, I'll do whatever I can."

The inspector raised an eyebrow as he paused beside her. He couldn't make out what she meant any more than Lyndy could. What could Stella possibly do?

"I appreciate that, miss," Inspector Brown said skeptically. He was shaking his head when he left the room.

"Thank you for letting me stay, Lord Atherly," Stella said,

"but I'm not going to be any use to anyone until I've had a long hot bath."

Lyndy tried desperately not to picture her in her bath but failed. At least he kept the grin off his face. Mr. Westwoode made his excuses, as well, and followed Stella out. Lyndy could barely wait until Fulton closed the door behind them. There was one more question to ask.

"If the horse isn't found, or is found . . ." Lyndy hesitated. He couldn't contemplate harm coming to the magnificent creature. The thief must know the horse's value. Lyndy prayed the thief would treat the stallion accordingly. "If Mr. Kendrick doesn't get his champion stud back, will you call off the wedding?"

"We've every right," Papa said.

Lyndy couldn't keep still. He began to rock on his heels. "But will you?"

Papa picked up a letter from his desk. It was dated this morning and was signed by Professor Gridley, the leader of Papa's newest expedition. "I suppose that's what you'd want."

"No." The word rushed from Lyndy's mouth.

Papa accepted Lyndy's answer with a nod and, continuing to read, sat behind the desk. Too engrossed in his letter, Papa hadn't heard him.

"Lyndy, my boy, did you say no?" Hugh said, a smug grin on his face.

Papa looked up from his letter.

Lyndy hesitated to answer. This time the acceptance that he wanted to go ahead with the wedding came slower. When had it happened? When he'd heard her talking to her beloved horse? When her father had forced her to her knees? When she'd got up again? When she'd let unabashed tears run down her face upon finding the dead vicar? When she'd cheered on Cicero at the top of her voice? When His Majesty had warned him not to let another gain her affection? When he'd touched the softness of her lips with his? When Mr. Kendrick had abruptly left the room, leaving unsaid what Lyndy dreaded most? When she'd promised to help when no one else would?

"I did."

Hugh's smirk widened. Papa raised a questioning brow.

"Well, then . . . ," Papa said, "we must hope the police apprehend the vicar's killer and find that horse, mustn't we?"

CHAPTER 15

"Anything?"

Constable Waterman shook his head. "Sorry, sir."

Inspector Brown was disappointed, but he was also determined. He'd been humiliated informing Lord Atherly of their progress, or lack thereof. That a prize horse had been stolen from the Earl of Atherly's stables during an active murder investigation was galling and embarrassing. But the lack of anything irregular in the stables, paddocks, or staff bedrooms, had convinced Brown more than ever that someone familiar with the stables had planned the theft. If so, Brown would find him.

"What about the coachmen, grooms, stable lads?"

Constable Waterman flipped open his notebook. "I've spoken to everyone except the groom Herbert Kitcher, the one found bound and gagged in the horse's loose box. I thought you'd want to talk to that one yourself."

"Right you are, Waterman. What could the others tell you?"

"Not much, sir. No one observed or heard anything unusual. Mr. Gates, the head coachman, was in Christchurch, visiting a niece. We've rung Christchurch, and they sent someone round the niece's house. She corroborates his account. He left the groom Kitcher in charge in his absence. According to the second groom, Leonard, the horse was in its loose box when he said good night to Kitcher before retiring. Kitcher and the head coachman are waiting for you in the harness room."

"Lead the way."

The groom was sitting on a bench, wrapped in a green and blue plaid horse blanket and sipping a cup of tea, when Brown and his constable found him. Pieces of straw stuck out of his unruly black hair, evidence of the groom's prior difficulty. Gates, the head coachman, leaned over a ledger set on a workbench. Both looked up when the policemen entered.

"Mr. Gates?"

The head coachman closed his ledger.

"I'm Inspector Brown. My constable tells me you're the one who found your groom bound and Mr. Elijah Kendrick's racehorse gone."

"Yes," Gates said. Brown looked over to make sure his constable was prepared to jot everything down. "What kind of person does something like that?"

Unfortunately, Brown could easily describe people he knew who were capable of it and worse. But he ignored the coachman's question. "Are you Herbert Kitcher?"

"I am." The fellow spoke through gritted teeth, as if challenging the inspector to dispute his identity.

"So, what happened, Mr. Kitcher?"

"I was waiting up for Mr. Gates, so I was in here, polishing the harnesses. I heard Orson snorting and got up to see what all the fuss was about."

"Then what happened?"

"I was checking on the horse when someone hit me over the head."

"Hit you over the head and what? Knocked you out?"

"Yeah, like the vicar."

"But the vicar's dead," Brown reminded him.

The fellow sneered. "I got a hard head."

And a bad temper.

Brown understood the fellow's hostility. Mr. Kitcher had been bound and gagged not thirty yards from where the rest of his mates slept peacefully in their beds. Not the best way to spend the end of Derby Day. But something else nagged at Brown. There was something about the fellow Brown didn't trust.

"And then what?"

"Then I woke up in Orson's box, all bound up and gagged."

"You never saw who hit you?"

"No."

"Do either of you have any idea who could've done this?"

"No," the groom said, without hesitation.

A bit too fast, perhaps?

"I can't make it out either, Inspector," Gates said, shaking his head. "I understand why someone would do it. That horse was worth thousands, if not millions, of pounds. But unless you forgot to lock the doors, Herbert, how did the thief get in?"

Brown couldn't have said it better. He waited patiently for the answer.

"And now that I'm thinking about it, how did that lad the other night get in?" Gates added.

"What lad?" Brown asked.

"I found some village lad poking about the coach house the other night. I'd assumed he'd come to see the Americans' motorcar. Now I wonder."

"I asked Leonard to lock the doors," the groom said, casting the blame elsewhere.

Gates put his palm against his forehead. "Ah, Herbert, what were you thinking?" The groom stared down into his tea. "The lad Leonard has been sick, Inspector. It's possible that he might've left the stables unlocked."

"Where were you between half past two and four Monday afternoon, Mr. Gates?"

The head coachman didn't hesitate. "I had a bite to eat around two and went up to the house right after to take care of the new thoroughbreds when the Americans arrived. Then I was in the paddocks with Beau, Lister, and Sugar."

"Can anyone corroborate that?"

"I saw the lad Charlie before I went up to the house. Lots of others saw me there. I walked backed here with Roy, the Kendricks' groom. Lord Lyndhurst and Miss Kendrick were with me in the stables, and then I was with several lads in the paddocks." Gates was clearly out of it, then.

"And you, Mr. Kitcher?"

"I was here in the stables when the new horses and the American lady arrived."

"And before that?"

"Where do you think I was? Here, in the stables."

"Anyone see you?"

"What are you asking me this for? I'm the one that was attacked."

Brown ignored his outburst. "After the American lady arrived, did you stay in the stables?"

The groom didn't answer.

"Mr. Kitcher?"

The groom took a sip of his tea. Brown waited. No answer.

"Where were you after Miss Kendrick arrived, Mr. Kitcher?"

Still no answer.

If the fellow wanted to play this game, the inspector welcomed the challenge. Brown knew a liar when he saw him. It was only a matter of time until Brown discovered the fellow's secret. "If you refuse to cooperate, I will be forced to escort you back to the station."

"I was out walking on the Forest, alone."

"Where?"

"Fletchers Green."

"Do you typically go walking alone on the Forest in the middle of the day?"

The groom refused to explain himself.

"Herbert made a bit of a fuss about that time and left," Mr. Gates said.

"Do you often lose your temper, Mr. Kitcher?"

Again, the groom refused to speak.

"Whomever this fuss was with, I'll need to speak to him."

"It was, ah . . ." The head coachman seemed uncharacteristically hesitant. "It was Miss Kendrick."

"Lord Lyndhurst's American fiancée?"

"Yes, I'm afraid so."

Now, this was interesting. Brown might have to interview the young lady again.

"Why were you up at the house, Mr. Kitcher?"

"Herbert wasn't up at the house, Inspector. Miss Kendrick had come to the stables to see to the settling in of her horses," Mr. Gates said.

"Right." The groom had no alibi and was furious for being humiliated by a woman. Men had sought revenge for less. "So, Mr. Kitcher, after you had this row with the earl's future daughter-in-law, you went walking on the Forest to cool off your temper? Or did you go up to the house and take it out on the vicar? To get back at Miss Kendrick, perhaps?"

"What? No!" The groom leaped to his feet, throwing the blanket and the cup and saucer to the floor. The unfinished tea in the cup spread like a stain across the wooden boards. Kitcher raised a finger at the inspector. "I never touched a hair on that priest's head."

Brown stared at the groom, unflinching. Mr. Gates open his mouth but shut it again. "What about his money?" Brown asked. "Did you also take that, Mr. Kitcher?"

"What are you talking about?" the groom said. "I'm the victim here." Herbert pushed past the inspector, crunching several pieces of the broken white porcelain teacup beneath his feet, and charged out of the room.

"Don't go anywhere, Mr. Kitcher," Brown yelled after him. "We'll need to talk to you again."

"Take a seat, Mr. Finn," Inspector Brown said, indicating the captain's chair opposite.

Once they had finished talking to the staff in the stables and had washed the muck from their shoes, Brown and his constable had taken over Lord Atherly's smoking room again. The scent of cigars and leather permeated the room.

It beat the smell of horse manure.

"I hope this isn't going to take long," the footman said, sitting down.

What was the fellow thinking? Brown didn't know what he expected to see in the footman's face—concern, fear, curiosity—but whatever it was, he didn't get it. Harry Finn focused on the wall again.

"You told us before, Mr. Finn, that no one saw you in Lord Lyndhurst's dressing room at the time of the vicar's murder."

"That's right."

"What if I told you that the tailor arrived with Lord Lyndhurst's wedding suit about that time?" Brown had discovered this bit of news when he'd finally been allowed to speak to Mr. Fulton. He'd been itching to see how the footman would react ever since.

"Yes. What of it? The tailor was expected."

"I would think that it would be your task to take charge of the wedding suit."

"Yes," the footman said slowly. Brown could see the suspicion in his eyes.

"Then why weren't you there to greet him?"

The footman said nothing.

"Since you were nowhere to be found, the second footman was sent up with it, as well as with Mr. Kendrick's trunk, which you say you retrieved. He visited the respective dressing rooms at the time you were supposed to be there, pressing the viscount's riding clothes. He didn't see you in either room. What do you say to that?" Brown folded his arms across his chest and leaned back. He had his man, and he knew it.

The footman sat silently, staring at a point over the inspector's shoulder, his head held high.

"Where were you, Mr. Finn, when someone bludgeoned the vicar to death?"

"I haven't done anything wrong."

"If we search your room, we won't find anything to incriminate you, such as ten thousand pounds hidden away?"

"Where would I get that kind of money?" the footman scoffed.

"From the money belt of the dead vicar."

The footman's eyes widened. The news had shaken the footman, but Brown couldn't say why. Was Harry Finn afraid they'd discovered his secret, or was he startled to learn the vicar had carried that amount of money around?

"Have you been to the stables lately, Mr. Finn?"

The footman frowned. The abrupt change in subject seemed to take him by surprise, as the inspector intended. "No."

"On friendly terms with any of the staff there? Herbert Kitcher, for instance?"

"Herbert, the groom?" Harry Finn relaxed his shoulders and unclenched his hands in his lap. Brown hoped his constable didn't return too soon and spoil it. Brown might actually learn something. "I heard the horse thief tied him up."

"Who told you that?"

"Mr. Gates told Mr. Fulton, and a kitchen maid overheard them talking. All the servants know about it by now."

Brown frowned. He should've known.

"Besides, Lord Lyndhurst is quite beside himself over it all," Harry Finn added.

"So, you would help Lord Lyndhurst get his horse back if he could?"

"Who wouldn't?"

"Would you do anything for Lord Lyndhurst? Would you kill the vicar to rid your lord of a marriage he didn't want?"

The footman shook his head vigorously. Anger flickered across his face as he made eye contact with Inspector Brown for the first time since he'd entered the room. "No, no, no!" Harry Finn shifted his gaze and stared over Brown's shoulder again. "Besides, you have it all wrong."

"Do I?"

The footman opened his mouth to say something but hesitated. Was he conjuring up a lie or debating whether to tell something he'd learned in confidence? Brown put his money on a lie.

"Mr. Fulton said that the death of the vicar won't stop the wedding. It's the missing horse that might do it. Mr. Fulton said Lord Atherly is within his rights to claim a breach of contract if the horse isn't returned."

"Thank you, Mr. Finn," Brown said sincerely. This wasn't the information he'd hoped to get from the footman, but this gossip was as welcome as it was unexpected. Brown waited a moment or two to say more. The footman licked his lips. There was more Harry Finn wanted to say.

When the footman wasn't forthcoming, Brown asked, "Is there anything else you wanted to tell me?"

Harry Finn licked his lips again. But as he opened his mouth to speak, Constable Waterman strode into the room. The footman clamped his jaw and stared at the wall again.

"What do you have for me, Waterman?" Brown said, irritated. Now Brown might never know what Harry Finn was going to say.

The constable held up a small worn brown leather-bound book. "Found this in Mr. Finn's room." They'd decided earlier that while Brown questioned the footman, his constable would be searching Harry Finn's room on the third floor.

"You searched my room?" Harry Finn's face was hard.

Brown ignored the footman. He was piqued at his constable. First, the constable had interrupted what Harry Finn was about to tell him, and now this. He had sent Constable Waterman to the footman's room to find the money, not a book. Why was the constable smiling? A surge of hope welled in the veteran policeman. "Did you find the money?"

"No, sir. I didn't." Constable Waterman handed the inspector the book. The gilded words *Common Prayer* were engraved on the cover. The constable reached over and opened the cover of the book. "I think you're going to want to have a look at this, sir."

"This better be good, Waterman," Brown grumbled.

Brown looked down at what his constable pointed to. In a large sprawling hand, Reverend John Bullmore had signed the inside cover. Miss Judd, the vicar's housekeeper, had mentioned a prayer book had gone missing the morning of the murder. Brown kept the smile from his face. It wouldn't do well for either the footman or the constable to know how pleased he was.

"If you'd never met the vicar before he arrived at Rosehurst a fortnight or so ago," Brown asked, "why do you have a book in your room that belongs to the victim, Mr. Finn?"

"He gave it to me."

"This is an expensive gift to give a stranger."

The footman said nothing.

"How is it you have his book, then, Mr. Finn?"

"As I said, he gave it to me. I introduced myself to him after his first sermon, and he gave me the book."

"Just like that?"

"Yes, just like that." The footman stared over the inspector's shoulder again.

Brown didn't believe him. Had the footman met the vicar a fortnight ago, or was the footman lying, and they'd known each other before Reverend Bullmore arrived in Rosehurst? The latter was more likely. But it didn't matter. What did matter was why Harry Finn had possession of the vicar's prayer book that went missing the day of the murder.

"You don't have an alibi, Mr. Finn, and you have in your possession the dead man's book that went missing the day of his murder. I say that warrants a trip to the station."

"I didn't kill him!" The footman leaped to his feet.

Constable Waterman immediately stepped over and placed a firm hand on Harry Finn's shoulder. Brown was grateful the constable's grip hadn't lessened any since the days his constable wrangled ponies.

"Take him away, Waterman."

CHAPTER 16

Stella leaned forward and glanced in the dressing-table mirror, the carved tiger maple framing her face. Normally, her skin looked pale against the ivory lace of her gown, but now splotches of pink colored her cheeks. What was she last thinking of? Not the death of the vicar, the theft of Orson, the arrest of the footman, the rush of Epsom and her audience with the king, not even the strangers gathering below. So much had happened in such a short time. She covered her cheeks with her hands as she blushed again, remembering what she had been thinking about—Lyndy's kiss.

What if she did marry Lyndy? Would she ever be anything but "the American"? Would she and her "strange ways" be merely tolerated by the Searlwyns, as it seemed she had always been by Daddy? Or was there hope? Lyndy seemed different, almost kind at times. The softness of Lyndy's lips, the firm hold of his arms. She blushed again. And yet the arrogance, the impudence . . .

"What do you think, miss?" Ethel, Stella's maid said, placing a string of pearls around her neck. Stella, wrapped up in her thoughts, started at the sound of the maid's voice.

"I think I've decided not to go down."

Lady Atherly had made good on her promise to hold a small gathering of friends and neighbors eager to meet and gawk at "the American." Stella had never fared well at society events back home. That garden party at the Vanderbilts' in Newport, that ball at the Astors' in New York . . . She could envision the blunders, the comments, the disaster that awaited her downstairs. They expected her to smile and nod and make small talk about the weather. They might ask her to sing or play the piano. How disenchanted they would be. She'd meant her comment to be a joke, but maybe she'd stay upstairs, after all.

"But everyone will be so disappointed, miss. You being called delightful by His Majesty, and all." Ethel pinned a few loose wisps of hair, then stepped back to check her work.

As the maid placed a comb, a swirl of tortoiseshell and pearls, in Stella's hair, Stella smiled. The comb perfectly matched the hand-embroidered silk charmeuse dress Stella wore for tonight's soiree. The maid was a natural. She was also friendly and kind and, dare Stella hope, a confidante? Stella could certainly use one right now.

Daddy hadn't allowed Stella to bring Decker, her lady's maid from home, with her. On the journey to England, she and Aunt Rachel had had to cope with each other's help. Stella hadn't minded. Daddy had hired Decker, and the woman had never been friendly, muttering as she wrangled with Stella's thick hair. But here, Lady Atherly had insisted Stella find a proper English lady's maid. Ethel, a housemaid, had been assigned the task temporarily. Stella liked Ethel: she was gentle, had a kind face, and seemed eager to please. The maid had a knack for doing Stella's hair. If it were up to Stella, she'd let Ethel stay on permanently as her lady's maid.

"But isn't it in bad taste to throw a party so soon after the vicar's murder and the arrest of their footman?" Stella meant it. It was exceptionally bad timing, though she suspected she'd say anything to get out of having to go downstairs. Her hands were shaking as she patted her hair, inspecting the superb job Ethel had done. "Ethel, I wonder . . . ?"

Stella paused at the sight of the maid's reflection in the mirror. Stella swiveled on her cushioned bench seat. Ethel, tight lipped and knotting her pinkie fingers, stepped back until she bumped into one of the four carved oak posts of the bed.

"What's wrong, Ethel?"

"Nothing, miss."

Stella rose and approached the maid. Ethel's hands stopped moving, and she grew rigid, as if, not being able to retreat, she rooted herself to the floor. Stella placed her hand lightly on the maid's shoulder. The maid flinched, reminding Stella that the English weren't familiar with their staff. She took her hand away.

"It's obviously not nothing," Stella said gently. "Perhaps I can help?"

The maid looked up at Stella, confusion and conflict on her face. Someone killed the vicar, someone stole a prize stallion, and the police had questioned Ethel about both. Stella knew from her interactions with Inspector Brown that he could be less than delicate. And to have a fellow servant hauled off to the police station on suspicion of murder . . . Who wouldn't be upset?

"Harry didn't kill Reverend Bullmore," Ethel said.

"It's upsetting to think so, I know."

Although it was ludicrous that the maid should have to carry the water upstairs, Stella was glad she'd taken a long hot bath. But because of it, she'd missed much of the police's comings and goings this afternoon. With Lyndy's early departure from afternoon tea, she'd had to glean what had happened from Mrs. Westwoode's subtle allusions and disparagements.

"You don't understand, Miss Kendrick. I know Harry didn't kill Reverend Bullmore." How could Ethel know such a thing?

As if reading Stella's mind, the maid added, "I know because I think I saw who did."

Stella stepped back without taking her eyes off the girl and plopped down when her legs met the edge of the dressing-table bench. "Who was it?"

"I don't know. A stranger, I think."

Not someone she knew, then. Relieved, Stella exhaled slowly. "Did you see much of the man's face?"

"No. I didn't see his face at all."

"Then how do you know it wasn't Harry if you didn't see his face?"

The maid hesitated, wringing her pinkie fingers together again.

"I can't help if you don't tell me, Ethel."

The maid stared down at the lilac-, green-, and cream-colored area rug. "I was with Harry." The maid's words were barely audible.

"You were? I heard no one admitted to seeing Harry during that time, and Harry refused to admit where he'd been. Why didn't you say something?"

The maid sniffled, choking back tears. Stella finally understood.

"You were alone with him, weren't you?"

"It's not what you think," Ethel blurted out, meeting Stella's shocked gaze with her own. "I've known Harry since childhood. We were neighbors in North Gorley."

"That doesn't excuse you, you know that. In fact, all the more reason to suspect—"

"No, miss, we weren't . . . He's like a brother to me. I was teaching him to read."

"Oh, Ethel."

What a heartbreaking conundrum. If Ethel admitted to being alone with Harry and then lying to the police and Lady Atherly about it, she would be dismissed without references, as would Harry. But if she said nothing, Harry could hang for a murder he didn't commit. So why did they put themselves in such a precarious situation in the first place?

"Teaching Harry to read is commendable, Ethel. Why do it in

secret? Why not do it in the servants' hall, where you wouldn't be alone?"

"His parents are so proud of how far and fast he's risen in the household. When he applied for the position of first footman, he claimed he could read. But he can't. He never learned and was afraid he'd lose his position if Mr. Fulton found out."

"But why teach him now, if you've known him for so long?"

"Because he'd gotten away with it. At least he had until the vicar handed him that prayer book, hinting that he'd somehow found Harry out. I don't know how. Harry asked me to help him that same day. So, you see, he couldn't have killed the vicar."

"I'm curious. How is it that Harry doesn't know how to read, but you do?"

"My aunt is a schoolteacher in Fordingbridge. She taught me and all my sisters to read." Since Ethel was literate and competent, maybe Stella could convince Lady Atherly to let her keep the housemaid, after all. If she wasn't dismissed summarily for her misconduct, that is.

"That's where you were when you saw the stranger near the library?"

The maid nodded. "We were in the music room. It's difficult to do anything in secret here. Someone is always around. But no one ever uses that room, except when the countess has her musical nights." They had stolen away while everyone was outside waiting for Stella to arrive.

"Describe the stranger to me."

Ethel told her what little she knew about the stranger and about going into the library.

"Is that what you told the police?"

The maid nodded and then paused. "I forgot to tell them about the clunking sound."

"Clucking sound?"

"I heard him running, and he made an odd clunking sound, like . . . like he was stomping and running at the same time."

Stella frowned.

"At least that's what I remember. I told the police everything else."

"Except the part about being with Harry."

The maid looked down at the rug again. "Yes, except that," she whispered.

"And Harry didn't see anything?"

The maid shook her head.

Stella so wanted to believe Ethel. One's maid had to be trustworthy. But Ethel's description of the strange man was vague. Did she see someone? If so, what caused the clunking sound of his gait? Stella didn't know what to think.

"You didn't take the vicar's money, did you?" Stella hated to ask, but she had to be certain she could trust her maid.

"No, miss. I didn't know about the money. Not until the police mentioned it."

Stella studied Ethel's face. She believed her. "You need to tell the police what you told me."

"But—"

"Ethel, I will do whatever I can to prevent your dismissal. In fact, I was going to ask if you could stay on permanently as my lady's maid."

"Miss!" The maid's eyes lit up.

"But you have to tell the police."

The maid's face clouded over again.

"Ethel, they believe Harry murdered Reverend Bullmore. Harry could hang."

The girl looked stricken. Had she never thought of it that way before?

"Promise me you'll go tomorrow."

Ethel nodded, her shoulders square, but tears dampened her eyes. "Will that be all, miss?"

Stella wanted to throw her arms around the girl and tell her that she'd been foolish, but for all the right reasons, and that Stella would never let Lady Atherly throw her out on the street. But that wasn't proper behavior between an English lady and her maid. Instead, she smiled, hoping to convey her feelings that way.

"Yes. Thank you, Ethel."

As the maid opened the door, the hum of murmured conversation mixed with the strands of soft music floated into the room from downstairs. Stella's stomach lurched at the sound. If only she didn't have to . . .

"Wait, Ethel. I have an idea." Stella rose from her bench and hoisted the train of her dress over her arm. "Grab my shawl, will you? Quickly."

"Certainly, miss, but it will ruin the effect of your dress."

"They won't care what I look like where we're going."

"*We*, miss?" Stella snatched the shawl Ethel had retrieved from the wardrobe and wrapped it tightly around her shoulders. She'd be cold, but there wasn't time to find her duster coat.

"Yes, Ethel. I'm driving you to Lyndhurst, to talk to the police."

"Now?"

Stella laughed, relief flowing through her body. If she was quick enough, no one would stop them. She wouldn't have to face the party downstairs. "I can't think of a better time, can you?"

The crunch of the horses' hooves on the gravel drive was rhythmical and reassuring as Lyndy led Tupper toward the house, the light fading quickly around them. He'd ridden the racehorse hard across open expanses of Furzley Common and Cadnam Green, steering clear of the brush and bracken. With both of their energy spent, he'd taken her up to Stagbury Hill to listen to distant birds call through the warm stillness, and admired the streaks of orange, red, and yellow stretch across the horizon as the sun set.

Lyndy had never been one to waste time in reflection, but

with the events of the past few days, he'd found little peace of mind. What with meeting Stella, finding the vicar murdered, having his dream of owning a champion thoroughbred nearly realized and then dashed with the cruel theft of the stallion, he could think of nothing else. He'd taken the ride on Tupper, hoping the challenge would clear his mind. It had. Time spent on the Forest was never wasted.

The distant roar of a motorcar had broken the serenity of the sunset. Who else had a motorcar besides . . . ? He'd hurried back.

What was Stella up to now?

Music wafted from the open door as the silhouette of a couple entered the house. Was that Alice playing Mozart? A carriage passed him and pulled around the drive. A couple alighted as Lyndy approached the house. *Mother's soiree!* He'd completely forgotten.

"She's magnificent, Lord Lyndhurst." Baron Branson-Hill, thin as a lath and rumored to own a hundred horses, patted the horse's neck as Lyndy motioned for the groom lingering in the shadows, waiting for his return.

"She is," Lyndy said as the groom led Tupper away.

"Any news on the thoroughbred stud?" Baron Branson-Hill asked. Lyndy wished he hadn't.

Lyndy swallowed down the sourness that rose in his throat. Lyndy's stomach churned from just thinking about the stolen horse. The police had been very tight lipped. Did they, like he, think the horse would never be found? The priceless animal had most likely been ferried to the Continent by now.

"You'll probably know as soon as I do."

The baron laughed as Lyndy followed him and his wife inside. But Lyndy hadn't been joking. Gossip traveled fast. Mother's soiree was evidence.

Despite the cost, every chandelier and wall sconce was lit. The scent of roses and gardenias filled the entrance hall and the grand saloon, as fresh bouquets adorned every tabletop. Music, now Debussy, soft and melodious, drifted in from the music room and accompanied the din of conversation and laughter. Two days ago, Mother couldn't find anyone but the West-woodes to witness the wedding. Now, after His Majesty had called Stella delightful, the house was full of "well-wishers" from the best families in Hampshire. He had to get out of there.

"Where is your delightful fiancée?" sneered Lady Philippa Fairbrother, a buxom, black-haired beauty in a green silk and velvet dress. Lyndy's gaze swept across the room. Stella wasn't in sight. Philippa put her hand on Lyndy's arm. Lyndy stiffened at her touch. "Poor Lyndy. Is she as uncouth as they say?"

Lyndy knew Philippa through her brother at Eton. She was Mother's favorite to marry Lyndy, before Papa's fossil expedition expenditures made it impossible. *Thank God for horse fossils.* The woman was a viper.

"Yes, and it's quite refreshing." Philippa frowned at Lyndy's retort and let her hand slip away. Lyndy brushed his sleeve where her hand had been.

"Lyndy, a word!" Mother called, weaving her way through the guests toward him. "How lovely you look, Lady Philippa. If you'll excuse us for a moment." Lady Philippa smiled and nodded knowingly as Mother wrapped her arm around Lyndy's and led him toward a quiet corner. "Where have you been?"

"Out riding. I needed to—"

"Do you know what Miss Kendrick has done? Do you?" How could he know? And then he remembered the roar of the motorcar on the heath. Mother smiled at Lady Yardley, a heavyset matron in a flouncy lavender lace gown, as she passed. "She left. Left!" Mother whispered through clenched teeth, determined to keep the smile on her face. "Without a word to me or any of my guests."

"Oh, dear. Why?"

"She told your father she had to take a housemaid to the police station."

Lyndy laughed. *How brilliant!* At least Stella had figured a way out of this charade.

"Do you find this amusing? Our guests came here to meet Miss Kendrick."

"Then invite them to the wedding."

Mother glared at him but said nothing. What could she say? She knew he was right.

Lyndy spied Lord Hugh chatting with Sir Alfred Goodkin, another chum from Eton. "Now, if you'll excuse me while I mingle with our guests."

"What's this about the footman?" Sir Alfred asked the moment Lyndy reached his side.

"He is also Lyndy's valet," Hugh added. "That makes it all the worse."

Yes, it does.

At first, Lyndy had been annoyed at Harry's arrest: it was bad enough when Papa let the third footman go last month and Harry had to serve at table. Lyndy had spent over a year molding Harry into his perfect gentleman's man. Harry was loyal, able, proud and, above all, discreet. Now who was going to dress him, who was going to shave him, and who was going to draw his bath? Who else was he going to be able to trust?

Lyndy had been equally insulted. How dare the police insinuate, with so little evidence against him, that Harry had done anything criminal? It reflected poorly on them, on Harry and, worst of all, on Lyndy.

But most of all, Lyndy had been troubled. Why would Harry have the vicar's prayer book? He knew Harry couldn't read. It was an unspoken secret between them. Lyndy didn't mind the pretense, as it had never interfered with Harry's duties. But having the prayer book didn't make Harry a killer. Harry wasn't capable of harming anyone. Unfortunately, Lyndy knew who was.

"You were in Rosehurst when they arrested Harry, weren't you?" Lyndy asked Hugh. Hugh nodded. What had taken

Hugh into Rosehurst? Hugh had never said. He'd been there the afternoon of the murder as well. "The police have the ridiculous notion that my man had something to do with the vicar's death."

"But didn't a maid see a strange man running from the library?" Despite being in Rosehurst at the time, Hugh, who reveled in gossip, was, not surprisingly, well informed.

"It appears they don't believe her."

"Oh, Lord Hugh, dear," Mrs. Westwoode called, pulling a hapless man in spectacles toward them.

"Drink?" Hugh said before dodging past Sir Alfred and into the crowd.

Lyndy gave his excuses to Sir Alfred as Mrs. Westwoode craned her neck in search of Hugh. Lyndy cast his gaze about as he caught up with Hugh heading toward the less crowded drawing room. "Have you seen my father?" Perhaps Papa knew more about Stella's spontaneous trip to the police station.

"Lord Atherly and Mr. Kendrick are holed up in the study. Something about a fossil expedition?" Hugh said.

Lyndy nodded knowingly. That was how Papa and Mr. Kendrick had met in the first place, through their mutual friend, Professor Gridley, the leader of Papa's latest expedition to find horse fossils in Wyoming. Ironically, the expedition, or more precisely its exorbitant cost, was the driving force behind Papa's decision to arrange Lyndy's marriage with an American heiress.

"Your mother is not pleased, with him or your Miss Kendrick. If Mrs. Westwoode introduces me one more time as her 'darling daughter's fiancé,' I, too, might have to make an escape."

"What took you into Rosehurst, Hugh?"

"Did you see Lady Philippa?" Hugh whispered. He didn't answer the question.

"You know I did," Lyndy said.

Hugh winked, nudging Lyndy with his elbow. Hugh was

one of those men who hoped to take a mistress the moment his wife produced an heir and a spare.

I'd been one too. But now?

"Well, I hear she and Lord Fairbrother aren't well suited," Hugh said, winking and smiling. No man could be well suited to Lady Philippa.

Except for a tête-à-tête of a young couple whispering and giggling by the mantel, the drawing room was empty. The couple bolted the moment Lyndy and Hugh walked in.

"Why do you think your man did it?" Hugh asked.

"I don't think he did."

Hugh raised an eyebrow in surprise. "Then why do the police think he did it?"

"Money. Supposedly, the vicar had the audacity to carry thousands of pounds strapped to his leg." Hugh flopped down into one of the wingback armchairs.

"What would a footman do with that kind of money, anyway?" Hugh asked, as Lyndy strolled over to the liquor tray on the side table.

Who knew about Harry? But Lyndy knew what Hugh would do. Hugh had debts. At the Derby, Hugh had wagered thousands more than Lyndy knew his friend had. Until recently His Grace the Duke of Tonnbridge had been indulgent with his second son, happy to have him return safely from that cursed war in Africa. But Hugh had confided a few days ago that the duke, hoping to encourage maturity and economy in his son, had recently cut back on his allowance. Obviously, the duke's hopes had yet to come to fruition.

"I have to admit I'm not surprised someone killed him," Hugh said.

Lyndy, having poured Hugh's whiskey, clanked glass against glass as he jammed the decanter stopper in with force. "Why is that?"

"Bully was not your typical God-fearing vicar."

"Bully? Clyde Harris called him that. I'd never heard that before."

Hugh chuckled as he took the glass Lyndy held out to him. "A nickname my father gave the good Reverend Bullmore years ago."

"I didn't realize you knew him."

That was a bit disingenuous on his part. He should've added, "Until the day before his murder, when you argued with the man." Lyndy had never mentioned the argument. Should he now?

"He was a favorite of my father's, being an oddity in His Majesty's circles—a vicar who was an unrepentant punter," Hugh said. "Bully used to come to Wellston Castle for the house party during Ascot every year."

Reverend Bullmore, a fixture of the Turf, associated with the then Prince of Wales and his social circle and an annual guest of the Duke of Tonnbridge? Lyndy had had no idea. If he was to believe the gossip, the vicar was also connected with the scandal at Carcroft House. Did Hugh know anything about it?

"That was before he dropped out of society," Hugh said. "If you listen to the gossip, he went to Everton Abbey."

Lyndy had heard of Everton Abbey. It was an Anglican monastery in eastern Hampshire, known for its extreme austerity. Lyndy cringed thinking about it. "Why would he do that?"

"Why, Lyndy, my good man. When have you ever listened to gossip?"

"Never. That's why I'm asking you."

Hugh laughed. They both knew Hugh was as bad as the women when it came to gossip. "Point taken. Supposedly, he went because he was involved in a notorious scandal."

"Clyde Harris implied Reverend Bullmore was paid off after the incident at Carcroft House. Is that what you're saying?"

Hugh shrugged. "That's why it's gossip, my friend. No one really knows the truth."

"The truth," Lyndy said. "Pity that has never stopped anyone's blathering."

"How true!" Hugh laughed before gulping down what was left in his glass. "Let's get fuddled, old chap!"

Hugh held out the empty glass, shaking it. Lyndy took the glass and returned to the liquor tray. The glow from the chandelier above glistened off the glass and the crystal bottles, throwing shards of light across the silver tray. That tired old tune Schubert's "Serenade" drifted in when a couple of old, drooping matrons, looking for somewhere quiet to sit, peeked in.

"Join us for a drink, ladies?" Hugh said, then laughed as the women slammed the door.

Lyndy loathed baiting his friend, but he knew Hugh hadn't told him everything. Those same rumors that accused the vicar of taking hush money also put Hugh at Carcroft House that scandalous night. Lyndy had never given the rumors about Hugh any credence, until now. Lyndy reached for the whiskey and, before pouring Hugh another drink, poured himself one.

CHAPTER 17

"I think she should carry a Princess Plume bouquet. Do you know what a Princess Plume bouquet is, Miss Kendrick?" Mrs. Westwoode did not hesitate a moment for Stella's response. "No, I can't imagine you would, would you? Being an American."

There it was. Another not so subtle insinuation that she wasn't a properly raised English lady. When Lady Atherly left to consult with the housekeeper about the day's menus, Mrs. Westwoode had commented on Stella's presumed ignorance of proper wedding menus. Now it was wedding flowers. And each insinuation carried a reference to Stella's "impolite and impetuous" failure to appear at the party last night. Stella preferred Lady Atherly's stern admonishment "not to embarrass me again" far better than Mrs. Westwoode's insidious droning.

"Baroness Branson-Hill carried one at her wedding. You would've met her last night if you'd only been there."

Stella ignored the hurtful comments, as she did Daddy's when they were at home. But unlike at home, she couldn't hide in the stables. Not that she hadn't tried. Stella had gone there early, only to have Lady Atherly send someone to fetch her for breakfast. She'd been trapped in the drawing room with the other women ever since.

But it had been worth it, hadn't it?

"It's a combination of white orchids and green Farleyencis fern. It's quite spectacular and dignified and requires much patience to design. Elizabeth seems determined to carry lilies of the valley. What are you planning to carry, Miss Kendrick? If you decide to attend your own wedding, that is."

Stella neglected the Jack London book in her lap—who could read with Mrs. Westwoode droning on like that?—and stared out the window longingly at a pair of snowy white swans drifting about on the pond down the hill. What she wouldn't give to be one of them right now.

"Perhaps a simple bouquet of lilacs, since everything about your nuptials is under a cloud. Poor Lady Atherly. What was she thinking? Do you even know when or where it will take place, Miss Kendrick? Perhaps that will be your excuse not to make an appearance?"

Wasn't providing Harry with an alibi a good excuse?

"Did I tell you Elizabeth and Lord Hugh are to be married at the His Grace's private chapel at Wellston Castle in three weeks' time?"

Stella barely heard the question. Mrs. Westwoode had rambled on and on about her daughter's wedding plans for . . . How long had it been? An hour or two, maybe more? Besides, Mrs. Westwoode had no interest in Stella's opinions. Was there no way to escape this woman's voice or her subtle reprimands?

"Should you become Lady Lyndhurst before my darling becomes Lady Hugh Drakeford, though I doubt—"

Lyndy walked past the window. "Excuse me," Stella said, snapping shut her book. Lady Alice and Miss Westwoode glanced up from their jigsaw puzzle, a scenic river scene from Switzerland. Stella tossed her book down, ignoring the look of consternation and surprise on Mrs. Westwoode's face.

"Where are you going now, Miss Kendrick?" Mrs. West-woode asked.

"Hold on, girlie," Aunt Rachel said, struggling to rise from her chair.

"It's all right, Aunt Rachel. You stay put." Stella wasn't about to wait for her.

Stella hurried from the drawing room and down the hall. She paused a moment when the second footman opened the front door; it should've been Harry.

Had Ethel's confession been worth it? Was it enough to get Harry released? Would Lady Atherly dismiss Ethel for breaking the rules? Would Inspector Brown speak with Ethel again? Would he believe the maid? And if Harry didn't kill the vicar, who did?

Stella, flustered by her frustration and doubt, rushed out the front door, hatless and gloveless, and straight into the path of a New Forest pony. The group, which had been grazing mere steps from Morrington Hall's front door, scattered a few yards away. Catching up to Lyndy momentarily forgotten, Stella stood, transfixed. She was transported back home, to a pasture full of horses in Kentucky. No, this was better. The ponies, though smaller than the horses she was used to, wandered freely. She would have loved that as a child. Did they all have names? Did this same group frequent Morrington Hall's lawn regularly? What would they do if she approached them?

"I wouldn't do that if I were you."

Stella, having crept up on the closest pony, a bay-colored mare, paused, the hand she'd raised to pet the animal frozen in the air. "And why not?"

Her tone was harsher than she'd intended. Her worry about Ethel and Harry, her frustration at being belittled and lectured to, her resentment for being trapped inside all morning were catching up to her. Why was she taking it out on him?

"They might not be wild, but don't tell them that. They'll sooner bite you than not."

"Thank you for the warning, Lord Lyndhurst," she said, dropping her hand to her side as the pony continued grazing.

Lyndy frowned. "Are we back to that again? It's Lyndy. After Derby Day I assumed . . ." He had the decency not to finish his thought.

"I've spent the entire morning cooped up with Mrs. West-woode, who's been chiding me and insulting me and insinuating again and again that I'm not a proper English lady. So, I will not be calling you by your nickname. It's not proper."

He looked over at her, his jaw set, his lips tight. He clutched his lapels. "Why do you insist on acting like something you're not?"

"Are you saying I'm not a lady?"

"Come walk with me."

Confused and frustrated, she did as he asked. He led her through the rose garden, where spindly stems bowed over from their lush, heady blooms, and down to the edge of the pond. She waited for him to say more, but he stared out at the swans, occasionally fiddling with the belt of his tweed jacket.

They stood in silence. Stella was used to silence. Having no one but Daddy and servants in the house, she had spent long periods back home without speaking or being spoken to. She'd sit and read for hours with only the sound of the clock ticking or birdsong to break the quiet. Until this morning, she hadn't fully appreciated the luxury of it. But she wasn't used to standing idle, in nervous anticipation of what the man next to her might say. Judging by his restlessness, tugging on this, brushing at that, neither was he.

She clasped her hands in front of her until the tips of her fingers turned numb from her ever-tightening grip. Then she bent down, found a smooth, flat stone, and flung it out across the water. The rock skipped five times, sending increasingly larger ripples in its wake, until it sank under the water. She chose another and flung that too. This time it skipped eight times and made it within inches of where the swans had glided out of reach. She looked down for another rock.

"Where did you go last night? Mother was not pleased." Was that a chuckle?

Stella had driven Ethel to the police station in Lyndhurst without incident. Unable to reach Inspector Brown at that time of night, the constable on duty had insisted they wait for Constable Waterman. Though Ethel had been a nervous wreck, wringing her hands until they turned red, Stella hadn't minded. She preferred the drab police station to Lady Atherly's music room. When Constable Waterman had arrived, he'd patiently written down Ethel's story and sent the pair of them home. To Stella's relief, the wait had saved her from having to mingle with strangers. The guests had gone home.

"I took Ethel to the police station in Lyndhurst."

"Why?"

Her words followed in a rush. "Because Harry couldn't have done it. Ethel was with him at the time of the murder. The police had to know." No reaction. Wasn't he relieved about the footman? "Besides, who wants to be the center of attention? I had to find some excuse to skip the party."

Why doesn't he smile or wink or say something?

"I know they face dismissal without references for lying and being alone together," she said, "but perhaps if you spoke to Lady Atherly on their behalf . . . ?"

He remained staring out at the pond. It was as smooth as glass. Yet Stella could feel the muscles in his body tense.

"Lyndy?"

He faced her, a slight smirk on his face. "Finally."

What did he mean by that? And then she remembered; she'd called him by his nickname. She chuckled. He always seemed to get his way, like Daddy. Yet she didn't mind. It was different with him.

Lyndy's face clouded over again. "I never did think Harry did it."

"What made you so certain?"

"Because I'm afraid I know who did." Lyndy pointed to the

folly across the pond. It looked like a larger stone version of the gazebo in her garden in Kentucky. "Hugh and the vicar argued the night before . . ."

Before what? Did Lyndy suspect his friend of the murder?

"No," Lyndy said when she asked. "I don't know."

"What do you think Lord Hugh wanted the vicar to give to him?"

"I think Hugh knew about the vicar's money and wanted it. Hugh has debts." Who would've known, the way Lord Hugh bet at the Derby? Or perhaps because of it.

"You don't suspect Lord Hugh was involved in Orson's theft, too, do you?"

Lyndy stared out at the pond again. He didn't deny it.

"Orson is worth tens of thousands of pounds, if not more," Lyndy said.

But why would Hugh steal the stallion if he'd robbed the vicar of thousands of pounds? Was he that over his head in debt? Besides, Lord Hugh was with them at Epsom Downs when the horse was taken.

Admiring the pink and white daylilies blooming around the base of the folly, Stella asked, "Where was Lord Hugh when the vicar was killed?"

"He says he was in Rosehurst."

"He says?" Stella glanced over at Lyndy. He pulled the cap from his head and ran his sleeve over his forehead, as if the morning sun was too hot. Stella couldn't picture it ever being too hot here. "Do you doubt him about that too?"

"I do. What business would Hugh have in Rosehurst that he won't discuss? It doesn't make sense." Lyndy frowned and began rocking on his heels. "It was almost better when the police suspected Harry did it."

"I have a favor to ask, Mother."

Lyndy had been dreading this encounter from the moment Stella suggested it. He was never comfortable being alone with his mother. She'd spent the requisite hour a day with him and Alice when they were children, but she'd made it clear that it was her duty to attend her children and not a desire. *Duty!* How Lyndy hated that word. He could count on one hand the number of times they'd had a private conversation that didn't entail Lyndy doing what Mother construed as his duty. He hoped this wouldn't be one of them.

And then there was the matter of Stella's absence at Mother's soiree last night.

"What is it, Lyndy?"

Sunlight streamed through the French windows of Mother's morning room, illuminating a painted center table laid out with wedding gifts: engraved silver candlesticks, a large silver platter, an intricately painted Chinese vase that stood several feet tall, numerous bejeweled brooches, hatpins and hair combs, a long string of immense pearls once belonging to Catherine the Great, and a diamond tiara tipped with large pear-shaped stones. Hidden behind the vase was a bronze sculpture of three polo players and their horses in a hideous tangle. It was an original work by the American artist Frederic Remington. Lyndy could guess who had sent that.

This was her sanctuary, with its pale blue and white palette, its heady scent coming from the large bouquets of white roses, and its prominent secretary desk. With its tall ceilings and light palette, Mother's morning room was the antithesis of Papa's study. Yet Lyndy didn't feel any more comfortable here than in Papa's room. Mother sat at the secretary, drafting a letter. She hadn't stopped writing on his account. Why had he agreed to do this?

"Harry, the first footman, is innocent. A maid gave him an alibi. They were together at the time of the vicar's death." Mother stopped writing and looked up, expectation and skeptical curiosity in her expression. "It was innocent enough. The maid was teaching Harry to read. The girl has already informed the police."

And now what? Would the police suspect Hugh, as, God forgive him, Lyndy did?

"What does that have to do with me?"

"I'd like you to give me your assurances that they won't be dismissed."

"Why should I?" Mother went back to her letter.

How could she be so callous? How could she not sense the conflict he was going through? How could he have expected anything else? Lyndy held his temper, but he began pacing the room. He couldn't wait to be away from here.

"Because the footman's innocent. Isn't that enough?"

"But the servants disregarded my rules, Lyndy."

"Miss Kendrick gave the maid her word. Otherwise, the girl never would've admitted to it."

Mother slowly set down her fountain pen. "Pity, Miss Kendrick didn't consider that before she acted so rashly."

Mother was livid about last night, and she had every reason to be; Stella shouldn't have dashed off as she had. Stella shouldn't have promised the maid anything either. But did that mean Mother would let Harry hang for breaking her rules? Or was she so petty that she'd let the maid and the footman suffer because Stella didn't present herself to be gawked at? Lyndy had been as shocked as the rest at Stella's conduct, but by God, he admired her audacity.

"Miss Kendrick didn't want Harry to hang, Mother. But you, you would dismiss them both without references? You might as well let him hang."

"Don't be so dramatic."

"Who will we get to replace them, then?" Mother flinched. Lyndy had hit on a sore subject. Papa's fossil expeditions had forced them to let several of the staff go, and keeping the staff they had was proving difficult. "Hasn't Mrs. Nelson hired three new maids in so many months, just to have them desert us? We'll be down to a single footman without Harry. Shall we allow the hall boy to serve at table, to dress me?"

"Very well. You made your point. I shall tell Mrs. Nelson not to dismiss the girl."

"And Harry?"

"I'll tell your father to inform Fulton that he is not to dismiss the footman."

"Thank you, Mother."

She tilted her face, tapping the side of it with her finger. Wrinkles stretched from the corner of her eye. Laughter lines, he'd heard them called. She used to laugh. Lyndy bent down and dutifully kissed his mother's cheek. When had she stopped?

CHAPTER 18

"Did you hear the news, Mr. Heppenstall?"

The boy held three wooden crates of empty ale bottles, stacked up to his chin. He couldn't see his feet, and that was never a good thing.

"Watch what you're doing there, lad," the publican of the Knightwood Oak said. "If you drop them bottles, it will come out of your wages."

"What news?" Old Joe looked up from the newspaper he had spread out across the bar.

"Don't encourage the boy, Joe," Tom Heppenstall chided. But Old Joe waited expectantly. Tom knew neither the boy nor the old man would be satisfied until the lad said his piece. "Well, then, tell us what you've learned."

"The police released Harry Finn, first footman at Morrington Hall."

"Did they now?" Old Joe said.

Tom glanced over toward the window where that grockle had sat last night. A couple of hands from Granger's farm occupied the table now. Tom had assumed he'd seen the last of the stranger. No such luck. After days away, the grockle had turned up again. Was the bloke a murderer or a harmless grockle? Who was he kidding? There was no such thing as a harmless grockle.

"What I hear," the boy said, resting the crates on the nearest table, "is that someone saw him doing something else at the time of the vicar's murder, so he couldn't have done it."

"Who's this someone else?" Old Joe said.

"I don't know."

"Then who did do it?" Old Joe said.

"I don't know. But from what I hear—"

"What you hear? What you hear?" Tom said. "You hear a lot of nonsense, that's what you hear. Now pick up those crates, lad. That table needs wiping down." He flung his towel over his shoulder and strode around from behind the bar.

"The argument I heard wasn't nonsense." Old Joe and Tom stared at the grumbling lad, who was focusing on balancing the crates against his chest as he lifted them up again.

"Put those crates down," Tom said.

"But . . . ," the boy said, even as he obediently set the crates on the table again. The publican grabbed the back of the lad's collar and pulled his face toward him.

"Now you listen here, boy," Tom said, the boy frozen in his grip. "If you heard something, anything, that pertains to the murder of our vicar, you say so, and you say so now." Tom, letting his frustration with the boy get the best of him, pushed the lad, who tumbled backward against the table. The glass bottles clinked as the boy collided with the crates.

"I heard someone arguing with the vicar," the boy stammered, "and before you ask, I don't know who it was. I couldn't see his face. Just that he wore posh clothes."

"When was this?"

"The night before . . . you know, before *it* happened."

"Where?"

This time the boy hesitated.

"Where did you hear it?"

"At Morrington Hall."

"At Morrington Hall? What in the name of—"

"Not by the house," the lad scrambled to explain. "On the other side of the pond. Near that little building with the columns."

"The folly?"

The boy nodded, his face as red as that of a drunkard on a binge. Tom didn't have to ask what the boy had been doing anywhere near there. He'd suspected for quite some time.

The boy looked at his boots. They had an inch of mud on them. How many times had he told the lad to scrape his boots before coming in? First the table, now the floor. Tom might have to hire a maid just to clean up after the boy.

"You should've told someone," Old Joe said.

"But I don't have permission to cut through—"

"Lord Atherly's land? No, you don't. You don't have any business . . . ," Tom said. "You cut through there to see the butcher's daughter." It wasn't a question. "That's why you haven't told anyone."

The lad nodded.

The publican leaned toward the boy. "You're going to tell the police now, though, aren't you, lad?" His voice was barely above a whisper. He wasn't happy. "For it's either you tell the police or I'll surprise the missus with a fresh side of bacon from the butcher's tonight. If you get my meaning."

The boy tripped over his own feet as he hurried toward the door. Old Joe chuckled. Tom didn't see the humor in it. If he weren't his wife's cousin's boy, he would've let the lad go long ago. Maybe he should tell the butcher, anyway, and be rid of the troublesome lad.

"And you'll put these bottles away when you get back," Tom yelled as the boy swung open the door and disappeared.

*   *   *

Papa conversed with Inspector Brown on the other side of the smoking room as Mr. Westwoode hurried past without a word. Lyndy didn't like the troubled look on Mr. Westwoode's normally placid face. As he hadn't liked the look on the coachman's face when Gates had alighted from the family carriage, charged with the unpleasant task of conveying the bad news. It hadn't mattered that he and Hugh were hip deep in the Beaulieu River, fishing. Or that Stella, in a simple but sumptuous pink linen and lace dress, along with Alice, Miss Westwoode, and Miss Luckett, the chaperone, were admiring Lyndy's fishing prowess from the comfort of a woolen blanket, spread with the remains of their picnic lunch, on the shore. The police summons had ruined a perfectly good afternoon.

"What's this all about? I've told you everything I know," Lyndy lied.

"Yes, and thank you, my lord," the inspector said. "We highly regret taking you away from the river, as it is Lord Hugh Drakeford we'd like to speak to."

"Me?" Hugh shrugged. "I had nothing to do with the vicar's death or the horse's disappearance."

"It's not only you, Hugh," Papa said, trying to explain. "They are asking everyone now that the footman has been exonerated."

"Papa, you're allowing them to question everyone?" Lyndy couldn't believe it. The intrusion, the implication was insulting. No wonder Mr. Westwoode had made such an unceremonious departure.

Papa nodded, insisting the inspector had assured him of his discretion.

If they were asking everyone, why the need to rush them back? Couldn't the police have waited until they returned from their afternoon excursion? Lyndy looked at the constable. The policeman hadn't uttered a word but held a pencil and notebook at the ready. Lyndy looked at the inspector. That man would win a staring contest with anyone, even Mother.

"Then let's get this over with," Lyndy said, settling into the nearest captain's chair. Hugh remained standing and faced the inspector.

"Right," the inspector said. "Could you tell me, Lord Hugh, where you were late in the afternoon last Sunday?"

The question took Lyndy by surprise. Why ask Hugh about the day before the murder? They all knew Hugh had spent the afternoon playing cricket at the local pitch. Hugh was the best bowler Lyndy knew. Hugh had come back, bragging and . . .

"The reason I ask is that someone was overheard arguing with Reverend Bullmore late that afternoon. It was described as heated. It was you, wasn't it, Lord Hugh?"

There it was. The secret Lyndy had been prepared to keep for the rest of his life. Did Stella, the sole person he'd confided in, tell the police? She'd given her word. She wasn't capable of such deception. Was she? *No.* Someone else must've overheard the argument. *But who?*

"Who says so?" Hugh said, obviously wondering the same thing.

"Then it's true?" The inspector sounded surprised. Had he been bluffing? Had he tricked Hugh into confessing? Lyndy wasn't sure whether to feel contempt or admiration for the inspector. "You were overheard saying, 'Either give it to me or leave me alone.' Is that correct, Lord Hugh?"

"So, what if I did?" The bitterness in Hugh's voice surprised Lyndy.

"What were you arguing about?" the inspector said. "What did you—"

"What the argument was about is irrelevant as Lord Hugh wasn't here when the vicar died," Papa interrupted. "We have all been quite cooperative, Inspector, but will be less so if you insist on asking my family and guests inappropriate questions."

The inspector opened his mouth as if to say something but snapped it closed again.

Lyndy didn't know what to think. He appreciated Papa's intervention, but Hugh had just admitted to arguing with the dead man. But with no explanation. Lyndy wanted to know more. What had he been arguing about? Who had overheard it besides Lyndy? What would the police do about it now? Did they suspect Hugh of stealing the horse?

"Right. Thank you for your cooperation, Lord Hugh. As our investigation continues, we may require your assistance again. Please do not leave the area without giving us fair warning." With that veiled threat, the inspector dismissed Hugh.

Hugh shrugged before turning on his heel. Lyndy followed his friend as Hugh hummed some ditty they'd heard at the theater in London last season. Why was Lyndy more troubled by all this than Hugh appeared to be?

Hugh caught the concerned expression on Lyndy's face and scoffed. "Don't worry, old chap. That policeman's gone off his chump."

If only Lyndy could believe that.

Stella set her elbows on the dressing table, picked up the glass perfume bottle, and lifted the stopper. She loved that scent. It always reminded her of spring in the woods back home. She caught a glimpse of Ethel in the dressing-table mirror as the maid tugged on Stella's hair. A small smile softened the girl's face as she worked.

They had done the right thing. Harry was a free man.

"Did you know the police came back today?" Stella asked, admiring the result of the maid's efforts, a long single braid draped over her shoulder, tied with a pink satin ribbon.

Mr. Gates had arrived at the scene of their picnic, apologetic but tight lipped. Stella, Lady Alice, and Miss Westwoode had stood guard outside the door after the policemen called Lyndy and Hugh into the smoking room. Mr. Westwoode had stormed past, not even acknowledging his daughter as she tried to take his hand. When Lyndy and Lord Hugh emerged from their interview, Lyndy had been indignant but unforthcoming. As Lord Hugh reassured Lady Alice and Miss Westwoode that there was nothing to fret about, Lyndy had glared at him. Stella had not been reassured.

"Yes, miss. I did hear the police came back," Ethel said, brushing a stray hair from the arm of Stella's nightgown. She turned and picked up Stella's evening gown from the bed.

"Have you heard any reason why? They summoned us from the banks of the river and never told us why." Stella swiveled around to look at her maid when the woman wasn't forthcoming. Had she overstepped her bounds again? No. The maid's head and shoulders were deep in the wardrobe as she fetched something. A dress had slipped from its peg.

"It was Lord Hugh, miss," Ethel said when she reemerged. "Seems he argued with the vicar the day before the murder."

Stella was shocked. She hadn't told anyone; Lyndy had been adamant. How did the police find out? What else did they know? Lord Hugh had seemed nonplussed when he'd finished his interview. Maybe he had a perfectly reasonable explanation for the argument, after all. But then why had Lyndy seemed so upset?

"And the Westwoodes, miss."

Stella stared at her maid. This was the first she had heard of their involvement. But it shouldn't have come as a surprise. The police had asked her and Lyndy about their whereabouts on the day they discovered the vicar's body. Between the two of them, they could account for everyone, except Lord Hugh and the Westwoodes.

"I'm assuming the police wanted to know their whereabouts at the time of the vicar's death?"

Ethel nodded, closing the wardrobe door. "They should've asked us instead of bothering Lord Atherly's guests," Ethel said, the first hint of disdain Stella had ever heard in the maid's voice.

"Do you know?"

The maid nodded. "Markham, Mrs. Westwoode's lady's maid, told us she'd dressed her missus for riding about that time, and I remember Millie being put out when she'd gone to make the beds, as Miss Westwoode was having a lie-down. Millie had to go back twice before the young miss left the room."

"What about Mr. Westwoode?"

"No one seems to know where he was. Will that be all, miss?"

"Help! Help!" A shrill cry reverberated through the closed bedroom door.

Without thinking, Stella leaped to her feet, snatched the silk embroidered robe Ethel had laid across the top rung of the needlepoint chair, and dashed across the room. She threw open the door, hurrying to don the robe, but paused the moment she crossed the threshold, realizing she had no idea which way to go. The vacant hallway, lined with paintings suitable for any museum, inlaid tables holding priceless Chinese vases and Japanese statuettes, artifacts accumulated by previous generations, stretched on and on in both directions. A well-polished silver suit of medieval armor stood on guard at each end.

"Help!"

The cry came again, echoing up from the grand saloon beneath them. Stella leaned over the carved oak railing as Mr. Fulton shuffled hurriedly across the parquet floor below. Miss Westwoode, her face as pale as a finish-line post, emerged from her room with a maid Stella hadn't seen before on her heels. She'd hastily wrapped a shawl around her shoulders. Her hair, flowing down her back, was only partially braided. They scurried toward the stairs. Stella, with Ethel mere steps behind her, followed.

Stella bound down the stairs, taking them as fast as she could, and followed a footman, still dressed in his evening livery, to the library. The library door was open, and several servants lingered, whispering, outside. Surprisingly, Miss Westwoode didn't hesitate and disappeared inside.

"Who is it?" Stella asked.

When no one responded, she approached the door. She'd known she would have to return to this room one day, but this wasn't how she'd hoped it would happen. Until now she had relied on the books she'd brought with her from Kentucky and hadn't had any reason to enter.

Please don't let there be another dead body inside. She stepped across the threshold.

But there was a body lying prone on the floor. In a swirl of gray and navy-blue silk, next to the side table, the same one that had held the vicar's last cup of tea, was Mrs. Westwoode. Lord Atherly and Lyndy knelt on the floor next to her. Miss Westwoode whimpered from the couch.

The room closed in on Stella. The stuffed birds in the display case leered at her. The shelves of books tilted toward her, as if to topple to the floor and bury her beneath them. Stella reached out for the nearest handhold and accidentally grabbed her father's arm.

"Let go of me, girl," he said, brushing her hand away. She snapped her hand back as if she'd been stung. When had he arrived? He pushed past her to gawk over Mrs. Westwoode's body. Stella stayed where she was. She didn't want to see the body or go anywhere near it.

"Get her to sit up, if you can," Lord Atherly said.

Stella gasped as Mrs. Westwoode's head and back, with Lyndy's firm grip around her shoulders, rose from the carpet.

Mrs. Westwoode looked around, blinking, as if seeing the room for the first time. Her cheeks were flushed, but otherwise, the matron appeared unharmed. Stella was astonished and relieved. Stray strands of hair, loosened from the elaborate knots on the back of Mrs. Westwoode's head, fell limp about the lady's shoulders. She clung to Lord Atherly, who, with Lyndy's aid, helped her to her feet. Her breath came quick and shallow.

"Take a moment to compose yourself," Lord Atherly said as others arrived—Lady Alice and Lady Atherly, who dismissed the gathering crowd of servants, and then Lord Hugh.

"What's everyone getting hot and bothered about?" Aunt Rachel said, clutching her robe about her, as she hobbled in behind them.

"Where's Augustus?" Mrs. Westwoode whined when the men set her down beside her daughter on the couch. "Elizabeth, darling, where's your father?"

Miss Westwoode reached for her mother's hand. "I don't know. What happened, Mummy?"

"I was attacked. That's what happened." Mrs. Westwoode put a hand to her throat and then to her head. "They stole my jewels."

Mrs. Westwoode began to ramble on about a gold amethyst pendant necklace and a tiara, about having matching earrings snatched away, and again and again, she mumbled something about the stench of the stables.

"I came in after dinner," Mrs. Westwoode said. "All I wanted was a book to take to bed."

Stella scoffed quietly. She didn't believe it. Unlike the other women, Mrs. Westwoode never had a book in her hand. She'd never even picked up one of Lady Alice's magazines. So, what was Mrs. Westwoode doing in this room, of all rooms? Stella could only guess.

Mrs. Westwoode went on. "I think he must've been lying in

wait for me. I started to scream, but he whispered in my ear that if I did, he'd kill me."

"Who was it, Mummy?" Miss Westwoode said.

"For God's sake, woman. Who did this to you?" Daddy said.

"It was him. Him!" Mrs. Westwoode declared. "The stranger. That man who killed the vicar."

CHAPTER 19

Leonard rubbed the callused palms of his hands over his face. He'd been dozing. He couldn't, wouldn't, let Mr. Gates down.

Lying in bed, sweating and shivering, Leonard had missed everything: the arrival of the new horses, the death of the new vicar, the Derby, seeing the viscount's American lady with muck on her shoes, the theft of the new stallion, Herbert tied up and gagged. Not that he hadn't heard about it all. Charlie, the young lad who never stopped talking, had made sure Leonard knew what he was missing when he'd brought up Leonard's beef tea.

But who can think of anything when your head pounds every time you move?

He shifted his weight on the stool. He had to be alert, just in case. Sugar sighed and sniffed, and it echoed in the silence of the stables. She was always the last horse to fall asleep. Leonard pinched his cheeks.

Now Herbert had gone. Packed up all his things sometime after dinner and left without so much as a by-your-leave to Mr. Gates. Leonard had never liked Herbert. The groom thought too much of himself, ordering others about while he sat with his feet up, daydreaming. About what Leonard could only guess. Tonight Herbert was supposed to relieve Leonard after his turn of the watch. But Herbert had never come. Mr. Gates had asked Leonard to take the second watch. Leonard didn't mind. It was important work, what with the theft of the prize stallion. Mr. Gates wasn't taking any chances. And Leonard wasn't going to miss out on anything else.

Leonard's eyelids fluttered closed. He shook his head to rouse himself. But two shifts . . . when he was weak yet. His chin fell toward his chest.

Click.

Leonard's head snapped up.

Creak. Click.

Someone had opened and closed the washing-yard gate.

"Who's there?" Leonard leaped to his feet. He snatched the lantern hanging from the hook near the stable door. It swayed in his hands, nearly banging against the wall. He grabbed the bottom rim, steadying the flickering light, before reaching for the metal bolt on the door, polished from use to a high shine on one end. He slammed it to the side, flipped the latch, and swung the door open.

Crunch, crunch, crunch. The would-be intruder, merely a dark shadow in the lantern's dim light, was running away through the gravel yard!

Clink! Crash! The washing-yard gate swung open and slammed against the outer wall.

"Stop!" Leonard tripped over the threshold as gaslight streamed down from the windows above. He'd woken Mr. Gates.

Leonard rushed through the gate and toward the fading sound of running feet until he cleared the practice yards. He stopped, unable to go farther, doubled over, and gasped for breath. His illness had left him short winded. With his hand on his knee for support, he looked up. Morrington Hall, a silent behemoth, cast a long shadow across the hill. There was no sign of the intruder. He straightened up and lumbered back toward the stables.

"Damn." Leonard couldn't believe it. He had had the culprit in his sights, and he had let him get away.

Mr. Gates, followed by every groom and stable hand, most in their stocking feet, rushed to meet up with Leonard. "What happened?"

"Someone tried to get in."

"Who was it?" Mr. Gates asked.

"He ran away when I opened the door."

"He got away?"

Leonard nodded slowly. With Herbert gone, Leonard had harbored thoughts of a promotion. Mr. Gates would never make him head groom now.

"Get yourself to bed, lad. I'll take the rest of the watch, in case they come back."

Leonard, his breath shallow, slumped his shoulders. He followed the others slowly as they headed back toward the stables, letting the lantern hang from his hand at his side. He was a full three yards behind when he reached the washing-yard gate.

"See to those bales before you find your bed, though, Leonard," Mr. Gates called. Several bales of straw were stacked inside by the gate. Herbert was supposed to see them put away.

As Leonard hung the lantern on the nearest hook, a glimmer in the straw caught his attention. Was it the flash of an animal's eye in the lantern light? He kicked at the straw. Nothing. But as he bent down to grab the first bale, he noticed it again. What animal wouldn't have scampered off by now? He retrieved the lantern, then hovered it above the straw. The fresh scent of the straw prompted the first deep breath he'd taken since his pursuit of the intruder. He loved that smell. He peered in closer, taking another deep inhale. A glint of gold and purple shone brightly in the light. He shoved his hand into the straw, then pushed it back to get a better look. His eyes widened. A large purple gem twinkled in the lantern light.

CHAPTER 20

"Good morning," Stella said, forcing a smile on her face, as she stepped into the warmth of the kitchen.

She didn't mean it. The morning had been as dreary as any since she'd arrived, except for the brief clearing when she first awoke. The promise of sun, as she'd already learned from morning after morning of the same tantalizing brightness, was a hollow promise indeed.

She'd barely slept. Too many questions without answers. Who was this man who had first murdered the vicar and now had attacked Mrs. Westwoode? Would he attack again? How could he sneak past maids and footmen, butler and lord without anyone suspecting? Could it be someone they all knew? The moment the sun shone through her window, she had dressed without ringing for Ethel and had headed straight for the stables. Barely fifty yards from the house, raindrops had splattered around her. She'd headed back toward the house, but the skies opened up completely before she'd reached the front door. Drenched, her blouse sticking to her skin, her wet hair dripping and loose about her shoulders, Stella had crept back to her bedroom, grateful no one was up yet. After changing into dry clothes, she'd headed for the kitchen. She craved answers, warmth, and Kentucky black cake.

It had been her mother's favorite. One of Stella's earliest memories of her mother was sitting in a warm kitchen with Cook and Mama and stealing raisins from the cake batter when no one was looking. Daddy hadn't allowed Cook to make it after Mama died. But Stella had, in secret, when she became old enough. The methodical steps of baking, the rich smell of cooking currants and raisins, and the memories of Mama tasting the batter with her pinkie could soothe away the worst of hurts. Oh, how she needed that now.

Clunk!

Mrs. Cole, a thick woman with a round, bespectacled face pulled taut by the severity of her bun, slammed the heavy black kettle back onto the stove. The other servants froze in place. The girl with flour on her cheek and her hands in the dough stopped kneading. They all stared at her.

"Miss Kendrick!" Mrs. Cole said, surprised and not particularly pleased.

At home, Stella would go into the servants' hall or kitchen at any time. Cook knew to expect Stella any day the weather prevented her from escaping to the stables, like today. She'd never seen a kitchen staff react this way before.

"Can I help you, Miss Kendrick?" Mrs. Cole wiped her hands on her apron as she approached Stella. A mere glance from the cook as she passed compelled everyone to resume their duties.

"I wanted to bake a Kentucky black cake for everyone and wondered if you had all the necessary ingredients."

Why was Mrs. Cole squinting at her like that? Stella looked down at herself. Her white blouse and pale brown and embroidered gold skirt hadn't a speck on them. She touched her ears and the back of her neck—no stray tendrils of hair had escaped from Ethel's skillfully placed pins. Her hair was nearly dry. She covered her mouth with her hand and ran her tongue across her teeth. Nothing.

Yet the others had again stopped what they were doing, their eyes wide or their mouths agape. One young maid held her apron up past her nose. Stella could hear the girl's muffled giggle.

"I beg your pardon?" Mrs. Cole said.

Stella caught the eye of the girl who was giggling. The maid dropped her apron and scampered toward the larder. "On such a dreary day as this, I hoped to share a recipe from home, Kentucky black cake, and wondered if I needed to take a trip into town to get anything for it."

"Yes, miss. I heard you the first time."

"Oh." Stella focused her attention back on the cook. "I assume you have plenty of the basics—flour, brown sugar, butter, eggs, brandy. But do you have allspice, citron, currants, and raisins? I'm not sure if these are staples in an English kitchen, as they would be back home."

"Yes, miss, I do indeed have all the ingredients."

Stella smiled in relief. By the reaction of the kitchen maids, she'd worried she'd made yet another faux pas. Perhaps once she started baking, she could encourage the maids to talk. Who knew what they might tell her that they wouldn't dare tell the police? "Do you have an apron I could wear, Mrs. Cole?"

"You want a what? To do what?" Mrs. Cole sputtered.

The quiet pounding of hands kneading bread against the wooden table, the click of a spoon as someone stirred a pot, the soft footfalls of the maids as they crossed the flagstones of the kitchen, fetching this and that, all stopped. Only the hissing of the steaming kettle left to boil too long broke the silence. All eyes were on her.

Stella's heart sank. "If this isn't a convenient time . . ." Mrs. Cole began shaking her head vehemently. Stella's voice trailed into silence.

"Never, miss," Mrs. Cole said, straining to contain her indignation. "It will never be convenient for you to come into my kitchen and bake your Kentucky black cake."

The quiet vehemence took Stella by surprise. The staff at home had always been so accommodating, so patient, after her mother had died, leaving Stella alone with Daddy. She didn't expect the same sympathy here, but she had never expected to be unwelcome. Suddenly, pots banged, hands pounded bread, feet shuffled, voices rose as the kitchen staff tried to act busy.

"I don't know what foolishness prevails in your own country, Miss Kendrick, but that is not the way things are done here!" Mrs. Cole folded her arms across her chest, daring Stella to contradict her.

There it was. Stella had done it again. She'd broken yet another of the unspoken rules of English etiquette. Would she ever learn?

So much for getting the maids to share their gossip with me.

"Miss Kendrick, is there something I can help you with?" Mrs. Nelson said, a cluster of keys jingling at the waist of her crisp black dress, as she descended the stairs.

"She wants to bake a cake in *my* kitchen," Mrs. Cole said without taking her eyes off Stella.

"Now, now," Mrs. Nelson said, her hands clasped against her chest. "I'm sure you misunderstood, Mrs. Cole. Miss Kendrick had a request? Is that it? Something from home to cheer her up in these troubling times? You know it was Miss Kendrick who found the vicar, don't you, Mrs. Cole? And today was to be her wedding day, after all."

Stella appreciated Mrs. Nelson's attempt to ease the situation, but her words were hollow. The message—that no matter how awkward or inappropriate her behavior, Stella was soon to be a member of the family and was to be tolerated as such—was clear. But Stella didn't want to be tolerated or placated or condescended to. Not by Lyndy, not by Lord and Lady Atherly, and not by the staff downstairs. She'd had enough of that from

Daddy to last her a lifetime. She wanted to be accepted, loved, for who she was. Was that too much to ask? Stella regarded Mrs. Cole, who hadn't relaxed her arms or the grim expression on her face. It might be.

"I'll make you a Kentucky black cake," the cook said, conceding. "If that is what you want."

"That would be fine, Mrs. Cole. Don't you agree, Miss Kendrick?" Mrs. Nelson said. "Though you'll speak to myself or Her Ladyship next time you have a request, won't you, Miss Kendrick?"

"Yes. Thank you," Stella said, knowing Mrs. Cole's black cake would be tasteless in her mouth. There wouldn't be a hint of her mother's touch or home in it.

The maid bit her fingernail and looked away. Stella tried to ignore her. Wasn't that how most of them regarded her, as a thing of curiosity? She was the one that had dropped her cap the day Stella arrived. Stella had seen her pass in the hall outside the kitchen a few minutes ago, fastening a coarse morning apron around her waist as she walked. Millie, wasn't it?

The maid had pressed up against the wall in the grand saloon, beside the grandfather clock, which towered over her. A brush stuck out of a metal pail beside her. As Mrs. Nelson had bid Stella good morning, the maid had stood silent and motionless, as if to hide in the clock's shadow. But to no avail. Mrs. Nelson had noticed her and had left to have a word. Stella couldn't hear what was said, but the maid looked stricken. She bobbed her head to the housekeeper, snatched up her bucket, and headed toward the staircase. She glanced over her shoulder at Stella before climbing the stairs. She was biting her nail again.

Could there be more in her gaze than curiosity? Stella, on an impulse, followed. Seeing Stella approach, the maid stopped. She curtsied as Stella gained the landing. The scent of smoke wafted up from the bucket.

"You don't have to curtsy to me. I'm the American, re-member?"

A hint of a smile crossed the maid's face but vanished at the *tap*, *tap*, *tap* of footsteps on the parquet floor nearby. "I'm sorry, miss. I didn't mean to disturb you."

"Wait," Stella said, reaching out and grabbing the sleeve of the maid's print dress as the young woman turned to leave. The maid dutifully stopped but hung her head and stared at the polished oak step beneath her feet. Stella quickly let go. "Did you want to speak with me?"

The maid peered around, making certain no one else was near, before pulling a charred piece of paper from the pocket of her apron, the bib soiled with what looked like strawberry jam. She handed it to Stella. All that was left of the yellowed typewritten paper was a fragment of the left side corner. It bore the word fragment *prom*, the partial monetary amount £*10*, and the word *Cork*. *A promissory note?* Stella handed the paper back toward the maid, who pushed it back toward Stella.

"It's for you, miss. Ethel told me you were helping the police find the vicar's killer." *She did?* "As you were so kind, miss, to convince Lady Atherly to keep Ethel and Harry on, I knew what to do when I found that."

All Stella had done was speak to the police about what she knew and convince Ethel to tell the police the truth. This was how rumors got started.

"It's Millie, is it?"

"You know my name." The maid sounded amazed.

"You clean my room every day, don't you?"

The maid nodded.

"Millie, I don't think—" Before she could set the record straight, the maid interrupted.

"But look, miss."

The maid leaned in, pointing to the writing at the top edge of the promissory note fragment. Stella examined it again. It read *y 29, 190.* A date. It could have been from January, February, or July of any of the past five years. Or it could've read *May 29, 1905*—the day the vicar died.

"That's not all. I found these too."

The maid produced two more fragments of burnt paper from her pocket, pieces of what had once been a handwritten letter. When they were put together, partial sentences that contained the words *Carcroft, silence, marriage,* and *money* were discernible. One fragment was only an inch or two long. The word *Bullmore* was clear. Stella shivered, and not only because this manor was the draftiest building she'd ever stayed in. She wrapped her arms around her shoulders.

"The vicar probably burnt them that morning, before he died." Stella remembered a fire had been lit that day. But even as she said it, she questioned her reasoning.

Why would the vicar have a promissory note when he had thousands of pounds strapped to his leg? And what about the letter? Whom was it addressed to? The vicar or someone else? How did the Carcroft scandal figure into all of this? Why would he burn the promissory note and the letter, and why at Morrington Hall and not at the vicarage? Was the word *silence* in the letter a threat? What did her and Lyndy's marriage have to do with it?

"But I didn't find them in the library, miss."

Stella blanched at the maid's revelation.

"I found them in Lord Hugh's room."

CHAPTER 21

Lyndy was annoyed. While dressing him, Harry had fussed over a mislaid tiepin Lyndy didn't even like, and Gates had summoned him from the breakfast table before he'd finished his morning racing paper and before Stella had arrived. Not to mention that he'd slept little after last night's dreary dinner and the return of the police. The attack on Mrs. Westwoode had put everyone on edge. Now Lyndy traipsed to the stables in the rain. Despite the fact that he was being escorted by a stable hand and had an umbrella, the bottom half of Lyndy's trouser legs were wet.

"What's this about, Gates? Why did I have to come all this blasted way in the rain?" Lyndy snatched the rough but dry towel the coachman held out for him. He rubbed his trouser leg more vigorously than necessary.

"I am sorry, but there's something you must see, my lord."

"They've found Orson?" Lyndy said, tossing away the towel. "Why didn't you say so?" *If that horse has been injured . . .*

Lyndy wouldn't let this affront go unanswered. Once, a footman had been caught taking three silver forks and a serving spoon. He'd been summarily dismissed without references. At

Eton, if a boy stole from you, he was sent to the headmaster for a good birching. The death of the vicar was monstrous, but Orson's theft felt personal. The perpetrators must be dealt with.

The head coachman shook his head. "No, I'm sorry to say. But the police have enlisted the help of the agisters now, my lord. If Orson is anywhere in the New Forest, they'll find him."

What if he's not in the New Forest? What if he's not in England anymore?

"Make this quick, Gates," Lyndy grumbled, his hopes dashed.

"If you would follow me, my lord."

Gates waited for Lyndy's impatient nod before heading down the aisle and out into the washing yard. A stable hand held the umbrella over Lyndy's head as they followed. Gates stopped next to a stack of straw bales set against the wall. Lyndy rubbed his arms with his hands to ward off the chill. Rain dripped from the eaves of the stables, from the brim of Gates's hat, from the umbrella above Lyndy's head. Lyndy regretted his abrupt departure from the house. Annoyed at Gates's summons, he'd stormed out without his overcoat.

"Why are we standing in the rain, Mr. Gates?" Lyndy did little to hide his annoyance.

"It's imperative I show you, in person. I don't want the police to say I did anything untoward."

"The police? Bloody hell, Gates. What's this about?"

Had Gates found another body? After the death of the vicar and the attack on Mrs. Westwoode, it wasn't as inconceivable as it had once seemed.

Gates leaned over a bale of completely useless straw, its drenched stalks now brown and limp in the rain, and widened a burrow that had already been made on one side. Then he stepped aside. Lyndy approached and peered in. A cache containing gold, an amethyst, and diamonds, wet and glimmering, lay within. Mrs. Westwoode's stolen jewels.

Well, at least the blackguard didn't get away with this.

But who was he? It pained Lyndy to give it too much thought. He pulled the tiara from the bale and picked off a stalk of straw caught between two diamonds.

"Leonard, the second groom, found this during last night's watch," Gates explained. Lyndy had fully approved of the night-watch scheme when Papa had told him about it. One couldn't be too careful. "Someone came through the washing-yard gate late in the night but fled when Leonard confronted them. In his pursuit, Leonard discovered these."

"An intruder? Why is this the first I'm hearing of it?"

"I informed Lord Atherly last night, my lord, but he requested you be shown everything this morning."

Lyndy nodded. Why would Papa leave the comfort of his study, set aside his work, planning out the details of this new fossil expedition, when he could get Lyndy to go out in the rain? "Do you trust the groom? Could he have been the attacker and hid the jewels here?"

"The lad could barely breathe after pursuing the intruder. He's been laid up in bed until not long ago."

"Then you've done right, Gates. I hate to do it, but the police must be informed." Were they ever going to be rid of them? "Give the jewels to Fulton to lock up until the police arrive. Now let's get out of this bloody rain."

Gates nodded. "Charlie, run up to the house and tell them to call the police. Tell them they're needed at the stables . . . again." The groom handed the umbrella to Gates, pulled up the collar of his raincoat, and ran toward the house.

"Why, Gates?" Lyndy said as soon as the two were safely out of the rain.

"Why what, my lord?"

"Why leave the jewels there, hidden in a bale of straw?"

If the same man as attacked Mrs. Westwoode also killed the vicar and stole the horse, why would he need her jewels? Weren't the vicar's thousands of pounds and a champion stud thoroughbred enough? Why not kill her too? A killer, a horse thief, a jewel thief. Could there be more than one perpetrator? Or two or three? Lyndy had suspected Hugh of needing the vicar's money. But he couldn't fathom why Hugh or anyone else would do all these such things. That brought him back to his question. *Why leave the jewels in the straw bale?*

"To recover them later, my lord?" Gates said.

Gates didn't have to elaborate. They both knew what he'd left unsaid. The culprit was someone living or working at Morrington Hall, as the police had been implying all along. As Lyndy had suspected all along.

"I didn't want to say this in front of Charlie," the head coachman said, shaking the rain from the umbrella, "but my head groom, Herbert, packed up his things and left after dinner last night, without a word or the pay coming to him. Not long after that, the intruder tried to get in, and we found the jewels."

"Do you suspect him?"

Gates shrugged. "At this point, aren't we all suspect, my lord?"

Stella went to breakfast, expecting to find Lyndy. She was eager to show him what the housemaid had given her. But when she entered the dining room, the long mahogany table reduced to two leaves and the buffet against the wall lined with silver warming trays filled with poached eggs on toast, sausages, roasted potatoes, and a smoked haddock dish called kedgeree, Lyndy wasn't there. No one was except Daddy, who was hidden behind his newspaper, and Mr. Westwoode, who was setting his fork down as she entered.

Stella enjoyed breakfast. The formidable dining room, with its dark paintings of men on horseback and its closed green damask drapes, was bright and cozy by day, even on a rainy one like today. She could sit where she liked, always across from the tall windows, and she could eat as much as she liked, of what she liked, without the comments or disapproving scowls of the married ladies, who took their breakfast in bed.

Stella filled her plate at the buffet—oh, how the scent of dill and lemon made her mouth water—and sat across from her father.

"If you'll excuse me," Mr. Westwoode said, pushing back from the table.

"Have you seen Lord Lyndhurst?" Stella asked.

Daddy said nothing.

"He was here but was called away," Mr. Westwoode said before leaving.

Stella ate in silence, gazing out the windows at the pond, a riot of splashes and ripples in the rain, while her father rustled his newspaper and occasionally grunted. Just like back home. When she finished, she left without a word. Her father didn't notice. As she crossed paths with Mr. Fulton, coming to check on breakfast, she learned Lyndy had gone to the stables.

If he wasn't daunted by the rain, neither would she be. She rushed toward the stairs to change.

"Are you going to help me or not?"

Stella paused. It was Lord Hugh's voice. But he was nowhere in sight. His tone startled Stella. She'd known Lord Hugh only to be the most congenial of men. But his tone reminded her of her daddy. She decided not to respond.

"What is that supposed to mean?"

It was Lord Hugh again. He hadn't been talking to her. But Stella listened and heard no one else. She looked around. Two footmen, carrying trays from the dining room, crossed the hall, but neither took any notice. Stella spied the cloakroom door ajar. The telephone cord stretched from the wall through the gap in the door.

"I should've known. You're as bad as the vicar."

She took a few steps closer. Why was he hiding in the cloakroom?

"Are you accusing me?"

The menace in Lord Hugh's voice sent a chill down Stella's back. She couldn't believe it was the gentleman she knew speaking. Whom was he talking to? Did someone else think Lord Hugh had killed the vicar?

"I've done everything you asked of me."

Silence.

Stella listened to the sound of her breathing, the hall clock ticking across the room, the tap-tapping of the footmen's shoes as they crossed the polished parquet floor again.

Suddenly, Lord Hugh roared, "You think I don't realize that? You think I'm not reminded of it every day? If you aren't going to help me, there's nothing more to say!"

Slam!

Horrified, Stella froze. The cloakroom door flew open. Lord Hugh, holding the wooden candlestick telephone in his hand, glared at her, an uncharacteristic frown etched on his face. Overcoats, raincoats, capes, Stella's and Daddy's duster coats, among others, lined the back wall behind him.

"Miss Kendrick. What are you doing?"

Caught eavesdropping, she should've cowered in guilt and fear, but his tone sounded too much like Daddy's when he scolded her like a child. She reacted without thinking.

"I'm looking for Lyndy."

"I'm afraid I have no idea where our friend the viscount has gotten off to," Lord Hugh said, trying to brighten his tone. His attempt at a smile was useless. Anger flashed in his eyes. The heat of fear radiated through her chest, urging her to flee. "I left the breakfast table before he did." He set the telephone on the top of a tall carved walnut plant stand just outside the door. "A tedious call from The Duke. He won't be able to make your and Lyndy's wedding, I'm afraid." He said nothing about taking the call in the cloakroom.

Lord Hugh nervously chuckled as Stella continued to stare

at him. He was trying his best to ease the tension between them. "I'm looking forward to it, though, whenever it finally takes place."

"Me too." Stella could think of nothing else to say. She had to get away from him, now. "If you'll excuse me."

Stella gingerly stepped past him, half expecting to feel his hand reach out to restrain her. But it never came. She walked deliberately toward the stairs. Was he standing there watching her? Did he suspect she'd heard everything? What would he do now? Were those footsteps coming toward her? She strained to hear, but her heart pounded louder in her ears than the clock. When she reached the stairs, she grabbed hold of the rounded finial on the oak newel post and peeked over her shoulder. Something, a bee or a fly, hovered over a bouquet of peonies, but otherwise, the hall was empty. Stella closed her eyes and sank to the nearest step.

CHAPTER 22

"I've been looking for you," Lyndy and Stella said simultaneously. They faced each other across the lawn: he, returning from the stables; Stella, dressed for riding, walking toward them. The rain had stopped. A small patch of blue sky shone through a break in the clouds.

"You go first," Stella said.

When Lyndy had spied Stella, a compulsion to confess every distressing thought in his head had superseded his annoyance at not finding her at breakfast. But he knew better. He'd wait at least until he'd sorted his thoughts out.

"Ladies first, as always."

"If only that were the truth," Stella scoffed. Her tone took him by surprise. What had her father done now?

"It's the truth if you're dealing with a gentleman."

"Are you claiming to be a gentleman, Lord Lyndhurst?" she teased.

She was right. He wasn't the gentleman Mother expected him to be. He wasn't the gentleman that Stella deserved.

I never claimed to be.

Lyndy brushed aside all thoughts of murder, theft, and betrayal and closed the gap between them. He looped his arm around Stella's tiny waist and, with the cool feel of her taut riding jacket beneath his hand, pulled her toward him and kissed her. When they parted, Lyndy regretted having to let go. Her closeness seemed to keep the unpleasantness at bay. At least the faint scent of rose from her tooth powder was still on his breath. Stella shyly looked around, pushing a strand of her hair behind her ear.

"Just as I suspected," she said, straightening her top hat. "Not a gentlemanly bone in your body." Then she smiled. How he adored that smile. "Why were you looking for me?"

"I have news." She looked at him expectantly. He motioned for her to follow him. He led her into the garden and invited her to sit on a wrought-iron bench beneath the ancient oak. Its branches, thick and gnarled, hung low toward the ground. When he was a child, it had been Lyndy's favorite climbing tree. "One of the grooms found Mrs. Westwoode's jewels in a straw bale in the washing yard last night."

"That means that whoever attacked Mrs. Westwoode didn't get any farther away with them than the stables. Could they have hidden them there, hoping to retrieve them at another time?"

She'd come to the same conclusion he and Gates had. "Gates suspects Herbert, the head groom. He's absconded."

"But Herbert was found bound and gagged when Orson was stolen. That would mean that one person couldn't have done all of this. Could there be two such horrible people? Or, God forbid, maybe even three?"

"That was my thinking, too, but I was hoping to be wrong."

"You, wrong?" She was teasing him again. He chuckled. Despite the odious topic, she'd put him at ease.

"Why were you looking for me?" he asked.

Her smile faded. "I have news too. You're not going to like

it." She pulled several pieces of charred, yellowed paper from her skirt pocket. She handed them to him. "A maid found these in Lord Hugh's fire grate."

Lyndy read what was legible on the letter and the promissory note. What did the letter mean? That Hugh knew of or suspected the vicar's involvement in the Carcroft scandal? Or that the vicar knew of or suspected Hugh's involvement? Since the maid recovered the letter in Hugh's room, Lyndy suspected the latter. The promissory note, on the other hand, was more encouraging. Hugh wouldn't have borrowed money if he'd stolen thousands of pounds from the vicar.

"There's more." She told him of the conversation she'd overheard Hugh having on the telephone. "He said he was speaking to his father but . . ."

Why wouldn't this go away?

Lyndy yanked down hard on his jacket. The hem was wet. He'd confronted Hugh, and Hugh had denied any involvement with the vicar's death. Why couldn't Lyndy believe him, his closest friend? What was Hugh hiding?

"Perhaps he was speaking to his father," Stella said hopefully. "Hugh might not be involved in any of this."

Lyndy could've kissed her again for her optimism, for her attempt to ease his distress, but his heart wasn't in it. He didn't believe for a moment she was right.

Mrs. Westwoode settled into the captain's chair Inspector Brown indicated. Mrs. Westwoode fiddled with the folds of her dark blue linen skirt before smoothing it across her lap. She fussed with her gloves, tugging at several fingers. She hadn't once looked Brown in the eye. He'd stood across from countless people in that chair. Could this be the interview that helped him catch the vicar's killer? Brown doubted it.

"I simply don't understand why you needed to speak to me again."

Brown apologized and patiently explained the police's need to interview people on multiple occasions, especially when there was a development that necessitated it.

"Well, I do hope it doesn't take long. Now that the rain has stopped, I'm to go with my daughter and some others in a motorcar."

The excitement and awe in her voice were undeniable. The lady was not nearly as bothered by last night's events as she'd appeared to be when he'd been called from the warmth of his bed to Morrington Hall late last night.

If only a good night's sleep could brush all my cares away.

Constable Waterman, his notebook open and ready, raised an eyebrow. He'd noticed the difference too.

"What is it you want from me?" She shifted in her chair.

Knowing the difference between impatience and nerves, maybe Brown would learn something valuable, after all. This woman was nervous. *But why?*

Brown retrieved the colorful cardboard Cadbury's chocolate box from the end table. The box had been sitting around the station since somebody's birthday last week. He'd been in a hurry when the call came in, and the box was empty, so he'd grabbed it. He lifted the lid.

"Do you recognize any of these, Mrs. Westwoode?" Sparkling jewels and gold, none the worse for their time spent in the straw, filled the chocolate box.

"You found them!" Mrs. Westwoode grasped at it. Brown took that as a yes. "Where were they? Are they all there? Have any been damaged?" Brown secured the lid and set the box out of the lady's reach. "I want my jewels back, Inspector."

"We need to keep them a little longer, Mrs. Westwoode. You understand." The scowl on her face said she didn't understand, but Brown couldn't care less. "As we found them alongside the fire iron that killed Reverend Bullmore."

That was a stroke of luck. When they'd inspected the bale of straw where the jewels were hidden, they'd also found the missing fire iron shoved deeper inside. It had been wiped clean, but Brown and, more importantly, the coroner had no doubt it was the weapon used to kill the vicar.

"Then I was right! My attacker was one and the same as the vicar's killer. Have you found the fiend?"

"We have our suspicions, but we haven't made any arrests yet."

"Why not? My maid said a stable hand disappeared last night. Perhaps it was him?" Yet again the rumor mill had preceded Brown, making his job more difficult.

"Yes, Herbert Kitcher, the head groom, is being sought for questioning. But—"

"But nothing, Inspector. I say you should arrest him."

"The one chink in the chain, if you'll beg my pardon, ma'am, is your description of your attacker. It doesn't match that of the groom."

Mrs. Westwoode had opened her mouth to object, to interrupt, to demand but snapped it shut at Brown's pronouncement. Mrs. Westwoode shifted in her chair again. She fiddled with the lace on her blouse. She cast a quick glance at Brown and then at the constable.

"Could you describe your attacker to me again, Mrs. Westwoode?" Brown asked.

"I am not obliged to relive my ordeal again and again for you or anyone," she said, sticking her chin out defiantly. Now Brown knew why she'd been nervous when she arrived. She was hiding something. Brown pinched the bridge of his nose.

Why wasn't he surprised?

"Forgive us, Mrs. Westwoode. We didn't consider your constitution might be too fragile to . . . ," Constable Waterman said.

"Fragile? Do you take me as the fragile type, young man?" Mrs. Westwoode said, turning an indignant stare at the constable.

Good ole Waterman. He was learning.

Mrs. Westwoode went on. "You have no idea—"

"Your attacker, Mrs. Westwoode?" Brown insisted.

"The beast had curly black hair, stood not much taller than me, and had rough hands," Mrs. Westwoode proclaimed. "And he smelled of the stables."

"Thank you. That description fits the groom perfectly."

Mrs. Westwoode stood up, her back ramrod straight. She smoothed her skirt again, as if merely the presence of the policemen had soiled it, and took a few steps toward the door.

"Before you leave, I'd like my constable to read you the description you gave to us last night."

The woman blanched, and Brown knew he'd been right. She was hiding something.

"The monster had fair hair, was at least a head taller, and had sun-spotted skin," the constable read, "and he smelled of the stables."

Last night Mrs. Westwoode had described Mr. Gates, the head coachman. Today she'd described the missing groom, Herbert, but only after she'd learned of his disappearance. What was she playing at?

"So, if we can agree the fellow smelled of the stables, we must consider that he could be anyone who worked in the stables, had recently visited the stables, had been out riding for an extended period, or had handled the horses for some other reason," Brown said.

"Why should I care? You're the policeman," the matron said. "That's for you to find out."

"Did your attacker have fair or dark hair, Mrs. Westwoode?" She said nothing.

"Was your attacker tall or similar to you in height?"

"How should I know?" she said, frustrated.

"What do you mean, you don't know? Mrs. Westwoode? What do you mean, you don't know?"

She plunked back down on the edge of the chair. "You can't

imagine what it was like, having a man steal your jewels and threaten your life like that. It was so sudden and frightful."

"You lied?" Brown said.

Mrs. Westwoode squinted at him. He couldn't read her expression, but he could guess she was weighing her options. Would she deny it and lie again? Would she admit it and explain why?

"I didn't lie. I simply couldn't remember. I was frightened. I'd been violently attacked. You were hounding me to say something, anything. So, I did."

Brown sighed. He was losing his patience. Then it came to him what she was hiding. If he was right, she had every reason to be nervous—lying to the police, obstructing the course of an investigation, not to mention wasting his time. Didn't she know a killer was on the loose? If he had his way, which was unlikely given she was a guest of Lord Atherly's, she'd be accompanying him in the police wagon instead of taking a joyride in a newfangled car.

"Did you even see your attacker, Mrs. Westwoode?" Brown asked through gritted teeth, already knowing the answer.

"How could I? He was behind me the whole time."

"You may go now, Mrs. Westwoode."

"I knew this would all be a waste of time," the lady said, brushing imaginary lint from her sleeve.

It took all Brown's years of training and restraint not to kick the woman's wide backside as she left.

CHAPTER 23

"I've never been in a motorcar before," Miss Westwoode said, lumbering into the backseat of Daddy's Daimler. She wore her heaviest overcoat and a sturdy short-brimmed straw hat with a wide green satin bow. Wearing borrowed goggles, she stepped on the hem of her skirt and landed in her mother's lap. Mrs. Westwoode sat buried in Daddy's driving coat.

"Be careful, darling!" Mrs. Westwoode said as she and her daughter untangled themselves from the driving veil Stella had lent the matron. The trip had been conceived after the rain had stopped, but with the exception of Stella, none of the other women owned appropriate driving clothes.

"Neither have I," Lady Alice said, nestled, smiling, next to Stella in the front seat, looking much like Miss Westwoode's twin in borrowed goggles, straw hat, and overcoat.

Their enthusiasm made Stella smile. She took driving the car for granted. Daddy had bought the first one three years ago, attempting to be the first man in Kentucky to own an automobile. After Daddy had fired four chauffeurs, Stella was taught to drive and had been doing it ever since.

"How kind of your father to loan us the motorcar," Mrs. Westwoode said.

Kind. That was not the word Stella would've used. The smile faded from her lips.

Upon returning to Morrington Hall with Lyndy, Daddy had instructed her to drive Mrs. Westwoode, her daughter, and Lady Alice into Rosehurst in the Daimler. No discussion, no explanation. She'd bristled at the command. But she'd acquiesced because she enjoyed driving, and it would give her a chance to see more of the New Forest. Driving Ethel to Lyndhurst in the dark didn't count.

"It's such a lovely day," Miss Westwoode said.

Stella looked at the gray sky, the muddy drive. *This, a nice day? A nice day in June is dry and warm, with a sky the color of sapphires, the pastures of bluegrass the color of emeralds, and the air smelling of gardenias.* But at least it had stopped raining. For now.

"Ready?"

The ladies giggled and nodded.

Stella, taking advantage of Daddy's absence, pushed the gas pedal hard and, to the sound of the women's delighted squeals, raced down the drive, a spray of wet pebbles flying up behind the wheels. A group of New Forest ponies grazing farther down the lawn bolted at the engine's roar. Stella let up on the gas, sorry to have frightened the animals. When she reached the end of the drive, she said, "Which way, Lady Alice?"

"Rosehurst is that way." Lady Alice pointed right. Stella turned left.

"You're going the wrong way," Mrs. Westwoode said, looking down the lane behind her.

"I thought we could tour a bit around the Forest first," Stella said.

"That's an excellent idea," Lady Alice said. "Turn here."

For over an hour they drove, passing through villages, clusters of whitewashed cottages with thick thatched roofs; rolling across miles of wide-open heathland, a patchwork of green lawn, flowering yellow gorse, sprawling carpets of heath, feathery stands of fern, and large, shallow puddles, dotted with grazing cows, horses, and donkeys; and winding through tunnels of ancient woodlands, the towering trees interlocking their upper branches, shielding them from the cloudy sky. Stella inhaled the salty air when they reached the windswept sandy hillocks of a coastal road, with its unimpeded view of the Solent and the towering white cliffs of the nearby Isle of Wight, before returning inland again. They drove across such places as Beaulieu Heath, Setley Plain, Widden Bottom, Lady Cross Walk, and Bagshot Moor. They encountered the villages of Boldre, Battramsley Cross, Norleywood, and Keyhaven, agreeing to circumvent the bustling port of Lymington, a destination better saved for another day.

Stella delighted in every encounter with this exotic landscape, hoping to explore it more. Preferably on horseback. But would it ever feel like home?

After seeing a sign for a village called Burley, Mrs. Westwoode said, "It has been a pleasant tour, Miss Kendrick, but time to go to Rosehurst now, I think." Mrs. Westwoode was right. Burley would have to wait.

"Which way, Lady Alice?" Stella said.

"A few miles down that lane."

Stella steered down the narrow lane, barely wide enough for the Daimler. She drove at a steady clip, splashing through shallow puddles, until the lane curved around a squat gray building hidden partially by the largest yew tree she'd ever seen. She didn't know yews could become trees.

"Is that . . . ?" Stella asked, slowing down as she rounded the curve and letting the car glide to a halt.

"It is," Lady Alice said cheerfully. "Our parish church, St. Peter's. That is where you and my brother will marry."

Stella had never seen anything like it. The ancient gray stone walls, tilting slightly askew from the redbrick steeple, a glaring modern addition, and topped with a red slate roof with several tiles missing, looked as if they had risen from the earth, not been crafted and molded by a man's hand.

"How old is it?"

"Most of it dates to about 1086. The Normans used part of a Saxon wall to build the present nave."

Stella tore her gaze from the church to stare at Lady Alice. Had she said 1086? And so casually? If this church were in the States, it would be a national treasure. Here it was a parish church hidden down a country lane. There was nothing, nothing in her experience to compare it to.

"The yew itself is about a thousand years old," Lady Alice added.

Stella had learned about redwood trees in California that were saplings when Columbus sailed from Spain, but she'd never seen one. This quiet giant could be a witness at her wedding? She didn't know what to say.

"The vicarage is down the lane a bit," Lady Alice said. That explained why Stella hadn't seen the church when she and Lyndy visited the vicarage. It was hidden by the trees and the curve in the lane. "I believe the new vicar is expected soon." Lady Alice hesitated. "I don't suppose they'll ever discover who killed Reverend Bullmore."

"Of course they will," Stella said.

"Mummy says we shouldn't discuss the vicar's death," Miss Westwoode said. "It's upsetting."

"So, it is, darling," Mrs. Westwoode said. "Shall we go, Miss Kendrick?"

Stella pulled the hand lever, releasing the side brakes, and put her foot on the gas. As she drove away, the ancient church and yew receded from view. A few days ago, the sight of the church would've repelled her, its squat, solid walls symbols of her daddy and his unbending demands. Now the yew, a shrub that had overcome all odds to grow tall and thrive for a thousand years, beckoned her to return, to put down roots of her own. Could she, with the pall of the vicar's murder casting a shadow across the marriage? Or was it the vicar's death that hinted at the need for a new beginning? Could she and Lyndy make it work, or could she defy her father and still start a new life?

Stella stared ahead as she approached the village, leaving the church and yew behind. Would she return? She didn't know.

"This way?" Stella asked.

Lady Alice nodded.

"Okay, if you say so."

Stella plunged the car into the water flowing across the road on the edge of the village of Rosehurst.

Splash!

"What are you doing?" Mrs. Westwoode said, peering into the water beneath the tires. "The road is flooded."

Lady Alice laughed. "No, Mrs. Westwoode. This is the water-splash. It's always like this. The road was built to let the stream flow across. The ponies and other livestock use it as a watering place. It's perfectly safe."

"Then what do you suppose happened there?" Mrs. Westwoode said, pointing down the road.

A string of two-story redbrick buildings, some with slate roofs, some with red clay tiled roofs, some with thatch, each with a chimney and a large storefront window, lined the curving road on both sides. A small crowd had gathered by the building closest to the far side of the watersplash. The storefront read WHITEHOUSE & SON, BUTCHERS. A man wiping his hands on his stained white apron leaned in the doorway. Stella drove clear of the water, pulled the car over, and parked.

"What are you doing?" Mrs. Westwoode said. "The stationer is at the other end of the high street."

Without answering, Stella pulled off her driving veil, climbed out of the car, and approached the crowd. A man in a tan cap, tall boots, and a green vest had laid his coat aside and was rolling up his shirtsleeves. He kneeled beside the gray New Forest pony lying on her side at the edge of the road.

"What happened?" Stella whispered to the woman next to her.

The woman, clutching a bolt of light gray wool to her chest, shrugged. "Just up and laid down in the middle of the street."

The man gently ran his hand from the pony's shoulder to its flank, to its hip, and then down its left leg. The pony wiggled its lips and flared its nostrils when the man's hand touched its fetlock. Not a good sign. The pony groaned as the man tried to move its leg. Stella flinched and took a step forward. She had to help her, poor thing.

Lady Alice, having joined the crowd, put her hand on Stella's shoulder as Stella stepped forward. Stella looked over her shoulder. Mrs. Westwoode and her daughter had stayed in the car. "Let the agister do his job," Lady Alice said.

Agister? Lyndy had mentioned the word in passing. Agisters were forest rangers, who might help the police find Orson.

"What happened to her?" Stella asked the agister after he managed to get the pony on her feet. He frowned as he searched the faces in the crowd until his eyes stopped on Stella in her duster coat.

"That your motorcar?" The agister pointed to the Daimler. Several heads turned to look at Daddy's automobile. Mrs. Westwoode, in the backseat, frowned from the sudden attention. "A pony was killed by one last week."

Stella stared at the car in horror. It had never struck her as something dangerous before. She would drive the Daimler into the pond before ever hurting a horse.

"Grockle," he muttered, shaking his head.

Stella cringed. She didn't like the sound of that.

"Have you made any progress in finding the stolen race-horse, Mr. Gerald?" Lady Alice said, drawing the agister's attention away.

"Begging your pardon, miss," he said, yanking the cap from his head. "I didn't see you there. I meant no disrespect."

"Well, Mr. Gerald, have you?"

"No, miss, not yet."

"Herbert," Stella said.

Beyond the humbled agister, a man with curly black hair crossed the street. It was the head groom from Morrington Hall.

"If he's involved, I'm sure Mr. Gerald will do all he can to help find him," Lady Alice said, misunderstanding Stella's meaning. "Won't you, Mr. Gerald?"

"No, I mean, there's Herbert." Stella pointed toward the groom.

Heads turned. Herbert, now the focus of attention, dashed into a squat whitewashed, thatched building set apart from the others. A few wrought-iron tables and chairs had been set here and there in front of it. A wooden sign with a massive oak tree in summer green foliage hung above the door. Stella pushed past the woman with the bolt of cloth and headed across the street.

"Miss Kendrick?" Lady Alice called after her. After catching up with her, Lady Alice put a hand on Stella's arm. "Where are you going?"

"To confront Herbert."

"But you can't go in there."

"Why not?"

"Why not?" Lady Alice's expression struck a close resemblance to her mother's haughty glare, and there was more to her tone than simply astonishment. "Because, Miss Kendrick, that's the pub."

"So?"

This time, Stella didn't let Lady Alice's hand restrain her. That man could be the key to the vicar's death. Stella shook off Lady Alice's hand and headed toward the Knightwood Oak.

Tom Heppenstall slid the tuppence across the smooth, polished surface of the bar with one hand and into the other. He tossed the coin into the till and slid the drawer shut. A rumble, like the purr of a giant mechanical cat, passed by outside. The boy, who was supposed to be washing the windows, had his face pressed against the glass.

"Oi, watch the nose prints!" What was so interesting that the lad would risk cleaning the window a second time?

The boy, his nose still pressed against the glass, motioned the owner of the Knightwood Oak pub toward the window with a fluttering wave of his hand. With an exasperated sigh, Tom strolled from behind the bar, skirted the tables, one of them cluttered with two dirty glasses and a plate of sausage grease and tomato seeds, and peered out the window. Parked across and down the street a bit was a motorcar, shiny and magnificent. A group of onlookers had gathered, not around the motorcar, but around a prostrate pony near the butchers' shop. Tom recognized Neil Gerald, the local agister, and didn't give the pony another thought; it was in good hands. But that motorcar. For once, the boy was right. That was something worth looking at.

"Can we go out and get a closer look?" the boy asked.

Tom hesitated, and that wasn't like him. He had a dozen customers, tables to clear, glasses to wash, yet . . .

"Who do you think it belongs to?" the boy said.

"The Americans."

Tom and the boy simultaneously turned their heads at the sound of the gruff voice behind them. Old Joe had left his perch at the bar, his newspaper left open to the sporting page, and was looking over Tom's shoulder, out the window.

"'Tis a beauty," Old Joe said. Tom and the boy nodded in

full agreement. "Saw a picture in the paper of His Majesty in one just like it. Here now, isn't that Lady Alice?"

Tom squinted. He had resisted the need for spectacles; he could see the labels on the taps, the keys on the till. What use did he have for spectacles?

"It's hard to tell, all bundled up like that," the boy said, "but I think so. Who's that with her?"

Tom squinted harder. He could make out two ladies among the onlookers, each wearing a long overcoat of some kind and a fancy wide-brimmed hat. Lady Alice must be the blonde.

"It must be the American," Old Joe pronounced. "Miss Kendrick."

Tom squinted even harder. He'd heard more than he'd asked for about the Kentucky horse breeder and his lovely daughter. Before Tom had started working at the Knightwood Oak, he would never have believed that men in pubs gossiped. Silently drowned themselves in a bitter, yes. Went on about who had heard what and when, like a gaggle of geese, never. One rumor had Lord Lyndhurst marrying the American heiress. Another insinuated Miss Kendrick was the one who had found the dead vicar's body. Yet another declared that the horse breeder, Mr. Kendrick, had won two hundred thousand pounds at the Derby and was trying to convince Lord Atherly to sell Morrington Hall. Tom didn't believe a word of any of it.

"I'm going out to get a closer look," the boy declared. Before Tom could stop him, the boy pushed a chair out of his way and, ducking his shoulder, avoided Tom snagging his vest.

Where did the lad think he was going? He had work to do.

"Oi!" Tom yelled at the boy as the door flew open and a man darted in. The boy, stumbling back to avoid colliding with the new arrival, smacked into the uncleared table, sending a glass shattering to the floor.

"Idiot boy," Tom muttered. "Oi, watch yourself. The glass."

Tom pointed to the jagged fragments on the floor as the newcomer crunched one under his boot. It was Herbert Kitcher, the groom from Morrington Hall. Tom hadn't expected to see him so soon, what with the way he was drinking last night. With only a quick glimpse at the floor, Herbert shoved the boy into a nearby chair and ran toward the back door.

For one long moment, a hush pervaded the pub as everyone silently stared at one another. Only after closing, when Tom turned the key in the lock at night, did it ever sound like this. And then pandemonium! Glasses slammed down, chairs scraped across the floor, the door banged closed, and voices rose, shouting over each other, complaining, questioning, demanding. What had just happened?

"Look!" Old Joe shouted above the din. He was staring out the window. Every able-bodied man in the pub rushed to find a place at a window. The boy, brooding over his rough treatment, stubbornly stayed where he was.

Tom wasn't sure what he'd expected to see—a runaway wagon on three wheels careening into the watersplash, a pack of stampeding ponies crashing into the greengrocer's, a flock of pigeons landing on the agister's head? But this? Never.

The American, Miss Kendrick, had crossed the street and was heading for his door. Two other ladies, one of them Lady Alice, skittered after her, while another clambered from the motorcar, shouting something. Men in the Knightwood Oak bolted away from the windows like skittish colts.

"Excuse me. Hello?" a sweet high voice called out.

Tom turned to see the young American heiress, her hat three times wider than the opening in the doorway, as she peered through, her blue eyes curious and wide. He'd heard rumors about how Americans were different. He'd dismissed the wild tales the cowhands and the delivery boys swapped while in their cups. But there she was, an heiress to a great fortune, standing on his doorstep, peeking in. Could all the rumors be true?

Tom, determined to keep his composure, made for the front door. A straggler, in his frantic need to disappear out the back, knocked into his shoulder.

"Oi!" Tom was annoyed. The customer had impeded his advance. Tom couldn't have the boy reaching the door first; he'd embarrass them all. "Watch where you're going."

It was the grockle. The one he'd told Inspector Brown about. When had he arrived? Tom hadn't noticed him before.

"Pardon," the bloke mumbled as he pushed past.

Old Joe reached the door first.

"Can we help you, miss?" Old Joe said, opening the door wider.

"Did you see Lord Atherly's groom, Herbert, come in here?" The lady glanced about, seeing what she could from the threshold.

The boy, his mouth hanging open, his eyes glazed and unblinking, pointed toward the back entrance. Tom hadn't needed to worry about him. The boy was frozen to his seat.

"Mr. Westwoode? Is that you?" Miss Kendrick said.

Mr. Westwoode? Tom didn't know anyone by that name. He followed the lady's gaze to the retreating figure of the bloke who had nearly knocked him off his feet. *The grockle.* Tom folded his arms across his chest as the bloke disappeared out the back door. Tom finally had a name for the stranger's face. Inspector Brown would soon know it too.

CHAPTER 24

Whack!

Stella struck the yellow ball with the mallet, sending it ricocheting off Miss Westwoode's blue ball and straight through the hoop.

"Brilliant shot, Miss Kendrick." Lyndy admired Stella's concentration and determination, not to mention the fine curve of her backside, as Stella took her stance behind her ball and smacked it again toward the next hoop. Croquet had never been so enjoyable.

And here is Mrs. Westwoode, to ruin everything.

"The sun is lovely, don't you agree, Lord Lyndhurst?" the matron said, strolling over to his side. "After such a dreary start to the day too."

Yes, the rain had stopped, and the sky had cleared. What did this woman want him to say? There were fewer things in life that Lyndy hated more than conversations about the weather.

"My daughter adores croquet. She's quite skilled at it, though I see Miss Kendrick has played a time or two herself." Stella expertly smacked her ball again, this time hitting Alice's ball, earning yet another stroke. "If I may be so bold, Lord

Lyndhurst," Mrs. Westwoode said, facing him. Lyndy kept his eyes on the croquet players. "You need to keep an eye on that future bride of yours."

"How so?"

"Hasn't anyone told you of our trip to Rosehurst?"

Lyndy, unable to find Hugh after Stella gave him the burnt letter and promissory note, had taken Beau out for a ride. He'd changed for tea, only to find the ladies had returned from their excursion and were on the lawn, playing croquet. He hadn't spoken to Stella yet. Hugh, standing beside his red ball, took a few playful practice swings with his mallet. Lyndy's chest tightened. Lyndy hadn't spoken to Hugh yet either.

Taking his silence as an answer, Mrs. Westwoode continued. "Miss Kendrick nearly stepped foot into the public house in Rosehurst today."

Almost went into the pub, did she? He suppressed a chuckle as Stella took another smack at her ball, sending it through the next hoop. Well, Mother would certainly not approve. For that alone, he wished she had gone in, despite the scandal that it would've caused. He had hoped for different, after all, hadn't he?

"And would have, if it hadn't been for my darling Elizabeth."

Lyndy doubted that. Miss Westwoode couldn't prevent an ant from crossing over her foot, let alone prevent Stella from crossing the threshold of the Knightwood Oak.

"Aren't you shocked?" Mrs. Westwoode pressed.

"Why is what I would like to know. Does Miss Kendrick have a penchant for cider? Or was it the colorful locals she aimed to gawk at?"

"She wanted to follow someone inside." That wasn't the answer Lyndy was expecting.

"Who?" he said, more churlish than he planned. Why wouldn't this woman just tell him what had happened?

Mrs. Westwoode hesitated, glancing first at the croquet players. Then she leaned in and whispered, "She said she saw the scoundrel accused of killing the vicar."

Mrs. Westwoode leaned back, satisfied no doubt by the look on Lyndy's face. He was stunned. Lyndy didn't know there was such a man. There were suspicions, yes, but no one had been openly accused. He glanced at Hugh, standing beside Miss Westwoode, laughing, at his own joke presumably, as they waited their turn. Could Stella have told Mrs. Westwoode, of all people, his concerns about Hugh?

"Who would that be?" Lyndy asked, fidgeting with his tie. Harry had tied the damn thing too tight.

"Herbert, the groom. Who else?" Mrs. Westwoode declared indignantly.

Lyndy relaxed his shoulders and sought Stella's gaze. She caught his eye and waved happily at him. She was enjoying herself. He smiled back.

"Who else would it be?" Mrs. Westwoode added.

Who else indeed? Lyndy glanced at Hugh again.

"And was it? Herbert?" he asked. Not very bright of the groom, showing his face in Rosehurst, and in the pub, of all places. Did he think the police wouldn't hear about it?

"We'll never know. As I said, Elizabeth prevented Miss Kendrick from following him inside. But she was most distressed when she returned to the motorcar. The scoundrel had escaped out the back."

"Then perhaps it wasn't such a prudent action on your daughter's part, after all."

"What? How could you say that?"

"If Miss Kendrick could've prevented Herbert from escaping, we might have had an end to this business."

Lyndy enjoyed the moment, as the affront crossed the lady's face, before calling to his friend. He had to do this now, before

Hugh's name, and not Herbert's, was on Mrs. Westwoode's lips.

"Hugh, a word?"

Hugh whispered something in the ear of Miss Westwoode, who smiled, and then, carrying his mallet, he jogged over to Lyndy. Stella had missed the last hoop. It was Miss Westwoode's turn again.

"What is it?" Hugh said, watching the game. Miss Westwoode hit her ball through the hoop. "Jolly good, Miss Westwoode."

"Shall we go somewhere more private?" Lyndy said.

That got Hugh's attention. Lyndy led him toward the hedge maze. Built by the fifth Earl of Atherly, using a thousand yews, the quarter-acre square maze had been a favorite hiding place for Lyndy and Alice when Nanny was in a temper. Lyndy hadn't completed the maze in years.

"What is this about?" Hugh asked when Lyndy stepped inside the hedges.

"Do you know anything about this?" Lyndy held out the burnt scrap with the vicar's name on it.

Hugh hesitated. "Why would I?"

"You're not a good liar, old chap," Lyndy said. "It was found in your room."

Hugh frowned. "How did you get it?" he asked, his voice tense.

Lyndy glanced down at the mallet in Hugh's hand. "A maid gave it to Miss Kendrick, and she gave it to me."

"Miss Kendrick knows about this?"

Lyndy nodded.

"In here." Hugh swung the mallet to his shoulder and motioned for Lyndy to follow him farther into the maze.

Hugh chose the first right turn and then the next left turn and then another left. Obviously, Hugh didn't know where he was going. When they reached the dead end, where the sound of the croquet players was muffled by the tall yew hedges, Hugh stopped. He swung around and raised the mallet. The stripe of red paint around the base of the handle, only a few inches from Lyndy's face, looked too much like a smear of blood.

"Bloody hell!" Hugh shouted. Hugh flung the mallet to the ground at their feet. Lyndy flinched. "Why can't I leave this behind me?" Hugh muttered a few curses under his breath as he ran his fingers through his hair. Hugh bent down and retrieved the mallet. "Will you trust me that it had nothing to do with the vicar's death?"

"If you say it doesn't," Lyndy said.

"It doesn't."

A cheer rose from beyond the maze. Both men turned toward the ruckus but could see nothing. The hedge was too tall.

"Who won? Your fiancée or mine? I wonder," Hugh said.

Lyndy was confident Stella had won, but at that moment he couldn't care less.

"Do you have debts?"

"Why do you say that?" Hugh's voice had an edge to it again.

"Steady on. I supposed you might, having to live on your reduced allowance while entertaining the Westwoodes."

Lyndy resisted mentioning the promissory note found in Hugh's fire grate. They both kept Clyde Harris's card handy. Every well-bred punter did. When they were younger, nothing could keep the two of them from the Turf, and if they placed a bet or two, so much more the fun. At any given house party, put the two of them at the same table for whist, and no one had a chance. But Hugh had abandoned cards, as well as the Turf, not even attending the Rosehurst Races, since he'd returned from the war. No, that wasn't quite right. Not since the war, but since the incident at Carcroft House. Lyndy had heard the rumors, the accusations, about someone caught cheating at cards while His Majesty King Edward was at the table. Had Hugh been there, as some rumors suggested? Had he been the one cheating?

And why the sudden change? Why attend this year's Derby? Two days after the death of the vicar. Can it be a coincidence? Lyndy wanted to think so. But he doubted it.

"Oh, that." Hugh shrugged. "I can handle it."

"Glad to hear it." Lyndy didn't believe him. He knew too much, about Hugh's argument with the vicar, his argument with his father on the telephone, the note from the moneylender. Hugh was in trouble, but how?

"Shall we?" Hugh raised the mallet to indicate the path leading back to the entrance of the maze. "Elizabeth already accuses me of neglect."

"Not having second thoughts, are you?" Lyndy said, leading the way back.

"Too late for that, I'm afraid. Elizabeth's a good enough sort, mind you, but the mother I could do without. I imagine you can relate."

Lyndy nodded. His soon-to-be father-in-law was a scoundrel, but unlike Mrs. Westwoode, he'd be returning to America after the wedding.

"Yes, but I won't have to put up with him much longer."

Hugh nodded. "There's a blessing. Though you still have to put up with the daughter."

"Yes, but at least she's a damn sight more attractive than the alternatives."

Hugh laughed at Lyndy's jest. "She is that. Now, if she'd only keep her bloody mouth shut."

Lyndy opened his mouth to agree and then stopped. Lyndy had said something in jest; Hugh was in earnest. *How dare Hugh?* Lyndy's defense of Stella, his explanation about how he admired her bluntness and her curiosity, died on his tongue. Instead, he said, a bit spitefully, "So, how is the old duke?"

Hugh stopped as they took a corner. He shot Lyndy an angry glance.

"You were heard, Hugh. Morrington is a big place, but there are many, many ears about."

"What did you hear?" Hugh demanded.

"That you accused your father of being 'as bad as the vicar' when he refused you something. That you slammed the telephone down on your own father's ear."

"That was between The Duke and me." Hugh's indignation put an end to the discussion.

"Very well."

Why had Lyndy said that? Nothing was at all well. He'd known Hugh for years; they'd met their first year at Eton. Yet Hugh was hiding a secret, one he wouldn't trust Lyndy with. Until Lyndy knew what Hugh was hiding, nothing would be well between them. Hugh misread regret for doubt on Lyndy's face.

"I promise you, Lyndy. I had absolutely nothing to do with the vicar's death." Hugh smiled and swung the mallet onto his shoulder. "Now, shall we rejoin the game?"

CHAPTER 25

"Who called it in?" Inspector Brown said, pulling his Wellingtons on. The morning's rain had left this patch of ground soft and muddy.

"The local agister, Neil Gerald," Constable Waterman said. The inspector nodded. He'd met Mr. Gerald before. He was as dedicated an agister as they came. "He'd noticed a set of tracks down that lane that doesn't match any horseshoe he's ever seen before. Thought it might be worth checking."

Brown stepped down from the wagon into a puddle in the gravel path. He checked the sky. The clouds were gray but were thinning. No rain again soon, then.

"Lead the way, Constable."

Constable Waterman headed down a narrow path, more a footpath than a lane, fenced off on both sides and thick with brambles. Footprints and horseshoe tracks appeared in the low, muddy spots. A hundred yards in, a wide puddle blocked the path. Constable Waterman and Brown strode single file across an old board someone had thrown over it. After a quarter of a mile or so, the brambles thinned, and tall oaks, planted there once long ago, lined the path. The constable stopped at the first gate in the fence. On the other side was an old brick barn. The roof needed retiling.

"Is the owner of this paddock at home?" Brown asked.

The constable shook his head. "No. I called in at the cottage before you arrived." Constable Waterman pointed back the way they had come. A well-maintained brick cottage with a brick barn and a vegetable patch stood not far from the lane. "But there was no answer. He is a registered commoner, but Mr. Gerald has no record of taking any of his stock off the Forest for any reason."

A confident neigh, with a bugle-like ring, sounded from the old barn on the other side of the gate.

"No legitimate reason he should have a pony or horse in the paddock, then?"

"Not that Mr. Gerald could think of."

"Let's have a look, shall we?"

The inspector swung open the iron gate and headed for the barn. A second neigh warned him to use caution as he rounded the dilapidated building. With his ears pricked forward, his tail lifted, the missing racehorse boldly looked Brown in the eye. He was a magnificent creature, his slick black coat shiny and clean. Despite his misadventure, Orson looked none the worse for wear as he chomped the hay piled up at his feet, never taking his eyes off Brown. He was tethered to a post, thank God. But would the tether hold if the horse had a mind to bolt? Brown didn't want to find out.

"What is the name of the commoner, Constable?"

Constable Waterman pulled out his notebook and flipped it open. "The property belongs to a Frank Dobbs."

A smile threaded its way across the inspector's face. "It does, does it?"

"Sir? Do you know Mr. Dobbs?"

"No, never met the fellow."

"Then you've lost me, sir."

"But I have met his brother-in-law, a certain groom at Mor-rington Hall."

As if on cue, a few rays of sun broke through the gloom. Brown couldn't have been happier.

"Tea is served, my lady," the butler announced.

"How ever did she learn to play like that?" Lord Hugh said, handing his mallet to the footman.

"All those garden parties in Newport, I expect," Daddy said, lumbering out of his white wrought-iron lawn chair.

Stella said nothing as the two talked about her as if she wasn't there. She didn't remind Daddy that she'd learned to play by spending hours alone on the lawn of their Kentucky home, striking each ball herself. When she had played at the sole garden party she attended in Newport, she had unequivocally defeated the other players and had been shunned by the other girls for the rest of the afternoon. She had retreated to the stables after that and hadn't played croquet since. Until today.

"I hope there's enough of those tiny sandwiches, Lady Atherly," Daddy continued. "I do love those."

Lady Atherly rose from her chair as if she had a wooden board sewn into her corset. "I suspect so, Mr. Kendrick. Mrs. Cole is not unaware of your . . . appetite."

"Has anyone seen Augustus lately?" Mrs. Westwoode asked for the third time since they'd returned from their drive. She glanced around, as if her husband might step from behind a hedge at any moment. Stella wasn't about to tell Mrs. Westwoode he'd been in the pub.

Had it been him? Had he heard her call his name? Was that where he spent all his time? Except at those times when Mrs. Westwoode asked after him, Stella rarely gave Mr. Westwoode's whereabouts a second thought. Until now. But why? What did she suspect him of: killing the vicar, stealing Orson, attacking his own wife? Simply because she'd seen him dashing out the back door of a pub? Or because, despite the police's best efforts, none of these crimes had been resolved? He'd always given Stella a sympathetic smile. Could it have been a façade?

"Where's Lyndy?" Lady Atherly said. "He knows I expect him at tea."

"I spied him heading toward the house earlier," Mrs. Westwoode said, "but I haven't seen him since."

"He had some business to take care of," Stella said. Lyndy had been somber when he and Lord Hugh rejoined the others. He had pulled her aside as Lady Alice made a particularly good shot, knocking Miss Westwoode's ball yards away from the wicket, and had whispered something about unfinished business. It concerned Lord Hugh. "He said he wouldn't be back until late."

"So, you're his confidante now," Lord Hugh said. It wasn't a question. Hugh was smiling, but he sounded bitter. He'd been a bit cool to her since their encounter outside the cloakroom. But what did he mean? What had Lyndy told him?

"Why shouldn't she be?" Lady Alice said. "They are to be married soon."

"Not soon enough," Daddy grumbled. "The girl's going to change her mind if they put it off for too long."

"As if you've ever given me a choice," Stella muttered. Unlike a few days ago, the truth of it left her more thoughtful than bitter. She was changing her mind, but not in the way her father proposed.

"But what about the horse, Mr. Kendrick? Wasn't the marriage contingent on its return?" Mrs. Westwoode said.

"They'll find it, or there'll be hell to pay," was Daddy's reply as the door to the hall opened and Daddy plodded through it, following the lady of the house.

Who would have to pay for it this time? Not Daddy. He'd make certain of that.

"I do hope they find him," Mrs. Westwoode said, putting her hand on Stella's arm. The woman's sudden compassion touched Stella.

"Thank you, Mrs. Westwoode. So do I."

"As you presumably know, Mr. Westwoode is quite respected and quite successful on the Turf. Indeed, he won considerably at Epsom. He so hoped to give our darling Elizabeth the first foal from that stud as a wedding present."

Stella's misjudgment of Westwoode's concern aside, Mrs. Westwoode's words were disturbing; Mr. Westwoode had blatantly lied to his wife. He hadn't won at the Derby. He had lost three hundred pounds on a long shot and had bet against Cicero. Who knew how much he had lost on that race?

"Ah, there you are, Augustus."

Mr. Westwoode was waiting at the door. He cast a quick glance at Stella before offering his arm to his wife.

"Where have you been?" Mrs. Westwoode demanded.

And what else have you been lying about?

CHAPTER 26

"Now, this is a surprise," Clyde Harris said, running his thumb and forefinger across his glossy black mustache. He pushed back from his deep wooden desk, a greasy newspaper with a half-eaten order of fish and chips spread out on top, and stood. He pulled out his handkerchief and, after wiping his fingers, indicated a curved, leather-covered tub chair across from him. "Please do have a seat, my lord."

"I'd rather not." Lyndy walked over to the window and looked down on Cork Street. Three stories below, two men carrying something covered with a cloth between them struggled to enter the five-story whitewashed town house across the street, their burden too wide to fit through the narrow door. London had long lost its appeal, owing to the loud parties, the shallow women, the dirt and the smell. He couldn't wait to get back to the New Forest. "This won't take long."

Lyndy crossed the room when he spied a photograph of Clyde Harris with Sir John Bremond and Lord Ramshaw in the winner's circle at Ascot. He wanted to blame the train ride up for his restlessness, but he knew better.

"What is it I can do for you, my lord?"

Lyndy pulled the charred remains of the promissory note from his waistcoat pocket. He held it out toward Harris. "I assume this is one of yours?"

The moneylender glanced at it. There wasn't much to go on, but Lyndy had recognized the signature paper and lettering Harris was known to use.

"It is."

Lyndy had never doubted it, but the man's confirmation steeled him to carry out the rest of his plan.

"Before we go further, you must promise me your utmost discretion. No one can know about this. No one." If the police found out, it would be regrettable. If Hugh knew he was making inquiries, it would be devastating. After Stella's overhearing of Hugh's conversation, Lyndy had recognized the risks of using the telephone. Why else would he have come up to London on such short notice? "With this murder business, it's important I discover the truth before the police do."

To his credit, the moneylender didn't flinch at the mention of the police. "I understand completely, Lord Lyndhurst."

Satisfied, Lyndy walked over to Harris's desk and took the seat previously offered him. He set the remains of the promissory note on the desk.

"I need to know who this belongs to."

Settling back in his desk chair, Clyde Harris pushed the newspaper and food to the side. He clasped a pair of spectacles to the bridge of his nose and pulled the charred paper fragment toward him, then inspected it closely.

"If I may ask, where did you find it?"

"As you might suspect, in a fire grate at my family's estate in Hampshire." Lyndy didn't want to say more, couldn't say more. Admitting that much diminished his hopes of it belonging to someone besides Hugh. Who else at Morrington would have borrowed from Harris?

"Then I will have to check my books." The moneylender swiveled his chair around, pulled a ledger from a file cabinet against the wall, swiveled back, and flipped it open on his desk. "This may take a few moments."

Lyndy hopped to his feet again and moved about the room, studying several pictures of well-known racehorses tacked up on the walls, looking out the window again—the movers were no longer there, having solved their problem—and admiring a glass vase filled halfway with the cream, tan, and white shells of cowries.

"Well, that narrows it down a bit," the moneylender muttered.

Lyndy stepped back toward the desk, leaned over it, and tried to read the ledger upside down.

"There are only two possibilities, as only two men at Morrington Hall have accounts with me, in addition to you."

Two? Lyndy's heart jumped. *Who else could it be?*

"Lord Hugh Drakeford and Mr. Augustus Westwoode."

Westwoode? Lyndy knew little about the man. He rarely spoke when he happened to be around, which was not often. Lyndy had never suspected. But why not? The old boy was a punter, like the rest of them. He had a daughter about to marry and a bothersome wife. Why wouldn't he borrow the odd bit of cash here and there?

"Is it Westwoode's or Lord Hugh's note?"

"Let me look." The moneylender retrieved two file folders from the cabinet. Each labeled with a particular man's name. Mr. Westwoode's folder was an inch thick. Lord Hugh's looked empty. Harris opened Mr. Westwoode's file first. "I don't see anything from that date."

The note had to be Hugh's. It was the truth Lyndy had suspected, the fact he'd come all this way to confirm. Then why did he feel like he'd eaten a spoiled oyster?

"How much does he owe?"

Misunderstanding Lyndy, who cared only about Hugh, Harris said, "Mr. Westwoode's account has been paid in full. Right after the Derby. There's a first time for everything."

"Lucky for him. A good tip can go a long way." Lyndy made no attempt to hide his sarcasm.

"Yes, and a bad one can land a man in my office." The moneylender chuckled at his jest. Lyndy wasn't in the mood.

"And Lord Hugh?" he asked.

Harris opened Hugh's file. A copy of the burnt promissory note was on top. Harris looked up at Lyndy. He didn't need to say more.

"How much does Hugh owe?"

"I'm afraid Lord Hugh is in arrears for a thousand pounds."

"What about other debts?" Lyndy pointed to the few sheets of paper beneath the promissory note

"That is the total debt. These"—Harris lifted up the edge of the other papers with his index finger—"were all paid years ago by His Grace, Lord Hugh's father."

"But not this one." It would explain the conversation Hugh had had with his father. "Thank you, Harris," Lyndy said, retrieving the charred promissory note from the desk.

He'd learned what he came to learn, and he'd confirmed what he suspected. Hugh was in debt, and his father wasn't helping him. It would explain Hugh's argument with the vicar as well. Hence, Hugh's comment that his father was as bad as the vicar. They had both refused to help him. But had Hugh then killed the vicar, determined to get the money, anyway?

"You're most welcome, my lord. Though I have to say, two surprise visits in a week is unusual."

"Two? Who else surprised you?"

"Why, Lord Hugh did. I hadn't seen him since, well, years. Before the war, I dare say."

"When was this?"

"The day on the note, May twenty-nine."

"Lord Hugh was here, in London, on the twenty-ninth?" Lyndy demanded.

Harris squinted at Lyndy from over the rim of his spectacles. "Yes. Is there something wrong, my lord?"

Lyndy could reach across and shake the man. "When? Do you remember exactly when?"

"Before tea. Around three o'clock, I'd say."

Lyndy banged his hand on the desk and laughed. Hugh had claimed to be in Rosehurst, when he had actually been in London, borrowing money. Hugh couldn't have killed the vicar.

A shadow crossed the window as Inspector Brown pounded on the door. Herbert was inside. Brown nodded to his constable, who disappeared around the corner. They'd catch the groom if he tried to escape out the back.

"Oi!" Herbert yelled. "Let go of me!"

Brown smiled. Got him!

"We have your brother-in-law, Mr. Dobbs," Brown yelled as Herbert Kitcher, struggling in the firm grip of Constable Waterman, was hauled into view of the front door. "Open the door."

The door creaked open, and the round face of a towheaded man appeared, the same face that had peered out through the lace curtain at them when they'd first approached the cottage. A cat, an orange and white tabby, darted through Brown's legs and straight in through the opening in the door. The cottage's owner launched backward and grabbed the cat by its tail. Brown seized the door and forced his way in. The cat screeched as the towheaded man pulled it toward him and picked it up by the scruff of its neck.

"It keeps trying to get at me female." The fellow pointed with his thumb behind him. A persistent high-pitched yowling sound emanated from a back room.

"Mr. Frank Dobbs, I presume?" Brown waved Constable Waterman and his captive into the house.

Frank Dobbs, sucking a finger scratched by the determined cat, nodded.

When his constable and Herbert were in the hall, Brown let Dobbs toss the tomcat onto the garden path before locking the door behind him.

"We need to ask you a few questions about a missing horse," Brown said. "Shall we?"

Brown indicated the first room off the hall. With plain white-washed walls, it was furnished with two wingback chairs with drab yellow upholstery; a center table, stacked with copies of the *Sporting Life* and the *Sporting Times* going back a few weeks; and a dining table, covered with dirty dishes on one end and several polishing cloths and horse tack on the other. The disarray had Brown wondering what had happened to Herbert's sister, Mrs. Dobbs.

"Should I make tea?" Frank offered, rubbing the stubble on his chin.

"No. Have a seat," Brown said.

"I didn't do it," Herbert said as Constable Waterman pushed him into one of the wingback chairs. Frank sat in the other.

"What are you denying, Herbert?" Brown asked. "That you didn't steal the horse or that you didn't kill the vicar?"

Herbert leaped to his feet. "I didn't kill the vicar! Tell them, Frank. Tell them I was with you," Herbert said, desperation in his voice. "Tell them!" Constable Waterman pushed him back into the chair.

"He was," Frank said. "He was with me."

"Right. You two were too busy planning the theft of a thoroughbred racehorse to have killed the vicar. Is that what I'm to believe?"

"That's right," Herbert said.

"It's true," Frank said.

"You heard that, didn't you, Waterman?" Brown said.

"Aye, I did," the constable said, smiling.

"Please make note that Herbert Kitcher and Frank Dobbs confessed to the theft of the racehorse known as Orson."

The constable scribbled something in his notebook.

"You never thought I killed the vicar, did you?" Herbert asked, slumped in his chair.

"No," Brown said. "A stableboy . . ."

"Charlie," the constable offered.

"Right. Charlie saw you around the time of the vicar's murder, talking to someone in the back paddock. I'm assuming that was you, Frank?"

Frank nodded.

"Why did you leave the estate so abruptly last night, Herbert? You didn't give notice," Brown asked.

"I left the minute I could."

"After you attacked Mrs. Westwoode in the library."

"Wait, what?" Herbert lifted his head, his eyebrows scrunched together. "Who?" To Brown's surprise, the groom seemed genuinely perplexed. "I've never even been inside the manor house."

"But you could've used her jewels, couldn't you?"

"No, no, you got it all wrong." Herbert shook his head, looking from Brown to Constable Waterman and back again. "I don't know anything about that lady, and I don't know anything about her jewels."

"Then where did you go?"

"I went straight to the pub. You can ask Tom Heppenstall if you don't believe me. I thought I had something to celebrate."

"How wrong you were," Brown said, chuckling. Herbert glared at him.

"No, Inspector, we did have something to celebrate," Frank said, misunderstanding Brown's gibe. "We had a buyer, Lord Islington. That's what we've been waiting for."

Lord Islington! He was a prominent and powerful member of parliament, and his name was synonymous with horse racing. He would do anything to win.

"Whose idea was it to tie Herbert up when you two stole the horse? Yours or Herbert's?"

Frank looked at his brother-in-law.

"Don't say anything, Frank," Herbert said.

"But it was a good idea, Herbert," Frank said. "I wouldn't have suspected you."

Herbert dropped his head and stared at his lap.

Yes, it had been a good idea. Brown was loath to admit he'd been fooled, but Herbert had done just that. If they hadn't been investigating the vicar's death at the same time, Brown might never have been suspicious of the groom. The vicar! Brown still hadn't found the killer. Who else was fooling them? Brown, hiding his frustration, walked over to the center table and riffled through the stack of racing newspapers.

"When did you plan it? Before or after the vicar's death?" he asked.

"Right after we heard that the Americans were bringing racehorses." Herbert grumbled something, but Frank continued. "We nearly didn't pull it off, though, did we? First, Herbert had that row with the American lady. We had to meet up at a different place than planned. Then, the night the vicar died, Mr. Gates nearly caught me in the coach house."

Brown asked, "You planned to do it on Derby Day?"

"That's when Herbert said everyone would be gone. We didn't know that the stallion's offspring would win the Derby, did we? That was just good luck, I guess."

"Yes, that was good luck, wasn't it?" Brown said, not hiding his sarcasm. "Get them out of my sight, Waterman."

CHAPTER 27

Hugh was squatting beside the birds' display case, examining the magpie. Lyndy had hated that unblinking bird as a child. When he had viewed it at the eye level of a four-year-old, the magpie had seemed ominous. Now its black feathers were faded and tattered on the edges. Perhaps someone should capture a new specimen for the case. Hugh straightened up as Lyndy joined him in the library. "Collect any of these, old boy?"

"No. Grandfather caught most of them. Papa helped as well." Lyndy looked around the room. The maids had scrubbed and dusted and polished. It was the picture of genteel sophistication. As if the vicar had never come to a violent end on the other side of the sofa.

"We'd thought you'd deserted us. Drink?" Hugh held up his glass.

Lyndy nodded. For what he had to say, Lyndy was going to need all the help he could get.

"We had a rousing game of bridge earlier," Hugh said, stepping over to the tray on the card table. There was a spare glass beside the decanter.

He's been expecting me.

"It seems your American isn't as skilled at cards as she is at croquet."

"Everyone else went to bed?" Lyndy asked, avoiding the inevitable. He feigned looking at a set of bound volumes of *The Hampshire Antiquary and Naturalist*. How many of the books in this room had ever been read? He spotted *The Romance of the Scarlet Leaf, and Other Poems*. Stella seemed to enjoy reading such things. Perhaps she would make a dent in them. Lyndy took Hugh's proffered drink but didn't sit down.

"Yes. A bit early, don't you think?" Hugh laughed. It was after two in the morning.

Lyndy tipped back his glass and emptied half its contents, the port heavy and sweet as it slid down his throat. "I have something I must admit."

"I don't like the sound of that."

"I suspected you of killing the vicar." The words tumbled out of his mouth as fast as he could say them.

"How could you think such a thing?"

Lyndy wanted to make excuses. He wanted to catalog the long list of suspicious behavior: the argument with the vicar, the argument with the duke in the cloakroom, Hugh's avoidance in answering questions about his whereabouts, the burnt letter, the burnt promissory note, the large bets at the Derby while complaining about a pinch in funds. Lyndy wanted to ask why Hugh had burned the vicar's letter, why he'd lied about being in Rosehurst when he'd been in London. Lyndy wanted to rail against Hugh for not trusting him with the truth. But instead, he said what came difficult to him.

"I'm sorry."

Hugh tipped his glass back, emptied the contents, and poured himself more port. He strolled over to the mantel and tossed another log on the fire. Lit to take off the late spring chill, it crackled and snapped. Lyndy never took his eyes off him. Was Hugh going to say anything?

"I spoke with Harris," Lyndy said, unable to stand the silence.

"How'd you find out?" Hugh said, without rancor. He stood with his back to Lyndy, warming his hands by the fire.

"A promissory note. It didn't burn completely either."

Hugh chuckled. "I shouldn't have trusted the fire, or the discretion of a housemaid, to hide my mistakes." Hugh turned to face Lyndy. "Oh, don't look at me like that. I'm not proud of what I did. Quite ashamed, to tell the truth." Hugh grabbed for the fire iron to poke the fire, but it hadn't yet been replaced.

"Your father has cut you to the quick, hasn't he?"

Hugh studied Lyndy intently. "You don't know anything, do you?"

"I know you and the vicar both were at Carcroft House the night of the scandal," Lyndy said, pacing about and counting off on his fingers. "I know a burnt letter with the vicar's name on it was found in your fire grate. I know you argued with the vicar the night before he died. I know you lied about where you were when he was killed. I know someone stole the vicar's money and you were in desperate need of funds. I know you didn't kill the vicar. What else is there?"

"I'm impressed. Knowing all that, I'd suspect me too. You didn't mention any of it to the police?"

"Certainly not."

Hugh took a sip of his port before settling onto the sofa. Lyndy eased into a leather club chair, his eyes never leaving Hugh. He waited, hoping to finally get some answers.

"Right after the war, I was in a bad way," Hugh said, staring into the fire. "Not myself, shall we say. It was during this time I attended the infamous house party at Carcroft House. His Grace, His Majesty, and Reverend Bullmore, among others, were in attendance. As you know, there was an illegal game of baccarat. It was all the rage at the time."

"I know all this," Lyndy said. "I know you were there. I

know the vicar cheated and was sent to Everton Abbey to do penance."

"No, Lyndy. It was me. I cheated."

Lyndy was dumbfounded. He'd had it backward all along.

"Excuse me, my lord." Lyndy started when the butler appeared. He would never admire Fulton's impeccable timing again.

"What is it, Fulton?" Lyndy snapped. The butler showed no signs of noticing Lyndy's irritation.

"Will you be needing anything more, my lord?"

Hugh held up his glass and rattled it. "More port!" he exclaimed. His voice, which was a bit too loud, echoed in the large room. The decanter was almost empty.

"No, Fulton," Lyndy said, ignoring his friend. "Get yourself to bed." The moment the butler was out of sight, Lyndy turned back to Hugh. "You were saying?"

"I was saying, I cheated. I wasn't myself. But in my arrogance, I still expected to win. It made me wild when I didn't. I drank more and more." Hugh smiled and took another sip of his drink. "I placed larger and larger wagers until I was on the brink of losing . . . Well, I won't go into the particulars, but we'll leave it at that. Unbeknownst to me, everyone was wise to my deceit. When the night was over, everyone agreed to keep the truth to themselves, but only after eliciting a promise from me never to gamble again." Hugh sat silent for several moments, tapping the rim of his glass to his lips but not drinking. "For his loyalty and his silence, The Duke gave Bully a large sum."

"Ten thousand pounds," Lyndy said.

Hugh nodded.

"But?"

"But someone talked, didn't they? I'll always blame their crafty butler. I woke up the next morning with a nagging headache, like the one I'm sure to have tomorrow, and a father near to disowning me, to learn that our host had banished Bully from Carcroft House and that the scandal had made it into the newspaper. I never crossed paths with Bully again, until this past Saturday."

"But the gossipmonger said only that someone cheated, not who?"

"Why do you suppose the old boy spent three years at that dreadful abbey?" Hugh said. "To avoid any hint of involvement by His Majesty, The Duke, or myself, Bully offered himself up, like the sacrificial lamb he was meant to be. He never said a word in his defense. Everyone assumed he'd been the cheat."

"He did your penance for you," Lyndy said. Hence the vicar's reference to the ten thousand pounds as his "penance."

"One could look at it that way. Though I'm sure Bully minded the rigors of monastic life far less than I would have." Hugh chuckled, and then he shivered, despite the warmth of the fire.

"But you didn't hold to your promise, did you?" Lyndy said.

Hugh emptied his glass again and reached for what remained of the port.

"Is that why you argued?"

"No. We argued because I asked him to give me some of that ten thousand pounds. He refused, in that blasted letter. I tried to change his mind," Hugh scoffed. "I was in debt. The Derby was two days away. Why not give me a couple of thousand pounds? It was part of my inheritance, really. What good was it doing strapped to the chap's leg?"

The full impact of the vicar's sacrifice for Hugh hit Lyndy hard. He hadn't known the vicar well, but the tragedy, the irony of the vicar's murder, and Hugh's betrayal of the man threatened to overwhelm him. Clearing Hugh's name of murder didn't bring the resolution or peace of mind he'd expected. Quite the opposite. Knowing what he knew now, would he ever sleep well again?

"Does Elizabeth know?" Lyndy asked, his mouth dry, his stomach churning.

Hugh shook his head. "None of them do, and I'd like to keep it that way. Mr. Westwoode would call off the engagement if he suspected, and The Duke would disown me. Bully hinted that he might tell, but he never did, thank God." Or didn't get the chance. Hugh finished the port in his glass and frowned. "You won't say anything, will you?"

"No, not to her or her parents or your father." Lyndy wouldn't promise not to tell Stella. He'd have to unburden this to someone someday. "But you must do something for me, Hugh. Keep your promise. Quit gambling." It was as much an entreaty as a requirement for his silence.

"But, Lyndy, I won nine hundred pounds on Cicero at the Derby. I couldn't possibly—" He slurred his words, but Hugh knew what he was saying.

"No more!"

Lyndy sprang up, upsetting the glass on the table beside him. The red liquid splashed across the table and dripped onto the carpet. Another mess for the maids to scrub away. Lyndy didn't care. He couldn't look at Hugh again or listen to his excuses. If he didn't get out of the room now, they would both regret it.

Lyndy?

Stella had waited all night for his return from London. Even the book Lady Alice had recommended, *Undine, A Romance*, hadn't been enough to distract her. She'd listened to every creak and tick and scurrying sound the quiet night hours revealed. Finally, she heard footsteps, loud footsteps, by someone not trying to hide his passing. She put her book down, crossed her bedroom in three steps, and cracked open her door. It was Lyndy.

She grabbed her robe from the top rung of her bedroom chair, put it on and poked her head out the door. No one was about. Lyndy had already disappeared behind his bedroom door.

Tightening the robe's sash about her, she slipped into the hall. She tiptoed down the carpet, barefoot, hoping to muffle any sound. But when she reached Lyndy's bedroom, she left her raised hand hovering a few inches from the door. What was she doing? It was after two in the morning, and she was outside a man's door, alone. Lady Atherly insisted Aunt Rachel chaperone the couple. Though they had circumvented Aunt Rachel's efforts on more than one occasion, what would Lady Atherly think if she saw Stella now? He was her fiancé, after all, though, wasn't he? Who else could she tell about seeing Mr. Westwoode in the pub? How else would she find out what he'd learned about Lord Hugh in London? Did he even know about Orson yet? Stella had to speak to him.

She glanced down the hall one more time and softly knocked. No answer.

He had come this way. He couldn't have fallen asleep yet; she'd seen him just moments ago. She knocked again. He had to be in there.

"Lyndy," Stella whispered.

"Good night, Hugh," Lyndy said, sounding quite surly.

She hesitated for only a moment. What made him think it was Lord Hugh at his door? Why was he angry? "It's Stella," she whispered.

Crash!

Stella jumped as the sound of metal clanging against metal reverberated from down the hall. Someone had bumped against a suit of armor as they staggered down the hallway in the darkness. Who was that?

The flowing sleeves and flouncy lace of Stella's robe fluttered as the door flung open. Lyndy grabbed her arm and yanked her into his room. He glanced up and down the hall before he closed the door carefully, quietly, behind her. He was wearing only his trousers and undershirt beneath his open dressing gown. Stella blushed. She'd never seen a man undressed before. She averted her eyes. The carpet was Persian, an explosion of tiny colorful flowers—red, gold, black, green, and blue—intricately woven together. Stella stared at a design that reminded her of bluebells from back home.

"Who was that out there?" she asked.

"Hugh. He's drunk." Lyndy tied the sash of his dressing gown around his waist. "You shouldn't be here."

"I need to talk to you. I'm not sure if you know, but while you were gone, the police—"

"Couldn't it wait?"

"Wait? I've been waiting for you for hours."

"Are you always this impatient?" he said irritably.

She placed her hands on her hips. "Are you always this rude?"

Lyndy glared at her, then crossed to the bed and dropped onto the edge of it. It was a carved mahogany four-poster bed like the one in Stella's room. Only the carving on the headboard differed. "I confronted Hugh," he grumbled.

A million questions swirled through her head, pushing aside what she'd come to tell him. But he obviously wasn't in the mood to indulge her curiosity. She restrained herself to one.

"And?"

"He didn't kill the vicar." He looked up at her, scowling. He'd cleared his friend's name of the murder. Why was he so upset? "He was in London at the time."

"But?"

He chuckled, and his shoulders relaxed. "You are relentless, aren't you?"

"I'm an American."

"Yes, there is that."

She fixed her eyes on him in anticipation.

"I discovered a secret best forgotten."

It couldn't be worse than killing the vicar.

"Then why aren't you relieved? Your friend isn't a murderer."

"Yes, but . . . he's not the man I believed he was."

She wanted to ask him what he meant. She wanted to put her arm around his shoulders and comfort him. She wrapped her arms around her shoulders instead.

"I'm sorry."

People had disappointed Stella her whole life: her father, her "friends," even Aunt Rachel. Only horses seemed to be honest about who they were, for good or bad. She looked at Lyndy. Would he disappoint her too?

"What was it that you wanted to tell me?" he said, reviving a little and fiddling with the collar of his dressing gown. The brown silk of the collar went well with his eyes.

"The police came while you were in London. They found Orson."

"They did?"

What was that in his voice? Surprise, concern, relief?

Stella nodded.

"Where? When? Who? Is he injured?"

"Who's the impatient one now? Maybe I should wait to tell you," Stella said, teasing.

"Fair enough," Lyndy said, a faint glint in his eyes, a crooked smirk on his face.

Stella smiled. "He's fine, thank goodness, though we'll have to have the vet around in the morning."

"Who took him?"

"Herbert, the groom, and his brother-in-law. The police found Orson in the brother-in-law's paddock a few miles from here this afternoon. They've both been arrested. Unfortunately, neither of them could've killed the vicar or attacked Mrs. Westwoode. But I have an idea about someone who might've." Stella ignored the skeptical look on Lyndy's face and continued.

"Yesterday I followed Herbert to the pub near the village green in Rosehurst."

"Yes, I heard about that. Mrs. Westwoode said her daughter prevented you from going inside."

"Well, it was actually Lady Alice, but Mrs. Westwoode was right that I didn't go inside. But I did get a good look. Who do you think I saw rushing out the back way?"

"Who?"

"Mr. Westwoode."

Lyndy laughed. It was little more than a loud chuckle, as Lyndy never laughed properly. No one she'd met since she arrived at Morrington Hall, besides the men in the stables, had laughed properly. It wasn't the response she'd expected, but she liked his loud chuckle, nonetheless.

"I don't blame him. I would've snuck out the back door too. If Mrs. Westwoode knew . . ." he said.

"That's not all. Mr. Westwoode lied to his wife about his gambling success. She claims he won, but I saw him tear up his ticket. Who knows how much he lost that day."

Lyndy hooked his finger over his dimpled chin. "Do you know, I learned something quite extraordinary about our Mr. Westwoode. Hugh wasn't the only one in this house to borrow money. Also, Westwoode paid off his debts on Derby Day. You don't think . . . ?"

"That he killed the vicar and paid off his debts with the money? It's possible. But did he attack his own wife?"

"Have you met Mrs. Westwoode?"

Lyndy had a point.

CHAPTER 28

As Papa, Mother, Alice, and the other parishioners filed out and greeted the new vicar, Lyndy glanced back at the family pew. Stella, clutching the curved back of the pew in front of her, worn smooth by generations of hands, stared straight up at the ceiling of St. Peter's Church. Miss Luckett sat patiently beside her.

Not wishing to jar his new peace of mind, Lyndy had heard little of the new vicar's sermon, a somber reminder of Reverend Bullmore's untimely death. Instead, he'd amused himself by watching Stella experience the awe of the Norman church. She hadn't listened attentively to the vicar's pontifications either. She'd gazed at the ancient stones, the hand-carved wooden beams holding up the roof, and the stained-glass windows of St. Peter and his fellow apostles, which were given to the church by the fourth Earl of Atherly. She'd strained to read the centuries-old inscriptions on the floor and walls, some more legible than others, revealing the crypts of those long buried, many of them Lyndy's ancestors. A power and reverence emanated from this place, though it was barely larger than their drawing room. From the look on her face, he knew her church in Kentucky was nothing like St. Peter's. But was that a good thing or not?

Lyndy breathed in the lingering scent of incense, relishing his relief. Orson was back in their stables, unharmed and feisty as ever. He'd tried to take a nip at Lyndy when he'd visited the stables before church.

"Lyndy, Miss Kendrick." Mother beckoned them with a sharp snap of her head.

Lyndy crossed the cold gray stone floor. Stella, hearing the tap of his shoes echo, pulled her gaze away from the ceiling.

"Mother would like us to join the others."

Stella nodded, shuffled between the wooden pews, and followed Lyndy toward the door. Miss Luckett followed not far behind. When they reached the vestibule, Stella reached out and touched the walls, irregular fieldstones set in rough plaster centuries ago. She shivered and pulled her shawl tighter around her shoulders. He offered his arm. Somber and thoughtful, she took it, and they stepped outside together. She hadn't uttered a sound. Perhaps she'd listened more carefully to the new vicar's sermon about Reverend Bullmore's death than Lyndy had. Would the police ever catch the killer?

The new vicar was speaking with Miss Westwoode and Mrs. Westwoode, his white and gold vestments brilliant despite the overcast sky. He was about ten years Lyndy's senior, with thick black hair, spectacles, and a beard. He had a habit of sticking his finger in his ear and wiggling it. Lyndy had already seen him do it twice. Without knowing why, Lyndy took an instant dislike to the man.

"Reverend Paine," Mother said, "may I introduce Lord Lyndhurst, my son?" Mother waved briefly to Mrs. Fisher, whom she knew from the annual Rosehurst floral show, as the lady exited the church. The vicar tipped his head.

"It is a pleasure to meet you, my lord."

"Vicar."

"And this is his betrothed, Miss Stella Kendrick."

Stella's hand tightened on Lyndy's arm. Was she still uncomfortable being introduced as such? Hadn't they come farther than that?

"*Enchanté*," the vicar said.

"Nice to meet you, Reverend Paine," Stella said. "May I introduce my great-aunt—"

"Elijah Kendrick, at your service, Vicar," Mr. Kendrick said, brushing Stella aside and shoving out his plump, stumpy hand. The vicar politely shook it. "Bad business about the first one. I presume you'll be as eager as I am to expedite my daughter's wedding to the viscount? It was supposed to be yesterday. I have to get back to the States, but I'll be damned if I leave before I see her wed. When a man only has one daughter, he has to see it's done right."

Several matrons, waiting their turn to greet the new vicar, murmured their disapproval at Mr. Kendrick's coarse behavior, his vulgarity.

"I don't think this is the time or the place to discuss this, Mr. Kendrick," Reverend Paine said. He indicated the line of parishioners behind them. Men cleared their throats; lads shifted from one foot to the next; women whispered to their neighbor behind gloved hands; children tugged on their mothers' sleeves. They were growing impatient.

"Why not? You're here, Lord and Lady Atherly are here, and I'm here. I think this is the perfect time and place."

"But others are waiting, Mr. Kendrick," Mrs. Westwoode hissed between her teeth. She glanced about to see necks craning as the line of parishioners condensed into a cluster that was slowly inching forward. The American horse breeder seemed oblivious to the growing impatience, and curiosity, of the crowd.

Mother's calm exterior couldn't hide her indignation at the impropriety of it all. "Mr. Kendrick, I think it best to discuss this inside, after Reverend Paine is done greeting everyone," Mother said, hoping to put an end to it.

"But this won't take long, will it, Reverend?" Mr. Kendrick said.

The vicar hesitated before answering. Doubt flickered in the vicar's eyes.

"Besides, they don't have to wait." Kendrick pointed over his shoulder with his thumb. "There's always next Sunday, right?"

"Well, if you insist, I must say, what with the death of Reverend Bullmore so fresh on everyone's mind—"

"Whose doing was that? Your sermon was—" Mr. Kendrick interrupted, but the vicar cut him short.

"I'd like to greet my other parishioners now, if you don't mind."

"What's all this hemming and hawing about?" Miss Luckett said. "Out with it, Preacher."

The vicar started, like a chicken seeing a fox. But he quickly regained his composure. "What I was saying is that I think we should postpone the wedding until—"

"I say, what's going on?" Hugh eyed the crowd as he strolled past to join them. He'd been last to leave the church.

Needing a few extra minutes to pray and ease your conscience, Hugh? Lyndy doubted it.

"Good news about the stolen stallion," Hugh said, slapping Lyndy on the back. Lyndy merely nodded. It wasn't good news. It was brilliant news. But Hugh's demonstration of callousness and greed still stung. "From what I hear, the horse was no worse for wear."

"Good thing too," Mr. Kendrick said. "I wasn't relishing calling in my lawyers."

Mrs. Westwoode reached over and tugged Hugh's arm. "This is my daughter's fiancé, Lord Hugh Drakeford, son of His Grace the Duke of Tonnbridge," she announced. "Lord Hugh, dear, this is the new vicar of Rosehurst, Reverend Paine."

"Yes, and I'm sure he is one, at that," Hugh said jovially.

Miss Luckett winked at him.

Lyndy hadn't expected to find Hugh abundantly cheerful this morning, especially considering last night's indulgences, but then, why not? With Lyndy's promise to keep Hugh's secret, for Hugh nothing had changed.

If only that were true for me.

The vicar bowed, but his smile faded. Several snickers and chuckles escaped from those parishioners closest to Hugh. Mr. Kendrick, having no couth, as usual, snorted with laughter.

"I bet you get sick of that joke, eh, Reverend?" Mr. Kendrick said, still chuckling.

Reverend Paine said nothing but waved the nearest person forward. The audience was over.

"I do believe we had the same brilliant idea," Lyndy said as Stella descended the stairs in her riding habit, the top hat the perfect extension of her elegant neck. Her long skirt swayed as she skipped off the last step. He, too, was dressed for riding.

He'd missed a golden opportunity, having Stella in his bedroom last night. He'd been upset with Hugh, yes, but he wasn't blind. The soft curves beneath her dressing gown made her as alluring as any woman he'd known. What was wrong with him? Had he been that angry with Hugh, or could it be something else?

Damn this new conscience!

"They say, 'Make hay while the sun shines,'" she said, smiling. "I say, 'Let's ride before the English rain falls.'"

"I couldn't agree more."

Fulton opened the door, and Lyndy, bowing, indicated for Stella to go first.

"Are you both going riding before tea?" Mother said, a fresh bunch of pink peonies in her arms. Since she'd had to dismiss much of the gardening staff, Mother had taken to keeping the flower vases full. "Miss Kendrick mustn't go without a chaperone."

Ignoring Mother, Lyndy grabbed Stella's hand and led her outside. Tully and Beau were waiting for them. Lyndy waved off the groom holding Tully's reins, and as he assisted Stella in mounting, he caught a glimpse of the trousers she wore beneath her skirt. He watched, transfixed, as Stella hooked her leg around the top pommel of her sidesaddle and smoothed her skirt across her knees.

"I think your mother has got it all wrong," Stella said, pulling the veil over her face. She adjusted the reins and crop in one hand before leaning over to pat the horse on the neck with the other.

"I agree with you," Lyndy said, looking up at her, the image of her leg still in his mind. "But in what way are you referring?"

"I think it is you who needs the chaperone." She'd caught him staring! With that, Stella clicked her tongue, spurring her horse into a trot.

"Hey!" Lyndy shouted, springing into his saddle. Stella was already across the lawn before Lyndy urged Beau into a canter to catch up.

Lyndy chased her across Butts Lawn, Fletchers Green and then through Queen Bower. Despite her inexperience with the Forest, Stella expertly navigated the gorse thickets, the heath patches, and the sprawling stands of bracken. Without hesitation, she and Tully leaped many small seasonal ponds left by the rain. He'd nearly caught up to her when they rode out on to Poundhill Heath, speckled with New Forest ponies, several head of cattle, and the old gray donkey, Headley, who had a penchant for brambles and carrots. The donkey belonged to a commoner from Minstead, but since childhood, Alice had pretended it was her pet.

Stella encouraged Tully to run faster. Lyndy couldn't tell

who was enjoying the ride more, the woman or the thorough-bred. The ponies, used to sharing the land, moved to make way, but Headley, who Lyndy suspected had lost most of his eye-sight years ago, didn't budge.

"Watch out for the donkey," Lyndy yelled, laughing and feeling ridiculous.

Stella showed no signs of hearing him or heeding him. She and Tully ran headlong toward the towering oaks that bordered the heath. Lyndy squeezed Beau hard with his thighs, spurring the horse to catch up, but Beau was no match for Tully.

"Watch out for the donkey!" Lyndy yelled again, the wind in his face muffling the sound of his warning.

Stella deftly steered Tully to the left to avoid the stubborn and blind old animal. Lyndy sat back in his saddle, relieved. How foolish he'd been for questioning the skill of the horse and her rider. Beau slowed, but Tully didn't as the thorough-bred approached the path through the wood. Like a brown and white spotted flag, a fallow deer leaped from its hiding place in Tully's path. The horse reared. Stella's top hat flipped off, flew over the horse's back, and landed upside down on the grass.

Lyndy kicked Beau with his heels, shouting at the horse to run. He couldn't get there fast enough.

Stella expertly clung to the horse's back and soon regained her seat. As Lyndy approached, she was trying to calm the horse, to little avail. Prancing nervously about, Tully flicked her ears back and forth and curled her lip. The horse was paw-ing the ground when more deer sprang to life, crashing through the wood, snapping twigs and stomping brush in their escape. Tully bucked and ran.

Stella, pitched forward by the jolt, was hurled over Tully's right shoulder. But instead of flying free of the horse, she hung, suspended a few inches above the ground, her hair catching on the tops of gorse bushes, her shoulder and back bouncing against the animal's flank. Her skirt had caught on the top pommel.

Lyndy was helpless to do anything but watch. Beau pinned his ears back as Tully's leather reins dropped and dragged along on the muddy ground. Then Stella's skirt ripped free of her waist, releasing her. She tumbled to the ground, somersaulting twice, before lying motionless on her side.

Lyndy leaped from the stirrups before Beau had stopped a few feet away, and staggered as he ran, trying to catch his balance. He fell to his knees at her side.

"Stella!"

"Ah, that hurt," she moaned.

He wanted to clasp her to him, cradle her, and kiss her. He wanted to rail at her for frightening him. He looked down helplessly at her instead. "Can you sit up?"

She rolled onto her back and stared up at him, her silky hair tangled and littered with bits of oak leaves, gorse twigs, and grass. Her face was unblemished but for a small scrape across her cheek. A rip in the left shoulder of her jacket revealed where she'd landed when she hit the ground. Cuts in the knees of her riding trousers revealed scrapes as well.

"Tully?" she said faintly.

Lyndy glanced back. Tully had sidled up to Beau as he grazed.

"Your horse is fine. I can't say the same for you."

"Owww," she groaned, rolling onto her side again. He expected her to curl up in pain, but she surprised him as she pushed up onto her elbow. She raised her hand to be helped up.

"Should you be getting up?"

"Unless you plan on carrying me all the way back . . ."

He grabbed hold of her offered hand and helped her to her feet. "Are you certain you're all right?"

"I'll heal," she said, brushing herself off and making a vain attempt to smooth her tangled hair. "Ow. I think I bruised a rib or two. Not my best fall."

"You've fallen before?"

"Many times. Haven't you?"

Of course he had. To be a good rider, one had to know how to fall.

"I'm more embarrassed than anything," she added.

Embarrassed? He'd never seen any woman, not even Lady Letitia Bentley-Sudder, who was the best female rider he knew, get up so quickly from a fall.

"Good thing I'm wearing trousers, huh? Can you get my skirt?"

"Of course," Lyndy said, admiring her legs, which, freed of the bulky skirt, were long and graceful in the tight riding trousers, and on view for all to see. He jogged over to where her skirt had fallen and brought it back to her. He turned his back as she slipped it around her waist.

"All done," she said. When he turned back around, she'd covered herself. "It seems ridiculous to wear both skirt and trousers."

"But you can't mean to ride only in trousers, like a man?" Lyndy said. *How ridiculous.* Next, she'd be suggesting she ride astride instead of sidesaddle.

"Why not? It would be safer and easier." She leaned on him as she limped back toward Tully. "Help me up." She grabbed hold of Tully's reins as the horse stood compliantly still.

"You don't mean to ride back, in your state?"

"Isn't there a saying?" She looked at him expectantly.

How could he argue with that?

CHAPTER 29

Lyndy lifted Stella off her horse, brushing aside the startled groom, and insisted she lean on him as they entered the house.

"Ring for Miss Kendrick's maid, will you, Fulton? She's taken a bit of a tumble," he said the moment the butler opened the door.

Stella, never having such fuss made about her falls before, wasn't sure she cared for it. She pulled away from him.

"As I told you already, I can walk by myself."

Her knees were scraped, but it was nothing cold, clean water wouldn't soothe. Her shoulder, on the other hand . . . That was going to smart for days.

"Obviously, I need to—" Stella's breath caught in her throat. She was going to say, "Wash and dress for afternoon tea," but she'd seen Mr. Westwoode striding down the hall at the end of the grand saloon. He hadn't been at church this morning. "We need to confront him," Stella said before rushing off in the direction in which she'd seen him go.

"Stella!" Lyndy called, in pursuit.

Stella had reached the edge of the grand saloon when a loud

gasp startled her. Ethel, emerging from the servants' doorway, gaped at her, one hand covering her mouth, Stella's pale blue beaded satin evening gown draped in the crook of the maid's arm. Ethel pointed at Stella with her other hand. Stella looked down at herself. Her white blouse was untied and dirty; her jacket and skirt needed a good brushing; patches of mud clung to the skirt hem. Strands of tangled hair fell loose about her face and neck. Yes, she looked frightful, but did her maid have to react like that? Perhaps Ethel had heard the fuss Lyndy made about her fall.

"That sound, miss, on the carpet. Those boots." Stella lifted her skirt and stared down at her feet. "That's what the killer wore. I'd swear on my mother's grave." Ethel covered her ears with her hands. "I'll never forget that sound. That sound of those boots running on this carpet."

"The killer was wearing riding boots?" Lyndy said, coming to Stella's side.

The maid nodded. Her face was as white as a sheet.

"Ethel, you didn't say before that the man you saw was dressed for riding," Stella said.

The maid shook her head. "I didn't realize it until now, when I heard you, miss. With the black boots, the black trousers, it was all a blur."

"But who could that have been?" Lyndy said.

"Good afternoon." A man's voice carried from the entrance hall, cutting off any speculation on Lyndy's rhetorical question. They turned to see Inspector Brown handing his hat to the butler. "I'd like to have a word with Mr. Augustus Westwoode, if you please."

"In here, if you don't mind, Mr. Westwoode," Inspector Brown said, pointing toward Lord Atherly's smoking room.

As lovely as it was, Brown hoped this was the last time he'd ever have to see this room again. As he stepped in behind Mr.

Westwoode, Lord Lyndhurst, accompanied by his American fiancée, followed behind him. From the way Miss Kendrick grimaced at the animal heads on the walls, she agreed with him.

"My lord? Can I help you?" Brown asked.

"We were just about to telephone you, Inspector Brown," Miss Kendrick said.

Were they now?

Before Brown could ask why, Lord Lyndhurst said, "I, we, would like to be present when you interview Mr. Westwoode."

Brown weighed the reasons to object. Lord Atherly, and Brown's superiors, would not take it kindly if he offended the viscount needlessly. But Brown still wondered why. "If Mr. Westwoode has no objections?"

That gentleman had already taken a seat. Westwoode shook his head. He began chewing on his upper lip. "What is this about, Inspector?"

Brown waited for the others to be seated. Lord Lyndhurst strolled the room, looking out the window, examining the gun cases, and studying the mounted animal heads, as if he'd never been in the room before. When Brown indicated a seat, the viscount waved it off and bid him to begin. Brown tried to dismiss the young lord's restlessness but kept the viscount always in the corner of his eye.

"When I interviewed you on a previous occasion, Mr. Westwoode, I asked for your whereabouts during the time of the vicar's death."

Mr. Westwoode stole a quick glance at Miss Kendrick. Now, why would he look at the young lady? Was she his alibi? Had she been lying to Brown as well? That would be a shame. Despite all the rumors and gossip surrounding her "unusual" behavior, he'd taken a liking to the young woman. Brown always prided himself on being a good judge of character. Had he been mistaken?

"If you recall, Mr. Westwoode, you told me you'd taken a walk. I took you at your word."

Mr. Westwoode said nothing but waited expectantly.

"Do you know what a grockle is, Mr. Westwoode?"

The fellow frowned. Brown's change in the subject had the desired effect. *Confuse the bugger.*

"No, I have no idea."

"It means 'stranger' or 'outsider,' someone from outside the New Forest."

"Then I must be a grockle, Inspector." Mr. Westwoode shrugged. "What does that have to do with anything?"

"Grockles get noticed, Mr. Westwoode, particularly in a man's local pub."

Mr. Westwoode's jaw dropped open, but it was Miss Kendrick who blurted, "How did you know?"

How did she know anything about this? What else hadn't she told him? Was that why the pair of them insisted on sitting in? Perhaps, he was wrong about her, after all. *Shame.*

"I'm the one that should be asking that question, Miss Kendrick," Brown chided.

"You saw me, didn't you?" Mr. Westwoode said to Miss Kendrick. "I was hoping I'd left in time."

"In time for what?" Brown didn't appreciate losing control of his own interview. "Explain yourself, Miss Kendrick."

Miss Kendrick confessed to following the groom Herbert to the door of the Knightwood Oak pub. Upon peeking inside, she observed Mr. Westwoode dashing for the rear entrance.

The rumors about this girl are true, then? Brown kept the astonishment from showing on his face. *She is an odd one.*

"How did you find out, Inspector?" Miss Kendrick asked.

Mr. Heppenstall had told him, but he wasn't going to reward her with an answer. "I will be the one asking the questions, Miss Kendrick."

Seemingly properly abashed, she nodded.

"Now, Mr. Westwoode, would you like to tell me where you were when the vicar was killed?"

"What? Now, hold on." He lowered his voice. "I didn't kill the vicar!"

"But his money would solve your problems, wouldn't it?" Lord Lyndhurst said.

A box of cigars labeled Por Larrañaga held the viscount's attention. Brown smelled them the moment Lord Lyndhurst opened the box. If things went as Brown hoped, perhaps the young lord would be kind enough to offer him one. But first things first. He waited for Mr. Westwoode to answer the question.

"I admit I have debts," Mr. Westwoode said. "But I didn't kill the vicar."

"But you knew about his money?" Lord Lyndhurst said.

Westwoode nodded.

It was happening again. Brown had to regain control. "You told my constable that you didn't know about the vicar's money, Mr. Westwoode."

"Well, I didn't know until luncheon that day. My wife overheard Lord Hugh mention it to the vicar. She later told me."

Brown sputtered curses under his breath. Could he believe a word out of anyone's mouth? Not only had Westwoode lied about knowing about the money, but his wife and his future son-in-law had too. Brown would have to reinterview Lord Hugh and Mrs. Westwoode. Nothing they had told him could be trusted. He'd arrest the lot of them if it wouldn't cost him his job.

"What about the Derby?" Miss Kendrick said.

"What about it?" Brown snapped.

Miss Kendrick recounted her conversation with Mrs. Westwoode about how the matron's husband won at the races. "I know that you lost, Mr. Westwoode. I saw you tear up your ticket."

"I did lose. I never claimed otherwise. But I never told Caroline either way. We never discuss it."

"Then how did you manage to pay back all that you owed to Clyde Harris?" Lord Lyndhurst said.

Clyde Harris? When had he gotten involved?

"Clyde Harris was the moneylender?" Miss Kendrick asked, her brows knitted in surprise.

Lord Lyndhurst nodded.

Brown sat down. A good policeman knew when to question and when to listen. He'd lost control of this interview the moment he allowed Lord Lyndhurst and Miss Kendrick into the room. He'd have a few choice words for the two young people about withholding evidence from him, but now was not the time; Westwoode was admitting to everything.

"I didn't pay Harris a farthing."

"I spoke to Clyde Harris," Lord Lyndhurst said. "I examined your accounts. You were in great debt, on the verge of bankruptcy even, and then you paid it all off at the Derby, two days after someone killed the vicar and robbed him of ten thousand pounds."

"I never!" Mr. Westwoode declared, leaping to his feet. "If you take the word of a money-grubber over a gentleman, then you, sir, are not one either!"

"Now, now, Mr. Westwoode," Brown said, indicating for the fellow to take his seat.

Did wonders never cease? In all his years, Brown had never seen someone insulted by an accusation of *paying off* a debt. Was he telling the truth or trying to cloud the issue with his dramatic denial? Brown honestly couldn't tell.

"Then explain why Harris would say you paid your debt," Lord Lyndhurst said.

"I can't possibly. The fellow must be mistaken."

"Right." Brown wasn't getting anywhere with this. "Which brings us back to your whereabouts when the vicar was killed, and when your wife was attacked."

"Are you implying that I attacked my wife?"

"It isn't as absurd as it sounds, Mr. Westwoode. Many a crime is between husband and wife."

Miss Kendrick shot a quick look at her betrothed. Was she having second thoughts?

"It is one way to get her jewels," the inspector added.

"For what purpose?"

"To pay your debts. It's one way to avoid having to tell the missus you're bankrupt."

Westwoode laughed. Brown couldn't fathom why.

"Are you saying you didn't use your wife's jewels to pay off your debt?"

"Don't you see, I couldn't have, because I've used them already, to pay off past debts."

"How's that?" Brown asked.

"All of her jewels are glass paste. Not a single true gem among them." Westwoode composed himself. "Caroline doesn't know, and I'd rather she didn't find out."

Lord Lyndhurst, a slight curl to his lip, turned away and strode back to the window. What was so compelling outside? Nothing, Brown suspected. Lord Lyndhurst, the true gentleman in the room, had accepted the honest debt but couldn't abide the deception. Maybe Brown had been too rash to judge these two young ones.

"Then, where were you, Mr. Westwoode?" Miss Kendrick said before Brown could.

"Ask the inspector. If the publican told him about me, he knows where I've been."

Miss Kendrick and Lord Lyndhurst looked expectantly at Brown.

"You tell them, Mr. Westwoode," Brown said.

Mr. Heppenstall had confirmed Westwoode's presence in the pub that afternoon, but the publican hadn't noticed the precise time when Westwoode arrived or left. Brown hoped he'd be able to trick Westwoode into telling him.

"I was in the pub."

"When the vicar was killed?" Lord Lyndhurst said.

Mr. Westwoode nodded. "When the vicar was killed, when my wife was attacked, when Miss Kendrick appeared on the doorstep. I escaped to the pub every chance I could."

Brown pinched the bridge of his nose and sighed. He'd needed Westwoode to be the killer. But, God help him, he believed the fellow. That left only Lord Hugh and members of the family; and without absolute proof, not just the word of the publican's lad, who thought he had witnessed the vicar and Lord Hugh arguing, Brown was never going to be able to accuse any of them.

"But why?" Miss Kendrick said.

"It's not what you think. I rarely drink more than two pints at any given time."

Brown could guess. He'd seen more than one married man crying in his cups. After meeting Mrs. Westwoode, Brown couldn't blame him.

"I can't imagine the men of Rosehurst would appreciate your presence," Lord Lyndhurst said. "They go to their local to relax, not to be judged by their betters."

"I go for that same reason," Mr. Westwoode said. "I don't have to be Mrs. Westwoode's husband or Miss Westwoode's father or Lord Hugh Drakeford's future father-in-law. All I am to them there is a . . . What did you call it, Inspector? A grockle?"

Miss Kendrick reached over and put her hand on Mr. Westwoode's arm. There was one who could empathize. Who would want to be the American horse breeder's daughter? Rumors said he was a brute.

"But you lied about it," she said.

"If Caroline found out, she'd put an end to it. 'We can't have Lord Hugh's future father-in-law patronizing a pub, can we?'" he said, mimicking his wife. The bitterness in his tone was palpable.

"How do you get away with it?" Lord Lyndhurst said. Was

he curious or envious? "Simply because you were wearing tweeds and not your morning coat? Who did they think you were? Our new gamekeeper?"

Brown had heard rumors that funds were tight at Morrington Hall and staff were being let go.

Mr. Westwoode shrugged and nodded.

Brown didn't want to disillusion Mr. Westwoode, but no one at the Knightwood Oak had mistaken him for anything but a gentleman.

"I should try that," Miss Kendrick muttered.

"Try what?" Brown asked.

"Dressing like a gamekeeper," Miss Kendrick said. "Think of the freedom it would give me."

"Don't get any ideas, Miss Kendrick," Lord Lyndhurst warned. Miss Kendrick stared at a blank point on the wainscot that ran along the wall. "I can't have . . ." Lord Lyndhurst continued admonishing her, but she was no longer listening.

"Please excuse me." Miss Kendrick abruptly stood. "I apologize, Mr. Westwoode, for ever doubting you," she said, her otherwise lively countenance a blank.

"Stella?" Lord Lyndhurst said, laying his hand lightly on her shoulder, his concern overriding his manners. "Are you in pain?"

She nodded her head. "Yes, that's it. I'd like to lie down now."

In answer to Brown's questioning stare, Lord Lyndhurst said, "She was thrown from her horse earlier."

"Then by all means," Brown said.

Relief washed over her face as she nearly fled the room. Lord Lyndhurst might believe his fiancée was in pain, but Brown hadn't spent years studying liars not to know one. What was that young woman up to now?

CHAPTER 30

"Is it going to rain today, do you suppose?" Papa said. "It has been threatening all day but hasn't produced a drop."

Lyndy silently groaned. He loathed talking about the weather. He took a sip of his tea, already growing cold, as he glanced over again at the drawing-room door. Where was Stella?

"Where is the girl?" Mr. Kendrick said, as if reading Lyndy's mind. The prospect was unnerving. Mr. Kendrick looked at Lyndy.

Why did the brute want to know? Had he learned of Stella's fall? Would he care?

"She never misses a meal," Mr. Kendrick said.

That was true enough; Stella's "healthy" appetite was part of her charm.

When she'd rushed off, complaining of pain, Lyndy had offered to escort her back. She'd refused him, insisting she simply needed to rest. But when she didn't arrive for afternoon tea, he suspected she'd injured herself more than she'd let on. He glanced at the door again. If she didn't send word or arrive soon, he intended to check on her, whether she wanted him to or not.

Mr. Kendrick tipped back his teacup and audibly slurped down its contents.

"Does anyone know where she is?" This Mr. Kendrick addressed to everyone else, before setting down his cup and biting off the end of a scone, the cream and lemon curd dripping back on to the plate. He lapped up the fallen cream with his finger and licked it off. Obviously, he wasn't overly concerned. "Rachel, aren't you supposed to be keeping an eye on her?"

Miss Luckett bristled at the accusation. She set her teacup in her lap. "Hold your britches on, Elijah. I reckon she's changing for tea."

Mother eyed Lyndy, a knowing, unapproving expression on her face. She knew Lyndy had ignored her admonition not to go riding with Stella without the chaperone. She suspected he wasn't telling all he knew about Stella's whereabouts and the reason behind her absence. Her stare was unusually compelling.

"She's resting," Lyndy said. "She had a bit of a tumble earlier."

Mother shook her head, as if to say, "I knew nothing good would come of it." As if the old chaperone could've prevented Stella from falling off the horse. She didn't seem overly concerned about Stella either.

"Is she unwell?" Alice asked, looking up from one of her magazines. Alice flipped through these magazines, mesmerized, for hours a day. Lyndy didn't see the draw. If it didn't have *sporting* in the title and give him details of the upcoming races, why bother?

The illustration on the left page of the magazine Alice held open in her hands was of a somber-looking couple with their eyes downcast, the woman in a wedding dress and veil. Were they simply being reverent? Lyndy bent his head to get a better look. No, they looked miserable. He glanced over at Hugh and Miss Westwoode. Hugh plucked the last madeleine from his plate and took a bite. Miss Westwoode sipped her tea, glancing up at Hugh now and then. Hugh appeared oblivious to his fiancée's need for attention. Must every marriage be miserable? Mother and Papa's certainly wasn't blissful. Lyndy glanced at the drawing-room door again. Would his be?

"She's late, that's what she is," Mr. Kendrick said. "I was afraid this would happen. She's getting disrespectful and full of herself." Mr. Kendrick dipped the remainder of his scone in his tea.

An audible groan arose from Mother's direction. If he kept talking about Stella like this, Lyndy might have to throttle the brute.

"I blame myself. I've let her have too much freedom. But I've always insisted that 'a lady must never be late.' Isn't that right, Lady Atherly?"

Mother, the tightness around her mouth the only indication that she'd rather chew her fingernails than agree with the American, said, "One must maintain the highest standards in all aspects of etiquette, Mr. Kendrick. Pity that's not always the case."

"Well, I've done my best by the girl. Seems it wasn't enough."

"No, it seems not," Mrs. Westwoode said, watching over the rim of her teacup for any reaction. Lyndy, suppressing his desire to throttle her too, was careful not to give her one. Mr. Kendrick frowned. He presumably didn't expect to be agreed with.

"Well, whatever's keeping her, I daresay Miss Kendrick will regret missing these lovely madeleines," Hugh said.

"They are delicious, aren't they?" Mrs. Westwoode said. "Don't you agree, Elizabeth, darling?"

Miss Westwoode nodded and sipped her tea.

"What did the police want to speak to you about, Augustus?" Mrs. Westwoode asked.

Mr. Westwoode, silent since the police had dismissed him and he had gone downstairs to have their tea, nibbled on a scone. "Nothing, dear. Just some clarification, is all."

Satisfied, Mrs. Westwoode turned the conversation to the weather, again. Between Mrs. Westwoode's surprise over how it hadn't rained on them while they greeted the new vicar after church this morning and Papa's hopes that it would be warmer tomorrow for his planned visit to the Bronze Age barrow that reportedly contained ancient horse bones, a footman arrived with the requested second tray of mushroom tartlets and egg and watercress sandwiches. Mr. Kendrick, holding out his plate, waved the footman to his side. Stella might partake more of a meal than the average Englishwoman, but her father was the one with the prodigious appetite. As Mr. Kendrick helped himself to the savories, the footman, an unveiled look of horror on his face, was helpless to stop him.

Lyndy struggled to recall the servant's name. The footman hadn't been at Morrington Hall long. Stella probably knew. Where was she?

"Aaahhh!"

Lyndy flinched, heat flashing through his chest. He'd never heard a scream like that before. Gasps and cries and the clattering of teacups and saucers and plates followed as the others dropped their china. The tartlets and sandwiches slid onto the carpet as the footman let the tray slip. Lyndy was on his feet before anyone else. He had to get to the library, where the scream had originated. It had come from Stella.

As he reached the adjoining door, the others weren't far behind. Lyndy swung it open and ran into the library. A stream of late afternoon sun stretched from the tall French windows across the carpet, the sofa, to light up the stuffed roseate spoonbill, now a beacon of pink, in the display case on the other side of the room. The library was empty.

"It's him! It's him!" Miss Westwoode screamed. "The man that attacked Mummy!"

The leg of a man in black boots and black riding trousers disappeared through the door opposite. The thud, thud, thud of running footfalls sent chills down Lyndy's spine. The man was wearing riding boots.

"What?" Mrs. Westwoode said as Lord Hugh and Mr. Westwoode made chase after the figure.

"Stella? Stella!" Lyndy's gaze darted about the room in confusion. It was her voice he'd heard. It was her scream. He was certain of it. Lyndy could still smell the scent of her perfume, hyacinth and moss. He turned over cushions; he threw aside curtains; he knelt and looked beneath furniture, desperate to find her, desperate not to. But she was gone.

He turned to the footman, who was peering over the heads of the ladies lingering in the doorway. "You," Lyndy barked, angry that he couldn't remember the footman's name, angry that he didn't know what had happened, angry that Stella wasn't there, angry that he cared so much. "Fetch the police downstairs."

"My lord? What's happened?" said a familiar voice.

Lyndy swiveled around at the questions. Inspector Brown was standing in the servants' doorway. A group of gaping maids stood on the steps behind him. Stella's scream must've reached the servants' hall.

"She's gone!" Lyndy said.

"Who's gone?" the inspector said.

"Miss Kendrick," Alice said, stepping into the room and putting her hand on Lyndy's arm. "They'll find her, Lyndy," she whispered.

He nodded. He had to believe she was right.

"We heard a terrible scream, and then we saw the intruder," Miss Westwoode said. "Perhaps the one that attacked Mummy."

Mrs. Westwoode's face paled.

"First, my horse, and now my daughter!" Mr. Kendrick declared, spreading the blame to everyone in the room. "What kind of people are you, anyway?"

His sister's gentle restraint kept Lyndy from striking the wretch, but no one would restrain his tongue.

"What kind of man are you?" Lyndy said. "Your daughter—"

"By God, I knew something like this would happen." Mr. Kendrick, ignoring Lyndy's rebuke, focused his gaze across the room. All eyes but Lyndy's followed. Lyndy hadn't finished saying what he had to say.

"Mr. Kendrick, you are the most—" Lyndy said.

"What's the meaning of this?" Papa demanded.

"What is she wearing?" Miss Westwoode whispered, scandalized.

Lyndy, interrupted by the others' declarations, tore his eyes away from Mr. Kendrick to see what all the fuss was about.

"Stella!"

Flanked by Mr. Westwoode and Lord Hugh, Stella was ushered into the library, her arm held tightly by the constable. She hadn't changed out of her riding habit but wore only her white blouse, jacket, and riding trousers. Her skirt was bundled up in her arms.

If they had harmed her . . .

The rip in her jacket's shoulder was from her fall, Lyndy reminded himself as he noticed the hint of white blouse beneath. She wasn't crying, but melancholy clouded her countenance. There was no sign of the terror Lyndy had heard in her scream. She was safe and seemingly unharmed.

What the bloody hell is happening?

"Constable Waterman," Inspector Brown snapped. "You have some explaining to do."

"She fits the general description. Black trousers, black boots, taller than the maid," the constable said.

"And?" Inspector Brown said, a darkness to his voice, which made the constable flinch.

"Miss Kendrick could be the vicar's killer."

Inspector Brown glowered at his constable and strode over to him. Hugh and Mr. Westwoode stepped aside.

"We caught her running away, sir."

"Miss Kendrick is not our killer, Constable Waterman," the inspector said, prying the constable's hand from Stella's arm.

"She could've attacked me," Mrs. Westwoode said feebly.

"No, Mrs. Westwoode," Lyndy said, refraining from adding, "You asinine woman." "Miss Kendrick was with her maid, dressing for dinner, when you were attacked." He approached Stella, trying to discover what had happened from her eyes. Fatigue and pain looked back at him.

"On behalf of myself and my constable, I humbly apologize for your detainment, Miss Kendrick."

Rubbing her arm, Stella said, "No apology is necessary, Inspector."

"I could not agree less, young lady," Mother said. Mother crossed the room, pinning Stella with her livid glare. "I insist on an apology and a great deal more from Inspector Brown, and from you, Miss Kendrick. Please cover yourself up."

Stella fastened the skirt about her waist.

"We thought you were dead," Miss Westwoode said.

"Don't be dramatic, Elizabeth," Mother said.

Mother might roll her eyes now, but Lyndy had seen the fear in them. Miss Westwoode wasn't far off the mark.

"I'm so sorry if I gave anyone a fright," Stella said.

A fright? Lyndy's heart flipped and fluttered in his chest. How dare she do that to him? He, like Mother, would demand more from her than an apology. But later, when they were alone.

"But I won't apologize for my tactics. It was the only way," Stella insisted.

"Only way to do what, Miss Kendrick?" Inspector Brown said.

"To prove who did kill Reverend Bullmore."

CHAPTER 31

"Right," Inspector Brown said, nodding to his constable. "No one leaves this room until Miss Kendrick tells me what she's talking about."

Mother, her face a picture of composure, but for the hardness of her stare, indicated for everyone to take a seat. She was not pleased. When was she ever?

Lyndy tugged on the sleeve of Stella's riding jacket. The strain of it rent the cut in the shoulder farther as he pulled her down onto the sofa beside him. He regretted his use of force when she groaned in pain. Her ribs must be giving her trouble. But he didn't release his grip. He was not letting her go until he knew exactly what was going on.

"I, for one, do not appreciate your use of theatrics, Miss Kendrick," Mother said. "You have disrupted afternoon tea."

Disrupted? Mother was a master of understatement. The tips of Lyndy's fingers tingled. He still wavered between rage and relief. Stella, with her bloodcurdling scream, had made fools of them, of him, making them believe she was in danger or worse. On the other hand, he wanted to cover her lovely face with kisses. He'd never been so pleased to be wrong.

"I wouldn't have done any of this if it wasn't necessary, Lady Atherly," Stella said.

"Does any of this pertain to the vicar's killer, Miss Kendrick?" Inspector Brown said, folding his arms across his chest. Lyndy was surprised not to see him tapping his foot, given the unveiled look of anticipation and impatience plain on his face. "If so, I think we'd all appreciate you illuminating us."

"I did it to prove a point," Stella said. "Two actually. The first relates to the mistaken assumption that a man murdered the vicar."

"Are you suggesting, Miss Kendrick, that a woman killed Reverend Bullmore?" Mother said, flabbergasted by the idea.

Papa fumbled to get out his lorgnette, as if he needed to see better to understand what was said. Miss Westwoode, her face pale, swayed, as if about to faint.

"Yes. Ethel saw the vicar's killer as the person ran away, wearing only her riding trousers, and assumed it was a man. As did all of you when you saw me."

"That's preposterous!" Mrs. Westwoode declared.

"Is it?" Lyndy said. Stella's charade was outlandish, but her reasoning was not.

"I think after Miss Kendrick's little demonstration," Inspector Brown said, "it's not only possible but highly likely. Jolly good, Miss Kendrick." The inspector grinned and nodded in approval. He was the only one.

Why was Lyndy looking about the room for the culprit? It had to be one of the maids, surely. Could it be one of them? Mother? Never. Alice? Lyndy hoped to God no. Mrs. Westwoode? She was attacked. Old Miss Luckett, the chaperone? She didn't have the strength. Miss Westwoode? She couldn't squash a ladybird. Then who?

The inspector and Stella both looked at the same person. Lyndy followed their gaze.

"Wouldn't you agree, Mrs. Westwoode?" Inspector Brown said.

"What?" Mrs. Westwoode clutched a fist to her throat as the constable stepped behind her to prevent her retreat. She looked about her, as if in a daze. "What are you talking about?"

"You killed Reverend Bullmore," Stella said.

"Now, that is preposterous," Mother said. "Mrs. Westwoode was attacked. She is a victim, not a villain."

"Quite so," Mrs. Westwoode said, nodding.

"I'm afraid, Lady Atherly, she is no more a victim than you or I am," Stella said. "She only wanted us to believe that. That was my second point."

Hence her need for the scream, Lyndy realized. Again, Stella's charade had proved the impossible.

"Miss Kendrick's right, Lady Atherly. Mrs. Westwoode only pretended to be attacked," Inspector Brown said. "Then she implicated the stable staff by hiding the jewels and the fire iron near the stables."

Mrs. Westwoode waved her hand dismissively at the inspector. Was she going to deny it?

"Mummy?" Miss Westwoode said.

Slouched in her chair, her lips loosely parted, Mother was visibly shaken. "Caroline, is this true?"

"I . . ." Mrs. Westwoode reached for Hugh's arm. Hugh jerked away from her in disgust. Mrs. Westwoode looked about her, as if hoping to find sympathy elsewhere. She didn't find it. "Well . . . if you must know, yes," she said, squaring her shoulders, "that pretense was an unfortunate necessity. You can rest assured, Lady Atherly, that unlike Miss Kendrick, I didn't find one moment of pleasure in all that screaming and panting and playacting."

"But?" Hugh asked.

"But what with the footman's release, Lord Hugh, dear, the police were suspecting you of the vicar's death. I couldn't have that. As to the stables, it's a den of thieves already, isn't it?"

"You couldn't have us suspecting you either," Inspector Brown said. "Isn't that right, Mrs. Westwoode?"

"That isn't it at all," Mrs. Westwoode scoffed.

"Mummy?" Miss Westwoode said. "Did you kill the vicar?"

"Elizabeth, darling. Don't you see, I had to?" she said, exasperated.

"But why, Caroline?" Mr. Westwoode said. "Why?"

"Because of you, Augustus!" she snarled, turning on her husband. "You and your horse races. What I haven't suffered because of you. You know nothing of the indignities I've been subjected to."

"Indignities?" Mr. Westwoode said, his voice barely audible. "You killed a man."

"Do you suppose I enjoyed smashing the head of a man of God with a fire iron? Do you think I would willingly demean myself by such violence? I had to rummage through a dead man's clothes because of you."

Mr. Westwoode, his face losing all color, dropped into the nearest chair. "To find his money?"

"Yes, to find the money that would pay off your debts. I had to strip it off his leg, Augustus. His bare leg!"

"But you could've sold your jewels, Mummy," Miss Westwoode whimpered.

"No, she couldn't," Inspector Brown said. "They are paste."

"How did you . . . ?" Mrs. Westwoode said, as if seeing the inspector for the first time. "Oh, it doesn't matter how you found out," she sighed. "But do you know how I found out?" She looked about, pinning every pair of eyes to her. "Forced to pay off my husband's debts, I visited a pawnbroker the last time we were in London. You can only imagine my humiliation when I discovered I'd been wearing glass."

"Then you overheard Reverend Bullmore and Lord Hugh talking about the money the vicar kept on his person," Stella said.

Mrs. Westwoode took her daughter's hands in hers. "Don't you see, Elizabeth? It was an answer to our prayers," she cooed.

"It was heaven sent. Besides, he was a vicar. What need did he have of the money?"

"But you killed him, Mummy," Miss Westwoode whined. "You hit him with a fire iron."

"Yes, darling, I hit him, and it was awful. But I needed to knock him out. I needed to get to his purse."

"But why the trousers?" Papa asked, staring in the general direction of his paleontology collection on the bookshelf. He was curious but couldn't look Mrs. Westwoode in the eye.

"Yet another indignity, Lord Atherly," Mrs. Westwoode said.

"Then Miss Kendrick is right?" Inspector Brown said. "You were dressed for riding?"

"I couldn't think of a way to hide the fire iron, so I took off my skirt and wrapped it in that. Besides, my skirt had blood on it already from kneeling beside the vicar."

"I don't understand, Caroline," Mr. Westwoode said. "I've been in debt before."

"You don't need to remind me," she said bitterly.

"Then why such desperate measures now?"

"Why now?" Mrs. Westwoode pointed at Hugh.

Fear shot through Lyndy. *Could I have been wrong?* Could Hugh have been involved in the murder, after all?

"Our daughter is engaged to Lord Hugh Drakeford, the second son of the Duke of Tonnbridge, now, that's why, Augustus," Mrs. Westwoode said, much to Lyndy's relief. "But what do you care? You do as you please, spend what you please, gamble what you don't have, while I bow and scrape to see our daughter married well. Tell me, Augustus? What else was I supposed to do, with you determined to see us in the poorhouse?"

"Mummy, no. Say you didn't do this for me," Miss Westwoode said.

"Elizabeth, darling, why else would a mother do anything

but for her child? Do you think His Grace will let his son marry the daughter of a pauper?"

His face red, Hugh leaped to his feet. "Do you think, Mrs. Westwoode," he said, spitting the words out like venom, "that my father will let me marry the daughter of a murderer?"

"What?" Mrs. Westwoode said, rising, reaching toward him. "No, as I said, it was an accident, Lord Hugh. I didn't mean to kill the vicar. I didn't even hit him that hard."

"Or the daughter of a thief?" Hugh said, his lip curled.

Mrs. Westwoode advanced on him until he backed up into the birds' display case. The birds inside swayed from the jolt. The magpie toppled from its perch.

"I explained all that," Mrs. Westwoode pleaded. "We needed his money. For you. I did this for you, for both of you." Hugh slid away from her as she reached to touch his arm.

"All you did, Mrs. Westwoode, was to embarrass me and involve me in scandal."

"What? No, Lord Hugh, you've misunderstood. The debts have all been paid. Tell him, Augustus."

Mr. Westwoode, his head in his hands, said nothing.

"Hugh?" Miss Westwoode said when Hugh strode across to the other side of the room.

"Where are you going? When will I see you again?"

"See me?" Hugh scoffed. "I trust we shall never see each other again. If you'll excuse me, Lord Atherly, Lady Atherly, I must leave at once."

Papa nodded. "If you must."

Lyndy had never seen his mother so pale.

Hugh bowed formally at the waist.

"Is that it?" Lyndy said. Lyndy had lied for his friend, lost sleep over his predicament, trusted him. Yet wasn't it Hugh's fragilities and faults that had led to the vicar's demise, however indirectly? He wanted to leap up and grab Hugh by the collar. "You have nothing more than that to say?" Somehow, Lyndy had expected more.

Lyndy caught Hugh's eye, but the Duke of Tonnbridge's second son shied away from his gaze and said nothing. *What a hypocrite.*

"No! You can't do this to me!" Mrs. Westwoode cried, fighting against her restraint as the constable grabbed hold of her arms. "You and Elizabeth are to be married in a fortnight, by the bishop!"

Hugh retreated from the room. When he reached the stairs, Lyndy could hear him taking them two at a time.

"Lord Hugh! Lord Hugh!" Mrs. Westwoode pleaded as the police constable led her to the door. Her calls continued to echo as the inspector and his constable escorted her down the hall.

Miss Westwoode dropped to the floor beside her father's chair and buried her head against his knee. Stella, regarding the unfortunate young woman, covered her mouth with her hands. Did she regret what she had done? Could she have done otherwise?

For one long moment, the library was silent. Lyndy heard only Stella's labored breathing. She had performed her spectacle with bruised ribs, had exerted herself far too much. The damn woman was exasperating, maddening, and foolish. Then why did he feel so proud? Lyndy put his arm around her shoulder.

"Lord Hugh!" Another of Mrs. Westwoode's desperate pleas reached them before Mr. Kendrick strode across the room and slammed the library door closed.

"Good riddance," Mr. Kendrick exclaimed.

CHAPTER 32

Stella Kendrick came to a decision. She took a deep breath before stepping into the drawing room. The portrait of a young woman, wearing a red silk and velvet bustled evening gown and a haughty, knowing smile, stared back at her. How could Stella not have seen the resemblance before? Lady Atherly was whispering something to her husband and hadn't noticed Stella's return.

"Ah, you're a lady once again," Lyndy said, setting down his cup of tea and standing. His expression was unreadable; only the tension in his chin gave him away. His tone might be flippant, but Stella knew he was concerned.

When Lady Atherly had insisted everyone return to the drawing room and finish tea, Stella had gladly changed into her tea gown, one of pale pink embroidered chiffon and lace. Without the constraints of a corset, her ribs didn't cause her as much pain.

But what about the pain she'd brought upon the Westwoodes? She'd have to learn to live with it. Stella doubted she would ever put her riding habit on again without thinking of them.

"I'm not sure you ever thought so," Stella said. She intended to match his playful tone but failed. For he'd be right.

Lady Atherly, glancing over her shoulder at Stella, frowned.

Stella crossed the room to join Lyndy on the sofa. The West-woodes were notably absent. As was Lady Alice, who perhaps was comforting her friend, who had retreated to her bedroom. Mr. Westwoode was most likely drowning his sorrows at the Knightwood Oak.

Reenacting Mrs. Westwoode's charade had done what Stella had set out to do, reveal the vicar's killer. But she hadn't antici-pated Lord Hugh's abrupt and devastating departure. What would Miss Westwoode do now? With the scandal of having a murderous mother, she might never marry. Was that such a ter-rible fate? Stella glanced at Lyndy as Lady Atherly handed her a cup of tea, the steam rising above it. Only a few short days ago, barely a week, she hadn't thought so. But now?

"I'm always going to be a bit different, aren't I?" she said.

Lyndy leaned toward her. "I wouldn't have you any other way." His breath as he whispered into her ear tickled her skin. Warmth radiated down her neck and into her chest. She couldn't help but smile at him.

"Ahem." Lady Atherly glared until Stella and Lyndy gave her their full attention. "You shall learn to be a lady," she said, as if her words alone could make it so. "If you are ever to be-come Lady Lyndhurst."

"Not if," Daddy said, "but when, and the sooner the better for everyone, if you ask me."

No one asked you, Daddy.

"You did send for the vicar, didn't you, Lord Atherly?"

"Yes, Mr. Kendrick," Lady Atherly said before her husband could respond. "Reverend Paine shall be here shortly."

"Good. The wedding's already been delayed too long. We'd agreed on a quick and quiet affair. You need your money, and I need to get back to the States."

"Pity you can't leave right now," Lady Atherly said, a feigned smile on her face.

Mr. Kendrick frowned.

"Inspector Brown to see you, milord," Fulton announced.

"Is there something more we can do for you?" Lord Atherly said. "We were hoping to put this whole terrible business behind us."

"If it's all right with you and Lady Atherly," the inspector said, clutching the brim of his hat, "I'd like to ask Miss Kendrick a few questions?"

"Whatever for?" Lyndy said, reaching for Stella's hand.

"It's nothing to be concerned about, my lord. But I've been puzzling over a few things, and I thought Miss Kendrick might be able to help."

"You think my girl can shed light on something that's got you stumped?" Daddy said.

Stella squeezed Lyndy's hand before folding both of her hands in her lap. She could feel her heart beating. Answering the inspector's questions bought her a little bit more time to get the courage to say what she must. "Ask me anything, Inspector."

"Right," Inspector Brown said. "How did you know Mrs. Westwoode was the killer?"

Stella admitted she'd first suspected Mr. Westwoode. He tried to escape notice when she visited the pub. He lied to his wife about winning at the Derby, or so she thought. Someone paid off his debt to the moneylender two days after the vicar was killed. She'd been so convinced it was him. She said nothing about Lord Hugh.

"Right. We suspected him as well. What persuaded you otherwise?"

"The discussion about how freeing a change of clothes can be. Lord Lyndhurst and I had a similar conversation about riding habits earlier. That made me think. We had all assumed the vicar's killer was a man because he was wearing pants."

"A reasonable assumption," Lady Atherly said.

"Yes, Lady Atherly, it is," Stella said. "But when all the men in the stables, on the grounds, in the house, and in the village were eliminated as suspects, it had to be an incorrect one. Dressed in a riding habit, a woman is only one riding skirt removed from being dressed like a man."

"That explains how you came to think a woman may have done it," Inspector Brown said, "but not how you knew it was Mrs. Westwoode. Why not one of the maids?"

"Again, it comes back to our conversation with Mr. Westwoode. When he denied paying a debt that Lord Lyndhurst confirmed with the moneylender had been paid, it follows that someone else must have paid it for him."

"Someone like his wife or daughter," Inspector Brown said.

Stella nodded.

"Then why not Miss Westwoode?"

"Because I'd seen Mrs. Westwoode give Mr. Harris an envelope at the Derby. I hadn't realized its significance at the time. I'd mistaken Mr. Harris for a bookmaker, not a moneylender. In hindsight, I realized Mrs. Westwoode was paying off her husband's debt."

"And where else could she have gotten the money but from the vicar?" the inspector said.

Stella nodded.

"And, according to my maid, Mrs. Westwoode had been dressed for riding at the time of the vicar's death."

"Why did the woman fake being attacked?" Daddy said.

"Because Mrs. Westwoode was clever," Inspector Brown said. "She tried to implicate the stable staff when she planted the fire iron and her jewels in the straw. I knew she was lying to me. I knew she had secrets. But because of her attack, I never suspected she was the killer. Her scheme almost worked."

"Indeed. Who would suspect a victim?" Lady Atherly said.

"Miss Kendrick did," Lyndy said, a hint of pride in his voice.

Lady Atherly frowned. Stella suspected Lady Atherly didn't take it as the compliment Lyndy intended.

"Yes, I did, because it didn't make sense. Why would the thief harm the vicar and not Mrs. Westwoode? Not out of some sort of chivalry, surely? And why Mrs. Westwoode, and only Mrs. Westwoode, who is traveling with a few of her jewels, when Lady Atherly and Lady Alice, as ladies of the house, have far more expensive pieces? Why not slip into the morning room and steal the wedding gifts? The timing was problematic as well. Why attack Mrs. Westwoode days after the vicar? The same day that the police clear Lord Lyndhurst's valet of suspicion?"

"Well done, Miss Kendrick," Inspector Brown said. "You have a keen eye for this."

"Don't flatter the girl," Daddy said. "She's already getting a big head."

"She shall certainly not be needing those skills again," Lady Atherly said.

"Let's hope not," the inspector said, winking at Stella. She smiled at her unexpected ally.

"Reverend Paine is here, my lady," Fulton announced.

The smile faded from Stella's lips. She'd been dreading this. It was now or never.

"Finally!" Daddy said.

"Please show him in, Fulton," Lord Atherly said. "If that will be all, Inspector?"

"Yes, thank you. Good day to you all." The inspector tipped his head, slapped his hat on, and strode from the room. The new vicar, his finger wiggling around in his ear, stepped hastily aside as not to cross paths with the inspector in the doorway.

"Ah, Reverend Paine," Lyndy said. "Twice in one day. What a pleasure."

"The pleasure is all mine, my lord," Reverend Paine said, oblivious to Lyndy's sarcasm. "I hear there is good news, my lord. Reverend Bullmore's killer has been apprehended?"

"Yes. So the wedding can go ahead at once," Daddy said.

Stella, steeling herself for this moment, squared her shoulders. "No, Daddy," she said.

"What?" Daddy said, shaking his head. "I knew this would happen." Daddy pointed his finger at Reverend Paine, as if Stella's obstinance were all his fault. "You delayed the wedding too long." As the new vicar sputtered his objection, Daddy threw his hands in the air. "Do you want to end up penniless and alone?"

Stella ignored her daddy, more concerned with the crack in Lyndy's countenance. He had been taken by surprise by her objection as much as her father had. She turned to him, then placed her hand lightly on his arm.

"Do you still have that gorgeous ring?" she asked.

Lyndy nodded. Surprisingly, he didn't have to have a servant fetch it. He pulled the box from the inside pocket of his waist-coat.

"Have you carried it every day since we . . ." Stella hesitated to mention the first time she'd seen the ring, right before they'd found the vicar.

Lyndy nodded. "All the good it did me," he said bitterly.

"Would you put it on my finger for me?"

Lyndy's brows furrowed. "But I thought?"

"Perhaps you should leave the thinking to me," she said teasingly. A suspicious smirk spread across Lyndy's lips. One day, she'd see him smile a real smile. Or at least she hoped so. Stella turned to her father. "You misunderstand me, Daddy. I no longer object to the engagement, but if we're going to do this . . ." She hesitated. There was no going back now. "If we're going to do this, I want to do it properly. Not under a cloud or in the dark of night." She looked first at Lyndy and then at her future mother-in-law. "I may not be a perfect Englishwoman, but I am nothing to be ashamed of."

She glanced at her father. If only she could say the same for him. The scowl on his lips distorted his face. He looked like an overindulged troll.

"I'd like it to be announced in New York and Lexington and London, if that's what's typically done," she said. "I'd like Lady Alice and me to go to London for my trousseau. I want to dine and dance and ride with my future husband and get to know him without the specter of a man's death between us."

"Properly chaperoned, of course," Lady Atherly said.

"Yes, with Aunt Rachel always at our side." Stella smiled at Lyndy's muttered protest.

"Like burrs on a hound dog's belly," Aunt Rachel said, winking at him. "Then y'all can have a wedding befitting the son of an earl."

"I would be happy to oblige," Reverend Paine said. "If it pleases Your Ladyship."

"I have no objections, Frances," Lord Atherly said. "As long as it doesn't interferc with the expedition in August."

"It would allow Miss Kendrick the time to learn, and perfect, her duties," Lady Atherly conceded. Stella inwardly sighed. She had her work cut out for her.

"What do you say, Mr. Kendrick?" Reverend Paine said. "Shall I put the wedding on my calendar for, say, October?"

"Would the bishop preside over the ceremony?" Daddy asked.

Stella closed her eyes. How did she not anticipate this? Daddy always wanted the best. She'd been surprised he'd agreed to a quiet, unpublicized wedding performed by a village vicar in the first place. Daddy waited for an answer.

"If that is your wish," Reverend Paine said, bowing his head. He was offended.

"Then it's settled," Mr. Kendrick said, rubbing his hands together.

"Is it?" Lady Atherly said. Stella had no idea what concerned the countess now. Lady Atherly looked at what her son was holding. "The ring?"

Stella laughed. How could she forget? She turned to Lyndy again and held out her left hand.

"Are you certain you want to do this?" he whispered, taking her hand in his.

"Do it quickly," Stella said. "Before I change my mind."

Lyndy, whether he took her in earnest or not, slipped the ring on her finger without hesitation. The diamonds glittered as Stella held her hand up to the light. It fit perfectly.

"We'll see if the marriage is as good a fit," he whispered, a smirk on his lips.

Stella pecked him lightly on those lips. The surprise in his eyes made her smile.

"Yes, we'll see."

AUTHOR'S NOTE

Although I write fiction, I always find inspiration in the history and culture of real people, places and events, such as the New Forest of England.

Now designated a national park, the New Forest is a magical place of ancient trees, open heath and wind-swept coastline. I couldn't have found a better place to set *A Murder at Morrington Hall*. Just west of the port of Southampton, within the county of Hampshire, it covers about 220 square miles with approximately fifteen miles of coastline directly across from the Isle of Wight off the south-central coast of England. William the Conqueror called the area *Nova Foresta* in 1079, not because it was thickly forested but because it was an ideal hunting ground flush with thriving populations of deer. The ancient heathland landscape, which has never been cultivated or intensely farmed, has changed little since. It has been maintained across the millennia through the use of commoning, shared use and management of natural resources, particularly by the grazing of free-range ponies (much to the delight of my equestrian loving heroine), donkeys and cattle. Once found throughout Northern Europe, this form of pastoral economy is believed to now only exist in The New Forest. As the New Forest is complete with colorful place names and landmarks, I only found the need to fictionalize the Earl of Atherly's estate of Morrington Hall and its associated village of Rosehurst.

One might think an arranged marriage between the daughter of an American horse breeder from Kentucky and the heir to a British earl something only found in fiction, but Stella Kendrick's predicament was inspired by a very real phenomenon. Between 1869 and 1911, more than a hundred American heiresses or "Million Dollar Princesses" crossed the Atlantic and married into the highest levels of British society. The money-strapped British aristocracy was in desperate need of an infusion of funds and America's new industrial millionaires needed to solidify their social standing back home. So, these daughters of bankers, industrialists and railroad barons, including a Colgate, Gould, Jerome, Vanderbilt and Whitney, exchanged dollars for titles. Some did so willingly; some were not given a choice. Consuelo Vanderbilt was a spectacular example of the latter. However they landed into the British aristocracy, these women left an indelible mark. Nancy Langhorne Astor of Virginia was the first woman to sit as a Member of Parliament. Jennie Jerome Spencer-Churchill of New York was Prime Minister Winston Churchill's mother. The future king of England Prince William's great-great grandmother was Francis Work Burke Roche of Ohio. Even the television series *Downton Abbey* was inspired by one of these real life pioneering American women. To read more, I recommend *To Marry an English Lord: Tales of Wealth and Marriage, Sex and Snobbery* by Gail MacColl and Carol McD. Wallace. This resource was invaluable to me in telling Stella Kendrick, my "dollar princess's" tale.

Wild-hearted Kentuckian Stella Kendrick cautiously navigates the strict demands of British high society as the future Lady of Morrington Hall. But when petty scandals lead to bloody murder, her outspoken nature could be all that keeps her alive . . .

Following a whirlwind engagement to Viscount "Lyndy" Lyndhurst, Stella is finding her footing within an elite social circle in picturesque rural England. Except tea time with refined friends can be more dangerous than etiquette faux pas—especially in the company of Lady Philippa, the woman Lyndy was once set to marry, and her husband, the ostentatious Lord Fairbrother . . .

Outrage erupts and accusations fly after Lord Fairbrother's pony wins best in breed for the seventh consecutive year. The man has his share of secrets and adversaries, but Stella and Lyndy are in for a brutal shock when they discover his body floating in the river during a quiet morning fishing trip . . .

Suddenly unwelcome around hardly grieving Lady Philippa and Lyndy's endlessly critical mother, Stella faces the bitter reality that she may always be an outsider—and one of her trusted new acquaintances may be a calculating killer. Now, Stella and her fiancé must fight against the current to catch the culprit, before they're the next couple torn apart by tragedy.

**Please turn the page for an exciting sneak peek of
Clara McKenna's next
Stella & Lyndy mystery
MURDER AT BLACKWATER BEND
coming soon wherever print and e-books are sold!**

CHAPTER 1

August 1905
Hampshire, England

Lady Atherly didn't dare look at her husband. She couldn't trust herself not to overreact. And then what would everyone think?

She'd once thought William exceedingly handsome. But she'd lived with him too many years, endured that self-satisfied glint in his eyes too many times. Instead, she stared straight ahead at the swirling assembly of colorfully dressed dancers, the brilliant light of the chandelier reflecting off the ladies' jewels, their dresses' sparkling embellishments, the highly polished floor. The musicians, as good as any you'd find up in London, had begun the Lehár piece, *Gold and Silver*. Lady Atherly was partial to Johann Strauss II, remembering a time when she'd whirled about on the arm of a well-turned-out beau to Strauss's *Viennese Blood*, but she loved all waltzes, even this new one. Lady Atherly's jaw ached in her attempt to keep a scowl from her face.

"You'd think you'd be pleased, Frances."

Pleased? William would say something like that. She knew why he was happy. He'd gotten everything he'd wanted. Besides, what did happiness have to do with it? This was about tradition, decorum, survival. And everything rested precariously on the shoulders of a young, ill-bred American girl. How could that possibly make her happy?

The girl in question whirled by, close enough the women's eyes would've met had Lady Atherly not avoided Miss Kendrick's gaze. The hem of Miss Kendrick's ivory lace and rose satin gown swished along the floor as she yet again took a misstep. Even in the arms of a highly capable partner (Hadn't she warned her son not to dance too often with the American?), the girl lacked grace.

"Isn't she lovely?" William said. Lady Atherly rolled her eyes and held her tongue. Fool.

Of course, all the men admired her. How could they not? Miss Kendrick was beautiful and offered smiles and compliments to everyone like they were sweets. Her persistent questions made them think she was interested in what they had to say. But the women knew better. Just look at the way Mrs. Cowperthwaite and Mrs. Hamnett whispered about Miss Kendrick behind their fans as the girl passed. No well-bred lady was interested in horse breeding or fossil hunting or fishing or who was elected to Parliament or any other such masculine pursuit.

And then Lady Philippa Fairbrother waltzed past. Lady Philippa was graceful. She was witty. She was stunningly beautiful. And she didn't show her teeth like a horse. In her emerald and ivory satin gown, she was the quintessence of good English breeding. And hadn't she adored Lyndy? As the daughter of a marquess, she was everything a mother-in-law could want.

If only Lady Philippa had married Lyndy and not Lord Fairbrother. Morrington could've been saved from ruin without

Lady Atherly suffering the humiliation that was the Americans. If only Lady Philippa had inherited more.

"You insisted Miss Kendrick attend, Frances. So why are you scowling when your future daughter-in-law is the belle of the ball?"

Because no well-bred lady laughed while she danced either, nor would she ignore the disapproving stares of the society matrons. What did Miss Kendrick even have to laugh about? It certainly wasn't something Lyndy had said. Her son was not that amusing.

From the beginning, Lady Atherly set out to put a stop to Miss Kendrick's outlandish behavior. No more stepping out with Lyndy unchaperoned or driving herself in the motorcar. No public displays of affection, no unauthorized visits to the stables, and no more shirking her social obligations. But despite Lady Atherly's best efforts, Miss Kendrick still acted on impulse, let herself be swept away by emotion and, worst of all, persisted in asking inappropriate questions. Lady Atherly had made the mistake of insisting Miss Kendrick and her insufferable family move out of Morrington Hall. With Miss Kendrick living at Pilley Manor though, Lady Atherly lost control over the girl. Who she fraternized with was a constant concern. Lady Atherly had already nipped the inappropriate friendship with that silversmith's daughter in the bud. But just tonight, Lady Atherly heard an untenable rumor that Miss Kendrick was well acquainted with the old village hermit, a snake catcher of all things.

Will the girl stop at nothing to embarrass this family?

"Lovely evening, isn't it?" the rotund wife of a minor landowner said, sidling up beside her. Her crimson silk dress clashed garishly with the woman's ginger hair, her scent a vulgar overuse of rosewater. Lady Atherly invited her to one garden party years ago, and the woman presumed to speak to her on familiar terms at every social gathering since. Lady Atherly acknowledged her with the barest of nods. The woman collapsed her fan and pointed it across the room. "Oh, dear. Whatever is your child up to?"

Lady Atherly, knowing her daughter, Alice, had gone into dinner, sought Lyndy on the ballroom floor. A cluster of dancers had stopped and had gathered on the far end. Lyndy and Miss Kendrick were among them. A footman, his expression uncharacteristically showing concern, spoke to the group and gestured toward the door. Before the footman had finished talking, Miss Kendrick hitched up the train of her skirt and dashed past him, disappearing from the room. Lyndy chased after her.

Lady Atherly let out a long, silent sigh. *What now?*

With all the self-control Lady Atherly could muster, she pinched her lips together, lightly pressed her fingertips against her the cold diamonds in her tiara and said, "If you'll excuse me."

What she wanted to do was scream at her husband, "See what you've done to this family, William? See what I must put up with?" But she didn't. She deliberately maneuvered her way across the crowded ballroom as she made her mind up. This was going to stop.

Tom Heppenstall flicked back the tap handle too late. The frothy head bubbled up over the rim and foam slid down the side of the glass. He shook his head in disgust as he reached for the towel draped across his shoulder. After wiping the glass dry, he set the pint down on the bar and collected the tuppence, all without glancing at who had ordered the stout. Instead, he stared across the sea of ruddy faces toward the door as it opened.

Ah, bloody hell.

Standing in the doorway, with an old potato sack flung across his shoulder, Harvey Milkham scowled beneath the dusty, worn hat that flopped down on both sides of his head. Had Tom ever seen him take it off? The snakecatcher's hair was greasy white, Tom knew, in part because everyone knew Harvey was as old as the New Forest. Some joked Harvey once met King Rufus himself before that royal's unfortunate premature demise. But also, Tom knew because of the thick, curly gray eyebrows that protruded wildly out from under the hat. It was a wonder the old man could see. But he had eyes as sharp as a tawny owl, and those eyes scanned the crowded pub.

On any given day, Tom would pour Harvey his usual before the old bloke reached the bar. The regulars didn't have a problem with the hermit; he kept himself to himself. On slow, rainy nights, Tom even enjoyed prodding the snakecatcher with questions. Had Harvey found a new barrow? Had he visited Lord Brice to feed his lordship's talking bird with snakes he'd caught that day? Had Harvey met with the gentlemen from the London Zoo? Or had he been to Pilley Manor yet again, to visit with the Americans? What an odd pair, those two, Miss Kendrick and the snakecatcher, but their friendship made a bit of sense; they were both a bit daft.

But (God help him), on a night like tonight, Harvey's arrival could spell disaster. Not all of the locals were as welcoming. And Harvey didn't help his case much. On more than one occasion, the snakecatcher had decided the crowd at the Knightsbridge Oak was too thick to traverse and had emptied the contents of his potato sack on the floor. The local greengrocer, and who knows who else, hadn't set foot across the threshold since.

Tom had to get to Harvey before the old snakecatcher decided to do it again.

Ignoring someone's call for a pint of bitter, Tom hobbled from behind the bar as fast as his swollen ankle would allow him and pushed into the lively crowd. If Harvey Milkham weren't standing in the doorway with that blasted sack on his shoulder, Tom would've been pleased with the uptick in business lately. Ever since the previous vicar's murder and rumors spread that the killer had spent his time pondering his crime in the Knightsbridge Oak, Tom has seen an influx of new customers. Mostly folk from the nearby villages; some traveled from as far away as Ringwood and Minstead to drink a pint in the same pub as a murderer. Luckily the rumors hadn't reached beyond the boundaries of the Forest. The moment grockles started pouring in, for all the trouble they're worth, Tom might have to put a stop to all the idle gossip. Until then, who was Tom to argue?

"How's the ankle, Tom?" a well-wisher asked, as the publican tried to push past. Tom answered with a grunt and a shake of his head, as he spied that good for nothing boy that was the bane of his existence and the cause of his swollen ankle. The boy held a tray piled with dirty pint glasses before him. As he tried to navigate by a cluster of men, the boy lifted it. The glassware, teetering dangerously above his head, clanked but didn't fall.

"Oi!" Tom yelled. "Watch what you're doing there, lad."

Yesterday, unbeknownst to Tom, the boy had spilled a glass of half-finished cider on the floor, purportedly after hearing the ghost of Old Bertie, the original proprietor of the pub. Tom knew it was just the wind blowing, not the moaning of an apparition of a man who'd died languishing in prison for smuggling more than a hundred years ago but the boy believed the legend. The boy also failed to clean the spilled cider up. This morning, after checking on the stores in the cellar, Tom slipped on the sticky liquid and twisted his ankle. Tom, not one to fuss, simply choked down a syrupy teaspoon of laudanum before demanding the boy mop the entire floor. But even he knew standing behind the bar all day wasn't doing himself any favors. Tom, his ankle throbbing, limped by the well-wisher toward the door.

"Harvey! Harvey!"

The shout, which rose above the din in the room as field

hands, clerks, merchant's assistants, and farmers unburdened themselves of the day with alcohol-loosened tongues, didn't come from inside the pub. Men looked up from their beer as Tom neared the open doorway. A groom from Morrington Hall leaped from a dogcart and pulled the horse into the gravel yard of the pub.

"Oi! Move your horse," Tom yelled. Nothing good came from mingling the scent of a fine bitter with that of sweating horseflesh. But the groom, his face flush, obviously anxious, ignored him and unwisely grabbed Harvey's arm with the hand not holding on to the reins of his horse.

"You have to come with me. Now."

Harvey, startled, swirled around to push the groom away. The burlap sack slipped from his shoulder to the threshold of the pub. Several men nearby jumped back. With spikes of pain shooting up his leg, Tom lumbered forward as fast as he could.

"Harvey, Miss Kendrick needs you," the groom added. At the mention of the American lady, Harvey rubbed his bristly chin and followed the groom to the dogcart.

"But isn't the lassie at a party?" the grizzled old voice asked.

"She is, but Tully's been bitten by an adder. You have to come quick."

The two men leaped into the cart, the old snakecatcher being nimbler than Tom would've credited him for, and were driving past the green before Tom reached the threshold. He carefully reached down toward the abandoned potato sack as something wriggled inside. Tom snatched up the burlap bag, twisting the open end tightly closed in his fist. He limped slowly out the door, across the gravel yard of the pub, past the wooden tables that had been there so long they looked rooted, across the lane and onto the village green. After approaching a dense flowerbed on the edge of the green, Tom set down the sack on its side and backed away. A long, thin tongue flicked out as a sleek brown head protruded from the bag. The rest of the body, marked with a dark brown zigzag on its back, followed, slithering out and disappeared under the brush.

"Bloody hell." Tom hated snakes. Who but Harvey Milkham didn't? But it wasn't only the snake he cursed. Tom was profiting, yes, but why must it always be off the misfortunes of those up at Morrington Hall?

Stella leaped out of the automobile and jerked to a stop. She twisted around to see what was holding her back. Her ballgown had snagged on the corner of the door.

"Augh. Let go."

She yanked on it with both hands, ignoring the tearing sound as a rent a foot long sliced up the side of her rose-colored satin skirt. Free of the door, she dashed toward the stables.

I told them something like this would happen.

Inside, darkness pervaded. The long orange rays of the setting sun, seeping through the half-open windows, barely lit the way. Why hadn't the lanterns been lit yet? She rushed down the aisle that she'd treaded a hundred times in the past two months, dodging the anxious, downcast eyes of stable boys lining her way like the suits of armor up at Morrington Hall. She passed the stalls of the other horses. Most of the horses were calm but curiously sticking their heads out of the stall doors. Orson, their Thoroughbred stallion, barely pulled his head away from his hay. But Tupper, their promising filly, whinnied as Stella passed, sensing something was wrong.

When Stella finally reached her horse's stall, she could barely make out the familiar shape of the prone figure on the straw-covered floor.

"Tully!"

She flung herself to her knees beside the horse, ignoring the prickly straw sticking into her silk stockings. Tully didn't respond, no welcoming nicker, no raised head, not even an acknowledging glance. The horse's eyes were closed and stayed that way, as Stella leaned down, snuggling her head against the Thoroughbred's sleek neck.

Please, God, let her just be sleeping.

A clean, white bandage was wrapped around Tully's swollen left front knee. With her hand shaking, Stella reached toward the inside back of Tully's uninjured right front knee. She nearly wept when she found a clear and consistent pulse. But it was faster than it should be.

Harvey had warned her that he'd seen a high number of snakes in the area lately. And with the adder breeding season in full swing, even she knew a pregnant adder was a dangerous snake. Stella had told Lyndy, but he'd explained that it wasn't his place to alert the estate manager. She'd warned Lord Atherly, but he'd been too preoccupied with the upcoming visit of Professor Gridley to care. Finally, she'd approached the estate manager herself. But without word from Lord Atherly, the estate manager merely shrugged at his inability to act. These hierarchical rules were maddening.

And they say Americans do stupid things.

A movement in the straw drew Stella's attention. Until now she'd ignored everyone but Tully. She lifted her head and recognized the old man kneeling nearby, his floppy, old hat nearly covering his eyes. She grabbed his rough hand in relief and hopeful desperation.

"Harvey, tell me she's going to be all right."

"Oh, aye, lass. She'll be lancing over the heath in no time." Harvey gently patted Tully on her rounded barrel. "She's sleeping soundly now." His voice was heavily accented and gravelly, but Stella didn't need to understand every word he said. His reassuring tone was enough. Stella flung her arms around him, clamped her eyes shut and hugged the old snakecatcher. He smelled of damp soil and sweet pipe tobacco, like Grandpa Luckett. Stella had loved Grandpa Luckett.

When the footman had told her about Tully at the ball,

Stella's heart had stopped. She'd thought only about getting to her beloved horse's side. Who cared if Daddy didn't have a way home? Who cared if Lady Atherly would disapprove of her abrupt departure? But now, in the grim silence of the stables, relief easing its way through her tense body, she missed the glittering ballroom, the music, dancing in Lyndy's arms. She'd been enjoying herself.

In the past few weeks, Stella had attended, and dreaded, countless dances, teas, dinner, card, and garden parties, smiling, making witty banter and learning to play whist. All in all, everyone, even Daddy and Lady Atherly, seemed surprised how charming she, the "American," could be. But Stella had enjoyed little of it. Until tonight. Tonight, despite Lady Atherly's objection, Stella had decided to dance only with Lyndy (and what a dancer he turned out to be!). It had made all the difference. In the past couple of months, she'd become quite fond of the Viscount.

"Eh-hem," someone coughed behind her.

Stella opened her eyes and glanced over her shoulder. Lyndy, as handsome as she'd ever seen him in top hat and coattails, stood in the door of the stall, his arms folded tightly against his chest. He'd ridden beside her in Daddy's Daimler. But so too in the door were Mr. Gates, the head coachman and several stablehands clustered behind Lyndy. Someone had lit the lanterns, and they could see everything. Stella, self-conscious, pulled away from Harvey. She sat back on her heels, pushing a loose strand of hair behind her ear. She wasn't wearing her hat. In her haste, she must've left it at the ball.

"Is Tully going to be alright, sir?" one of the stablehands stammered, his eyes wide as he cranked his neck to look around Leonard, the taller groom. It was Charlie, the boy who mucked out Tully's stall and fed her every day. "I saw her trembling and sweating not long before."

"Oh, aye," Harvey said slowly. "She'll be right as rain.

Adders can't kill a horse, but they sure can make it uncomfortable. What you saw, laddie, was the poison working its way."

"But you've given her the antidote ointment, right?" Stella asked.

Could it have only been a few weeks ago, when Stella, sneaking away, just her and Tully, without even a groom knowing, had come across this odd, grisly old man in a floppy hat, knee-high boots, and wooden cleft stick? She'd led Tully to a narrow stream running through Whitley Wood. Mr. Harvey Milkham, or the snakecatcher as she would later learn the locals called him, had been on the other side, poking his stick under a pile of mossy rocks. Stella had watched to see what he was doing. He must've known she was there; Tully never drank very quietly, but he never acknowledged her presence. After a moment or two, Harvey had pulled a long, wriggling snake up with his stick and had draped it around his neck. He'd done the same again until three snakes dangled about his shoulders. Looking over at Stella and Tully on the other bank of the creek, he'd unwrapped the snakes from his neck, picked up a burlap sack and dropped them in.

"You be the American lassie staying at Pilley Manor, I presume?" he'd said.

"Yes, I'm Stella Kendrick."

"Lovely to meet you, lass." He'd promptly launched himself across the creek, swiped his palm against his dusty coat and jut out his hand. "Welcome to the New Forest."

Without hesitation, Stella had shaken it, grateful for the hearty, honest introduction. His hand had been rough and gnarled like a tree trunk but, like everything about the old man kneeling beside her, unexpectedly strong and reassuring.

"Aye, lassie," Harvey said. "Always carry a bit of antidote about with us."

He stood and brushed the straw from his well-worn clothes. Stella did the same, only now realizing she'd ruined her gown and her leg to the knee was showing. Mr. Gates quickly turned his head as he vainly tried to shoo the gawking stablehands away. No one budged.

After that first meeting, Stella had continued to seek out Harvey, even visiting him once at his home. They'd drank tea with a splash of scotch (what the doctor had ordered, he'd said) from tin cups. She'd relished lounging in his abandoned coal-burner's hut made of tree branches and covered with sod, listening, not to yet another conversation about the weather but of the sprains, bruises and adder bites Harvey had healed with his antivenom ointment. Instead of a future English Viscountess on display, she'd been a character in Robinson Crusoe. What a refreshing change.

For that memory alone, she wanted to hug him again. Instead, she looked down at Tully, resting comfortably in the thick straw, and pulled the torn pieces of her skirt back together.

"How much do we owe you?" Lyndy said, stepping into the stall, carefully avoiding Stella's gaze. Was he angry or trying desperately not to laugh? Stella still couldn't read Lyndy's expressions right.

"Tuppence for a pint wouldn't be turned down, your lordship."

"My father will pay far more than tuppence, Harvey," Stella said. "You've saved a precious horse today. How can we possibly repay you?"

"No need for that, lass. This fine, strong mare did most of the work." Harvey smiled as he took off his hat and swatted at a fly buzzing around Tully's head. His two front teeth were missing.

"You won't get off that easily," Stella said. "Mark my words, Harvey Milkham, I will find a way to pay you back for your kindness, whether you like it or not."

"I've no doubt, lass, no doubt at all that you'll do whatever you set your mind to." He nodded slightly to Stella and then to Lyndy before plopping his hat back on his head. "Congratulations, milord, on your upcoming nuptials." As he made his way through, the stablehands crowding the door, he indicated Stella with his thumb. "And good luck with that one."

Lyndy chuckled as he plucked a piece of straw from Stella's hair. "Thank you, my good fellow," Lyndy said, congenially. "I'm going to need it."